"And what made you think you could come barging in here in the middle of the night, invading my privacy?" Tessie demanded.

"Hush! You'll disturb the household." Jason's lips came down on hers, muffling further protest. She knew she should fight against the embrace but it was so sweet. . . .

"I heard you crying in your sleep," he murmured into the soft unbound coils of her hair. "Could I leave you to weep alone?"

"I didn't ask you to come. . . ."

"I'm tired," said Jason with sudden ferocity, "of waiting to be asked."

His hands moved over her body with practiced skill, palms warm and rough against her bare skin. The weight of his body held her close and he took her with an urgency that Tessie could no more have stopped than she could have halted a river in full flood. . . .

Books by Catherine Lyndell

Ariane
Border Fires
Journey to Desire
Stolen Dreams

Published by POCKET BOOKS

JOURNEY TO DESIRE

Catherine Lyndell

POCKET BOOKS

New York   London   Toronto   Sydney   Tokyo   Singapore

An *Original* Publication of POCKET BOOKS

POCKET BOOKS, a division of Simon & Schuster
1230 Avenue of the Americas, New York, NY 10020

ISBN: 0-671-73917-4

First Pocket Books printing May 1991

10 9 8 7 6 5 4 3 2 1

POCKET and colophon are registered trademarks of Simon & Schuster.

Printed in the U.S.A.

JOURNEY TO DESIRE

Chapter One

Tessie Gallagher leaned perilously over the rail of the steamer to catch her first glimpse of Yokohama. Above and behind the bustling city, Mount Fuji rose in a series of rosy curves, half-hidden in the morning mist. The mountain had been visible long before they came within sight of land, the first promise that her long-held dream was coming true. Streaks of rosy light, blue reflections from the water, the foggy green of distant hills, and the snow-crowned mountain rising above all—her first sight of Japan.

They had actually reached the bay. She could see junks and steamers and small boats, rowers whose blue-and-white robes fluttered in the breeze and others, laboring harder, who had cast off their robes and were wearing only—

Tessie blushed and looked away from the laughing, naked men in the nearest boat. She knew, of course, that the Japanese attitude toward the human body was quite different from that of Westerners. Uncle Morgan had told her often enough that they regarded nudity as a simply practical matter, that there was no shame in exposing the body to nurse a baby or take a bath. What Japanese would find shameful, he had said, was the Western custom of ladies in low-cut evening dresses, exposing their bare skin merely to have it seen.

So it was not that she was surprised, exactly, or disapproving. It was just that—like Fuji—the reality was more impressive than the mental picture she had formed.

Tessie leaned over the rail again, this time concentrating on the busy trading city with its low tiled houses around the quays, the narrow streets, and the high semicircle of elegant Western-style homes above the harbor.

"Trying to pick out your future residence, Miss Gallagher?"

It was Dr. Ashton, the elderly scholar who had become Tessie's friend during the weeks of sea travel from San Francisco. Tessie smiled at the sound of his voice and turned toward him. His bright eyes beneath snowy white brows twinkled at her, sharing her delight without a word.

"Do you hope your brother and his wife will choose to rent one of those fine Western houses on the Bluff?"

"I am afraid so," Tessie answered with a dimple. "Nothing less would suit Hartley's dignity!"

"Afraid?"

Tessie gave a little sigh. "Oh, it's not—I really shouldn't care where we live, should I? Not when everything else is so wonderful! After all, I have dreamed of coming to Japan ever since Uncle Morgan used to come back from sea and tell me about his voyages here. And if Hartley and Sophia hadn't very kindly invited me to accompany them, I should never have been able to make the trip."

Mama, nearing sixty now and used to being the autocrat of the household, would never have released the spinster daughter she'd kept at home to wait on her all these years. But Hartley was even more selfish than Mama—that is, Tessie corrected her own thoughts with a wince of guilt, Hartley and Sophia needed her so much more now, and so they'd been able to persuade Mama that she could get along for a year without Tessie.

"It's a dream come true," Tessie finished firmly, setting her errant thoughts back into place as if they'd been a crooked dust ruffle or a wrinkled antimacassar. "And I shall be eternally grateful to Hartley and Sophia for giving me this opportunity! It's just that I had rather dreamed of staying in one of those dear little Japanese houses Uncle Morgan described to me, with wooden walls and rice-paper screens and a charcoal stove and everything so neat and clean and simple. And those houses on—what did you call it?—the Bluff?—well, they look just like the houses in San Francisco!" Even from this distance, Tessie could tell that they would be full of overstuffed prickly horsehair chairs and sofas and ottomans, with mantel-pieces and little tables covered with miniature china ornaments and boxes made of shells and silver-framed photographs.

"Never mind," said Dr. Ashton kindly. "I think you will not find life in Yokohama *precisely* like San Francisco!"

"No, I don't suppose I shall." Tessie agreed. "Just imagine—all this to explore, and learn, and love!" She waved her arm in a sweeping circle that encompassed the city, the harbor, and the deck of the steamer. Her outflung hand nearly caught one of the hurrying sailors on the jaw. He ducked, slipped, staggered, recovered his balance, and decided not to curse the clumsy passenger after all when he saw the beaming grin that lit up her freckled face. That little Miss Gallagher would be pretty if she'd ever sit still and dress her hair properly and wear a fine silk dress like the ones her sister-in-law sported; but as she was, with her hair flying in the wind and not caring about saltwater stains on her old gray dress, and with that generous, big-toothed smile making you feel like the whole world was smiling on you—well! She had something better than being pretty, and that was a fact, but he was blest if he could put a name to it.

Dr. Ashton, watching Tessie's glowing face, had somewhat the same thoughts, but he was troubled by misgivings for her sake. "I hope you find Japan everything you have dreamed."

"If Mount Fuji is any omen," Tessie replied, pointing to where the gleaming cone rose out of the mists behind the city, "it will be far more. I can't *wait* to get ashore and start exploring the city!"

"Yes. Well, I hope you'll get the chance to do so. You're here with your brother and his wife, are you not, to oversee their household and to take care of their children? Hiring servants, a strange country, an unfamiliar language—it could be rather a lot of work. You must make sure to get some free time for yourself, to see something of the country while you are here."

Don't let them make a slave of you, was what he wanted to say, but he couldn't think of a polite way of phrasing the warning. And it was probably useless anyway. From what he'd seen on the voyage, Tessie's brother and sister-in-law were already quite used to having her at their beck and call, and she accepted her so-called duty without ever questioning the vague illnesses that kept Sophia abed and unable to deal with her own children.

"Oh, I'm sure everything will be wonderful, once we get settled," Tessie assured him. "And the language is not exactly unfamiliar to me, you know. I've been studying Japanese for years, though without ever hoping that I'd have the chance to use it."

"Yes, I do know." Dr. Ashton stifled a laugh. "I'll never forget the sight of you walking Mrs. Rugsby's baby, crooning Japanese lullabies to the little mite and telling it *'Oyasu mi nasai!'* when you wanted it to go to sleep. But Tessie—Miss Gallagher, I mean—that is

4

exactly my point. There you were with your sister-in-law's three children to look after, and you had to take a strange female's baby into the bargain."

"Well, poor Mrs. Rugsby was so seasick. Somebody had to help her!"

"And if it had to be you, couldn't your sister-in-law have taken care of her own children for a mere while to give you a little rest?"

"Sophia suffers from a very nervous disposition."

"Hmm." From what he'd seen, it was the people around Sophia Gallagher who suffered from her nervous disposition. But there were limits to how far one could go in criticizing other people's relatives. "Well, my dear, I must go below and pack my few possessions now. If you do get a free day—or if you need help of any sort—I should be delighted if you would call on me. I shall be staying in Yokohama for several days, visiting an old friend who runs a curio shop here, before I go on to my own residence in Tokyo. The shop is called Samurai Shokai, and my friend's name is Yozo Nomura. Here is one of the shop cards, with his address on it."

Tessie slipped the card into her reticule and promised Dr. Ashton that she would try to visit the shop before he left for Tokyo. *Though it may be difficult,* she thought with a slight frown. Naturally, Sophia would need her to take care of the children until they were settled in the English-language school. Then there would be the business of hiring servants, and Sophia was very difficult to please. One of the problems of her nervous disposition was that she always suspected servants of dishonesty. And, of course, she would have to find out all about how to get food and coal and newspapers delivered—

The boatmen circling the steamer called to one another in their fishers' dialect, a gull screeched overhead, a fish leaped gleaming out of the water, and Tessie's frown smoothed itself away. What was she worrying about? She was in Japan, and that was miracle enough for one day, for plain unmarried Tessie Gallagher from San Francisco, the spinster sister whose destiny was to become a maiden aunt helping out wherever she was needed in the family. She leaned over the railing again, her features twisted up into a ferocious squint as she tried to make out details of the wharves and quays and harbor buildings and the men trotting back and forth with bundles on their heads—all so deliciously new and foreign. Japan was like a wonderful package waiting for her to unwrap it. Who knew what marvels might lie within?

"Tessie! Aunt Tessie! You have to come below and braid my hair now. Mama says so!"

That was Seraphina Jessamine Gallagher, Sophia's nine-year-old daughter. As she tugged at Tessie's skirt, her voice rose into an irritating, high-pitched whine that carried an uncanny echo of her mother.

"In a minute, Sally," Tessie murmured, smoothing the little girl's tangled hair as she gazed out into the entrancing misty scene before her. There were Japanese men in long robes, and other Japanese looking peculiarly uncomfortable in adaptations of Western clothes, and an occasional foreigner looming above the Japanese—well, one, anyway. His back was to her, but as his companion pointed to the ship, he turned and seemed to be staring right at them.

Tessie's heart beat faster as she peered through the mist, trying to make out the foreign man's features. The arrogant cocked tilt of that black head was the same, and the loose-jointed, lazy walk. But it couldn't be—could it? Not here, thousands of miles from San Francisco.

"Aunt Tessie! Get me a cake from the cabin!" seven-year-old Eustace Neville Gallagher demanded.

"I want a drink of water!" chimed in five-year-old Forbes Montague Gallagher.

"You're supposed to comb my hair *now*. Mama said

so, and I want French braids tied with my new pink silk ribbon!" Seraphina Jessamine whined.

The foreigner on the quay turned away again, and Tessie let out her pent-up breath with a sigh of relief. One thing was clear even from this distance: the silver streak that ran through the man's thick black hair. Jason Lancaster's black-haired, blue-eyed intensity had been softened by no such magpie streak.

"What's the matter, Aunt Tessie?" asked Forbes Montague as she turned away from the rail, taking his hand. "You look sad."

Tessie stooped and hugged the little boy. For some reason, just at that moment, she badly needed the comfort of a child's wriggling body in her arms. "Not sad, Freddy. How could I possibly be sad when we're all about to start on a wonderfully exciting adventure? For a moment I thought I saw someone I used to know, that's all." Her voice trembled shamefully on the last sentence. Straightening up, she forced herself to go on as brightly and cheerfully as the children expected. "Let's go below now, shall we, and get you all nicely dressed to go ashore. It's going to be a wonderful, wonderful day, one we shall always remember—our first day in Japan!"

But for some reason, a little of the bright shining gloss on the day was unaccountably dimmed for Tessie. It wasn't that she'd seriously expected to run into Jason Lancaster again, ten years later and thousands of miles from home. And it surely wasn't that she'd wanted the man on the quay to be him. How could she want to meet him ever again, after the way he'd treated her the last time? Indeed, it was a good thing that man wasn't Jason, not if the mere thought of him after all these years could still bring a silly lump into her throat.

By the time Hartley, Sophia, the children, and their trunks had all been brought ashore, Tessie's natural

7

lively spirits had returned, and she was able to enjoy the short ride through the streets of Yokohama to the fullest. A Japanese agent of Benten and Company, the trading firm that had employed Hartley, had been waiting for them on the quay. He had bowed and explained in slow, careful English that everything had already been arranged for their arrival. The head of the firm had personally rented a house for them and had hired the servants they would need. The house came furnished, and the English-language school for children of foreigners was on the same street.

"I might like to choose my own furnishings," sniffed Sophia. "And how do we know this place is clean?"

Mr. Nakamura bowed again. "You will, of course, make any alterations you find desirable. If the house is unsuitable, I will assist you in finding a better one. The *jinrikshas* are waiting. Will your ladyship condescend to ride to the house and view it now?"

Sophia sniffed again at being asked to climb into such a shoddy foreign contraption as the little two-wheeled carriage. "Actually drawn by a native—in harness—like a horse!"

Tessie waited until the rest of the family had taken their seats in the little carriages before she mounted into the last one.

"Arigato," she ventured to Mr. Nakamura.

A broad, delighted smile split his face, and he bowed three times, quite briskly. "Ah, the lady learns our language!"

"Only a little." Tessie apologized, wincing at the rough, uncultured sound of her voice. The few minutes on the quay, hearing Japanese spoken so smoothly and naturally by laborers and tradesmen and little children, had made her painfully aware of how little she had learned in all those lessons with Masao in San Francisco.

Mr. Nakamura beamed again and unleashed a torrent of friendly Japanese phrases upon Tessie. Through the hail of unfamiliar syllables, she understood him to be politely contradicting her, lavishing undeserved compliments upon her miserable phrases and predicting a happy stay in Japan for the learned lady foreigner. Tessie felt positively relieved when the man pulling her *jinriksha* started off at a dead run, leaving Mr. Nakamura in mid-sentence and freeing her from the obligation of trying to follow his flowery phrases.

All the same, it was an auspicious beginning. The Japanese were quite friendly, not at all the foreigner-hating inscrutables her fellow passengers predicted. Her accent and grammar might be lamentable, but Mr. Nakamura's reaction proved that she could get along without being trailed by an interpreter wherever she might go. And with the house and servants already provided, a school for the children close at hand, she might soon have all the freedom she could desire to go about Yokohama at her leisure. What could be better? Tessie leaned back in the light carriage and drank in her first sights of Yokohama with an easy mind.

To one used to expansive American cities, everything seemed small and strange and mysterious: little blue-roofed houses, shops hung with blue and white banners inscribed with mysterious symbols, smiling little people in indigo-blue robes patterned with white flowers. The streets were a fluttering wonderland of flags and draperies and paper screens, with each corner offering some new delight to catch the eye: a gilded signboard with a wonderful red lacquered dragon, a little brown baby staring solemnly at Tessie from under his brocaded cap, a miniature tree in a pot full of miniature rocks that somehow suggested a whole mountain covered with wind-twisted pines.

Presently they reached the high crescent that Dr. Ashton had called the Bluff, with its semicircle of two-story Western-style houses facing the harbor, and Tessie felt some of the exhilaration of being in a foreign country flee her. Here all was neat and orderly in a way she knew all too well—white lace curtains covering windows, housemaids in white aprons and nurses in starched white caps promenading with their little charges. At least Sophia should feel quite at home here, and the sooner she felt settled, the sooner Tessie would be free to explore the delights of the lower town. She might even manage a brief foray today; Sophia would want to explore her new domain and might be quite pleased to have the children taken away for a time. They could walk back down the hill, Tessie thought, and buy some of the sweet cakes that had smelled so enticing where they sizzled in the street vendors' stalls. The children would enjoy that.

Sophia soon disabused her of that notion.

"Take my precious babies down into that dirty foreign quarter? You must be mad, Teresa!"

"Here," said Tessie wearily, "we are the foreigners, Sophia. And what's more, they just might think we are the dirty ones. Remember how shocked Masao was when he found out that we just sponge and air our woolen dresses all winter, instead of washing them?"

"No," said Sophia. "I never approved of your parents taking in boarders, and I certainly did not approve of your spending so much time associating with foreign riffraff. Besides, I want you here. Someone must take inventory of all the furnishings and bric-a-brac that came with the house. I don't want the owners claiming we stole or broke anything, when at last we get out of this horrible country."

Masao had been a quiet young engineering student who paid for his room and board by tutoring Tessie in Japanese. Though he was not rich, his manners were impeccable, and Tessie suspected that he came from one of the proud old samurai families that had been impoverished by the changes of the last thirty years. She had been fond of Masao; it made her red hair curl tighter and her cheeks burn to hear Sophia dismissing him as "foreign riffraff."

But quarreling with Sophia would only make her seem ungrateful. It was very kind of Hartley and Sophia to bring her with them. She'd always longed to travel but had never expected to have the opportunity. So Tessie smoothed down her red hair with one hand, bit her tongue until the urge to answer back had passed, and took the notebook Sophia had handed her for the purpose of taking inventory. While she painstakingly listed the contents of each room, Sophia lay down in an upstairs chamber. The bright sunlight dancing on the harbor water had given her a headache. She wanted a cup of tea, with milk and sugar, as soon as possible, and Tessie was to make it herself. Sophia was sure these foreign girls couldn't possibly make a decent cup of tea.

It took three days before the inventory was completed to Sophia's satisfaction, and even then she would have kept Tessie to copy it over in a fair hand if Hartley hadn't demanded Tessie's services in his downstairs office. The head of Benten and Company had not yet called to tell him when he should come to the office, but every day a messenger sent up stacks of papers and invoices and local newspapers, "so that you can familiarize yourself with the customs of the country," Mr. Nakamura politely explained. Hartley sweated over the invoices, read the racing news in the local papers, and ignored the rest. He shoved the pile of paperwork, written in Japanese, into a corner until Tessie could deal with it.

"But Hartley," Tessie exclaimed when she saw the stack of rough-cut papers covered with flowing brush strokes, "Masao only taught me enough to speak with people and to read a few simple little folk tales like the ones I translated for the children. I don't know all these business terms, even in English, much less in Japanese!"

"Well then, you'd better learn them, hadn't you?" Hartley grumbled. "After all, it's your fault I'm in this spot."

That hadn't been the way he saw it when the letter from Benten and Company came to his house in San Francisco, Tessie remembered. Phrases like "golden opportunity" and "a chance to get out of this dead-end desk job" had been freely used in those happy days. Certainly Hartley had had no thought of refusing this job offer and explaining the mistake that had caused it.

It was those children's stories Tessie had been translating. She'd turned one of them into a little poem. Seraphina Jessamine had learned the poem and chanted it for some of Hartley and Sophia's dinner guests one night. The distinguished guests were charmed by the Oriental tale and even more charmed when they learned that it had been translated by a member of the family. Exactly which member of the family was not made clear. Hartley had made modest noises about his long-standing interest in things Oriental and had, in consequence, acquired a wholly undeserved reputation as a brilliant young man who spent his spare time studying Oriental languages.

Somehow that reputation had reached the American branch of the international trading firm Benten and Company. The letter had mentioned the need for a young man of energy and responsibility to train in the Yokohama branch of the firm for a year, with an implication that Hartley might then return to a very senior position in the States. The man who interviewed Hartley in San Francisco had complimented him several times on his supposed knowledge of Japanese but had not exactly asked if Hartley really could speak the language. Hartley hadn't felt it necessary to set the matter straight.

That, at least, had not changed. Hartley might now be seeing his position in Yokohama as more of a trap than an opportunity, but he certainly didn't intend to confess his deception to the mysterious head of Benten and Company, the man who kept sending these stacks of paper up the hill. And Tessie didn't really want him to do so. She didn't want to return to America in disgrace, and what would happen to her opportunity to travel in the Orient? Far better, she thought, to get a good dictionary and work through these papers with Hartley. Once she'd learned the specialized vocabulary of the import-export business, it shouldn't take her long to give him rough translations of the more important papers—and then, at last, she would be free to go out.

"Good, good," said Hartley when Tessie was settled with her dictionary, pen, inkwell, and sheets of blank paper. "Let me know when you're done, will you? I'm going to the races. I don't mind telling you, it's been pretty damn frustrating, sitting here and reading the racing column in the *Japan Gazette* every day and never having a chance to get out and look at some of this prize horseflesh for myself. You'll zip through these papers in no time. Don't write it all out—well, no, I guess you'd better do that, but make a summary, too. I don't want to plow through all the details." He gave her a perfunctory brotherly peck on the cheek and was gone before she'd picked up her pen.

For a day and a half, Tessie managed to quash her restless desire to explore, turning all her attention to the papers Hartley had left with her. She even derived some amusement from the quaint English-language phrases mixed into the business letters.

Then Sophia commandeered her services for a morning of sorting and airing the children's clothes. Everything had been packed away in trunks for the sea voyage. The morning of stooping and shaking out clothes and settling fights among the children left her too tired after lunch to pick up the thread of her translations again.

"Don't grumble," she told herself sternly. She'd done more than half the work already. If she worked straight through this afternoon, without stopping for tea, and came back after dinner, she might actually have Hartley's desk cleared by midnight. Then she'd be free to explore Yokohama in the morning. She thought with a little guilty excitement that it might be wise to rise early and leave the house while Sophia was still abed, just to avoid any problems. Ah, but the harbor city would be beautiful in the early morning, with mist pearling the masts of the ships and draping the quays in jeweled beads! Wasn't that enough of a reward to look forward to?

Tessie set to work with a will, pen scratching over the sheets of foolscap as she made summaries of the letters and documents for Hartley to read when he returned. By late afternoon she was thirsty, and her back ached from bending over the desk for so many hours, but she had made quite a respectable dent in the mass of work.

"Miss Gallagher?"

The soft foreign voice startled Tessie. She dropped her dictionary, spun around on her stool, and gave a low involuntary cry of dismay at the sight of Mr. Nakamura standing in the door.

"Forgive me—I did not mean to startle you." Mr. Nakamura gave three quick, precise bobbing bows in succession. "Your legal sister—I have that correct?"

"Sister-in-law."

"Ah. Your sister of law told me that you will be in

14

this room, but she cannot spare a servant to announce you." Mr. Nakamura frowned. "To announce me? I announce myself."

"It's perfectly all right, Mr. Nakamura. I was startled for a moment, but that doesn't matter." Her dismay had really been at the thought of more papers to translate, more work to keep her in this prim English-style house on the Bluff when she longed to be down in the crowded noisy streets of the Japanese city. "You have more work for Hartley? I will give it to him when he comes in. I'm sorry, he is out just now, some matter of business. I was just using his office for some private correspondence of my own," Tessie lied with a flaming blush. It would never do to let this soft-spoken representative of Benten and Company know that Hartley was spending his days at the races. It would never do to let him know that Hartley depended on his sister to translate his Japanese correspondence, either. With her foot, Tessie felt for the fallen dictionary and tried to nudge it under the desk.

"Please do not be concerned. If I had wished to speak your brother, I would have gone to the Yokohama racing track."

Tessie felt her blush growing several degrees redder, until her cheeks matched the tendrils of hair that had sprung free from her bun.

Mr. Nakamura's black eyes twinkled like little round jade buttons. "Yokohama is a very small town for foreigners, Miss Gallagher. And it is my business to know what your brother does." He bowed again and stooped to pick up the dictionary. "I have come to see you, not Mr. Hartley Gallagher."

"M-me?"

"Yes—and *not* with more papers to translate! Dr. Ashton is leaving for Tokyo tomorrow. He is sad that you have not been to call on him. I am to bring you to drink tea at the shop of his friend. Samurai Shokai."

"Yes, I know. But how did you—"

"Yokohama," said Mr. Nakamura again, "is a very small community. For foreigners. You will come?"

A pang of guilt assailed Tessie at the sight of the work she was leaving undone. "I ought not—I have all this—"

She gestured hopelessly at the stack of letters and bills and invoices and brochures. Mr. Nakamura seemed to know everything already; she might as well be frank with him. "Your employer, this mysterious head of Benten and Company, is expecting Hartley to be familiar with all this material. And Hartley is expecting me to have it ready for him. Tonight," she lied. "He—he plans to work late, to make up for taking the afternoon off. Your employer—"

"Sent me," Mr. Nakamura interrupted, "to be sure that you have an opportunity to visit with Dr. Ashton before his departure." He bowed and strode out of the room without giving Tessie a chance to make any more excuses.

"Your employer! And what business is it of his, may I ask?" Tessie muttered as she followed. She felt grumpy at being pushed around like this, perhaps even grumpier because she was being forced to do something she had been longing to do. Somehow, she felt, she was being deprived of a legitimate sense of grievance.

"No." Mr. Nakamura had come in a light open carriage rather than a jinriksha. He offered Tessie his arm to help her climb in.

"What?"

"No. You may not ask. Or rather, I may not answer. Be careful of the step, Miss Gallagher, it is rather high."

"I don't even know his *name!* None of us has even met him yet—not even Hartley!"

The carriage rattled out of the drive and down the steep slope leading to the lower town.

"You shall meet him," Mr. Nakamura promised. "In due course of events. Now is not the time. Now is the time to take tea with Dr. Ashton. You will be a charming young leisure lady for an hour—is that right?"

"Lady of leisure," Tessie corrected, still feeling slightly unnerved.

"Ah. Like sister of law. English is a very logical language, is it not?" Mr. Nakamura beamed on Tessie with such innocent good will that she could not bring herself to question him further.

Mr. Nakamura left Tessie at the door of the curio shop of Samurai Shokai. "Just ring the bell," he instructed her, "and go on in. Doctor Ashton is expecting you." Tessie moved slowly into the shadowy interior, pausing at every step to exclaim over some new sight. It was a wonderland of quaint and fantastic Japanese art. Her fingers traced the lacquered patterns of red and gold on an antique chest until she glanced upward and met the benign gaze of a fat bronze Buddha, seated cross-legged on the top of the high chest with a length of green-and-blue silk draped over his lap. A string of carved ivory beads dangled from the corner post of a folding screen painted with white cranes on a gold background; beads of lapis lazuli and cloisonné work were twisted around another bundle of silk dyed in glowing patterns of flowers and butterflies.

But the glory of the shop was its collection of swords and armor. A cuirass of woven metal strips, brightly patterned in black and red enamels, hung overhead; a row of helmets glared empty-faced from a spiked iron railing at the back of the shop; every wall was sharp with swords and daggers and throwing knives, glittering with danger, sharp and bright and beautiful.

"You admire my friend's collection?"

It was Dr. Ashton, rising from a wicker chair beside the gilt folding screen. Tessie moved forward, painfully conscious of her trailing full skirt and wide puffed sleeves brushing against pretty, fragile treasures, and took his outstretched hand.

"Forgive me—I did not see you at first," she apologized.

"It is rather dark," Dr. Ashton agreed. "I am glad you found the time to humor an old man with your visit. I was afraid you would find it too boring to spend an hour with me."

"Oh, no!" Had his feelings been hurt because she hadn't come to see him earlier? "I wanted to come sooner, truly I did, but there was so much to do. Well, Sophia needed some help, and so did Hartley, actually." She rushed to explain about the household inventory, and the masses of papers that the mysterious head of Benten and Company had been sending for Hartley to read, and how she had had to translate the Japanese for him because his employer must not know that Hartley couldn't do it himself.

Dr. Ashton's smile turned cynical as she finished her long and somewhat tangled explanation. "I thought so," he said. "No time for yourself. Used like a servant. And the worst is, Tessie, that you let them do it. Now, don't get angry." He held up a hand as if to defend himself. "I'm an old man. I grew to know you on the ship. Let's pretend for a minute that I am an old family friend. Tessie, there will not always be a Mr. Nakamura to come and whisk you away from your family's demands. You must learn to take some time for yourself when you need it."

"I have a duty to my family. They need me." If Dr. Ashton had ever felt thoroughly unwanted, perhaps he would understand how important it was to be needed. Tessie still could not think of Jason Lancaster without a sliver of ice piercing her chest. Hartley's need for her, the children's clinging hands, even Sophia's whiny complaints helped to melt that ice sliver. It was good to be part of a family, even if she wasn't a very important part.

"You have a duty to yourself, too." The doctor took both her hands in his and looked down at her with a piercing gaze under his bushy brows. "If you do not nourish yourself and your soul's needs, if you do not discover what is really important to you and take care of that, then you will be nothing. You will be no use to your family or anyone else, and least of all to yourself." He shook his head and smiled. "I apologize. Even the oldest of family friends is not entitled to read a pretty young lady such a lecture as this! I am concerned for your well-being; let that be my excuse. Now, promise to visit me in Tokyo one day next month, and then let us drop the subject. What do you think of my friend's shop?"

"I've never seen anything like it," Tessie said honestly. "There are so many beautiful things here!"

"There are indeed. Yozo Nomura is a connoisseur of art, and he has been collecting the treasures of his country for a very long time. If he could bring himself to sell more of them, he would be a rich man."

"They're not for sale?" Tessie looked regretfully at the length of flowered silk under the lapis beads.

Dr. Ashton shrugged. "Oh, the jewelry, the silks, the statues and lacquerware—all those little trinkets, he sells these, of course he does, it's his livelihood. But this is the heart of his collection." He gestured toward one of the walls full of swords and daggers and other wicked-looking spiked implements. "These things should be in a museum."

"You persuade me—almost." A short, dark man had come silently out of a back room, pushing aside the hanging of woven silk that concealed the doorway. He grinned. "But they should be in a museum of my own people, Ashton-*san*. You would carry them across the ocean for your barbarian countrymen to stare at, is it not so?"

A breeze from the open front door whiffled through the room, blowing aside the silk hanging at the back. Tessie had an impression of a tall, dark figure moving hastily out of sight—a man too tall for a Japanese, surely? And—of course, the light was deceptive—but something about his head had gleamed white, like a streak of silver. Could it be the man she'd seen on the quay? He'd been talking to Mr. Nakamura, the Benten and Company agent, then. And now he was hiding in the back of the curio shop to which Mr. Nakamura had brought her. Tessie felt suddenly, irrationally sure that this mysterious Westerner was the head of Benten and Company, Mr. Nakamura's employer—her brother's.

She'd been distracted for a moment from Dr. Ashton's conversation with the shop proprietor, but it didn't seem to matter; they were evidently repeating an old friendly argument. Dr. Ashton wanted to buy the entire collection of antique swords for a museum in America. Yozo Nomura insisted that these swords were the heart of his people's culture and history and that it would be a desecration to send them out of the country.

"Your colleagues don't have such tender consciences about selling their old swords to foreign barbarians."

"My colleagues," said Yozo Nomura, "have no consciences at all. My friend, please let us end this argument. You know what his sword was to a samurai —his honor, his very soul. A samurai who lost his sword in battle considered himself a dead man. I have bought these swords from honorable men, men deeply shamed that they must give up the way of the samurai. With every purchase I promised the sellers that these treasures of their families would be treated honorably.

Someday we Japanese will cease running after foreign ways and will revere our glorious past again. When that day comes, the Samurai Shokai collection of swords will be in a museum—a museum built by Japanese, for Japanese, in Japan!" He bowed low as if to take the sting out of his words. "Please, let us not bore your young visitor with this old argument. You will do me the honor to take tea now?"

"We should wait for my other guest," Dr. Ashton murmured.

Tessie felt an old familiar impatience rising inside her, overwhelming caution and manners. She *knew,* as well as she knew her own name, that the head of Benten and Company was eavesdropping on their conversation. He would already have heard her confession to Dr. Ashton that she was doing the Japanese translation Hartley was supposed to do. What more did she have to lose?

"Oh, let's just call him now and get it over with!" She marched past the two men and pushed open the silk curtain at the back of the shop. "Mr. Benten," she addressed a pole hung with antique silk kimonos, "you might as well come out and join us. I can see your shoes under the kimonos."

Folds of burgundy and plum and scarlet silk quivered slightly; woven parrots and tie-dyed flowers and embroidered lozenges shivered as the pole was set aside. Tessie looked up into a face she had once known as well as her own; but when she'd kissed him under the summer vines, he had not had that broad streak of silver in his black hair.

"I might have known you wouldn't have the manners to let me meet you in my own good time," said Jason Lancaster.

At the sound of his voice, Tessie was a thousand miles away and ten years younger, surrounded by the flowers of a summer garden.

Chapter Two

The gazebo in the far corner of the Gallaghers' backyard was a rotting, ramshackle structure of sagging latticework and peeling white paint, almost totally overgrown with morning glory vines. None of the adults in the family would have gone in there for fear of rotting floorboards. But the seven Gallagher children had played many a game of pirates and Indians and highway robbers there. Tessie had been the last child to play there, and now that she was a young lady of sixteen with high-piled red hair and cascading scallops of lace-trimmed petticoats, no one would expect to find her there.

It was the perfect place for a secret meeting.

"I don't see *why* we have to be so secret," murmured Jason Lancaster in between the kisses he pressed on Tessie's white neck.

"Don't you?" It was perfectly clear to Tessie, who was sinking into the languorous, drowsy haze that Jason's kisses always induced in her. A bee buzzed outside; sunlight slanted through the green vines and turned the inside of the arbor into a green shadow jeweled with the stained-glass colors of sun striking through morning glory flowers. Glory of the morning, indeed, Tessie thought drowsily, and why did people have to wear so many clothes? In her lazy dream she was somewhere far away with only Jason beside her, in some cloudy mountain land where clothes were an inconvenience to be discarded at will and where Jason's hand, now cupping her breast through layers of ribboned chemise and starched lace, could pass directly over the skin that ached for his touch.

"No, I don't," said Jason irritably. He raised his head from her neck. "Why can't I simply court you openly? I love you. I want to marry you. I'm going to marry you. I'm free and twenty-one, and your uncle Morgan will vouch that I'm a steady seaman of responsible habits. I want to call on you by the front door, Tessie my love, instead of sneaking over the back fence and hiding in this arbor until you can steal a moment to come running to me. I want to sit in the parlor and balance a teacup on my knee and be introduced to all of your sisters and your cousins and your aunts and say polite, boring things to them until they're convinced I'm a nice fellow. And then . . ."

He paused with one black eyebrow raised, looking down at her with a teasing grin.

"And then?" Tessie prompted him. She looked up, lips parted slightly.

"And then," Jason finished, suiting the action to the words, "once I've got the approval of your whole family, I want to take you out to the little arbor in the back garden and kiss you until you're too breathless to resist my advances!"

The bee circled the arbor, lighted on a flower, and buzzed irritably away when Tessie and Jason leaned against one of the lattice walls and shook his flower.

"I think—I'm already—too breathless to resist," murmured Tessie when Jason's lips finally left hers. "What happens next?"

Jason backed away from her, hands behind his back, and took several deep breaths. His shoulders were quivering with the effort of keeping his hands locked. *"Next,"* he said firmly, "we go up to the house and you introduce me to your parents."

"They've already met you."

"As your fiancé."

Tessie shook her head. "They'll never let me marry you."

"Why not?"

Tessie raised one hand and started counting off the reasons on her fingers. "I'm too young. Mother needs me at home. You're only a common sailor."

"So's your uncle Morgan!"

"I know. They don't much approve of Morgan, either, you know. He was supposed to go into the family business with Papa. Mother always gets that *look* on her face when he's in town and comes to see us." Pinched nostrils, lips downturned, an air of long-suffering martyrdom in the gestures with which she offered Morgan a piece of cake and poured out tea in his cup.

And besides that—Tessie sighed and shook her head. The other children, as they grew older, had been granted their moments of freedom. The girls went to dances and met young men from the best families of San Francisco; the boys went to college and then into respectable positions in the best firms of San Francisco. Tessie would rather go to college than to dances, but to judge from her mother's reaction when she broached the subject, she wasn't going to get the opportunity to do either any time soon. Her mother had shrieked and cried that she couldn't lose her little baby girl.

"You're too young to be gallivanting around," her father had said.

"Next year?"

"No. Women don't need higher education. It's dangerous, too. Why, just the other day I heard a medical man explaining that excessive study in women disturbs the delicate balance of the reproductive—well, never mind that."

"I wouldn't study excessively," Tessie had promised, trying to win a laugh from him.

"You won't study at all!"

"But I don't want to just go to dances and teas and socials and get married like my sisters." There had to be something more to life, though she didn't know what. Of course, that was before she'd met Jason.

"That's all right, Tessie," her father had said. "We're in no hurry to see you married. Your mother needs her baby at home. She's not getting any younger, you know. You'll be the comfort of her old age."

Now, remembering that conversation, Tessie shook her head again. "Even if you were rich, I don't think they'd accept it, Jason."

"There's only one way to find out, isn't there?" He pushed aside the green veil of vines that covered the entrance to the arbor.

"Jason! No!" Tessie caught his arm and tried to drag him back. Grinning, he wrapped both arms about her waist, lifted her off the ground, and carried her across the unkempt wilderness of the Gallaghers' backyard. Tessie flung her arms around Jason's neck and prayed that the rip she'd heard was only a seam in her petticoat and not the lace fringe she loved so dearly. The Chinese cook came out of his shed next to the back porch and yipped excitedly to his family. Two upstairs maids hung over the balcony and giggled at the sight of Miss Tessie being carried over some strange man's shoulder in a flurry of lace and slim legs.

"Teresa! What, may I ask, is the meaning of this?"

In her morning dress of puce satin with the butterfly bustle, Mrs. Gallagher was formidable as a battleship and hardly more maneuverable. It had taken her some time to navigate through the house to investigate the commotion in the backyard, but now that she was there, Tessie felt the excitement and the giggles ebbing away. Jason's arms relaxed; she slid to her feet and took his hand. The warm, steady strength of his fingers gave her the courage to say what came next.

"M-mama, this is Jason Lancaster. M-my fiancé."

"No such thing!" snorted Mrs. Gallagher. As she descended the steps, Tessie saw her father and two of her brothers behind her, and the servants crowding interestedly behind them. She closed her eyes with a little moan. It was going to be a *very* public scene. And a very bad one.

It was both of those things—and just how bad, Tessie could never have imagined beforehand. Even that night, when she had thankfully gained the privacy of her own little room above the back porch, she was still trembling with the memory of the things that had been said. As twilight fell, the lamp on her dressing table turned her little room into a white and rosy cave like the inside of the conch shell Uncle Morgan had given her. White curtains were trimmed with pink scallops, pink chintz canopy overhung the high mahogany posts of the bed, white lace doilies covered the polished wood of dressing table and night stand. Tessie sat before the window, wrapped in layers of white batiste trimmed with pink ribbons. She stared into the mirror, at her own white face with its frame of red curls, and for the first time it occurred to her that all this pink clashed abominably with her hair. But then, no one had ever considered what was suitable for Teresa Mary Alice Gallagher; they had simply designed a room suitable for a sweet young girl, the last daughter in the family, and expected her to fit into it.

They also expected her to fit into a life designed the same way, to stay at home helping Mama forever. Tessie had suspected that when she tried to talk to her father about college; today she'd become certain of it, and today for the first time she'd briefly—ever so briefly—rebelled against her duty.

Now she stared into her reflection, at eyes shadowed with the events of the day, and concluded soberly that she had no choice.

In those first brave moments, she'd thought she could actually do it—introduce Jason to her family and defy their snobbery and force their consent to the marriage. But then her brothers Hartley and Eugene started talking about horsewhips, and Jason began rolling up his sleeves and offering to take on any three Gallaghers in a fair fight.

She'd begged him to leave then, before matters got worse.

"And leave you with *them?* You'd better come with me."

"I can't. I'll explain. I'll make them understand. *Please,* Jason! It will only get worse if you're here."

He'd left then, but only with the promise—or was it a threat?—that he'd be back for her later, after she'd had it out with her family.

"A common sailor!" Mama had attacked before he was out of earshot. "How could you, Tessie? And sneaking around behind our backs. How could you lower yourself to behave so shamelessly?"

There was more in the same vein, much more, and whenever Mama stopped for breath, Hartley and Eugene chimed in. Papa, mercifully, just stood on the back steps glowering. He didn't need to say much. Mama and Hartley and Eugene said it all for him. And Tessie couldn't get a word in edgewise to say anything in her own defense.

She could have pointed out that Uncle Morgan had introduced them and that he, at least, approved of Jason. She could have explained that Jason was not a common deck hand but an educated man who'd chosen to work as first mate on a ship rather than depend on his older brothers to support him. She could have mentioned that the Gallaghers themselves were not of such exalted stock as all that. Hadn't Grandfather Gallagher first landed on these shores as a barefoot Irish lad fleeing the potato famine? And finally, she could have said that she was meeting Jason in secret for the excellent reason that she feared exactly such a scene as this.

Some of those things, said at the right time and in the right way, might have slowed the torrent of denunciations falling about her ears. But then again, they might not. Tessie gave a small, defeated sigh and shook her head at the white-faced girl reflected in the window. She had never been famous for her ability to say the right thing in the right way; of all her family, she was the one who'd inherited the biggest share of Grandfather Gallagher's fiery temper. And in any case, it was too late now. By the time Mama, Hartley, and Eugene had run out of words to describe her behavior, Tessie had been too furious to meet them with calm, reasoned arguments. She'd been stuttering in her rage, threatening to run away with Jason that very night, shouting that they didn't really care who he was, they just wanted to keep her from having a life of her own.

"That a daughter of mine should say such things! That these should be the last words my ears should hear! Oh, sharper than a serpent's tooth!" Mama exclaimed, pressing one hand against her ample bosom. "The pain—ah, it rends my heart! It—"

She'd stopped in mid-sentence, struggling for breath, an almost comical look of surprise on her face. Then she moaned, "Ah, it *hurts!*" in a pained whimper quite unlike her ringing theatrical tones of a moment earlier.

Papa and Hartley caught her as she fell.

There was water and burnt feathers and the shrieking of the upstairs maids, and through all the commotion the dreadful wheezing sound of Mama trying to breathe. Her eyes followed Tessie with a look of hopeless begging. Finally Dr. Chamberlain arrived with his black bag and some drops that miraculously helped Mama to breathe when she lay back on a pile of pillows.

"She's had similar attacks before? Yes, yes, I thought so. You should have called me in earlier. A bad history, a bad history. Agitation? Some shock? The stress of caring for this large family."

"There's only Teresa left at home now," said Papa.

The doctor shot Tessie a sharp, questioning look. She felt her cheeks growing hot. "Ah? Young girls can be very trying—very trying indeed. Well, Missie, your mother must not be troubled again. She needs rest and quiet and a regular course of treatment. I'll be visiting daily until she is out of danger."

"Nothing will trouble her again," Tessie vowed, and she meant it. How could she be so selfish as to upset Mama with her own desires at a time like this? She was young. So was Jason. They could wait until his next voyage was over. For now, her duty lay at home, with Mama, whose very life depended upon her.

A tiny rattling sound came from outside the curtained window. Tessie started and blew out the lamp. She heard it again, a series of minute sharp clicks, like tiny hailstones blowing across the windowpane. But outside the night sky was clear, illuminated by a moon that turned the lawn into a mysterious mosaic of black shadows and silver lights.

The sound came again, and this time Tessie knew what had caused it: a handful of sand and pebbles. Jason was in the backyard. He'd come back for her as he promised.

Her knees were shaking as she went to the closet and pulled out a dark cloak. There was no time to dress. But the cloak would cover her nightgown, and she could hide the bright gleam of her loosened hair under the hood.

The third, fifth, and seventeenth steps of the back stairs were given to protesting creaks. Tessie felt her way barefoot down the stairs and managed, with some strain, to skip over those three betrayers. Then there was the heavy latch of the back door in the kitchen to negotiate, and after that she had to thread her way through the empty pails and drying pans that littered the floor of the scullery. One last door, and then she was flying barefoot across the dew-wet grass.

He was in the gazebo already. Had he been so sure she would come to his call, then? Tessie felt a moment of irritation, and then she was lost as always in the rough, warm strength of his embrace, his cheek next to hers, his lips hot and demanding, large hands reaching inside her cloak, inside the loosened neckline of her nightdress, touching and caressing and roving over all the places on her skin where she had longed to know him. The cloak was a puddle on the floor, and her nightdress was off one shoulder entirely, and if he tugged on the other ribbon tie she would be completely naked. They had not yet said one word of greeting. It didn't matter. Nothing mattered but being with Jason.

"Will your father receive me," Jason murmured into her neck, "if I come to call by the front door next time?"

"No."

"Does he understand that we're promised to each other?"

"No."

"Then it has to be this way. Tessie, you'll trust me? I'll take care of you. I swear it. I'll—"

"I'd trust you with my life," Tessie whispered. His shirt was loose. She followed the vow by placing her lips on the dark, crisp hair that curled up to the base of his throat. Jason groaned, and his hands shook on her body as her lips moved down across the muscled expanse of his chest.

30

"Tessie—I can't—do you know what you're do-ing?"

"Yes," Tessie said. "I love you."

And then the nightdress was off entirely, and Jason's shirt followed it to the floor, and his hands and lips were all over her, lighting fires everywhere at once, and she wondered how she could ever have thought that kissing was the single nicest thing about being in love. This, whatever he was doing to her now, was far better, and she wanted it to go on forever. No, she didn't. It was too much, too sweet to be borne, and she moaned and pressed against him without knowing what she wanted, only driven on by a terrible need and urgency unlike anything she'd ever known before.

His thighs were rough against hers. She shivered with delight and expectancy and pulled him closer to her. All the love and longing that had built through their summer's secret meetings was welling up in her now until she wanted nothing more than to be close to Jason, to belong to him completely. Whatever he did had to be right, because he was Jason and he loved her—and she was aching with the need for more of his touch. His skin against hers was silk and fire and delight, too sweet to be borne. She did not know what to do, but they were doing it anyway.

There was a moment of pain somewhere at the center of her body, and for just that heartbeat of time she was afraid and remembered how her married sisters sighed and complained with mysterious side-long glances about men's needs and a wife's duties. But then the fires of need were burning inside her as well as outside, and the only thing that would quench them was Jason. She held him close to her and forgot the pain in the glory of the new sensations that blossomed inside her like fireworks in the night sky, pale moonlight all given over now to red and gold and blue and emerald sparks going off all at once.

And then it was quiet again, the pile of clothes

under them hard and cool and slightly damp for some reason, and Jason was holding her gently and stroking her forehead and apologizing.

"I never meant things to go so far, Tessie. I love you, I respect you—you know that. You're so beautiful—and coming to me half-naked like that, it's more than a man can stand. And anyway, we'll be married as soon as possible, so it's all right, isn't it? Listen, I've been thinking. I talked to Morgan, too. You'll have to come away with me at once, Tessie, tonight, before they think of sending you off someplace or watching you. Can you get back up to your room and pack any little things you want to take?"

"No." Tessie sat up and pushed the tangle of damp curls back from her forehead. She felt cold now that the warmth of Jason's body was no longer covering her, and awkward to be naked in front of a man now that their madness had passed. She scrambled into her nightgown, getting it on backward and ripping off the last of the pearl buttons in her haste, and wrapped the cloak around her.

"Well, then," said Jason, "you'll just have to come with me as you are, though where we'll get a dress for you I don't know. You'll have to stay inside my lodgings until I've got our marriage arranged. Then I'll get you a place to stay while I'm at sea, because the ship's leaving day after tomorrow. Morgan said he'll stand up for me at the marriage and sign as a witness, so that should be some help if your family comes after you."

"Wait. Wait, Jason. I don't understand. You're talking about getting married? Now? I can't do that. I came down here to explain to you. We have to wait."

"Tessie," said Jason, "we can't wait. Not after what just happened. Don't you understand? You have to marry me now."

"I will," Tessie promised. "Eventually. But not

now. Maybe after your next voyage. I can't just run away with you, Jason; it would kill my mother."

Jason snorted.

"Don't laugh! You don't know what happened this afternoon after you left. Mama had a heart attack. The doctor said he wouldn't answer for her life if she were to be upset or anxious about anything in the next few weeks, maybe months. Jason, I *have* to stay with her. It's my duty."

"Ah, yes," Jason said in a subtly altered tone. "Morgan told me something about your mother's heart problem."

"Then you understand why I have to stay?" Tessie felt almost disappointed that Jason accepted her decision so easily.

"No. What Morgan told me is that your mother has had 'heart attacks' for years, every time somebody in the family crosses her will, and that she's called in just about every doctor in San Francisco. After a time they all see through her."

"That's not true!" Tessie protested. "It can't be. Mama wouldn't do that. Besides, we all know she has a weak heart. We've known for ages—ever since that time when I was a baby, when Letitia Janet wanted to go to a dance with that wild O'Kelley boy and Mama simply collapsed in the middle of the argument."

"Just as she did today?"

"Well—yes."

"And I don't suppose the same doctor attended her both times, and all the times in between?"

"Well, no. This Dr. Chamberlain, he's just recently set up his practice in San Francisco. But that doesn't prove anything, Jason. You should have seen her. Nobody could have thought she was pretending."

"She has had," Jason reminded her, "a number of years to perfect her act. Well, Tessie? Are you coming with me or not?"

33

Tessie stood silent, biting her lower lip. There *was* a pattern to Mama's attacks. How could she not have noticed it before? But what if she was wrong, what if this time it was real and Tessie's elopement killed her?

"How can I take the chance?" she wailed. "If she dies, and it's my doing, I'll never, never forgive myself." Jason couldn't expect her to make a decision like that. "Can't you wait? Perhaps when you come back from this next voyage things will be different."

"And if they aren't?"

Then they would just have to wait even longer. Couldn't he see that? Tessie stared up at him, mutely beseeching his understanding.

"If you love me," Jason said, "you'll come with me."

"I'm afraid—" What if her mother died of the shock? How could he ask her to take that responsibility?

"I know you are. Too afraid to take a chance on me?"

What did that have to do with it? It wasn't Jason she was afraid of, but her own conscience.

"Tessie." Jason's voice was slow and measured. She felt as if some sentence of doom were being pronounced upon her. "Come with me now. I won't dangle for years on your mother's string, jumping to her commands every time she decides to pretend illness. And I won't have a wife who does that, either. You'll come now, or—"

If he insisted, how could she resist him? He was bigger and stronger than she was, and she was already morally his wife. It might even be wrong to refuse. And if he forced her to come with him now, if he picked her up and carried her away to marry him, it wouldn't be her fault.

But he didn't lay a hand on her.

"Or what?" Tessie asked at last.

"Come now," Jason said, "or not at all. It's your decision."

How could he be so cruel? Couldn't he see that if he left it to her conscience, there was only one decision she could make?

"Your mother won't die of chagrin," Jason said. "And I won't waste my life waiting for things to magically become different, waiting for a girl who won't lift a finger to change things for herself when she has the chance. Next voyage? Ha! I could ship 'round the world a dozen times, and your parents wouldn't like me any better, and you wouldn't be any braver. Come with me now, Tessie. I'm asking you for the last time."

He didn't mean that, he couldn't mean that. Not after the way they had loved each other tonight. Tessie knew she would die if Jason left her life. He had to feel the same way. "I will be waiting for you," she said, "when you come back from this next voyage."

Jason's face was blank in the moonlight. "Don't hold your breath."

He had left her then, and she had never seen him again—until this day in the Japanese curio shop.

Chapter Three

Tessie never could quite remember how she got out of the curio shop and away from Jason Lancaster. The shock of seeing Jason again left her as dizzy as if she'd been smitten with sunstroke. She mumbled some incoherent apologies to Dr. Ashton and fled the shop. Behind her she could hear Jason saying something about sudden illness and the shock to the system in one's first days in a foreign climate, and promising that he would personally escort Miss Gallagher home.

"No!" she gasped when he appeared to hand her into the carriage.

"As you wish," Jason agreed, his face a courteous mask. He stood back and let Mr. Nakamura drive her away.

Tessie longed for privacy, but when they reached home again she found Forbes Montague and Eustace Neville brandishing cardboard samurai swords and fighting to the death for the favors of Seraphina Jessamine, who had been tied to a bush by her new pink silk ribbons, awaiting the outcome of the battle. By the time Tessie had confiscated the swords, dried Seraphina's tears, and calmed Sophia, who was having hysterics on the balcony, nobody thought to ask where she'd been or why, and for this she was profoundly grateful. Subsequent domestic crises kept her too busy to think for the rest of the evening and too tired to lie awake brooding over the past when at last she fell into bed.

The next few days were not so easy to get through. From being an invisible presence brooding over the house, Jason Lancaster became an extremely visible employer. He didn't seem upset at the discovery that Tessie was managing Hartley's Japanese translations for him, or that Hartley had been spending his days at the Yokohama racetrack. She remembered that Mr. Nakamura had said several times, rather pointedly, what a small community the foreign enclave in Yokohama was. If he knew about Hartley, then it was logical to suppose Jason did, too. And if Jason Lancaster didn't mind Tessie's doing the Japanese side of the work, Hartley asked, what was she so worried about?

"I don't know," Tessie said miserably. "I don't trust him. It doesn't make sense. Why would he spend all this money to bring you here and then not be upset to discover that you're useless to him?"

Hartley threw back his sloping shoulders, puffed up his narrow chest like an offended cockerel, and explained to Tessie patronizingly and at some length that he had many things besides a mere clerk's translation skills to offer Benten and Company. Sound business sense, years of practical experience, an understanding of the American market—why, knowing Japanese was the least of the things a fellow needed to do business over here!

"Doesn't it bother you at all," Tessie demanded, "working for a man you once threatened to horsewhip?"

"Jason's a good fellow when you get to know him," Hartley told her. "He's put that little incident completely behind him, Teresa, and I recommend that you do the same, and soon. He wants the whole family to accompany him to the Baptist missionary picnic."

Tessie was able, without much maneuvering, to spend the whole of the Baptist missionary picnic surrounded by small children—trying Seraphina Jessamine's sash, wiping Forbes Montague's chin, holding Eustace Neville's head when he ate too much cherry trifle and was sick behind the bushes. She noted with some relief that Jason Lancaster did not seek her out. Naturally, she was not in the least disappointed.

She was less successful, however, in avoiding him on subsequent social occasions. The foreign community in Yokohama had a bustling social life, and Jason Lancaster was a prominent member of that community. He seemed to want his new manager and the new manager's family at each and every occasion. If it wasn't a garden party, it was a regatta or a horse show or a light opera company touring the Pacific by steamship or their very own Yokohama Amateur Thespian Society putting on a medley of Gilbert and Sullivan songs. Tessie managed to escape from a few invitations by pleading that somebody had to stay home with the children. Jason hired a starched German governess to watch the children and managed, by what tact Tessie never knew, to persuade Sophia that the governess had been her own idea. Since Sophia wasn't paying her wages, she was relatively easy to convince. When Tessie pleaded illness, Jason called on her at home, while everybody else was at the show, to express his concern and his hope that she would soon feel better. Tessie had actually been potting flowering plants on the back porch when he called, and while their Japanese houseboy was making excuses for her she had to crouch in the scullery for fear of being discovered out of her bed. It was all very undignified.

And, between Sophia's nerves and Hartley's translations and the social life Jason Lancaster had created for them, not only was she spending her days wondering where Jason would pop up next, but she hadn't had a minute to herself to explore the tantalizing Japan that lay just out of reach.

She was almost relieved when Mr. Nakamura appeared one morning and requested that she visit the Benten and Company offices "on a matter of business."

"You mean me," Hartley corrected. "Not my sister. I'm the office manager, remember?"

"Mr. Lancaster requires someone who speaks Japanese. And he has requested me to remind you that he expects the pleasure of your company at the race meeting this afternoon."

So Jason wouldn't be there. Tessie was curious about why he'd sent for her on a matter involving Japanese translation when he had Mr. Nakamura, whose English was infinitely better than her Japanese. Maybe it was something involving women's dress or American customs? Or maybe he just wanted to demonstrate his power over the Gallagher family—that he, who'd once been a poor seaman they wouldn't let in the door, could now snap his fingers and have Tessie or Hartley come running at his command.

He probably expected her to be irritated at this peremptory demand. How little he knew her, after all! Tessie was delighted at the prospect of getting out of another stultifying afternoon race meeting. Whatever she was to do for Jason, she would be doing it in the Yokohama office of Benten and Company, right down by the harbor in the Japanese part of town. And Jason wouldn't be there. Tessie told herself that she was delighted about that, too.

But he was waiting for her at the door of Benten and Company. Tessie paused in the narrow street. Had he just been leaving? What bad luck that she should have

encountered him just then. If only she hadn't answered his command so promptly, she might have
missed seeing him altogether. What bad luck, she
repeated fiercely to herself while her eyes drank in
raven-black hair with a silver streak, a tall broad-
shouldered form, an impatient face. It didn't mean
anything. The man was unreasonably handsome; naturally, it was a pleasure to look at him, but that didn't
mean she was glad to run into him like this. If she felt
a little short of breath, that was only because she had
been in a hurry; the trembling sensation in her
diaphragm had nothing at all to do with the unexpected sight of Jason Lancaster. Nothing whatever.

She waited for him to step out of the office and pass
her with a nod. Instead he beckoned to her. "Come
on. We'll miss the train," he snapped, and strode off
without looking to see if she could keep up with him.

"Train? But I thought—"

"We're going to the Tokyo office today."

"Why?"

"I need your help there."

Not another word of explanation did he vouchsafe
until they were seated in one of the little cars that
made the twenty-mile run to Tokyo daily. And even
then, when Tessie asked exactly what he wanted her to
do in Tokyo, he said only that they would discuss the
matter at the appropriate time.

"Why don't you sit back and look at the scenery?"
he suggested. "This is your first sight of Japan outside
Yokohama, isn't it? Surely you don't want to waste
these precious moments in arguing."

She didn't. That was true, though she was infuriated
that he should have pointed it out just a second before
she had been going to say the exact same thing. She
turned to the window, fighting the urge to say something rude.

On the misty horizon she could make out low hills
dotted with the twisted Japanese pines, so familiar to

her from prints she had seen. Here and there a little building with peaked roof and up-pointed corners appeared on the hillsides. Temples? She drew a breath to ask Jason, then remembered that she was not feeling friendly toward him. That did seem a pity. It would have been so pleasant to see this new and entrancing land with a friend beside her to explain it all. That was all she felt, Tessie told herself—mild regret that they couldn't enjoy common, cordial relations. And she was really a fool to sit here staring at him when there was all of Japan passing by outside the window!

Tessie turned back to the window and concentrated on the passing scenery. There was so much to see, if only she paid proper attention to it instead of thinking about the provoking black-haired man beside her!

The land stretched out flat on either side of the track to the distant hillsides. It was alive with color and life. The rice fields were quivering mirrors under the rising sun, sprinkled with fresh green spikes and interlaced with myriad winding paths. Here a crane spread its wings above the water and then sank back; there a group of men and women in indigo-dyed gowns stood knee-deep in the water and weeded the paddy. All the ditches that carried water to the paddies were blossoming with pink flowers. Occasionally they passed an arch, seemingly placed in the middle of nowhere, but as the train went by Tessie would look between the pillars and see a glimpse of Fuji's cone, or a perfectly framed pine tree on a hill, and she would almost understand why the arch had been placed just there.

The misty, subtle landscape reminded Tessie of herself with Jason: a series of moments half glimpsed and never fully realized. Whenever she felt on the verge of understanding what was going on between them, the inexorable passage of time carried her away from the moment of insight, just as the train sped past the views framed by the arches and reduced them to dots of insignificance in the distance.

As the train drew closer to Tokyo, the road that ran beside the tracks was crowded with people. "Oh, look!" Tessie exclaimed at the sight of one group of travelers, forgetting that she was not in charity with Jason. "Aren't the babies sweet? And they can see everything, riding on their mothers' backs like that. Look at their little black eyes taking everything in."

"You look as interested as they are," Jason teased.

"Well, it's as new to me, or even more so! What are we to do in Tokyo? Will there be time to look around the city a little bit?"

"I hope so. In fact, we're to go to the Kameido temple first. You'll like that."

The railway station was crowded with Japanese of all classes—mincing ladies with their black hair piled into high, glossy knots, Japanese businessmen wearing various strange combinations of Western and Eastern costume, barefoot coolies swinging their baskets of plaited straw, Buddhist priests with shaven heads, pilgrims in white dresses, and ragged beggars who exposed their running sores to the passersby. Jason strode through the station, keeping up a running commentary on the classes of people they saw. A beggar grasped Tessie's skirt and whined a long Japanese sentence at her. She was proud of herself for being able to understand that he was begging for a penny for food.

"No, my friend," Jason replied in Japanese. "From the look of your fat ribs, you're not short of food at all."

The beggar let go of Tessie's skirt, laughing and raising cupped hands. "Then a penny for luck, for the sake of your beautiful Fox Lady Barbarian!"

Jason tossed him a coin and took Tessie by the hand.

"Come on now. I can't afford to be rescuing you

42

from every street layabout between here and the Kameido!"

"You speak Japanese better than I do!" Tessie accused him.

"I have," Jason pointed out, "been doing business in this country for nine years."

"Most of the foreigners in Yokohama don't speak any Japanese at all, and some of them have been here for *thirty* years. Why did you deceive me?"

"Deceive you?"

"You pretended you needed me to come with you because I spoke a little Japanese. But clearly you don't need any interpreter. What are you up to?"

"Come *on,*" Jason said. "Let's get a *jinriksha.* The Tokyo railway station is no place for a private chat. I'll explain everything when we get to the Kameido."

The Kameido temple grounds were a network of broad paths around pools of water, covered with a roof of wisteria vines. The vines were blooming now, and the lavender and purple flowers drooped so low that they brushed Tessie's hair and filled the air with their sweet scent. She could barely catch a glimpse of pale blue sky between the thick hanging clusters of flowers. Drifts of loose petals—pale lilac, lavender, rosy pink, and deep royal purple—floated down to the still pools where goldfish swam lazily in the depths.

From the moment they stepped into the shaded paths, Tessie was breathless with delight.

"I thought you'd like it," Jason said after a while. "It's too bad that cherry blossom season is over already; next year we will come to see them. But this is the next best thing."

"It's wonderful," Tessie said honestly. She gazed with parted lips at an arbor covered with white wisteria, like a drift of new-fallen snow in the midst of summer's bounty. A low bench was placed below the arch of white blossoms.

"Sit down," Jason prompted. "Would you like tea?"

He ordered tea for her and sake for himself, and a platter of rice balls.

"I don't think I really want anything to eat," said Tessie, eyeing the cold, glutinous mounds of rice with a dubious look.

"Good. It's not for you. It's for the goldfish." Jason crumbled one of the rice balls into the water, and the fallen wisteria blossoms were immediately pushed aside by a swirl of red and gold. The rice crumbs disappeared, and three fat gaping mouths quested around the surface of the water for more. Tessie laughed and took some rice to throw to them herself.

"They're like fat spoiled little babies, aren't they?"

"Fat and spoiled, certainly," Jason agreed. "Everyone in Tokyo comes here in wisteria season to feed them. I wouldn't know about babies. I don't have much experience along those lines. Do you? You never married, did you?"

Tessie flushed. Did he think she'd had nothing better to do, all these years, but grieve for him? "Oh, well—nieces and nephews, you know," she murmured while thinking how best to strip Jason of his egotistical notions.

"Ah, yes. Hartley and Sophia's brats?"

"They were babies once, you know."

"And they're thoroughly spoiled now," Jason continued.

She didn't want to quarrel with him. Besides, it was true. "Tell me why we came here."

"Because I thought you'd like to see the wisteria," Jason said with a smile.

"No, really. You keep putting me off. Why was it so important to bring me to Tokyo today?"

"Well, in another week or so it will be too hot for the wisteria, and the blossoms won't be at their peak, and—all right, all right, don't hit me!" Jason held up his hands mock-defensively, laughing.

"I wasn't going to hit you." But he was balancing on the bench like a schoolboy, temptingly close to the goldfish pool. And Tessie was beginning to feel sorely tempted. She had to remember that he was her employer—well, Hartley's, anyway. "I just want to know what's going on."

"I thought we needed to spend some time together," Jason told her. "You've been avoiding me like a skittish pony, bridling and sidling and putting your ears back whenever I come around. I thought it was time to clear the air. If you're afraid I'll talk about our previous relationship, don't worry. My lips are sealed."

"I have no desire to discuss the past."

"Exactly." He looked relieved. Had he been afraid she would throw herself at him? "We need a good, sensible business relationship, Tessie, not some feminine emotionalism cluttering things up. I hired a Westerner who knew Japanese, and I got one. I'm perfectly satisfied with the arrangement if you are."

"I don't see that you need any help in that department."

"I don't stay in Yokohama year-round," Jason explained. "How do you think I built up this business out of nothing but a seaman's pay? Oh, doubtless you never gave it a thought. Why should you?"

He sounded piqued. Tessie decided not to tell him that she'd been intensely curious about how he'd achieved such a great success in so short a time. But the man's ego was so overinflated that she'd chosen not to ask.

"I spend most of the year traveling around Japan, talking to artists and craftsmen and seeking out new sources," Jason went on. "Most of those import-export dealers in Yokohama sit in their houses on the Bluff and wait for Japanese to bring things to them. You don't get the best prices that way, *or* the best craftsmanship, or the most unusual and interesting work. I know the country. I know the people. Benten and Company has a better stock of trade goods than any other dealer in Japan, and I mean to keep it that way."

"I still don't see why you pretend to need our help," Tessie murmured when he paused in his orgy of self-congratulation.

"Dammit, I'm getting to that! Can't you trust me for five minutes?"

"My experience has not led me to trust you for five *seconds*," Tessie flashed back.

"I thought we were putting the past behind us."

"You were. I've made no promises. But don't worry. That little episode between us was supremely unimportant to me. It's just that I would like to have my natural curiosity satisfied before I die of old age right here in the Kameido temple grounds."

Jason sighed. "I can see I had a lucky escape. It's quite simple, Tessie. The business has grown to the point where I need an office manager in Yokohama full-time. I can't stay there; I have to keep traveling around the country, seeking out new sources. Nakamura can't take the position; too much of the work involves keeping up with paperwork for English shippers and American warehouses, and his written English is pitiable."

"He speaks well enough."

Jason nodded. "I know. But something seems to happen to Japanese, even the ones who seem quite fluent in English, when they try to compose a business letter. You must have seen some examples of what I mean."

Tessie smiled. "There were a few such letters in the papers you sent for Hartley to look over. One announcing a name change said, 'In futura the o-title of our frim will be for new name Yoshimwra.'"

"Exactly. Nakamura can't handle the correspondence. I need Hartley to do that—and, it seems, I need you to translate the Japanese for Hartley."

"Can't Mr. Nakamura do that? His English is certainly much better than my Japanese."

Jason looked away and drummed his fingers on one knee. "It wouldn't work out," he said eventually. "Most of the Western trading firms here rely heavily on Japanese interpreters—and as a result, the men who are supposed to be in charge never really know what's going on. They know only as much as the interpreter chooses to tell them. Benten and Company has built a solid reputation based on my knowledge of the country and the language; everybody knows I can't be cheated by slipshod or dishonest translations. I want to continue that tradition by putting another Japanese-speaking manager in the Yokohama office."

"Don't you trust Mr. Nakamura?"

"That's not the point. It's the principle of the thing!" Jason raked his fingers through his black hair and stared angrily at Tessie. "Damn women, you never understand abstract principles. Look. I hired a Japanese-speaking office manager for Yokohama, and that's what I got—in two parts. Hartley is the office manager part, and you're the Japanese part. I want both parts to function well for my business; Hartley alone is useless to me. Your services are an important part of the job. And the job won't be done right if you keep trying to avoid me. We have to establish a normal, unsentimental business relationship. Do you think you can manage that?"

Tessie closed her eyes and counted to ten very slowly. The colossal arrogance of the man! How dared he insinuate that she was still in love with him? What made him imagine she'd ever given him another thought after the way he callously walked out of her life?

"Tessie?" His hands enclosed hers, warm and caressing. Tessie jerked her fingers away, feeling the shock of his touch through her entire body. Not, of course, that she desired him to touch her. It was just that she was surprised.

"If it's too hard for you, Tessie, we can work out something. Perhaps you need more time to get used to being with me again. We could go out again, spend time together in places like this where you don't have to be businesslike, until it gets easier for you."

Counting to ten really wasn't enough. Tessie started going through ten Hail Marys, her lips moving soundlessly as she prayed for calm.

"I'm sorry," said Jason, looking anything but sorry. "I didn't realize my presence would bring back so many painful memories. How could I have guessed you would still feel so strongly for me after all these years?"

Tessie abandoned the Blessed Virgin in mid-prayer and gave in to the promptings of her lowest self. "As it happens," she said icily, "I never gave you another thought. The only thing that worries me about our association now, Jason Lancaster, is that Ricardo might misunderstand. He's extremely jealous of me and very hot-tempered."

"Ricardo," Jason repeated.

"My fiancé."

"Hartley didn't say anything about your being engaged."

"He doesn't know anything about it. The—the engagement is a secret for the time being."

"Ah. Still afraid of your family? This Ricardo is as unsuitable as I was? A young man, no property, seeking to better himself by a good marriage?"

"No such thing," Tessie snapped. "As a matter of fact, it's Ricardo's family who might object. He comes of a fine old Castilian family, some of the first settlers in California—the Espiñosas—you must have heard of them?"

"Can't say I have."

"No," Tessie agreed cruelly. "You would hardly have moved in those circles. When Ricardo and I met, we fell in love at once. I hardly dared dream that such a man could truly love me, for he is everything a woman could desire and more. Tall, handsome, fair-haired, and beautiful as the sun."

"Ah, yes. Some of those fine old families do run to weak, pretty boys."

"Not Ricardo! His hobby happens to be breaking wild mustangs on the family ranch. He's a real man in every way, Jason, one who knows how to protect and cherish a woman."

"But not, evidently, to the point of introducing her to his family?"

"That will come in due course," Tessie said, trying to sound more confident than she felt. "These things take time."

"Indeed. My own crass, untutored instincts would suggest that when a man loves a woman, he wants to marry her and have her for himself—not let her go off to a foreign country for an unspecified period. Of course, I wouldn't understand how these fine Castilian families operate—not, as you point out, moving in those circles myself."

He sounded definitely piqued, and Tessie allowed herself a moment of private satisfaction. It was good for Jason Lancaster to be reminded that he wasn't the only man in the world. He should be reminded of that more often.

"Well," said Jason after a moment of waiting for Tessie's response, "I'm certainly glad to hear that your feelings present no bar to our working together in a businesslike way. Very glad indeed. As long as that's settled, I suppose I might as well take you back to Yokohama."

"I suppose so," Tessie agreed. She felt slightly disappointed at this abrupt end to the day. Which was silly of her, really. The Kameido temple was much more pleasant than the race meeting they were supposed to attend in Yokohama. But she would come again to Tokyo on her own, or with a companion of her own choosing, rather than with this arrogant, self-centered man. Anybody with any sense would be delighted that he wanted to cut their outing short.

"After all," Jason added, eyeing her narrowly, "I wouldn't want Ricardo to get the wrong idea about our association."

"When I next write to him," Tessie said, "I shall be sure to make it quite clear that it's purely a matter of business."

The train ride back to Yokohama was as dull and disappointing as the journey up had been exciting. The only consolation was that they would arrive too late to join the race meeting after all; she could go straight home and rest. That seemed appropriate. For some reason Tessie could take no pleasure, now, in the repeated vista of rice paddies, misty hillsides, temples, and arches. Flat, dull, featureless—the scenery was a mirror of her own life. A day trip to Tokyo with her employer, an evening listening to Hartley recount which horse came in first in the sixth race—such were the pleasures of a spinster sister's life.

Her glimpse of the bustling life of Tokyo had only made her feel even more caged at the thought of Yokohama's imitation of proper English society. She could hardly bear to hear the click of the railway carriage wheels conveying her from Japan to pseudo-England. From girls in kimonos and farmers wading knee-deep in the rice paddies to ladies in bustles and gentlemen in starched collars—from impudent friendly beggars and chanting priests to Hartley droning on about the race meeting while Sophia whined complaints about the servants and the smell of boiled cabbage drifted through the house. Tessie felt wild and desperate, ready to do anything to get out of this confined life. Japan was waiting for her, right around the corner, and she had nothing to look forward to except an infinity of inane meetings with Hartley and Sophia's friends, punctuated by painfully polite business conferences with Jason Lancaster.

When Hartley began describing the finish of the fifth race for the third time, Tessie picked up the folded copy of the *Japan Gazette* and began scanning its columns as he talked. In her present tired, discontented mood, the paper seemed almost as boring as anything else; still, there was food for dreams in the advertisements. A steamship company advertised tours of the Inland Sea; perhaps she could get ahead with Hartley's translations and leave the children with their new governess and take one of those tours. There was an advertisement for a Yokohama silk shop with weavings and antique kimonos and obis "brought at great expense from remote corners of the Japan Islands." Was that the sort of buying trip Jason Lancaster went on? Perhaps she could accompany him one day—not that she wanted to be near him, of course, but it would be a way to see something of Japan.

There was even a "Personals" column, just like in the papers back home. Tessie wondered idly why anybody would trust their personal lives to the doubtful anonymity of a newspaper's advertising section. Who read these plaintive pleas for "Major's Pussy-Willow" to "Return to Her Loving Hearth"? Who cared if "Single Young Man of Impeccable Connections" sought "Japanese-speaking Pillow Friend for Conversation and Companionship"? Actually, the last one sounded mildly improper. All right—now she knew who read these ads—lonely, frustrated spinsters like her, looking for vicarious thrills. But who on earth answered them?

Down in the lower right-hand corner of the page, a familiar nickname caught her eye and startled her into a long indrawn breath.

"Maggie T.—For news of a legacy, call upon the yamabushi of Kiritsumi. S. and C. and very U!"

For the second time since her arrival in Japan, Tessie was plunged into a whirlpool of memories that carried her back to happier, more innocent days. Ten years, fifteen years passed before her eyes in a blur of tears.

"Is something the matter, Teresa?" Her shocked stillness had penetrated Hartley's self-absorption. He broke off his monologue on horse racing in Yokohama and looked closely at his little sister for the first time in years. "You look quite pale. Was the day too tiring for you?"

"Perhaps I am a little tired," Tessie agreed, rising unsteadily to her feet. Her right hand pleated the newspaper in little folds, keeping the Personals column inside the folds and out of sight. "If you will excuse me to Sophia, I think I should like to rest for a while."

Chapter Four

Above and behind the shadowy, cluttered rooms of the Samurai Shokai curio shop was a second set of rooms—airy, open, almost empty, furnished only with low tables and a few heavy floor mats. Pearly light entered through rice-paper screens; a dark vase in a niche held a single spray of flowers and three bare twigs. This, too, Tessie thought, was Japan, but a Japan that might have been a thousand miles away from the busy street and the crowded shop below.

"I am so glad you had not yet left for Tokyo, Dr. Ashton," she told her host. "I did not know who else to turn to. It was so long ago, you see—almost ten years now—and none of the American authorities here was in Japan then. There might be someone at the embassy in Tokyo who remembers what happened, but I have a feeling they are under instructions to tell me nothing."

Dr. Ashton sighed and shook his silvery head. "I may not be able to tell you much more, Teresa. But it's true, I do remember the incident. What had you been told at the time?"

Tessie paused, trying to set her thoughts in order.

The day since she'd seen that advertisement in the Personals column had been one of frustrated searching and fruitless inquiries, ending at last in the serenity of these rooms above the Samurai Shokai, where Dr. Ashton offered her tea in a small round bowl and persuaded her to sit cross-legged on the mat before the lacquered table.

"It was ten years ago, or almost that," she began slowly. "In 1875. My uncle Morgan Gallagher was a seaman with a line of trading ships that made a regular run from California to Japan and back. Whenever he was in port he used to come to see us—me, really, the rest of the family didn't like him—but that doesn't matter now." She closed her eyes against the sudden sting of tears and memories. Morgan's curly red hair grizzled with white, his blue eyes crinkled at the corners from years of staring out at distant horizons, his songs and jokes and stories, the trinkets he used to produce out of hidden pockets delighted a little girl. And, as she grew older, she recalled the hours of listening to his fascinating tales of Japan, the mysterious land so recently opened to Americans, the country Morgan was growing to love almost better than his own. Fox devils and samurai warriors and pale, ghostly ladies in silk kimonos glided through Tessie's dreams in those days, beginning the fascination with Japan that had lasted all her life.

"This time, when his ship returned, there was a letter for us from the American embassy. Not from the ambassador—some clerk, I think. It didn't say very much, only that Morgan had met with a fatal accident on the voyage. Condolences. That sort of thing. It didn't even say where he was buried. I assumed he'd died on the way to Japan and had been buried at sea."

The actual contents of the letter hadn't been too important to Tessie then, only the crushing fact that Morgan was never coming back. First she'd lost Jason, who was somewhere on a ship bound for South America, and now Morgan. For a time life had seemed too crushingly heavy a weight to be borne. But Mama needed her, and then her sister Geraldine had the triplets and needed Tessie to help out. So Tessie locked her grieving inside her and went on doing her duty and telling herself it was enough, and gradually, over the years, it had somehow become almost enough.

Until this shattering voyage to Japan, when she'd been faced all at once with everything she thought she'd lost forever. First Jason—well, that love was lost forever, Tessie told herself firmly. But Morgan—that was something else again.

"No," said Dr. Ashton, abruptly breaking in on her thoughts. "No, he wasn't buried at sea. It happened here."

"Yes. I know that now." No one in Yokohama had been able—or willing—to tell her anything; but in the yellowing back issues of the *Japan Gazette,* Tessie had read the tantalizingly brief account of a fracas between "Morgan Gallagher, an American sailor," and "two of the *ronin,* or masterless samurai, who have recently had the impudence to attack our people for no cause other than some fancied resentment against the benefits of free trade and free converse with civilised nations." The writer of the article had gone on at some length about the ingratitude of these Japanese, who didn't seem to appreciate America's disinterested generosity in forcing them to open their country to Western trade. He'd said very little about the actual incident, only that one of the samurai was dead and the other severely wounded. Their names were not given, and there was no mention of what had happened to Morgan.

"No one seems to know what happened to him. Was he killed in the fight?"

Dr. Ashton sighed again and shook his head. "No.

He disappeared that night and was never seen again. It must have been a revenge killing; the dead samurai's friends would have waylaid him. He should have been on watch."

"Revenge!" Tessie protested, her voice unsteady. "But it said quite clearly in the newspaper that *they* attacked *him*. He was only defending himself. How could their friends have taken revenge on him for self-defense?"

"It's a different code of honor," Dr. Ashton told her. "I remember the incident well. It may not have received much attention in the press, but it did cause quite a little stir in the American community here. Some people thought the murderers ought to be tracked down and arrested. That was impossible, of course; we had no clues to their identity, and they had plenty of time to vanish before we realized that Morgan had disappeared. And as I recall, there were some delicate treaty negotiations going on at that time. The ambassador didn't want to disturb the negotiations with complaints about an American sea-man whose death couldn't be proved to be the fault of the Japanese. In the end it was hushed up. After all, no one knew exactly what had happened. Morgan was the only person who could have told us how the original fight started, and he had disappeared without a trace."

"What about the other samurai?"

"What?"

"The newspaper said there were two. One was killed, the other only wounded."

"Oh. He killed himself before he could be questioned. Shame at having failed, one presumes. So you see, Tessie, there was really nothing that could be done. And since Morgan was dead already, there seemed to be no benefit to anybody in pursuing the matter."

"If he was dead," Tessie said.

"If he wasn't, why didn't he come forward?"

"I don't know. But from what you are telling me, nobody ever saw him dead. And I have reason to believe that he is alive. Look at this!"

Tessie pulled the folded page of yesterday's *Japan Gazette* out of her skirt pocket and showed the advertisement to Dr. Ashton.

"Yes—well—very strange, the things people will put in the papers," Dr. Ashton muttered, examining the column of fine print. "A *yamabushi,* you know, would be a priest of Shugendo—the mountain worshippers—but of course the new Japanese government has outlawed all those old superstitions. I doubt that there is a Shugendo priest in Kiritsumi now, and if there were, he would hardly dare to identify himself to a foreigner. And what has this to do with you and your uncle, Miss Gallagher?"

"For one thing," Tessie said, "it's addressed to me."

"Maggie T.?"

"That's the next point. It's a silly nickname Morgan made up for me once, when I told him I was tired of my given name, Teresa Mary Alice Gallagher."

Teresa M.A.G., Morgan had said instantly. *How would you like to be called Mag?*

Ten-year-old Tessie had wrinkled her nose. *No. It sounds like hag.*

Maggie, then. Maggie Teresa—Maggie T. That'll be your secret name.

"Very interesting," Dr. Ashton allowed. "But I hardly see—"

"The initials are a secret code we used when he wrote me letters. They stand for Secret and Confidential and Very Urgent." Morgan had never been too dignified to play silly games with Tessie; even when he was away on his long voyages, those letters had come to brighten her day.

"Um, yes. They could stand for that—or for many other things," Dr. Ashton said grudgingly.

"And finally," Tessie said triumphantly, "that's not the copy of the *Japan Gazette* that Hartley takes!"

"No?"

"No. I happened to see the advertisement in there first, and I kept that page of the paper and took it to my room. But when I got there, someone had put *this* copy of the paper on my bed, folded open to the Personals column, with this advertisement circled in red."

"It certainly does seem that someone wants you to go to Kiritsumi," Dr. Ashton agreed. "But isn't it rather a slender thread on which to tie all your hopes? My dear Tessie, I don't want to see you disappointed, or worse. If your uncle were alive, surely he would have returned to America long ago. At the very least, he would have made himself known to you in some other way."

"If he could." Tessie's chin came up, and the light of battle danced in her eyes. "Don't you see, perhaps he is hiding—perhaps he has been hiding all these years —and he needs my help. That is why he is asking for it in such an oblique way, in a message nobody else would understand."

"*Is* he?"

"Who else would have placed the advertisement?"

"I don't know. That is what worries me."

"Well," said Tessie blithely, "there's only one way to find out, isn't there? I'll just have to go to Kiritsumi."

Dr. Ashton tried for some time without success to talk Tessie out of her plan. Kiritsumi was a remote village; the people there were not accustomed to foreigners and might be hostile. She didn't know for sure that Morgan had anything to do with this mysterious message. He could not honestly feel that the chances of Morgan's still being alive were very high.

"Ten years!"

"Nobody ever saw his body." Tessie had been

sparkling with barely suppressed excitement ever since Dr. Ashton let that fact slip. "And nobody else could have known his secret name for me. He's alive. And he needs me. I have to go."

A man who had known Tessie longer than Dr. Ashton might have recognized that there was now no stopping her, once she'd found that magic word. Dr. Ashton let her go at last only upon her promise that she would think it over very carefully before doing anything.

"And after all," he mused after she had taken her departure, "what else can she do?" He knew, as Tessie evidently did not, that there was a very good reason why she could not simply take off for Kiritsumi in the morning. If good sense did not force her to slow down and think things over, the governmental bureaucracy of the new Japan would achieve the same end.

Tessie, happily ignorant of bureaucratic restrictions, dismissed the waiting *jinriksha* and strode up the steep streets leading to the Bluff, rapt in her own thoughts. The Baptist minister, the head of the Catholic orphanage, and three wives of American traders all nodded civilly to Tessie as she made her way up the hill, and all were astonished to be completely ignored. Really, the manners of Hartley Gallagher's spinster sister were beyond comprehension! Was she getting a little odd, as maiden ladies sometimes did? The wives enjoyed the prospect of a little malicious gossip to enliven their restricted society, and were almost grateful to Tessie for her bad manners.

Tessie was as cheerfully oblivious to the people she'd offended as she was to the rules of the Japanese government. By the time she'd reached the crescent drive at the top of the Bluff, she had settled in her mind exactly which small satchel would suffice for her traveling needs and how early in the morning she would present herself at the train station to find out the route to Kiritsumi. Other matters could be resolved as she went along; the important thing was that her beloved Uncle Morgan was alive, he needed her, and it was positively her duty to go off into the interior of Japan to save him.

She had not thought out in any great detail how she was going to explain this duty to Hartley and Sophia. So when she entered the English-style house to find a scene of confusion and hysterics, with Sophia sobbing on the couch and Hartley demanding an immediate explanation for her disappearance, she simply told the truth.

"I've just found out that Uncle Morgan is still alive. He needs me to come to him at a village called Kiritsumi. I'm leaving tomorrow morning."

Sophia shrieked aloud, and Hartley patiently told Tessie that she was mad or suffering from sunstroke. Morgan had died at sea years ago. What was she talking about?

The more Tessie tried to explain, the less Hartley heard. The original letter from the consul, Dr. Ashton's story, the yellowing newspaper in the files of the *Japan Gazette,* the mysterious personal advertisement in yesterday's paper—all this got hopelessly mixed up with the translation needs of Benten and Company, Sophia's nerves, the need of Seraphina and Eustace and Forbes for their loving aunt, and that time in 1878 when Tessie was so unkind to their poor dear mother.

Before long, Tessie gave up trying to explain anything at all in a logical fashion. It was easier just to sit down and let her family do what they wanted. Hartley pounded on the nearest table and announced that Tessie was going nowhere at all without his permission. Sophia screamed that she was on the brink of collapse and that she'd always known Teresa Mary Alice Gallagher was a wicked, wicked girl who would bring shame and sorrow to the family. Seraphina Jessamine clung to her mother and wailed in sympathy. Forbes Montague reminded Tessie reproachfully that she'd promised faithfully to teach him how to fly one of the big Japanese kites in the shape of a dragon. Eustace Neville quietly collected all the iced cakes that had been laid out for the children's tea, retreated under the piano with his loot, and wolfed down pink icing. For the first time in her twenty-six years, Tessie did absolutely nothing to help. They probably wouldn't settle down until tomorrow, by which time she would be on her way to Kiritsumi.

"Pardon me for interrupting," said a silky-smooth, deeply amused voice from the doorway. "There is some difficulty?"

Jason Lancaster. Tessie closed her eyes for a moment and prayed for strength, patience, and purity of heart. Positively the last thing she needed was to have this infuriating, egotistical, selfish man intruding on the family quarrel.

None of the graces for which she had prayed was granted her—at least, not in the form she'd been expecting.

"What seems to be the matter?"

She felt his bulk settling on the sofa beside her, a warm hand enfolding hers. Tessie's eyes flew open. She was quivering with some feeling, shocked at his familiarity. How dare he presume to fondle her like this? Ten years ago she might have been young and foolish enough to let his embraces sway her. Now she was older, wiser, sadder—and so it couldn't be a thrill of treacherous pleasure she was feeling, just because his fingers had brushed across the inside of her wrist for a moment!

Shocked and confused, she jumped to her feet and announced her plan with the same lamentable lack of tact that had characterized her first statement of it.

"I'm going to Kiritsumi tomorrow," she told him, "and you can't stop me!"

"Why on earth should I wish to stop you? But you're not, you know."

"I knew you'd say that," said Tessie with bitter triumph. "You think I'm your slave, to stay locked in an office translating Japanese letters for you! Well, it so happens you are mistaken!"

Sophia gave a faint shriek and fell back against the cushions of her armchair, fanning herself with quick, nervous movements. "Teresa Mary Alice Gallagher, you ungrateful girl, how can you speak so to our benefactor?"

"At least I haven't threatened to horsewhip him yet," Tessie pointed out.

Hartley pushed between Tessie and Jason and began an incoherent, stammering statement in which he tried to convey simultaneously his devotion to Benten and Company, his hopes that the unfortunate incident ten years ago could be forgotten, and his apologies for his hysterical little sister. At the same time, Sophia began enumerating the wonderful things she and Hartley had done for Tessie and thanking Jason for his support.

"Do stop gobbling, Hartley. It makes you sound like a turkey cock on his way to the chopping block," Tessie advised. "As for you, Sophia, if you will compute the current wages of a nurse, governess, and housekeeper, I think you will find that I have already repaid the cost of my travel to Japan and the three very plain dresses you purchased for me."

"There was also the brass-bound trunk," Sophia gasped between sobs of indignation.

Tessie waved one hand in the air as if to shoo away the swarms of invisible flies. "I'm leaving that here. It's too heavy for me to carry by myself; a small satchel will suffice for my personal necessities on the trip. I shouldn't be gone more than two or three days; I haven't found out just how long it takes to get to Kiritsumi." Nor was she sure what she would find when she got there. This journey might be considerably longer than two or three days. But she saw no reason to bring that up now. "You'll just have to manage the children yourself for a few days, Sophia—with Fräulein's help, of course." The German governess hired by Jason had had an easy time of it so far, as the children were used to turning to Tessie for everything. She might as well start earning her keep now. "Hartley, you can stack the Japanese correspondence on my desk in your office, and I'll catch up on it when I get back. I'm sorry if that arrangement doesn't suit you, Mr. Lancaster, but you must remember that I, unlike Hartley, am not your paid employee. I have another and a higher duty elsewhere."

Jason was lounging against the door, arms folded, looking down at her with an infuriating grin. "Oh, I've never forgotten that, Tessie," he promised her. "And I'm most grateful to you for satisfying my curiosity. I always wondered what would happen when the worm finally turned, and what it would take to bring you to that point. You wouldn't do it for love of me, and you wouldn't do it for Ricardo. Who *is* the lucky man who's waiting for you in Kiritsumi? Or unlucky, I should say," he added as an afterthought, "since you won't be going there."

"I most certainly will!" Tessie blazed at him. "Morgan needs me, and I shall be there for him."

"Morgan?" Jason looked momentarily shaken. "But he's—"

"Dead," said Hartley.

"Been dead for years," Sophia added.

"Tessie's hysterical. Imagining things."

"I am not!" Tessie pulled the sadly crumpled page of the *Japan Gazette* out and waved it at Jason Lancaster. "It's perfectly plain."

Somehow, between bossy interruptions from Hartley and hysterical ones from Sophia and whines from Seraphina Jessamine, Tessie got her story out. She was glad to see that Jason seemed to take it a little more seriously than Hartley and Sophia had. She was also a little worried that by the time she'd finished explaining, Forbes Montague and Eustace Neville hadn't joined Seraphina in her whines for attention. What were the two boys up to? With an effort of will, she reminded herself that starting tomorrow—no, starting *now*—the children were Sophia's responsibility, not hers.

"You see?"

"Hmm. It's interesting," Jason allowed. "I was never quite satisfied with the official story of Morgan's death, myself."

Tessie stared. "You? But you were on the South American run that year."

Jason's brow darkened. "Yes, and if I'd been with Morgan, he'd never have gotten into whatever damn fool trouble caused his demise. I signed back on the Japan line for the next voyage and stayed here for several months trying to find out what had really happened. But nobody would tell me a damned thing. I didn't speak much Japanese then, and foreigners were pretty unpopular. I was attacked myself a time or two when I went into the wrong districts, barely got away with my life. And I wasn't taken by surprise, the way Morgan would have been—you know how he was, thinking all the world was his friend."

"I remember." Tessie blinked back tears, swallowed the lump in her throat. "You said *was.*"

"At the time," said Jason, "I'd no reason to hope he was still alive. This might put a different complexion on things." He smoothed out the page, folded it carefully, and put it in his pocket. Tessie was about to protest when she remembered that she had another copy of the advertisement upstairs.

"Then you understand why I *must* go to Kiritsumi?" Not that it mattered. She was going anyway. But after the burst of righteous anger in

64

which she'd defied Hartley and Sophia, her knees were trembling, and she was a little afraid of the adventure ahead of her. It would be nice to have one person in the world who believed in her—and Jason Lancaster, for all he'd betrayed her once already, somehow seemed at that moment like a very good source of support.

"I understand. But you can't go." He was smiling a little, as if he derived some secret pleasure from thwarting her.

Tessie felt betrayed all over again. And the strange thing was, it hurt nearly as much as it had the last time. "I do not see that it is within your power to stop me." At least she didn't have to let him see how much it hurt.

"Not me. The Japanese government."

"What interest is it of theirs?"

"No foreigner is allowed to travel anywhere in Japan without a pass from the government, to be inspected and recorded by a police officer at train stations, crossroads, ports, and all inns," Jason recited in a toneless voice, as if from memory.

Tessie stared at him. "But that's—you know that isn't true! We went to Tokyo yesterday, and nobody said anything about a pass!"

Jason cleared his throat. "Ah. Well. Travelers between Tokyo and Yokohama are excepted from this rule, because there are so many of them. But believe me, Tessie, you wouldn't get very far toward any other destination without being stopped, asked for your pass, and very politely escorted back to Yokohama."

"And a good thing, too!" Hartley joined in. "Young girls should be protected from their foolish impulses."

"Tessie is hardly a *young girl* anymore," said Sophia waspishly from her chair.

"And I believe the same law would apply to you, Hartley, so you needn't gloat like that!"

"I," Hartley pointed out with pious smugness,

"have no desire to waste my employer's time and money with pointless jaunts into the country. I am not in the least inconvenienced by this law. Come, Sophia. There is no need for your delicate nerves to be upset in this fashion. Tessie is going nowhere, and as soon as Mr. Lancaster has made her understand that fact, she can return to her duties."

Jason leaned back against the door frame after Hartley and Sophia marched out of the room. "Alone at last!"

He was laughing quietly to himself. Tessie couldn't bear it. Was everything in her life to be thwarted by this self-centered man? "You enjoy this, don't you?" she accused him. "You're just like Hartley and Sophia. You want to keep me in my place, being useful to you, and you think it's ever so funny that I didn't know about one stupid minor bureaucratic regulation! I might have known you'd find some way to stop me. You're too selfish to consider anything but your own pleasure and comfort."

Jason held up his hands before him in mocking self-defense. "Really, Tessie, you can hardly hold me personally responsible for the policies of the Japanese government!"

"No, but I can blame you for *enjoying* them! Oh, I should have known better than to look for help from you, Jason Lancaster! Bone-selfish, that's what you are, never a thought for anybody except as it concerns your own comfort. Look at the way you jilted me before, just because I wouldn't leave my home and family and my duty to them and run off with you at a moment's notice—"

"Dammit, Tessie, that's too much!" Jason interrupted her. He moved forward, and for a moment she quailed at the look of fury in his eyes, but then the sense of her own righteous anger upheld her.

"What do you mean, it's too much? Oh, yes," Tessie said, "I know, you wanted me to pretend that never happened, because it was more comfortable for you that way! Well, I'm terribly sorry, Jason Lancaster, but I can't quite manage that feat of mental gymnastics. What you did then has some bearing on what you are now, and I should have known that a man who'd callously abandon a young girl who loved and trusted him—"

She caught her breath, aghast at the trap her own tongue had led her into. She had never, *never* meant to admit that she had loved Jason Lancaster. A moment's infatuation in the moonlight—that was all it had been. The man was egotistical enough without adding to his towering conceit, without letting him know what a thorough conquest he'd made of the young Tessie.

Admit she'd loved him then, and he'd be conceited enough to think it meant she still did.

Fortunately, he didn't seem to have taken in her last words. He was too angry. His blue eyes flashed like lightning across a sultry summer sky, his hands were raised to take her by the shoulders and shake her into silence. Tessie retreated, step by silent step, before the fury she had unleashed.

"I didn't mean," said Jason, his voice deceptively gentle, "I didn't mean that you shouldn't remember what there was between us. I only ask that you should remember it correctly. The way it really happened. I didn't abandon you, Tessie. Callously or otherwise. *You* jilted *me*. I was ready to marry you; you refused me because you preferred the safety of home and mother to the uncertainty of life as a sailor's wife."

"Because it was my duty to stay with Mama. She was ill."

"Whatever. The fact remains. You refused to go with me, Tessie; you can't hold that against me now. What did you expect me to do—throw you over my shoulder and carry you away?"

"Why not? If you really loved me, you wouldn't

have *let* me sacrifice myself to my duty! A real man wouldn't have accepted that refusal!"

"Oh? I don't notice your Ricardo being so forceful as all that?"

"Who? Oh!" Tessie's face burned. "Ricardo! That's different. You, you see, I, he, we don't, that is . . ."

Jason's lips cut off her stammered attempts at an explanation; his arms closed around her with a need too long denied. Tessie gasped once with shock, then his mouth was over hers, and the length of his lean, hard body was pressed against her, burning through the muffling layers of skirts and petticoats until it seemed she knew every inch of him more intimately than she had on that night ten years ago. The intense sweetness of his kiss spread through her entire body until she was bereft of reason, wanting only to melt into unity with him. Why were her hands still curled into fists, pushing impotently at his hard shoulders?

She couldn't give in, not when all he wanted was to prove a point. Why he should want to prove that she still desired him was beyond her; yesterday, in Tokyo, he'd made it all too clear that he wanted only a business relationship. Presumably his male ego couldn't stand the thought that she had chosen another man above him. He wanted it both ways; he wanted to keep her at a distance, but he wanted to be the one who rejected anything closer.

As she slowly, painfully reasoned it out, Tessie found herself able to resist the violence of Jason's assault on her senses. With an aching sense of infinite loss, she pushed at his shoulders again, this time felt him release her, and stepped back into the cold emptiness of her self-contained shell. Not a wanton, redheaded slut, flushed with passion for a man who despised her. Tessie Gallagher. The sensible sister, the one the whole family could depend on.

The one Morgan was depending on.

With trembling, nerveless fingers, Tessie reached up

and pushed back the strands of curly red hair that had fallen over her forehead while Jason kissed her.

"If you're quite through," she said, "I should like to go and apply for a pass to Kiritsumi." She gave Jason her most withering look, the one she customarily reserved for Eustace Neville caught in a blatant lie. "After all, if the Japanese government lets a man like *you* travel all over the country on buying trips, they'll hardly object to giving one quiet, decent American lady a pass for a short trip into the mountains."

Chapter Five

Tessie was wrong. Just how wrong, she didn't discover immediately. Forbes Montague and Eustace Neville had employed the period of the grown-ups' quarrel to build a complicated tower of levers, pulleys, and buckets full of water on the balcony overlooking the front door. When Hartley came to the door to see Jason off, the tower collapsed and the water poured over his head. Tessie spent the remainder of the evening mopping Hartley off, protecting the two boys from an immediate whipping, listening to Forbes Montague's tearful explanation that they had only been trying to construct a water mill, holding Eustace Neville's head while he was sick, and looking for Sophia's smelling salts.

The smelling salts were eventually discovered in Seraphina Jessamine's doll's tea set, and peace returned to the family. But by then Tessie had a furious headache herself and had to agree with Hartley that it was far too late for her to go looking for whatever office granted travel passes to foreigners.

In the morning, a series of small, infuriating emergencies delayed her. Hartley needed a letter translated at once; he left the house swearing that his job depended on it and that he'd be back within the hour to pick up the translation. Before she could get to work, Sophia drew her off into a long and ultimately pointless discussion of the menus for the next week. Forbes Montague broke up that discussion by falling off the balcony. Sophia fainted, or nearly fainted, and it was left for Tessie to disentangle Forbes from the wreckage of his experimental flying machine, ascertain that no bones were broken, and explain to him that he really shouldn't have taken Eustace's word that the machine would fly.

She couldn't blame Hartley for the accident with Forbes and his flying machine, but she had a strong suspicion that the other two delays were his idea. The suspicion grew stronger when she translated enough of the "very urgent letter" to realize that it was an advertising circular explaining the merits of Japanese tinned beef. When she finally reached the Yokohama police station, she was met with polite, smiling, bland incomprehension at her request for a pass. Why did the foreign lady wish to go to Kiritsumi? Was it the custom in America for young ladies to travel alone? What if she met with some accident on the journey, would not the Japanese government be blamed for allowing her to go off alone?

When the fourth official in a row smiled and suggested that Tessie should consult with her brother about the advisability of such a journey, her suspicions of Hartley crystallized into absolute certainty.

She was even depressed enough to complain to Jason Lancaster when she saw him on the street outside the Benten and Company offices.

"Why, Tessie, you look like a thundercloud! Who's going to be murdered?"

"Hartley," Tessie said between her teeth. She had been on the point of marching into the Benten and Company office to inform Hartley that she saw through his scoundrelly plan and that it wasn't going to work. But since she didn't have any idea how to outwit him, it was relatively easy for Jason to deflect her from her intention when she explained her problems.

"Don't do it," Jason advised. "He's your excuse for staying in this country, remember? Come for a ride with me instead, and tell me all about it. Maybe I can help."

Tessie looked at him with suspicion. Jason had been amused at her difficulties yesterday. Why would he help her today? Perhaps he'd thought it over and now believed that Morgan was still alive and wanting her help. Perhaps even he, selfish and conceited though he was, had some rudimentary sense of duty toward his old friend.

"How could you help?"

"Hartley's used his influence to keep you from getting a pass, I take it," said Jason. "I have considerably more influence than Hartley."

"And even Hartley has more than I," Tessie sighed.

"Well, of course." Jason's blue eyes twinkled with an inner amusement. "The Japanese are a nation of real men. Their women know their place; they're not going to let some little snip of a redheaded barbarian girl tell them what to do. They expect you to keep quiet and obey your brother, just as a good Japanese girl would do."

Tessie only half listened to this sarcastic speech. It all seemed beside the point. "Well? Can you get me a pass or not?" she demanded when Jason paused at last.

"Come for a ride with me, and let's discuss it."

"Why should I go riding with you?"

"Because," said Jason silkily, "that is the price of my help. You may not object to discussing Morgan's life and death on the public streets of Yokohama, but I should prefer somewhat more privacy."

72

"That is sensible," Tessie allowed. She ignored Jason's proffered hand and stepped up into the carriage without assistance. "All right, let's talk."

"Later. I have an errand first."

She might have known he couldn't do anything in a simple, straightforward manner. Tessie sighed loudly and made a small production of settling herself against the cushioned seat.

"All comfortable?"

"Yes, thank you."

"Good," said Jason briskly, setting the horses into a canter. "It's rather a long ride."

It was. Within a few minutes, they were on the dusty road leading out of Yokohama. Shops and offices were replaced by wayside teahouses under the shade of ancient trees, then by fields of green vegetables and groves of bamboo. Tessie leaned forward, eagerly soaking up each detail as it came into her view, and quite forgot to look bored and impatient with the long journey.

"We're going to visit a paper maker," Jason vouchsafed after a while.

"I didn't know Japan had any modern industries." Tessie felt disappointed; so a factory was their destination! Not a very pleasant trip, compared with their visit to the wisteria-draped gardens of the Kameido temple yesterday. But then, yesterday Jason had been trying to get something out of her. Today she was tagging along on his errands, waiting for the moment when he might be inspired to do her a favor.

"It's not exactly an industry," Jason chuckled. "More of a cottage craft. Have you never seen Japanese paper? It's made by hand, very strong, with fine subtle variations of texture and color depending on the kind of barks used and the processes the craftsman employs. In the past it's been greatly in demand in the West. Even when Japan was totally secluded under the

Shogunate, theoretically admitting no foreign trade or contacts, Rembrandt was able to get his Japanese paper for sketches and etchings."

"I didn't know that!"

"If I can find someone to supply me regularly with a good quality of paper, I could add it to Benten and Company's stock. It would be a unique item, the sort of thing that built the company in the first place." Jason glanced sidewise at Tessie. "Didn't you ever wonder how I rose from a seaman's life to head of a major import-export firm in such a short time?"

The time hadn't seemed short to Tessie. Ten interminable years! And the first two or three years had been the hardest, when she'd still secretly hoped that Jason would come back for her. Instead, it seemed, he'd forgotten her almost at once. He must never, never guess how long she'd looked for him, how bleak and desperate she'd felt on the day when she knew for certain that his ship was in the harbor and that he was avoiding the street where she lived.

"If I had cared enough about you to wonder," she said, "I would have assumed you cheated some old man out of his life's savings, or married the shopkeeper's daughter!"

Infuriatingly, Jason only chuckled again. "No, Tessie, I'm not married. Kind of you to wonder, though."

Tessie compressed her lips and stared at the roadside.

"I came by my fortune quite honestly," Jason went on. "I love this country. I've learned a little of the language. I spent my shore time traveling and learning more. While my shipmates were drinking up their pay as fast as they got it, I was buying whatever little Japanese articles I could afford and selling them on the other end of the voyage. Gradually I built up a reputation as a man who knew where the best work in Japanese arts and crafts was to be found. With nothing more than that reputation, and my small savings, I left the sea to start Benten and Company—oh, just about eight years ago, it was, I guess. I had plenty of time to devote to the company. My best friend had been reported dead in a Japanese street brawl, and the girl I loved had given in to family pressure and jilted me."

Jason heaved a long artistic sigh and glanced at Tessie. "Ah, well, I see you are really not interested in the story of my life. Too bad. Some of the earlier episodes concern you intimately."

"I prefer true stories to romantically embroidered fictions," said Tessie coldly. It was ten years too late for Jason to pretend he'd felt true love for her. If he'd really loved her, he would never have accepted her talk of duty to stay with Mama. Instead he'd been secretly relieved; only that could explain why he'd vanished so quickly and completely from her life.

They were both silent until they reached the paper maker's house. Here Tessie was glad to be almost forgotten while Jason and the old Japanese man engaged in an animated conversation in Japanese about quantities and qualities of paper, grades of mulberry bark, and the need for extra drying frames if he was to produce the amount of paper Jason would be needing. While they talked, she glanced around the house and yard, enjoying the busy scene. In front of the house were two women sitting on the ground, taking strips of bark out of a vat of cold water and scraping them to remove every trace of the black outside portion of the strips. To the side of the house were rows and rows of drying boards propped up on racks, each board covered with sheets of tough, coarse paper.

Inside the house, several boys stirred vats of wood pulp. An apprentice stood over one vat, rhythmically lowering and raising a bamboo screen in a wooden frame. Each time he raised the screen, it bore a thin film of clinging wood pulp fibers, which he peeled off and set in a pile to be carried to the drying boards.

All the people worked quickly and surely, with only a word or two of guidance from the old man with whom Jason was dealing. Tessie was amazed at the deft certainty with which they handled the sheets of paper, and at the simplicity of the whole process. From tree bark to paper, it was all before her eyes in this one open house with its surrounding work sheds and yards.

"The paper is dry," the old man said, abruptly breaking off his conversation with Jason. Tessie wondered what sixth sense had alerted him; he hadn't even been looking at the drying frames. They followed him over to the frames. "Forgive me; it must be removed immediately. Overdrying hurts the fibers," he explained over his shoulder. One by one, the heavy paper sheets were lifted off the boards with a loud snap. The grain of the wood on which they had been drying covered the underside with a delicate pattern of swirling lines.

"Gampi," the old man said, handing a sheet to Tessie with a bow.

"Wild thyme," Jason explained in an undertone. "It makes the finest paper."

"Elegant but tough; fragile seeming, but strong in the spirit. Like your wife." The old man beamed with such innocent good will that Tessie had not the heart to correct his mistake.

On the road back to Yokohama, she finally broke down and asked Jason how he thought he could help her get a pass. She'd been waiting for him to mention it first, but she was beginning to think he never would. If his half-promise of help had been only a bait to get her to go on a carriage ride with him, then she wanted to know it now, while she still had a chance to tell him what she thought of such sneaking behavior.

"A pass?" Jason's expression of surprise was perfect —too perfect to be real. "Why, Tessie, I never promised to help you get a pass."

"I knew it!" Tessie drew a deep breath. Before she could launch into the blistering speech she had prepared, Jason pulled a white folded document inscribed in Japanese characters from his vest pocket.

"Now, now, don't say anything you might regret later," he warned her. "I'm not going to help you get a pass because . . ." He dangled the document enticingly before her face.

"You've already got one!"

"I've already got one," Jason agreed, with a meaningful emphasis on the first word.

Tessie frowned over the document. "I can't make it all out," she complained. "I *wish* they wouldn't throw Chinese characters into the middle of a Japanese syllabary!"

"Oh, well, basically it just says that I can travel anywhere I want to in Japan," Jason said with a shrug, as if to indicate that a little favor like a general travel pass was nothing to a man with his connections. "You can use it, subject to certain conditions, of course."

"Such as?" The tone of that last statement had been too casual; he had to be hiding something.

"Nothing much. It's just that you'll have to travel with me."

"What?"

"Don't frighten the horses," Jason murmured. "The gray mare is a nervous beast—rather like your sister-in-law, actually, doesn't like to work and takes little nips out of the bystanders with her sharp teeth. If you screech and jump up and down like that again, I won't be answerable for the consequences."

Tessie folded the pass to a tiny square in her fists and spoke slowly through clenched teeth. "What makes you think I would consent to such a ridiculous condition as that, Jason Lancaster? And for that matter, why would the Japanese police put something like that on the pass? I don't believe you!"

"Oh, it's not on the pass," Jason agreed, "not in so many words, that is. The problem, Tessie dear, is that the pass is not made out to you. If you will glance down at the space where the names of the foreign travelers are recorded, you will see that it is made out to 'Jason Lancaster and one woman.'"

Tessie studied the pass suspiciously. Her face burned. "Why is it written this way? Anybody would think the police made it out for your convenience, so that you could travel with any woman of easy virtue you fancied to take along on your buying trips!"

"That," agreed Jason with a hint of complacency, "is doubtless exactly what the police believe."

Tessie's fingers closed over the pass, and she sat very straight on the carriage seat. "Apart from the pleasure of blackening my name among the foreign community of Yokohama, did you have any particular reason for having the pass made out in this insulting and humiliating fashion?"

"My, my," said Jason, "what an impressive vocabulary. Tessie, don't be so quick to take offense. Your name is not on the pass, so I don't think you can fairly say that I've blackened it. And yes, I had a very good reason for letting the Yokohama police make their own assumptions about my desire for this pass. Do you really think your brother Hartley had enough influence and was able to move quickly enough to block your application?"

"I thought he would try. I was surprised that he succeeded."

Jason gave her a long, sober look. "Perhaps he did, perhaps not. But think, Tessie. If that advertisement was indeed placed by Morgan—or by some friend of his, for I can hardly believe that Morgan is still alive after ten years' silence—then there must have been some reason for communicating with you in such a secret and roundabout manner. There is mention of a legacy. Perhaps someone in Yokohama doesn't want you to collect that legacy; perhaps there is someone who wants to delay you so that he can get there first. It seemed to me that it might be safer if no one knew that you were planning to leave for Kiritsumi immediately. Of course, you've spoiled that bit of my plan now, by marching into the police station and demanding a pass on the spot."

"What was I supposed to do—ask your permission first?"

"It might have been a good idea."

Tessie bit her lip. She hated to give up the fine flush of her righteous anger toward Jason, but there was some sense in what he said. She wouldn't agree with him that Morgan must be dead by now. But she could certainly agree that whoever placed the advertisement had been secretive, possibly in danger, and that her impetuous action in demanding a pass for Kiritsumi hadn't done much to help keep the secret. Anyway, now Jason had a pass, and she didn't. It was definitely not a good time to quarrel with him.

"All right," she said at last. "Maybe you're right. I suppose I shouldn't have been so angry. I didn't realize that this was just a ruse to get me a pass without my name on it. I thought you really wanted to travel with me."

"I do."

Jason laughed at her expression of surprise.

"Think, Tessie. The pass is in my name. If you try to use it without me, the first policeman who examines your papers will want to know where I am. And if you can't produce me, he'll think there is something suspicious going on and have you sent right back to the bosom of your loving family in Yokohama."

"Yes, but I *can't* take you with me," Tessie protested. "It's not proper! I don't know how far away

79

Kiritsumi is, or what sort of town it is, or where I'll stay, or—or anything!" And most of all, she did not know how to frame her real objection. If seeing Jason daily in Yokohama had been bad, traveling with him would be sheer torture. Days and nights of watching his eyes flash with humor or darken with ill temper, of following the line of his mobile lips, of enduring his references to the past—she could never survive such an ordeal without giving him a hint of her present feelings.

Not, of course, that she still loved him. She despised him. It was just that she did feel some remnant of purely physical longing, some memory engraved on her senses of their brief time together. It was just that she continually had to fight the urge to brush her fingers across his lips, to sit closer to him on the narrow carriage bench, to imagine him stopping on this deserted country road and kissing her as he'd done the day before in Hartley's drawing room.

It was just that she was having enough trouble concealing her humiliating desires now, when they met in the circumscribed bounds of polite Yokohama society. On a long journey into the middle of nowhere, with no other company, no other duties, how could she ever keep him at a proper distance? No, the thing was impossible.

"If you don't know what you're doing," Jason said softly, "all the more reason you need me with you, Tessie."

"I wish I knew why you were doing this." Tessie dared a direct glance at him. "And don't try to tell me that you couldn't have found another way to get me a pass if you wanted to. I may not like or respect you, Jason Lancaster, but I do know that you are a very clever man."

"Your compliments overwhelm me. Yes, I probably could have found some other solution, but this one pleased me. Your name is mentioned nowhere. I'm known for going on buying trips all over Japan, so my departure for the Kiritsumi area should arouse no comment. And . . ." Jason paused for so long that Tessie began to think he'd run out of things to say. "I have personal reasons for wishing to accompany you," he ended at last.

"What?"

"So suspicious! Would you believe it's from sheer frivolous desire to spend a few days in the country with a lovely young lady?"

"Not for a minute. I already know that I'm twenty-six, redheaded, and too plump."

"Grave disabilities," Jason murmured with a mocking gleam in his blue eyes, "which, of course, make you completely unattractive to any man in his right mind. How good of Ricardo to court you in spite of them!"

Tessie flushed. "Oh. Ricardo. Well . . . that's different. Never mind about me and Ricardo, Jason. I'm still waiting to hear why you insist on forcing your company upon me."

"Would you credit a chivalrous desire to protect a lady going into possible danger?"

"No."

"Desire to rescue my old friend Morgan?"

"That's somewhat more credible," Tessie allowed, "but you've already said that you're convinced he's dead. And you've been in Japan several years without, as far as I know, making the least push to find him. I'm afraid I don't believe that, either."

"You're not very much fun to talk to," mourned Jason. He heaved a deep sigh. "All right. I can see it's time to confess. Benten and Company isn't doing well, Tessie. That is, the company is thriving, but I'm not. My own savings weren't nearly enough to start a major import-export business. I had to take out some very large loans when I got started, and for several years I could do no more than pay the interest. Now the loans are coming due. If they'd extend for another two or three years, I'd be able to pay them off, but my creditors don't want that. They'd rather take over the thriving business I've built from nothing."

"And what does all this have to do with Morgan and me?"

"The advertisement mentioned a legacy . . ."

Money.

Tessie felt unreasonably crushed. "Oh, Jason! Is that all your fine words amounted to? You want *money?*"

"Now, don't be complaining. You wanted a good, sound, commercial reason. I've given you one. If I get your pass, escort you on the trip, protect you from whatever dangers you meet on the way, and eventually help you to collect the legacy, wouldn't you agree that I'm entitled to half the proceeds?"

"It may not even be money."

"A really good curio—an antique vase, say, or a Heian painting—could be sold for a sizable amount."

Tessie gave him a disgusted look. "You really do think of nothing but money! And how do you know your services are going to be worth so much? I'm perfectly capable of taking a train to Kiritsumi by myself."

"The train doesn't go as far into the mountains as that," Jason told her. "We'll need to go by *kago* for the last part of the journey."

"What's that?"

"You'll find out. Tomorrow. If you agree to split the legacy?"

Tessie didn't care about the money, but she was disgusted to find that Jason's motives were so base.

"Remember," Jason prompted softly, "without this pass, you can't even leave Yokohama."

Chapter Six

Long before they reached Kiritsumi, Tessie had cause to be grateful that Jason had insisted on coming with her.

The day had begun well enough. They left very early in the morning, before Sophia and Hartley were awake. Tessie simply left a note for them, then quietly carried her satchel out of the house and down the steep road to the railway station. Jason was waiting for her there. He yawned several times and said he was too sleepy to quarrel this morning; could they please just board the train and get on with the journey?

"Feel perfectly free to go back to bed and have your sleep out," Tessie advised. "*I* don't insist on your company."

Jason held up the pass. "Regulations, Teresa, my dear. Regulations! Don't mind me; I'll nap in the carriage."

Tessie watched the pearly gray skies of early morning change to a brilliant blue flecked with wisps of white cloud. The train ran through the rice paddy fields she'd seen on the way to Tokyo, then on into hilly country where each valley was a splash of emerald green in which blue lilies sparkled like sapphires. Above the steady *chug-chug* of the train's little engine, she could hear the twittering of songbirds in the fields.

They had to change trains twice, and at each stop a Japanese policeman, uncomfortably formal in his Western-style uniform of shirt and trousers, politely requested to see their pass. Each examined the pass for long minutes, then solemnly studied them as if he suspected they might be concealing a third, illicit traveler in Tessie's satchel.

"You see?" Jason murmured to Tessie the first time their papers were inspected. "It really was necessary for me to come with you."

"What I see is that you made it necessary." Tessie suspected that she had given in too easily; perhaps if she'd stayed in Yokohama another day or so, or if she'd requested the help of Dr. Ashton or the American ambassador in Tokyo, she might have been able to get a pass for herself after all.

The railway line did not go into the high hills where the village of Kiritsumi was nestled among trees and clouds. Indeed, to judge from the reactions of the *kago* bearers Jason tried to hire, nobody went to Kiritsumi. The men shook their heads, backed away, and conversed in low, troubled voices with many sidewise glances at the foreigners.

"What's the trouble?" Tessie asked. Jason had made her stand back like a proper Japanese woman while he conducted negotiations with the bearers, and she hadn't been able to catch more than a few words of their discussion.

"Superstition. They say Kiritsumi is on the other side of a *tengu* valley, and they don't want to risk going through there after dark. In fact, now that they think it over, they don't want to go there at all." Jason shook his head. "We'll hire them to take us as far as Karuizawa. They won't object to that. It's a popular resort; lots of people go there. From there I'm afraid we'll have to walk."

"What are *tengu?* And what's a *kago?*" According to her Japanese dictionary, the word meant "basket." But surely they weren't going to ride up the mountain in baskets!

As it turned out, they were. The *kago* bearers happily accepted the change of destination and trotted off to fetch their vehicles, which were nothing more than large baskets, about three feet long, hung from a long pole.

Tessie fancied that Jason was watching her for signs of dismay. "Oh, how charming!" she exclaimed. "How do we get in?" She managed an ungraceful but enthusiastic scramble over the side of the nearest basket. Jason climbed into his own basket, the bearers picked up their long poles, and they set off up the mountain path at a swaying, bone-jolting pace.

After the first few miles, she grew accustomed to the swaying movement of the *kago.* She also, less happily, grew accustomed to the limitations of its shape and design. One could neither sit up nor recline in the short basket; the only possible posture was to sit cross-legged like a Japanese, and even then you had to crook your head to one side to avoid hitting the ridge pole. At least her long full skirts made it possible for her to sit cross-legged and maintain some degree of decency.

Thank goodness she didn't have to make light conversation with Jason. Indeed, any conversation at all was virtually impossible, with his basket lurching some ten feet behind hers and with their bearers chanting a rhythmic song as they walked. The only thing to do was to hunch over sideways and admire the scenery.

Fortunately, there was plenty of it to admire. The steep, shady path wound through pine woods and small clearings where wisteria and hydrangea grew like wildflowers. Now and then they reached a turning point from which Tessie could glance down over a green sea of forested ridges, interlaced with rivers that made winding ribbons of light through the many shades of green. Once or twice the bearers stopped to rest at little open-fronted houses where they brewed tiny cups of pale golden tea, and Tessie seized the opportunity to slip out of the *kago* and stretch her cramped limbs.

"You'll have plenty of chance to walk after we send the bearers back," Jason warned her. "Better rest now. We'll have to make good time if you don't want to be caught in the valley of the *tengu* after dark."

Tessie looked closely at his dark, impassive face. "Are you trying to frighten me? So I'll agree that your services are worth half of this mysterious legacy, whatever it may be?"

"Mmm. I hadn't considered that. Is it working?"

"It might work better if you told me what *tengu* are." The word was vaguely familiar from some of Morgan's stories—some kind of supernatural beings, Tessie thought—but she couldn't remember exactly what they were.

"Oh, just a kind of mountain goblin. They steal children, start earthquakes and avalanches, light fires, and impersonate the Buddha."

Tessie laughed. "I can't wait. When do we see these mysterious beings?"

"You won't *see* them," Jason said solemnly in sepulchral tones. "You'll only *feel* them—a mysterious, brooding presence, never quite visible, but always watching you from the heart of the forest."

"I shall be quite as grateful as I ought for your protection," Tessie said demurely.

It was almost four o'clock when the bearers deposited them in front of the Mampei Hotel in Karuizawa, and the cool mountain day was turning chilly as clouds drifted over the sun. Tessie felt an illogical shiver of distaste at the sight of the deep woods and the narrow rocky path that lay before them. And she *was* tired. Should she tell Jason that she wanted to rest here at the hotel tonight and go on to the little village of Kiritsumi tomorrow? No—he might think his silly teasing had actually made her nervous, and that would never do!

"Let's go," she said, raising her satchel to her shoulder. "I wouldn't want you to be caught in the woods after dark, since you're so concerned about *tengu.*"

Before they'd covered half the rocky way to the village of Kiritsumi, Tessie was wishing she had not been quite so sarcastic. She might have annoyed Jason. Worse, she might have annoyed the mountain goblins, whose presence did indeed seem to hover over this narrow valley as Jason had predicted. She didn't think it was entirely the effect of Jason's stories, or the refusal of a local guide to accompany them, that had made her so nervous. She was not an imaginative, sensitive, easily upset sort of person; she left all that sort of thing to Mama, with her weak heart, and Sophia, with her nervous disposition. She was plain, sensible Aunt Tessie who cleared up messes and packed luggage and hired servants, the one who never fell to pieces in a crisis.

Only why did she feel the need to remind herself of this just now? And what was that flickering light she'd glimpsed behind the trees? And that noise—

Something touched her shoulder. Tessie gasped and jerked away. Her satchel broke loose from its leather carrying strap and bounded down the side of the path.

"I just wanted to know if you needed to rest," said Jason.

"You startled me."

"Sorry. Well? It's a long, steep way."

Tessie glanced around at the dark, encircling woods. The pine trees seemed to have grown closer to the path since a moment ago, and the way ahead seemed even darker. Well, of course it was darker, she told herself. Getting on for evening, wasn't it? And rain clouds massing overhead. Nothing unnatural in that. It got dark at night. Nothing at all to be nervous about.

"Thank you, I'd just as soon go on," she said. "If you'd retrieve my satchel?"

Jason lay down and stretched one long arm down the side of the path, fingers straining for the broken leather strap. It seemed an excessively uncomfortable way to get the satchel. Tessie thought it would have been easier to scramble down and back up again.

"It's not a good idea to leave the path in *tengu* territory," Jason said when at last he'd drawn the satchel back up, just as if he had read Tessie's thoughts. "They don't like people who break leaves or twigs off their trees."

"I do wish you'd stop talking as if you believed in the goblins," Tessie said crossly.

"I'm not the only one," Jason replied with a grin. "Have you noticed the signboards?"

There had been boards with inscriptions in Japanese characters posted at several places along the path, but Tessie had not paused long enough to translate them. Now Jason pointed to the one directly ahead of them and read it to her.

"To the *tengu* and other demons: Whereas our minister of forestry intends to visit the Karuizawa district next summer, now therefore ye *tengu* and other demons inhabiting these mountains must move elsewhere until the visit is concluded."

"Well, so much the better," Tessie said. "If the goblins have any respect for authority, obviously they will have gone somewhere else for the summer! Now can we get on our way without any more silly talk?"

"Why?" Jason inquired. "Because it's unbefitting a grown man? Or"—this very softly, almost whispered in her ear—"because you're beginning to believe in them too? Here, take my arm if you're afraid."

Tessie had a blistering retort at the tip of her tongue, but she never got to use it. A light flashed just before them on the path, a roar like an explosion of blasting powder deafened her, and she found herself in Jason's arms, clinging to him for dear life while a torrential rainstorm beat on their unprotected heads. The government notice warning the goblins away was scorched into a blackened smear of paper that was pulped by the violence of the rainstorm.

The storm passed as suddenly as it had come, having lasted just long enough to soak them both to the skin. Tired and wet and shivering, Tessie slowly left the protection of Jason's arms. She felt unreasonably depressed as she did so.

"As I said," Jason remarked, examining the scorch marks on the tree and the pulped remains of the notice, *"tengu* set fires, call lightning, and bring down rainstorms on those who offend them."

"A typical superstitious response to natural phenomena! It was a freak localized storm, nothing more." Tessie picked up her satchel and started up the path. There was no particular reason why she skirted the scorched stone; it was just easier to walk around it than over it.

"In a hurry? Afraid the goblins will get you?"

"I don't know about you," Tessie retorted over her shoulder, "but I am wet, cold, tired, and hungry. I want to reach the inn at Kiritsumi." A horrid thought struck her. "It does have an inn, doesn't it? I mean, if nobody goes there—"

"I don't know." Jason caught up with her easily; two of his long strides equaled three of hers, and he wasn't hampered by wet, clinging skirts. "We'll just have to find out when we get there."

Tessie lost count of ridges and level stretches. Several times they passed little shrines where a carved mask of a long-nosed goblin face kept watch over offerings of rice cakes and bits of fish. She tried not to think about those shrines. She also tried not to think about the flickering lights that she kept almost seeing out of the corners of her eyes, or the way the mist hung in strange shapes on either side of the path, or the eerie cries of birds like wailing women. But she could not conceal the rush of relief she felt when at last they came over a ridge and looked down on a cluster of high-peaked thatched roofs, with honest yellow candlelight flickering behind rice-paper screens in all the windows.

And there was an inn, a little, weather-beaten old building in the heart of the village. As they made their way there, the villagers silently slipped out of their houses to look at the mad foreigners who had come all the way to this remote village—and through the valley of the *tengu,* too!

The innkeeper smilingly made them welcome, but he denied all knowledge of a *yamabushi* in the village.

"Honored sir, how can this be?" he protested, hands outspread. "The gentleman perhaps is not aware that the *yamabushi* were the priests of the Shugendo religion, which has been outlawed for many years."

Tessie nodded impatiently. "I know that, and you know that, but are you absolutely sure all these people in the village know it?" Any place backward enough to put out offerings of rice cakes to the mountain goblins might well have clung to the old Shugendo cult long after the government in Tokyo tried to extirpate it.

The innkeeper would not answer her directly; he looked only at Jason. Tessie swallowed her impatience and tried again. "There *must* be somebody in the village," she pleaded. "Perhaps a man who was a *yamabushi* in the old days but who has, of course, given up his priesthood now in accordance with the law. We are not interested in making trouble for your people; we do not accuse anyone of breaking the law. But it is very important that I find this man. I was—we were sent here. It is a matter of duty."

"It is a matter of the honor of the family," Jason put in quietly, and Tessie thought she saw a flicker of sympathy in the innkeeper's dark eyes.

"I know nothing," he repeated, "but perhaps—since you both speak Japanese—perhaps the honored guests would condescend to spend some time in the common room of the inn, where most of our villagers gather in the evenings, after you have bathed and refreshed yourselves. It might be that some traveler perhaps has heard of the man you seek."

And with that half-promise Tessie had to be content for the time being.

She was so tired and wet and cold that it was not difficult to be content in the steaming luxury of the bath, or to be pleased with the polished simplicity of the room to which she was shown afterward. Mats on the floors, a bronze and porcelain tea service in a wall niche, and a pile of tattered old books left by previous foreign travelers comprised the entire furnishings of the room. Tessie sat cross-legged on the mat, sipped the tea brought to her by a scared little maid of twelve or thirteen, and leafed idly through the books. None of them had Morgan Gallagher's name on the flyleaf. She hadn't really expected to find a clue to his whereabouts in two popular novels and an old copy of *Murray's Guide to Japan.* But as the moon rose through the pine trees outside, and the song of the crickets in the garden drifted through her open window, she felt charged with a curious bubbly expectation. Something wonderful was about to happen; she was going to find Morgan again, everything was going to be as fresh and beautiful as it had been in the summer when she was sixteen and did not know about loss and betrayal. The next person through the door would know the magic word that would set her free.

Though the next person through the door was merely Jason Lancaster, he was carrying something as welcome to Tessie as a magic word: a tray piled high with bowls of rice, fish, steamed vegetables, and the salty black sauce called *shoyu* that the Japanese placed on everything except sweets.

"The landlord apologized for the simple fare that is all he can set before the honored guests," Jason said with a straight face. He staggered slightly as he set down the lacquered tray with its heavy burden of food.

Tessie discovered that she was ravenous. "Tell him it's perfectly all right," she said between mouthfuls of rice. "We'll manage. What's this crunchy stuff in the blue dish?"

"Pickled sea urchin?" Jason hazarded. "No, too stringy. Preserved pine tree bark. Sugared soy crystals. Thousand-year-old cucumbers . . ."

Tessie spluttered and clapped one hand over her mouth. "Don't make me laugh so hard when I'm eating," she warned Jason when she could talk.

"I wasn't trying to make you laugh," said Jason, mournfully eyeing the rapidly emptying bowls between them. "I was trying to make you lose your appetite."

"Why?"

"So there'd be some left for me, what d'you think?" Jason took up a pair of wooden chopsticks and began laying vegetables and fish on top of his own bowl of rice. "Nice tray. Do you think it's made locally? I saw some woodworking tools out back. Perhaps the landlord does woodwork and lacquering in his spare time; there can't be many visitors to an isolated place like this. Not many places for him to sell his work, either. And it's good work. Look at the way this lacquer flower glows in the light; you only get that effect with many, many layers applied very patiently."

While Jason was admiring the woodwork, Tessie took the last of the unidentified crunchy preserves and most of the steamed vegetables. Some of the tastes were unfamiliar to her, a curious mixture of sweet and sour with strange smoky aftertastes, but she was hungry enough to be willing to experiment.

"Come on," she said, "you can buy out the landlord's woodshop later. I want to get down to the common room and listen for gossip. And I need you to listen, too; your Japanese is better than mine."

"You are a hard-hearted, single-minded, driving woman, Tessie," said Jason. "But it's nice to know you need me for something." He rose and bowed from the waist. "Your interpreter awaits, my lady. Shall we descend and mingle with the commoners?"

Downstairs, sliding screens had been moved back, and the entire first floor of the inn had been opened up into a single great room for the evening's entertainment. Villagers were already sitting in a circle around the edges of the room, and in the center a low lacquered table supported a blazing mass of candles.

"Uh-oh," Jason murmured. "No gossip tonight, I'm afraid."

"Why, because they're about to burn the place down?" Tessie couldn't keep from thinking about all those candles and the rice-paper screens and the low wooden roof beams.

"No. They're about to blow the candles out. It looks as if the evening's entertainment is to be the One Hundred Candles game."

Tessie started counting while Jason explained the game. It was quite simple: each member of the party in turn told a ghost story, and after each story a candle was blown out. As the room got darker and the shadows creepier, everybody enjoyed thrills of mystery and terror until the extinguishing of the last candle provided an excuse for screams, ghost sightings, and a little quiet cuddling in corners.

"We might as well listen," Tessie decided. "The landlord suggested we join the group. Maybe he knew they were going to do this tonight. Maybe there'll be a clue." She caught Jason's sleeve as he started to rise. "No you don't! You can buy local crafts for Benten and Company tomorrow. I need you to help me listen tonight. Remember," she warned him, "if you don't help me get Morgan's legacy, you won't have any money to buy crafts anyway." Since Jason's dreams and motives were only of money, she might as well use his greed to control him.

The first few stories were mild enough and simple enough for Tessie to follow the tales without Jason's help. A monkey cheated a crab out of his rice cake; an envious woodcutter was punished by the *tengu;* a blind man teased by children turned out to be a *tengu* in disguise and almost carried off one of the children but was thwarted by the boy's quick wits. Tessie relaxed and began to enjoy the cozy atmosphere of the inn for its own sake. She wished she had brought a notebook to record the stories; it would be fun to make them into a little book for Sophia's children.

Then, as the candles were extinguished one by one, the mood of the gathering grew darker. There were tales of ghostly heads issuing supernatural warnings, drowned women rising from the river to avenge their betrayers, ghosts returning with the tide to take over a ship. Revenge and violent death were constant motifs.

Only one candle remained by the time the storytellers of the village had exhausted their repertoire.

"Blow it out!"

"No, we need another story first!"

"*I* will tell the last story," volunteered a hooded man squatting in the corner farthest from Jason and Tessie.

"Yes, that's fair, Grandfather, since you proposed the game in the first place!"

The old man pushed his hood an inch back, revealing little of his face but a very long hooked nose surmounted by two bristling eyebrows, and began his tale. His voice was deep and vibrant, surprisingly so for such an old man, and the story he told fascinated Tessie more than the tales of revenge and violence that had preceded it. It was a story about a wanderer in a foreign land who got into trouble through no fault of his own. In a fight, he accidentally killed two men and fled into the mountains for sanctuary. There he met a priest who directed him to go to the Fountain of Jizo for forgiveness.

"Jizo," the old man repeated in his deep voice. "Jizo, who nurses the little children left motherless; Jizo, who reunites families long parted; Jizo had mercy even on the foreigner!"

The crowd of villagers sighed and agreed that the mercy of Jizo was boundless and much to be admired.

"When he came to the Fountain of Jizo," the old man went on, "he found . . ."

One of the shutters on the front window came loose with a bang. A wild, errant gust of wind blew through the inn with a wailing sound and extinguished the last candle. The villagers screamed as Jason had predicted, scrambled to their feet, and trampled through the room looking for a way out.

"I feel it, my dead wife's hand. Make her let me go!" wailed one man.

"Aiee! My head is being cut off!" cried another.

Jason grasped Tessie by the arm and pulled her to her feet. "Stand in the corner here, they're going to trample you!" He pushed her into the corner and shielded her with his body. Tessie caught a gleam of a horrible glowing face that danced in the air just behind Jason's shoulder. The face had a long nose and bushy eyebrows, just like the old man who had told that last story.

The story about the foreigner who had killed two men.

She had a clue after all. Now she had to find that old man and get him to finish the story! She pushed against Jason's chest, trying to get free, but he couldn't hear her protests over the cries of the frightened villagers.

"Don't be afraid," he said into her ear. His strong arms encircled her, holding her so tight she could not get away, and his mouth covered hers in the dark. The sweet, sensual pleasure of his touch robbed her of strength to protest. She stared wide-eyed into the darkened room with its glowing mask while the villagers pushed and screamed around them and Jason's tongue thrust deep between her lips and her traitor body reminded her just how much she had loved him once upon a time, ten years ago and thousands of miles away.

"Do not be afraid! Good people, do not be afraid. Here is light!" the landlord called. Jason slowly, reluctantly released Tessie as candles burst into flame, showing a room with mats kicked awry and rice-paper screens torn and a shutter hanging loose, with sheepish villagers blinking in the light and patting each other for reassurance. Robes were torn and hair was coming down and there were bruised shins and feet from the moments of panic, but there was no sign of any demons.

There was a narrow cord set just about shoulder height, where a man could blunder into it and think something was trying to cut off his head. A wet kimono swung from a nail on the wall, just high enough to brush someone's cheek like a cold dead hand.

The villagers looked at the evidence and laughed at

each other. "To think of you being taken in by such tricks!"

"Me, is it? And didn't I hear you praying to your ancestors to save you?"

But the old man with the long nose and bushy eyebrows had vanished, and the innkeeper could tell them only that he was a traveler who'd arrived at the inn after dark, while Tessie and Jason were eating. And that the game of One Hundred Candles had been his idea.

"It's all right," the landlord's little son piped up when he saw how distressed Tessie was by this information. "I know who he is."

"You do?"

"Of course. He's a *tengu*. Who else would play such nasty jokes?"

"Who else, indeed," said Jason, and he went off with the innkeeper to inspect his stock of carved and lacquered trays.

Chapter Seven

Jason had had every intention of staying strictly away from Tessie for what remained of the evening. It was getting too hard to control himself around her, much harder than he'd anticipated when he got the pass that would force them to travel together.

In Yokohama it had all seemed so simple. When his American agent reported meeting a young man named Gallagher who exhibited an astonishing knowledge of Japanese manners and language, Jason had immediately guessed that the man must be one of Tessie's numerous brothers. A very little investigation had confirmed that the man was Hartley Gallagher, and that the real expert on Japanese in his family was an unmarried sister named Teresa.

Unmarried! That was when the real mischief had started. Until he heard that word, Jason had been able to convince himself that he took only a mild interest in the fortunes of a family with whom he had once been acquainted. Once he knew that Tessie had never married, his imagination took off in a wild manner that would have astonished his sober business colleagues. He had never dared to hope that such a lush, lovely, sensual creature would remain unclaimed for long. Could it be that she had never forgotten her first love—just as he had never forgotten her?

There was only one way to find out. They had to meet again. And this time Jason was determined that the meeting should be on his own ground. With the wealth and resources of Benten and Company at his control, it had been a simple matter to arrange Hartley's extremely tempting job offer. A gamble, perhaps, that Hartley would bring his little sister with him rather than turn down the job and confess his ignorance, but the gamble had paid off.

Or so it seemed. Here was Tessie, living in the same little foreign community on the shores of Japan, where she could not help but encounter him at every turn; here was Tessie, practically working for him, as Hartley's job depended on her translations. He should have been able to court and win her again in no time at all. How had he failed?

For one thing, there was Tessie's own provoking coolness. Even when he tried to force her into admitting that she still remembered their summer of love, she remained calm and collected and entirely businesslike. But worse than that was the same obstacle that had stopped him before: her blasted family. Last time she'd had brothers and sisters in and out of the house at all hours and a mother given to announcing heart attacks at the slightest frustration. This time she was hiding behind a whining sister-in-law and three bratty children. If Jason invited Hartley and his womenfolk to the races, Tessie was sure to stay at home with the children, and Jason was stuck entertaining Hartley and Sophia. If he dragooned the entire family into the Baptist missionary picnic, Tessie would be holding a child's head while he was sick in the bushes and Jason would be stuck talking to the Baptist missionaries.

And if he pressed her too hard, she just might decide to go home and marry this Ricardo, who was clearly not worthy of her or he wouldn't have let her go to Japan without him in the first place.

It was Jason's plain duty to protect Tessie from marrying a worthless weakling of a man like that. This trip of hers had been a godsend, a way to get her away from her family for once, out in the remote mountains of Japan where they would be thrown together as the only foreigners within a hundred miles. And with his connections, it had been easy enough to arrange the pass. A little harder to account to Tessie for his desire to go with her, without confessing that he still loved her. He could hardly afford to confess that while she was still being so cool and calm.

Jason flattered himself that his story of financial ruin threatening Benten and Company had been a masterstroke. Of course, the slightest inquiry in Yokohama would have proved him a liar; anybody there could have told Tessie that Jason Lancaster's trading company was a flourishing success, that instead of taking out loans he was making them to help other businessmen get their start. But when did women ever think to inquire over such matters? Tessie had swallowed the story. He had a perfect excuse to travel with her.

There were just three things wrong with the arrangement.

The first was that they'd come all the way to this romantic mountain inn and Tessie hardly seemed to be aware that she was alone with him. All she wanted to do was listen to the villagers tell ghost stories—as if that would give her some clue to Morgan's fate!

The second problem was the increasing difficulty he felt in keeping his hands off her. He'd kissed her twice now, once to stop a quarrel and once in the darkness of the inn when he could pretend to be protecting her. Each time had been like a series of small explosions going off from his toes to his head, making him ache with desire for this redheaded, quarrelsome, infuriating, beautiful woman, with a body made for love and a mind set in the habits of a maiden aunt. He needed her so badly it hurt, and she barely knew he existed.

The third problem was that he really didn't know why they were here. The advertisement in the Yokohama paper had been a great idea; if Jason had thought of it, if he'd known the key words to insert that convinced Tessie the advertisement came from Morgan, he certainly would have done so. But he hadn't placed the advertisement. And he didn't have any idea who had done so. He was almost desperate enough to believe that Morgan really was alive and signaling for help; except that men did not disappear for ten years and then show up hale and hearty. There had to be some other explanation.

Jason felt annoyed with the world. He was a man who liked to know what was going on and to be in control of his fate. And here he was in the mountains of Japan, plunged into a mystery beyond his unraveling, courting, for the second time, a girl who'd jilted him once already, afraid even to admit that he was courting her. Jason had a dark suspicion that he was making a very great fool of himself.

So he went off and discussed lacquerware and carved bowls and purchase prices and terms of delivery with the innkeeper—that being his business, and something he could both understand and control.

He managed to achieve a cool, rational mood that lasted for all of fifteen seconds after he left the innkeeper's workshop and mounted the stairs to his room. Then he saw Tessie again.

"Psst! Jason!" she whispered. She was leaning out of the doorway to her own room, holding a candle that cast a glimmer of gold over her brocaded robe and turned her loosened hair into a red-gold flame of glory about her face.

Jason's heart turned a somersault. She wanted him. She hadn't been as unresponsive as she pretended to that kiss in the darkened common room. She, too, had been tortured by memories of their brief time together. He took the remaining stairs three at a time.

"Not so loud!" Tessie whispered reprovingly.

"I'm sorry, my love." Jason took the candle from her hand and blew out the flame.

"What did you call me? And why did you let the candle go out? Fortunate that I've got another one lit in the room, otherwise we'd have to talk in darkness," Tessie scolded under her breath.

"Er—yes, fortunate, isn't it? What exactly did you want to talk about?" Jason followed Tessie into her room and decided not to mention that the kind of conversation he'd had in mind was best conducted in darkness and under the bedcovers.

"The clue, of course." Tessie regarded him with the same exasperated look she gave to Forbes Montague when he forgot to take the frogs out of his pockets before sending his clothes to the wash.

"What clue?"

"It should be obvious to the meanest intelligence," said Tessie patiently, "that the old man who told that last story, and then disappeared, was Morgan's messenger. Didn't you notice the striking resemblance of that story to the way Morgan disappeared? Apparently it's not safe for him to meet us here. He wants us to go to the Fountain of Jizo—wherever that is. That's what I wanted to ask you about."

"Fountain of Jizo? Oh. Yes. Right," said Jason, rapidly revising his ideas once again. He had not actually noticed that the last story could be interpreted as a retelling of Morgan's misadventures. But Tessie would think him hopelessly stupid if he admitted that, and he could hardly plead the true reason for his stupidity: instead of thinking about the story, he'd been staring at the curve of Tessie's cheek and wondering exactly how many pins he would have to remove before all her glorious, fiery hair tumbled down over that smooth white skin. Now her hair was loose, and even more lovely than he'd imagined or remembered. He longed to bury his face in the springy red-gold curls. For some reason, he imagined that they would smell like jasmine; he wondered whether he could survive without finding out whether that was true.

"Well?"

"Well what?"

Tessie crossed her arms and tapped one slippered foot on the floor. "The Fountain of Jizo. Where is it, Jason?"

"Oh. I'm not exactly sure. But I'll find out," he promised, and meant it. He'd been racking his brains for a way to prolong this fruitless journey; if Tessie wanted to go off to some other remote spot in Japan, with him as her traveling companion, who was he to resist? The Fountain of Jizo. Jason's overheated brain conjured up visions of a woodland glade, a cool trickle of green water over age-old weathered stones, a bower wreathed with flowering vines, Tessie in the bower, that silly wrapper sliding off to reveal the glorious wealth of her body . . .

"How?"

"Trust me. I have ways of finding out things, you know." If he kept staring at the spot where the brocaded folds of her wrapper crossed, just above her breasts, he would be incapable of rational conversation. And for some reason Jason wanted to prolong this conversation, delicious torture that it was. He fixed his gaze sternly on the tip of her nose and told himself to think of higher things. "Remember how I found out the exact schedule of your father's evening walk so I could nip down the alley and get over the fence in your backyard while he was down at the other end of the block?"

Tessie giggled. The motion made her nose twitch at the end. It was a cute little nose, freckled on the bridge

103

and just slightly turned up, setting off the curve of her lips beneath . . . *No,* Jason admonished himself. *Don't think about lips. That's liable to make you think about kissing, and then you'll reach for her again. You have to go slowly, make her want you first, don't go grabbing at her again the way you keep doing.*

"We were incredibly devious in those days, weren't we? Did you know I had to bribe my nephews not to spy on us in the summerhouse?"

"No. What did you bribe them with?"

"Snakes. I spent every morning of that July helping those two boys catch snakes for their collection."

"Good God," murmured Jason. "Greater love had no woman. I didn't appreciate you at the time, Tessie. Why didn't you tell me? I would gladly have helped you catch them!"

"You probably would," Tessie agreed with a reminiscent smile. "But I was afraid it would be beneath your dignity."

"After the episode at the carnival, with the cotton candy and the Pig-Faced Lady and the crooked dice, I don't see how you could have thought I had any dignity left!"

Tessie giggled again. "Oh, dear. I'd forgotten all about that scene you made, just because you thought the carnie was cheating me and you were determined I should have my stuffed bear!" How long ago it all seemed. How carefree and careless they'd been in those days, when she made up any excuse to slip away for a few moments with Jason and he took her all around the city on silly excursions mixed with love talk and games. "Oh, we had such fun together then," she said, almost sadly. "What went wrong?"

It was too much, Jason thought. First she jilted him, then she dragged him all around Japan and used him as a tour guide and interpreter, and now she wanted to pretend she had no idea why they were no longer lovers. "I think I should be asking you that," he said. *"I* never wanted the fun to stop."

Tessie's laughter caught in her throat. "Yes. I remember now." That had been exactly it; she had a duty to her family, and he didn't want her when the price was waiting and sacrifice instead of sex in the summerhouse. "I wanted something more than fun from the man to whom I gave my heart."

She pulled the wrapper more closely about her and gave Jason a cool nod. "I mustn't keep you up any longer, Mr. Lancaster. I'm sure someone in the village will be able to inform me of the location of the Fountain of Jizo, since you are so sadly ignorant."

Brave words, but they were no cure for the ache in her heart after Jason left her to the solitude of her little room. Tessie leaned on the windowsill for a long time, watching the stars in the pines and following the dark silhouette of the mountain with her eyes. Was she only chasing a will-o'-the-wisp, a dream as evanescent as the lights of the mountain goblins in the deep forest? What was she doing here in this remote mountain village, searching for traces of a man ten years dead, traveling with another man whom she could neither trust nor forget? Jason teased her with kisses, tantalized her with reminiscences of that summer when they'd been so madly in love, then withdrew into the remote fastnesses of his own soul and acted as if she, not he, had been the one to spoil everything.

"Enough of that!" Tessie admonished herself. If she had a reason for being here at all, it was to find Morgan. The fact that to accomplish this mission she had to travel with Jason Lancaster was simply that—a fact—an annoying, heart-wrenching, miserable fact that, like so much else in her life, simply had to be put up with. And there was absolutely no use in staring out her window at the low summer moon, brooding over a summer ten years ago, and rehearsing in her own mind all the reasons why Jason had been entirely in the wrong to leave her as he had. If she couldn't sleep, she might at least read some literature.

That left a choice between the romantic novels and *Murray's Guide to Japan*. Tessie squinted at the fine italic print of the first novel for a few seconds and decided that she preferred learning more about Japan to going blind over the misfortunes of Araminta and Devon. Besides, she might find some information about the Fountain of Jizo.

Jizo was not listed in the appendix, nor were any fountains mentioned. Oh, well. Tessie opened the book at random to the section on the western coast of Japan. Murray described it as predominantly a section of "unbeaten tracks, with poor inns and few sights." Well! That was surely dry and dull and sensible enough to take her mind off *that man*. Pointless, too, since they were miles from the region described; so she needn't worry about the remoteness of the villages or the difficulties of travel. What sights did Murray recommend? Well, there was the city of Matsue, on the Shinji Lagoon. Noted for silk weaving and paper manufactures. Jason had probably been there. Then there were islands in the lagoon, some with interesting caves. Legends associated with these caves . . .

It was probably the first time in the history of Kiritsumi that the occupants of the inn had been awakened by a Western war whoop. The innkeeper and his wife huddled at the foot of the stairs, discussing spirits. They were joined by the three servants, discussing *tengu*. Upstairs, Jason rolled out of his sleeping mat, pulled on his pants, and dashed into Tessie's room to rescue her from whatever danger had threatened her, without considering whether it was spirits, goblins, or mere mortal beings.

He was somewhat disconcerted to find Tessie dancing about the room, her brocaded wrapper crumpled on the sleeping mat, her voluptuous body outlined inside her thin batiste nightgown by the candle burning on the windowsill. In one hand she was waving a tattered, dog-eared copy of a popular tourist guide to Japan.

"Oh, Jason," she exclaimed, "I've found it! The Fountain of Jizo! I mean, I know where it is now! Isn't that wonderful? I'm *sure* Uncle Morgan will be waiting for us there. We must leave first thing in the morning."

Jason felt like an idiot for having come charging to her rescue. When would he learn that his Tessie neither wanted nor desired to be rescued? Self-sufficient, self-possessed, nothing stirred her except duty to her family. The hope of tracking down a man ten years dead meant more to her than the love of a man who was very much alive and sleeping in the next room. She didn't even understand what the sight of her, all creamy skin and thin white nightgown and hair like a forest fire, was doing to him right this minute. She wanted him to sit down and read the damned guidebook with her.

"Put your robe on before you scream like that again," Jason suggested. "I'll look at the guidebook in the morning. I'm going to get some sleep. You should do the same."

And he withdrew before he could be tempted to act on any of the baser impulses that apparently never bothered Tessie.

Alone in his room, though, Jason remembered the section of the guidebook Tessie had been reading, and his hopes for the journey sprang up anew. The west coast? The city of Matsue? He knew some very slow ways to get there—and some very romantic routes. A steamer trip on the scenic Inland Sea sounded much better than a quick return to Yokohama. He would have another chance at Tessie after all.

Chapter Eight

The mists that hung over the Inland Sea were fragile as gossamer, swirling and parting with every breeze to reveal pictures of a coastline so lovely that Tessie was almost speechless with delight. The pine-covered hills rose in delicate curves to sharp points that looked as if they had been snipped out of paper with a clever pair of scissors, set in place by some Japanese landscape artist. At one moment they were mysterious dark green shapes half veiled in a thousand wisps of mist; a heartbeat later, the sun struck at random through the cloudy air and gilded the pine branches with evanescent tints of copper and bronze.

Tessie clung to the steamer railing against a sudden movement of the choppy sea.

"It's getting rough," Jason said. "Do you want to go below?"

"No. I don't want to miss anything."

The steamer lurched as she spoke, and Tessie almost lost her footing on the slippery deck. Jason's arm was about her before she had a chance to feel insecure, warm and steadying and holding her for just an infinitesimal second longer than absolutely necessary for her to regain a steady stance. Then he withdrew his support—but too late. The casual touch had been enough to unveil all those feelings she'd been trying so hard to suppress.

Tessie gripped the steamer rail and stared blindly at the mist-veiled vistas of coastline and sea. It would have been so easy to have leaned a little more on Jason just then, to have pretended that she needed the support of his shoulder and the comforting strength of his arms.

She did need them. But not because the sea was growing rough. Her own feelings were tossed like the waves around them, churning into a despairing froth of desire and longing and fear. Each time Jason touched her, he rekindled fires that she'd tried for lonely years to put out. It was not proper for Tessie Gallagher, the good daughter, the unmarried sister who remained at home, to lie awake at night aching for the touch of a man's hand. It was foolish beyond belief to dream for ten years of the man who'd abandoned her without a word rather than share her time of waiting and self-sacrifice.

And it was infinitely dangerous to entertain the faintest whisper of such thoughts now, when she was traveling alone with that same man into the heart of a secret country.

So Tessie gripped the rail until her fingers hurt, and stared into the thickening mists until her eyes burned, and reminded herself that she had a very good reason for being on this steamer—a reason that had nothing at all to do with Jason Lancaster.

That her duty required her to travel with a man who ought to be thoroughly repugnant to her was merely one of life's unfortunate coincidences, one of those matters that high-souled and proper-minded people simply rose above without a moment's worry.

Tessie concentrated on elevating her soul and maintaining the propriety of her mind until, when Jason spoke again, she was able to answer him without betraying the least sign of the fever that had momentarily consumed her.

"If I'd known how you would love this landscape, I'd have taken you on a tour of Japan the day after you arrived in Yokohama."

"I should think you couldn't afford to neglect your business to that extent."

"My business," said Jason, "such as it is, is founded upon my love of this country and its arts. I had a hard, lonely time building it up, for there are very few of our countrymen who care to know anything of Japan beyond the superficial view they get from foreign enclaves in Yokohama and Tokyo. Sometimes I dreamed of finding a friend with whom I could share the Japan I've discovered for myself. But I never dared dream that the friend would be you, Tessie."

His hand covered her cold fingers. Tessie moved away as naturally as she could, using the ship's motion to make it seem as if she was only trying to keep her balance.

"If I'm paying close attention to the country, that doesn't necessarily mean I love Japan," she said. "This country took my uncle." *And the man I loved.* No. She mustn't think like that. Japan hadn't taken Jason from her, for he had never been hers; if he had loved her, he would not have accepted her decision to stay at home with Mama.

"But you find it beautiful."

"I find it a puzzle to be solved," Tessie lied. She dared not open her heart to the beauty of Japan, for Jason was waiting there to share his love of his adopted country with her. One kind of shared love could lead to another, too easily, for she knew her own weakness toward this man. Tessie did not think she could make love with Jason without loving him again. She could not bear to love him again and then have him show again how little her love meant to him. She was only a challenge to Jason, and so Japan must remain only a puzzle to her. "All I care about is finding Morgan and getting home as quickly as possible." If she said it often enough, maybe it would be true.

"I don't believe that, you know." Jason's voice was tinged with laughter. If she looked at him, his eyes would be crinkled at the corners, his lips twitching upward; she would be drawn into laughing with him, and then she'd be lost indeed.

"It is a matter of complete indifference to me what you do or do not believe," Tessie said.

A moment later, Jason excused himself to go below, and Tessie told herself that she felt vastly relieved to be free of his company.

The city of Matsue, the closest town to the lagoon of caves that was their goal, lay across a hilly arm of land from the Inland Sea. The last three days of their journey were made by *jinriksha*. Tessie had felt a little disappointment when their time on the steamer was at an end. The coastal scenery had been so beautiful, the water for the most part so peaceful. And now, packed into separate *jinrikshas,* she and Jason would scarcely even be able to converse—for which, of course, she ought to be grateful. She told herself firmly that she *was* grateful, and settled herself to endure the long *jinriksha* ride in dignified silence.

It didn't work out quite that way. The *jinriksha* coolies Jason had hired were peasants from Japan's west coast, babbling and cheerful and infinitely curious about the redheaded barbarian woman. They had no sense of caste or place; they expected Tessie to get out and walk up steep places, apologized with cheerful laughter when they raced too quickly down a tempting slope and spilled her into the soft grass at the roadside, and told her all about their wives and babies and mothers-in-law. All of this was infinitely more to her taste than the tight-lipped formality of the *jinriksha* coolies in Yokohama, who had been well taught their place as servants by stiff-necked foreign diplomats and their ladies. Tessie had a wonderful time laughing and gossiping with the coolies, learning a little Japanese and a lot about the family life of the poor in Japan.

The only trouble was that in this cheerful, friendly atmosphere it was hard for her to keep Jason in his place. He was always by her side, taking her elbow to help her up a steep path, picking her up after an undignified spill from the *jinriksha,* adding his knowledge of Japanese to help unravel a tangled story about the head coolie's mother-in-law's sister's silkworms and the neighbor's geese.

He made no more flirtatious overtures, and for that, of course, Tessie could only be grateful. She did wonder from time to time—mostly at night—why he was behaving so gentlemanly. But it wasn't hard for her to come up with reasons. She had been such an easy conquest for him before, an innocent girl of sixteen. Doubtless he'd thought the spinster of twenty-six would fall into his arms and his bed just as easily, and he had been willing to try a few kisses to see if he could win her without too much trouble. But when she did not respond, he'd not thought her worth the trouble of pursuing, just as he'd not thought it worth his while to wait for her or fight for her before.

She was not, Tessie concluded soberly in the dark hours of those nights, a woman that any man wanted greatly or desperately. Her red curls and generous curves gave her a certain superficial charm, enough to be a momentary attraction to a superficial man like Jason. But if she wasn't willing to come at his first whistle, he wouldn't bother to try again.

Lucky for her that he hadn't guessed how shamingly much she still wanted him! He'd have taken her for his mistress on this journey, just for amusement, and then he'd have dropped her again as soon as he had what he wanted—another taste of her body and half of Morgan's promised legacy.

Lucky, indeed, whispered the traitorous voice within her. *At least you'd have a few nights of love to remember. What have you now?*

"I have my pride," Tessie told herself.

On those same nights, in the little country inns, Jason was fighting his own battle with pride. Tessie had rejected him so firmly, so decisively on the steamer. She'd made it humiliatingly clear that she wanted nothing from him but his help in solving this puzzle—no, not even that. She'd been quite prepared to set off into an unknown country alone. She didn't want or need Jason Lancaster. Not as a lover, not as a friend, not even as an escort into a strange land.

So he'd quit trying to court the vixen. Maybe, if he stopped offering himself, she'd discover that she really wanted the goods she'd spurned when they were so freely displayed. For the rest of the steamer voyage and for these days of travel he'd intended to be nothing but a courteous, somewhat distant traveling companion.

The trouble was that it was deucedly hard to keep Tessie at a distance. She was so happy with every little detail of the journey, from a moss-covered old house to a turquoise-blue flower growing in a hillside crevice, that he wanted to kiss her just for appreciating this land that he had grown to love so well. She was so tantalizing, flushed and wind-blown, with her hair coming down and her skirts flying every which way after a tumble from the *jinriksha*, and totally unaware of the tempting picture she presented. She was such a good sport, trudging up hills and adapting herself to the limited accommodation of these country inns without a word of complaint.

He could have asked nothing better than to travel around Japan with such a companion forever, laughing and seeing sights and buying artwork during the day, sharing a sleeping mat in some little inn at night, and after every such excursion returning to his Yokohama house. True, he might have to take a larger house . . .

Jason shook his head and laughed sourly at himself. What a romantic fool he was, mentally furnishing a house in Yokohama with servants and draperies and half a dozen redheaded babies, all for the sake of a woman who didn't care two pins for him! Maybe he could force a response of sorts from her by kissing her, but what was that worth when, as soon as he let her go again, she withdrew into her cool shell and asked him pointed intellectual questions about the legends of Jizo and the puzzle Morgan had set them? He didn't want a woman who had to be forced into his arms. He wasn't a caveman who'd carry an unwilling bride away, or even a Japanese husband who'd treat his wife like an upper servant who existed only to carry out his every whim. He wanted a wife, a companion, a friend. Someone who could share his love of Japan as well as his bed.

And he would be damned if he'd humble himself further by continuing to court a woman who'd jilted him once without a thought, and who would doubtless refuse him now as casually as if she were refusing an invitation to afternoon tea. Jason tossed and turned and pounded his sleeping mat and vowed that he was through courting Tessie this time. Pride might be a poor bedfellow, but it was better than humiliation, which was all the pursuit of Teresa Mary Alice Gallagher had ever brought him.

Jason had never forgotten those enchanted summer moments. Not for a single day of his life. But what was the good of remembering, when they'd evidently meant less than nothing to Tessie?

And so, separated by pride and drawn together by a longing neither would acknowledge, on the fourth morning of their journey by *jinriksha* across this barren hilly arm of Japan, they came to Matsue, a mist-enshrouded city of peaked mossy roofs and ancient temples, on the shores of a blue lagoon, framed by the blue horizon of rising hills with the goblin-haunted mountain of Daisen rising above all— Matsue, the city of gods and ghosts, the Venice of Japan, with its canals intersecting every quarter and its little humpbacked bridges punctuating the streets.

"If we stay here long," Jason told Tessie, "I shall take you to the shrines in and around the city. You will climb the six hundred and forty steps to the temple of Ichibata-no-Yakushi, who gives sight to the blind. And then we shall go to the shrine of Kwannon of the Eleven Faces, who gives mercy to all; and last to Yaegaki."

"And what," Tessie inquired, "is the special virtue of Yaegaki?"

"That is where lovers go to pray for unions with their beloved."

"I think," said Tessie, "that first we should go to the Fountain of Jizo." She glanced at him suspiciously. "And how does it happen that you know of all these places? You've been here before, have you, on your travels to buy artwork?"

Jason nodded. "There's a maker of silk sashes in the Street of the New Timber. And an excellent potter behind the great Shinto temple."

"And with all this local knowledge of yours, you just never happened to hear of the Fountain of Jizo?"

Jason's cheeks darkened, and he scowled at her. "What are you suggesting? That I was trying to mislead you? And for what purpose, pray tell?"

"So you could get here first and get the next clue to Morgan's legacy," Tessie said.

"Damn the legacy. For your information, the locals don't refer to it as the Fountain of Jizo. We're going to the sea caves of Kaka-ura. There happen to be dozens of legends associated with those caves. The one I'm most familiar with," Jason told her, "is about a *kappa* that lurks under the water for the express purpose of drowning and eating quarrelsome, suspicious red-headed women."

"Poor *kappa*," said Tessie demurely. "He must be very hungry, since there are so few redheaded women in Japan. We'd better set off for Kaka-ura at once."

But their coolies had contracted only to take them as far as Matsue, and they balked at the prospect of another day's journey away from their homes—at least so Jason informed Tessie.

"They say we can hire new *jinrikshas* and coolies at the Izumo Hotel," he reported. "It's only a short walk. Do you good to stretch your legs." He picked up Tessie's satchel and his own bag, offered her his arm, and set off down one of the narrow streets like a man who knew exactly where he was going.

If this was indeed the case, then he had misled her regarding the distance to the Izumo Hotel. The walk took up half the morning. Tessie did not object, though she felt vaguely guilty at not keeping more control of their journey. After three days of sitting in a *jinriksha*—and occasionally being spilled out—it was quite pleasant to wander through the narrow, canal-crossed streets of this ancient city, listening to the morning sounds of street vendors, the *clop-clop* of wooden sandals, the singing of birds in the trees and of crickets in tiny wooden cages.

"Matsue has three districts," Jason told her. "This is the district of the merchant families. Some of them are quite wealthy; see how tall and old the houses are? Then, across the canal is the temple district." He led her through these two areas, chatting with easy familiarity about the landmarks they passed, while Tessie looked about her and enjoyed the brief abdication from responsibility.

"What's the third district?" she asked when he

paused at the edge of the square where the Izumo Hotel was situated.

"Homes of the old families, the samurai." Jason nodded at the central hill of the town, crowned by its gray pagoda-shaped castle and with old walled courtyards and houses crowding down the slopes to the rest of the town.

"You're not going to lead me around on a tour of that part, too?"

"Wouldn't be much to see," Jason told her. "Everything's behind gates. Even today, the samurai families keep very much to themselves. They certainly wouldn't want anything to do with barbarian foreigners like you and me. In all the years I've lived here, I've hardly met any of that class socially, and the few I have spoken to—"

Jason's opinion of the old samurai families was drowned out by the clatter of many wooden sandals and the excited chatter of dozens of young people who came pouring out of one of the buildings on the square. In a hurry to get to their noontime diversions, they filled the square with a stream of laughing, oblivious boys and girls. Tessie and Jason were separated by the stream of young people; she could see his mouth moving but could not hear what he said. Suddenly his face showed a look of alarm. At the same moment, Tessie felt the ground shift under her feet. She looked down and discovered that she had been gently pushed to the very brink of the canal that bisected the square. Before she could move forward to firmer footing, something struck the backs of her knees. A hand gripped her shoulder and pushed her back with such force that she could not resist. She went tumbling down the damp, slippery bank and into the cold, still waters of the canal.

It was only a fall of a few feet. Tessie could not believe that she was in danger so suddenly. But somehow her skirts had become wrapped around her legs, hampering her movements, and the flow of the water was strong enough to drag her under the bridge. Something struck the back of her head, and the world exploded into blackness and stars. A slimy green taste filled her mouth and nostrils.

"Tessie! Tessie, damn you, breathe!"

It was rude of Jason to shout so loudly, and when she had a headache, too! Tessie opened her mouth to protest, but all that came out was a sort of strangled croak. Jason's face quivered before her eyes, separated into two quite separate faces, then shimmied into a revolting vista of green and pink vibrating hues.

"Hold still," Tessie said severely. "How can I listen to you if you keep changing color?"

"Are you all right? Sit up! Let me help you. There, that's better."

Now there was only one of Jason—a considerable improvement, Tessie thought, on two of him. Her vision had cleared, and she could see Jason quite plainly, soaking wet and incongruously crowned with a strand of green weeds from the canal. But her mind was still fuzzy. She couldn't shake the feeling that there really had been two people helping her out of the water. "You pulled me out."

Somehow Jason's arm was around her, and she was reclining on his shoulder. It was a very comfortable position; Tessie found herself disinclined to move.

"Yes, I did. And when we get back to Yokohama," Jason said severely, "you're having swimming lessons. I am ashamed of you, Tessie, damn near drowning in a few feet of stagnant water."

"I can swim," Tessie protested. "Someone pushed me. And then—I hit my head under the bridge?" Or had someone struck her? Her memories were dim, confused. Everything had happened so suddenly.

"I do not think anyone meant to push you. There was quite a crowd. I am sure it was an accident," interposed a new voice. Tessie looked up, wincing at the glare of the sun, and blinked in surprise. The man who knelt at her other side was a young Japanese, as wet as Jason and, like him, festooned with green weeds from the canal. And she knew him—though the last time she'd seen him he had been wearing a Western-style suit instead of a damp kimono.

"Masao! What are you doing here?"

"I have friends in Matsue, and my family home is not far from here," Masao told her. "I might more properly ask, Tessie, what you are doing in my country—apart from swimming in the canal, that is!"

"And I," put in Jason, "might ask who the hell you are to be calling Miss Gallagher by her first name! That is, I'm very grateful to you for helping me pull her out of the canal, of course, but—"

"Oh, Masao and I are very old friends," Tessie told Jason. "He taught me Japanese. When he was studying engineering in San Francisco, he lodged with my family, you see. But we'd lost touch since he came back to Japan. It's wonderful to see you again, Masao!"

The young Japanese rose to his feet and bowed formally. "And I am pleased to see you, too, Tessie—Miss Teresa," he corrected himself, slurring the *r* slightly. "Perhaps we might renew our acquaintance in more comfortable surroundings?"

"The Izumo Hotel," Jason said at once. "I'll see if they have rooms for us."

"On no account," Masao protested. "I, too, need to change my clothes. We will all be more comfortable at the home of my friend."

And, oblivious to Jason's protests, he led them up the hill toward the Oshiroyama castle.

"Your friend is a samurai?" Tessie asked when he paused before one of the ancient gates, with its ornament of greenish-bronze family crest and carved wooden gods.

Masao gave her an amused glance. "There are no more samurai in the new Japan, Miss Teresa. But yes, most of my friends are of the same class as my own family."

Tessie dimpled wickedly at Jason. "A pity these ancient families are so snobbishly exclusive," she murmured under her breath, too low for Masao to hear, "or I'd introduce you. Maybe you'd like to go 'round back to the servants' quarters?"

Chapter Nine

It wasn't a full day's journey from Matsue to Mitsu-ura, the seaside village from which one took a boat to the island of Kaka and the sea caves. Masao informed them that, at worst, the trip would take only three hours by *jinriksha*.

"It is only seven miles to the village," he explained.

"Then why does it take so long?"

"The road is very bad." Masao paused and smoothed the folds of his black silk kimono. "It is better, I think, if I accompany you. The fisher folk are not accustomed to barbar—foreign visitors," he corrected smoothly.

"Oh, thank you," Tessie exclaimed.

At the same moment, Jason said, "Very kind to offer, but we—"

A sharp pain shot up from his foot, and his polite refusal turned into a strangled gasp. Tessie and Masao went on discussing the details of the journey, Tessie thanking Masao for his help and Masao protesting smoothly that it was no trouble. He had nothing else to do, and it would be the greatest of pleasures for him to spend some time in the company of his dear Miss Teresa.

"And on the way to Mitsu-ura," he said, "you can tell me all about the rest of your family."

While Masao was arranging with his friend's servants to have *jinrikshas* brought for them, Jason drew Tessie aside for a moment. "Damn it, why are you letting that fellow trail along with us? We don't need some damned inquisitive Japanese poking his nose into our private business."

"We," said Tessie, "have no private business. *I* have a duty to perform—to find my uncle. I think Masao's local knowledge may prove very useful to us. You, as I recall, did not even know where the Fountain of Jizo was. Masao knows exactly how long it will take us to get there and what we should pay the *jinriksha* coolies."

"So do the coolies," muttered Jason. "And don't step on my foot like that again. I think you've broken two of my toes."

"I won't," said Tessie, "if you don't interfere with my decisions again. Remember, this is *my* search."

Jason gave her an evil grin and tapped his breast pocket, where the all-important pass from the Japanese government resided. "And my passport."

Tessie had other, less practical reasons for being pleased that Masao was to accompany them. With each day of their slow, romantic journey through the Inland Sea and across the western hills, she had found it more and more difficult to resist the magnetic attraction of Jason. Dreams of that sweet summer ten years ago tormented her nights; glimpses of Jason and chance touches kept her days aflame. She had come very close, a dozen times, to betraying herself with dropped glances, blushes, stammers, a thousand little signs.

It would be a relief to have a third party along, someone toward whom her feelings were simply friendly. She could chat with Masao, improve her

Japanese, and keep him as a buffer between herself and Jason at all times. With any luck, he would stay with them until the end of the quest. After all, they had not far to go now—a short journey overland to Mitsu-ura, then a boat ride to the caves. By nightfall it would all be over, and Masao's presence would simply ensure that she didn't do anything foolish on these last hours of their journey together.

It was all very sensible and rather dull.

The road to Mitsu-ura, however, was anything but dull. The path went up and over sharp ridges of hills, each ridge sheltering a flat field of rice paddies fenced in by deep forests. Ever since she'd fallen into the canal that morning, Tessie had suffered a vague sense of uneasiness, a feeling of being watched by unfriendly eyes. She had thought the feeling would vanish when they left the city of Matsue, but in these forest-enclosed plains she felt it even more strongly; and on the narrow sections of path leading up and over the hill ridges, she could almost hear the breathing of unseen presences hovering behind the rocks.

The last ridge before the sea was far too steep for the *jinrikshas,* and the path degenerated into a series of rocky stepping stones that no wheeled vehicle could manage. Here they had to get out and walk, and Tessie was glad of it. Masao walked beside her wherever the path permitted, distracting her from the uncanny sense that their every move was watched. When a great black crow took off from a tree before them with a shrieking caw, swooping so close that its wings all but brushed Tessie's hair, she shrieked and jumped like a silly young girl.

"It's only a crow," said Masao, taking her arm to steady her.

"Unless," Jason put in from behind them, "it's a *tengu* in disguise. Don't they like to take the forms of crows?"

"My people no longer believe in such foolish superstitions," said Masao. "The *tengu* are only a story to frighten children."

"Ah," said Jason. "I know that, and you know that. But are you absolutely sure the *tengu* know it?"

Using Masao as a buffer between her and Jason was not working quite as Tessie had envisioned it. Instead, it was she who seemed to have the uncomfortable position of standing between the two men and their polite bickering.

At least they had distracted her from her own childish fears. And as they came to the height of this last ridge above the village, the sight before her made her forget everything else. A tumbled steep path led almost directly down to a tiny village nestled at the end of a deep blue bay, surrounded on three sides by cliffs. The crescent curve of the beach was splashed with the bright colors of boats and fishing nets, and the little houses with their curved sides and strange angles gave the impression of having been built out of wrecked boats.

"It's so beautiful," Tessie murmured.

"It's a damned steep way down," Jason said. "Mind you don't slip." And somehow he interposed himself between her and Masao, taking her arm himself in a firm grip that defied her even to think of slipping on the precipitous steps.

"It is forbidden to go to Kaka if there be wind enough to move three hairs."

The old boatman quoted the adage without a smile. No expression whatever showed on his wrinkled, impassive face; his eyes might have been carved of black stone, his tanned face out of the sea-weathered wood that was rescued from wrecked boats and used to build the houses of the village.

"Do you mean we have to wait for an absolutely calm day?" Tessie cried in exasperation. "That could

124

take weeks!" How long would Morgan wait for them? How long dared he wait?

The boatman nodded reassuringly and told Masao, "Explain to the barbarian woman that it is usually calm at dawn. We will set out then if she likes. We could not go now in any case; all the boats are needed for the festival tonight. We go out to bless the fishes, so that they will love Mitsu-ura and stay close to our bay. You will stay in the village tonight and see the festival. We have an inn," he said proudly, pointing to a low wooden building no larger than any of the other houses set along the single street. "Tomorrow we will go to the sea caves. Does the barbarian woman wish to implore Jizo for the blessing of children? She is wise to come to Jizo, who loves children and has mercy on all. I have only known one other barbarian who was so wise. Do all barbarians have red hair?"

Tessie clutched Masao's arm. "The other foreigner who came—what was his name?"

The boatman shook his head, signifying ignorance.

"When was he here? Recently? And he had red hair, too?" It must have been Morgan—it had to be Morgan!

"You go to Jizo," the boatman mumbled. "Jizo has mercy, will give you children."

Tessie felt her own red hair uncoiling in snaky crescents. "I don't *want* to ask Jizo for children! I want to find—"

Masao was tense beside her, and Jason placed a warning hand on her arm. Abruptly Tessie recalled her feelings of being watched, her certainty that somebody had deliberately pushed her into the canal back in Matsue. Morgan might well be in danger, and she would be doing him no favor to use his name here or to make a scene in the village street.

"Very well," she said, relaxing. "We will see the festival tonight, and tomorrow you will take us to Jizo."

"I thought so." The boatman nodded in satisfaction. "All women want children."

The inn was a tiny, boxy place with no real privacy; the rice-paper screens that separated one little cubicle from the next were pockmarked with holes, and wherever Tessie went she could see the silhouettes of dozens of curious villagers, all but leaning against the screens from outside in their desire to see more of the redheaded barbarian woman. It was impossible to rest. After she had shaken out her dress for the next day and run a comb through her hair, she met Jason in the hall and learned that he had had the same problems.

"It's nearly sunset," he said. "Let's go for a walk on the beach, then come back and eat. The villagers will go to bed when it gets dark—I hope."

"Where's Masao?"

Jason made an irritated gesture with one hand. "How should I know? Off about some business of his own, I suppose. Maybe he's taken himself back to Matsue."

"Not without saying good-bye!"

"Does it matter? I, for one, can perfectly well enjoy a sunset stroll on the beach without the company of a lisping Japanese. 'Miss Telesa, Miss Telesa!'" Jason mimicked, and Tessie stared at him in surprise. She had not thought him capable of such rudeness.

"I don't think it's very wise of you to criticize Masao's accent," she said. "You probably sound even funnier to a Japanese than he does to us."

They walked on down to the beach, together but apart, with six inches of air and a storm cloud of dark thoughts separating them.

It turned out to be a bad time for a walk, but the spectacle that greeted them on the beach more than compensated Tessie for the loss of her stroll. At sunset the fishing net that had been stretched across the bay earlier was drawn in, by the combined labor of all the men in the village. They formed a line on the sands, each man gripping the rope that led to the edge of the great net, and chanting regularly as they hauled from hand to hand. Their half-naked bodies shone like bronze statues; the last glimmering rays of the sun struck echoes of bronze and gold from the sea and caught the gleaming rainbow iridescence of the fish leaping against the net. For half an hour Tessie and Jason watched, fascinated, as the day's catch was slowly brought in to the accompaniment of chants and songs and the cry of scavenging birds.

When they turned away at last, darkness had cast a cloak of velvety blue over the village, and the streets were lined on either side with tiny twinkling stars of green fire.

"Oh, what is it?" cried Tessie.

"Fireflies," said Masao, materializing out of the darkness beside her. He fell into step with her and Jason as they crossed the sands back to the village street. "They catch them in little cages for the night of the festival. Also there will be stalls selling cakes and straw toys for the children. This is only a poor fishing village, but these things they can make or catch themselves. Would you like to see the stalls where they are selling their trinkets?"

There was no word of explanation for his disappearance, no hint that any explanation was needed. Well, Tessie told herself, it wasn't. Japanese manners were different from Western ways; she was a guest in Masao's country and must accept that whatever this son of an ancient samurai family chose to do was proper, just as he had politely accepted the strange ways of her own family when he boarded with them in San Francisco.

They walked slowly up the single lane of the village. Masao bought Tessie a package of sweet cakes marked with good-luck symbols in red, and a little dancing straw whirligig that spun around when she blew on it.

127

"For good fortune in your quest," he said gravely.

"I don't recall Tessie mentioning why she wanted to come here," Jason drawled.

Masao had to look up at Jason, but he was in no way dwarfed by the taller man with his obvious antagonism. "Nor have I questioned her. But when I stayed with the family in San Francisco, she was sad about the loss of her beloved uncle who had disappeared mysteriously in Japan. It is a small matter to deduce that she is traveling in Japan now with the hope of learning something about her uncle's disappearance; particularly when she is so excited to learn that another redhaired foreigner had visited this remote village. And I do not recall," he added in meditative tones, "that *you* were present to comfort Miss Teresa in her bereavement at that sad time, Lancaster-*sama*."

"Oh, look at the fireflies!" Tessie exclaimed, feigning girlish excitement at the sight of the little insects crawling and fidgeting inside their black horsehair cages. "Aren't they lovely?"

"Let me get you one," said Masao instantly.

Tessie shook her head. "No, I hate to see things caged. They are beautiful here, but they would be far more beautiful flying free above the village."

"Poor Princess Splendor," said Masao. "If you freed her she would only fly about and tire herself out in a hopeless quest. She is better off in her cage. Do you not know the story?" he asked when Tessie looked questioningly at him.

She shook her head. "Morgan told me many folk tales of Japan, but I do not recall that name."

"Ah! Well," Masao said. "Princess Splendor was the child of the moon, tiny like these fireflies and giving off a bright light. One night when she was visiting the earth, an old woodman picked her off a bamboo branch in the moonlight and brought her home to his wife, and they brought her to the emperor, who loved her and wanted to keep her. And she loved the emperor, too, but she had promised to return to her mother the moon and not to stay with any mortal man. So she went back on the path of a moonbeam, crying silver tears, and when she reached the moon she died of sorrow for the emperor, who was grieving for her. And all her tears became fireflies, and on summer nights they go flying about the woods looking for the emperor whom their princess loved, and they do not know that he died hundreds of years ago."

"It's a beautiful story," Tessie said, blinking back tears of her own. Poor lonely princess, doomed always to fly about looking for a man who did not even exist! "But so sad."

"There is always sadness in love," said Masao quietly, "particularly when it conflicts with honor. We Japanese esteem honor above all things."

"But must that always stand in the way of love?" Tessie cried, thinking of her own case.

"All too often it does."

"But it is not inevitable. People who truly love each other will find a way to satisfy both love and duty. It is only weak souls who give up at once." She meant every word to be a barb in Jason's heart, to let him know how thoroughly she saw through him. She knew that if he'd really cared about her before, he would not have let her sense of duty keep them apart. She used that as a yardstick to measure his hints that he could care for her now.

But it was unsatisfactory, planting her barbs in a silent victim. "Don't you agree, Jason?" Tessie prodded.

Jason was no longer beside her.

"I wonder where he went? We'd better go back and look for him."

Masao shrugged. "He is a grown man. I do not

think he will have found any trouble in this little village. Let us walk a little farther. There is a garden behind the inn where you can rest."

Just before they reached the garden, Tessie glanced over her shoulder and cried out in alarm. A gigantic black shadow, outlined in swaying stars of green light, was overtaking them with rapid strides.

"Here they are," said Jason, breathing a little heavily from his hurry to catch up with them. "Wasn't easy to persuade the stall keeper to sell me all his wares, but I made it worth his while. Here you are, Tessie, all the captive Princess Splendors in the village."

And he handed her, one by one, the little horsehair cages, each containing a single firefly, that he had been carrying strung on long rods across his shoulders and down his arms.

"What a strange gift," said Masao coldly, "when Miss Teresa has already informed us that she does not love to see things caged."

"No," Tessie corrected him. In the safety of the darkness, she could smile up at Jason without fearing that he would misinterpret her happiness and gratitude, without trying to conceal the rush of tenderness that filled her. He had understood what she wanted to do, had put into action what she'd only dreamed of for fear it would antagonize the villagers. "I do not love caged things, that's true. Jason bought me the fireflies so that I could set them free."

And in the semiprivate garden behind the inn, while Jason and Masao sat on a rustic bench and the villagers thronged quietly outside the gate to observe the antics of the barbarians, Tessie opened the little horsehair prisons one by one and set their occupants free on the night air. A few took wing at once and flew about the garden, their little green lights flashing like jewels against the gentler glow of the candles behind the rice-paper screens; one cluster made a tiny green lantern in the ancient pine tree that shaded a corner of the garden. But most, bewildered by their sudden freedom, clung to Tessie's hands, crawled up her sleeves and skirt, and nestled into the braided coils of her hair as if afraid to leave their benefactress. She glowed with their subtle radiance, all outlined with tiny sparkling lights, and the villagers beyond the gate murmured that she must have some magic to enchant the fireflies into staying with her.

"Princess Splendor, indeed," Jason murmured.

Masao gave him a hard look. "Miss Teresa was very kind to me when I was in America. I would not wish to see her hurt."

"Neither would I," Jason said. "How fortunate that we are in agreement." And he wondered for a moment just how kind Tessie had been to Masao, and just what might explain the seeming coincidence of their meeting in this faraway corner of Japan. Could she somehow have arranged it? He knew so little about her; only that, at sixteen, she'd been cold and self-possessed enough to send him away without a backward glance, when he loved her more than life itself. It was only rational to assume that she had not become any gentler with the passing years, that her appearance of warmth and friendliness and trust was only a facade over a cold heart that knew not how to love.

Tessie, oblivious to the scrutiny of the two men, gently brushed the fireflies from her skirt and urged the ones still in her palms to taste the freedom of the warm summer night. "Go on, little princesses," she murmured, raising her cupped hands to lift a handful of fireflies into the open air. "Fly about, be free, seek your love!"

Jason sighed and shook his head. It would be easier to bear his loss if he could think ill of Tessie, convince himself that she was a cold-hearted, scheming woman who took lovers as easily as another woman changed dressmakers, who would connive to meet her Japanese "friend" while towing her discarded American lover behind her like a trophy. But he couldn't make that picture real in his mind. Tessie was just what she seemed—warm-hearted, innocent, courageous, and loving. There was not an ounce of deceit in her, and there was too much love for every living thing—for her worthless brother, for his bratty, whining children, for the demanding parents who'd eaten up her young life, even for the fireflies of Mitsu-ura.

The only thing wrong with her, from Jason's point of view, was that she did not have any of that love to spare for *him*.

And he had completely run out of ideas on how to remedy that situation.

The last of the fireflies left Tessie's head, circling above her for a few seconds like a green halo, before it sped off to join its friends in the sheltering branches of the great pine. She came toward the two men, adopting a deliberately cheerful tone to cover the slight ache of longing that had assailed her when she thought of Princess Splendor searching for her lost love.

"Didn't that old boatman say something about a torchlight festival after dark? Shall we go back down to the beach and watch the spectacle?"

"I'll be happy to escort you, Tessie," Jason said at once, rising from the bench while with one hand he held Masao down. "Masao is tired, though. I think he might find the night air unhealthy."

Masao accepted the veiled hint. When Jason moved his hand from his shoulder, he rose and bowed to Tessie. "I will come with you in the morning," he promised. To Jason, he murmured in Japanese, too low and swift for Tessie to catch, "Tonight is yours—but tomorrow is my turn!"

Jason shook his head at his own folly as he guided Tessie down the dark narrow street. Most of the villagers had already gone back down to the water's edge, the torchlight procession of the boats proving a

132

greater attraction than the incomprehensible conversation of two foreigners and a gentleman of the old samurai class. He and Tessie were alone now—and what good would it do him? If he hadn't been able to make her love him by a gentlemanly courtship in Yokohama, if she hadn't turned to him for help after that frightening evening in Kiritsumi, if she hadn't been touched by the romantic beauty of the Inland Sea—what good would one more evening do, except to lacerate his feelings and prove once more that he could not attract the one woman he needed to complete his life? He was letting his sense of rivalry toward Masao push him into acting foolishly. Well, they would have their walk, but he wouldn't make any advances that would give Tessie another chance to reject him. He'd laid his heart at her feet once before only to have her spurn it, and she'd given no sign in all this journey that her feelings toward him had grown any warmer. He would not make that mistake again.

As they drew closer to the beach, a hurrying throng of villagers filled the street. A drum began beating somewhere behind them, and the silver voices of young girls singing filled the warm night air. Suddenly the narrow street blazed in a circle of golden light, as dozens of torches were lighted at once. Laughing and singing, the villagers in their festival robes of shimmering silk hurried past the barbarians to hand the torches to the waiting fishermen. The little boats went out into the darkness of the bay, each one illumined with a dozen bobbing torches that grew as tiny as fireflies' sparks in the distance, until the entire bay sparkled with little golden lights.

The throbbing, insistent beat of the drum pulled at Tessie's feet, making her want to join one of the dancing circles on the sand. But that would never do. She was a foreigner here, an outsider, and the villagers might resent her joining their ancient rites.

She stole a glance at Jason who was mesmerized by

the torches bobbing up and down in the bay. She could take a long look at him without fear that he would see her conflicting feelings for him written on her face.

How perfect this night would be, Tessie thought wistfully, if only she could share it with someone she loved and trusted. But to cast Jason in that role would be as foolish as trying to join the village dance. Unsuitable. Dangerous, maybe. Impossible, in the long run.

He was a good traveling companion. He might be a good friend. But he would never be the husband and lover of her dreams, desiring her above all else, sweeping aside all obstacles to get to her, demanding total possession. The man she'd dreamed of would have carried her away with him that night ten years ago, forced her to marry him and stay with him forever. Jason's "love" had lacked that power. He would have married her if it had been made easy for him, because it was the honorable thing to do; but presented with a single obstacle, he faded away at once into the free scafaring life that was all he really wanted.

Tessie tried to imagine Ricardo, the proud, possessive, imaginary lover, beside her on the beach in Jason's place. It didn't work. A man as dominant and possessive as her imaginary fiancé would surely have refused to help her embark on such a risky mission. He would never have behaved like Jason, letting her choose her own dangers and take her own risks, always there with a helping hand when she needed one. Jason was actually a better friend, a better traveling companion, than the perfect lover she'd created for herself.

Tessie sighed and looked sadly at Jason's strong profile, dimly outlined against the faint glow of torch-light from the bay. Somehow, without her noticing it, her hand had crept into his. The steady warmth of his fingers encircling hers, the touch of palm to palm, made her heart beat faster and left her dizzy with a sense of vague anticipation.

The low beat of the drum, the silver threads of song, the golden lights of the torches all wove a web of enchantment about her senses. For a moment it seemed to Tessie that all her doubts and fears would be resolved if only Jason would turn to her and take her in his arms once again. The ache of longing inside her would be assuaged at last, and she would be able to forget the past in the sweetness of the summer night.

But he did not look at her, and the moment of madness passed. Tessie sternly quashed her errant thoughts and removed her hand from Jason's for fear that he would feel the wild throbbing of her errant pulse. What was she dreaming of? Once before she'd made the mistake of letting herself love this charming, unworthy man, and he'd proved himself too weak to keep her. She would not make that same mistake again.

Chapter Ten

In the clear blue morning, the water of the little bay was transparent and calm as glass. The boat skimmed over the smooth surface, and the morning breeze cooled Tessie's face. She felt almost as if she were flying. Resolutely, she turned her face away from Jason and Masao, sitting in silent competition behind her, and looked forward to the sea. Somewhere out there, past the safe waters of the bay, was the cave where the Fountain of Jizo was to be found; and there Morgan would meet her and explain, at last, what sort of trouble he was in and how she could help him come home to his family. That was all that mattered now—rescuing the beloved uncle who had teased her and played with her and told her stories of Japan and brought her little presents from the sea. She would not think of Jason Lancaster at all; he was an inconvenience, nothing more.

A great splash sprinkled the back of her neck and her dress with cold, salty droplets. Tessie turned and gripped the edge of the boat. Only one man was sitting behind her now: Masao, arms folded, looking very stiff and dignified in the folds of his formal old-fashioned kimono.

"Jason!" she screamed, forgetting her resolve of a moment ago. "What have you done to him? We must turn back!"

Masao lifted one arm and wordlessly gestured behind them, where a sleek, seal-like head rose from the water, a lithe, strong body turned and flipped for all the world like a dolphin at play.

"Delightful swim," said Jason a few minutes later, hauling himself back aboard the boat. "Couldn't resist the water. And the boat is so slow here inside the bay, no trouble at all to keep up. Care to join me for a dip, Tessie?"

Tessie shook her head and modestly averted her eyes as Jason swung his long legs aboard and began toweling himself dry with his own shirt. She caught just a glimpse of muscular, tanned thighs and a flat stomach with a dark downward-pointing arrow of curling hair. Tanned all over his body! He must be used to making this sort of shocking display of himself; of course he'd been living in Japan so long that he was almost Japanese himself in some ways, and Tessie had seen on her very first day in Yokohama how little the natives thought of nudity. She was sorely tempted to sneak another glance back, to see if he was really tanned *all over*. Temptation, Tessie reminded herself, as Mama had so often said, temptation existed only to be resisted.

Mama's words didn't have quite the strength, here in these foreign waters, that they'd had at home in the white-curtained house on the hill. The water *was* beautiful; clear and blue and cool. Tessie could just imagine how it would feel to shed her layers of hot, constricting clothes and slide through that clear blueness, feeling the cool edge of water against her bare skin.

Good heavens, what was she thinking of! Her fingers were actually plucking at the buttons at the neck of her dress, for all the world as if she'd contemplated taking Jason's mocking invitation seriously! Tessie snatched her hand away from the button like a child caught at the sugar bowl. Madness, that's what it would be, sheer madness. She would never consider behaving so improperly with any man, least of all a dangerous, shallow-hearted, deceiving rogue like Jason Lancaster. Only think how shocked Masao would be!

If Masao weren't there, Tessie thought, there would only be the old boatman to witness her shocking behavior; and he, not knowing Western customs, might not even know how shocking it was. Without Masao's stern, disapproving presence, she might have been even more sorely tempted to join Jason in the cool water of the bay.

It was certainly a good thing that Masao had chosen to accompany them!

Within a few minutes the temptation had passed, for as the boat left the safe confines of the bay the water grew cold and dark and menacing. Tessie felt that they were sailing over immeasurable depths, where any mystery could hide. Jason's stories about the *kappa* didn't seem quite so funny now; nor did the tales they'd heard in Kiritsumi, about the ghosts of drowned sailors climbing aboard fishing boats to return to land.

The sheer black cliffs that marked the edge of land added to the sense of vague menace. The boat skirted the cliffs, passing closer than Tessie liked to jagged gaps with masses of rock poised atop their heights, crevasses sinking into oblivion beneath the sea, tortured shelves of ancient strata tossed like a child's jackstraws by some upheaval of the earth, pillars of black rock watching them like silent sentinels.

Finally, just after they passed the highest of the sentinel rocks, Tessie saw a roughly arch-shaped opening in the cliff. The boatman guided his vessel through the arch and into a shadowy grotto floored with clear, still water. The rocks at the bottom must have been twenty or thirty feet below them, but Tessie could see them as clearly as though she were looking through thin air.

As they glided through the water, the narrow entrance widened into a high, lofty cave with smooth walls. Tessie was looking up, marveling at the glistening walls with their dancing reflections of light from outside, when Jason cried out and threw himself forward over her, pinning her down in the smelly, damp bottom of the boat. A shower of water cascaded over them both, and there was a splintering crash at the midpoint of the boat, right where Tessie had been sitting. Water rose up around them, and the boat rocked wildly back and forth while the boatman struggled to control it.

"What *was* that?" Tessie breathed when at last Jason released her and she could sit upright again. The side of the boat was broken and splintered just above the water line, as though some giant had kicked it in passing.

"Boulder. Fell from the opening where that spring of fresh water comes through. Saw it teetering," Jason said tersely. "Looked like it was going to hit the middle of the boat. Didn't have time to warn the boatman. I thought if I threw our weight to one side, it might just miss us. And so it did," he finished, looking more cheerful.

"Oh! I thought you were shielding me." Tessie felt obscurely disappointed.

"No, it wouldn't have come near you," Jason assured her. "But if the boat were wrecked—well, it's a long swim back to the bay from here."

Tessie nodded her agreement, thinking of the harsh, rocky cliffs and the steel-gray waves outside the cavern. A fit of shivering overtook her for a moment. Her clothes were wet through in several places, and it was cool inside the shadowy cavern.

"I beg to differ," Masao put in with his usual calm politeness. "Miss Teresa might have been seriously injured if the rock had struck her."

"I *told* you," Jason reiterated, "it wasn't anywhere near her."

"All the same, I do not think that this is a safe expedition for you. Miss Teresa, I shall order the boatman to escort you back to the bay of Mitsu-ura at once. You may remain at the inn while I explore these caves and make sure there are no further dangers awaiting you. If there is any message from your uncle, I will bring it to you."

"You don't set foot inside these caves without me," Jason told Masao.

"And who," Masao inquired, "will stay at the inn to protect Miss Teresa?"

"You can do that, since you're so concerned for her. *I* will explore the caves."

"Wait a minute!" Tessie's fit of shivering had passed, and she was able to speak at last. "What makes either of you think I'll wait at the inn? This is *my* search. Morgan's original message was addressed to *me*. I've seen no sign that he has any desire to speak with either of you gentlemen. Indeed, if you hadn't insisted on sticking your nose in at Kiritsumi, Jason, maybe Morgan would have met me there and this further journey would have been unnecessary."

"Now, Tessie, that's not fair!" Jason protested. "Dammit, you asked me yourself to come along and help you translate the Japanese stories!"

"Yes, but I didn't want you at Kiritsumi in the first place," Tessie argued. She knew she was being slightly illogical, but that didn't seem to matter beside the monstrous interference of the two men. "Now listen closely, both of you. If anybody goes on to the Fountain of Jizo, it's going to be me—and if either of you gives me any trouble about it, I'll send you straight back to the inn at Mitsu-ura to think over your bad behavior!"

Since Tessie had no idea how she would carry out this threat, she was rather relieved when the boatman entered the conversation with a long, impassioned speech about the spirits protecting the caves. She felt somewhat less relieved as she slowly grasped the point of his speech. Legend had it, he said, that the caves of Jizo were protected from persons of evil heart by a guardian spirit. If any evil-intentioned person tried to enter the caves, a rock would fall on them at the point they had just passed. Clearly one of his passengers was not a good person and should not be taken on to Jizo's fountain. "Possibly more than one," he finished, with a dark scowl at each of them in turn—the uppity fire-haired barbarian woman, the foreign man who let her speak to him so rudely without punishing her, and the fine gentleman of the samurai class who ought never to have been consorting with such dubious types.

"Actually," Jason said with a ferocious grin, "we are *all* desperately evil-hearted, and if you do not take us on to the Fountain of Jizo—"

Tessie kicked him in the shin. "I'll pay double what you asked for," she said while Jason was still in shock. "Three times."

The boatman's qualms of conscience were eased by this offer, and the boat glided on while Jason moaned quietly and nursed his shin. "I don't know why I travel with you, Tessie," he muttered. "A few more sightseeing excursions with you and I'll be maimed for life."

"I do hope you learn to stop interfering in my business before that happens," Tessie said sweetly.

At least there was no more talk about anybody's returning to the inn. Jason and Masao both seemed to have grasped that once this boatman got back to Mitsu-ura with his tale of superstition and danger, they'd have some trouble hiring anybody to take them out again.

As they moved deeper into the cavern, Tessie thought she could see a mysterious green light glimmering ahead. Soon all the water seemed to be suffused with radiance from below. She held her breath, marveling at the enchantment of the undersea world, until the boat passed under another arch and Jason tapped her arm. He pointed to the left, and she saw the source of the light: another opening into the cave, through which she could see a strip of green coast far away. He pointed to the right, and she looked up to the roof and saw a projecting white rock on which, from above, a trickle of whitish fluid slowly dripped.

"The Fountain of Jizo?" he queried in a low voice.

"Yes, yes, Jizo!" the boatman exclaimed with satisfaction. As he guided the boat toward the sandy strip at the back of the cavern, he told the foreigners that the whitish fluid was indeed the milk of Jizo, produced to nourish the souls of dead children. Mothers who had not enough milk for their children prayed to Jizo, and she gave them the power to suckle their babies; mothers whose milk came in abundance prayed to Jizo that their excess might be given to those in need, and their milk diminished.

There was a strip of sandy shore at the back of the cavern where the party could disembark and walk around, and from there paths opened into a network of other caverns, some underwater, some above it. In the dim light here at the back, Tessie could faintly discern the smiling face of a goddess carved in pale stone and, behind her, shapes so blurred and indistinct that they might have been carved by the force of the waves.

The sand at her feet was heaped with little towers of stones, as if children had been playing there. The boatman saw her curious glance and explained that the stones were piled up by dead children, in thanks for the milk of Jizo that nourished them until their souls were ready to go on.

"Are all the legends of Japan beautiful—and sad?" Tessie murmured to Masao.

He gave her an enigmatic glance. "We Japanese do not seek to deny the sadness of life." With a gesture at once delicate and remote, he lifted the hem of his kimono so as not to disturb the piles of stones at his feet.

The legends of dead children had left Tessie feeling quiet and melancholy. The mood of cheerful expectation with which she had set off that morning had quite vanished. The blue-lit, echoing cavern with its sad legends and the eternal whisper of the waves was no place in which to entertain bright hopes of reunions. She could not believe that Morgan would be waiting for her in such a place—and if he was waiting, where was he? Why hadn't he shown himself?

She'd hinted to Jason, in a fit of temper, that perhaps Morgan was hanging back because of his intrusion. She hadn't really meant it at the time, but now she wondered. Morgan—for she refused to believe the message had come from somebody else after her uncle's death—had set a message in a place where she would read it, worded in such a way that only she would understand it. He had wanted her to come to him. He hadn't said a thing about wanting Jason and Masao and some Japanese boatman from the village.

Perhaps, if she could separate herself from the others, Morgan would show himself to her and tell her why all this secrecy was necessary.

It wasn't difficult to slip away. The boatman was dozing quietly on the beached boat while his clients explored. Jason and Masao were arguing in coldly polite tones about the date of carving of the stone goddess, peering and poking all over her poor weather-worn features to prove their points. They hardly noticed when Tessie casually strolled through the passageway that led to the network of caves. She permitted herself an ironic smile. How quickly they forgot their pretence of concern for her! Jason, of course, had only been plotting to get to the caves without her, to get whatever clue to the legacy he thought might be there; and Masao—what *was* Masao's reason? Perhaps he'd been truly concerned for her safety, but then he forgot her the next minute!

"Oh, stop it," Tessie told herself. "Traveling with two men has upset your judgment. You are beginning to think like a pretty young girl who expects men to fight over her and flirt with her, instead of Hartley's spinster sister and everybody's favorite maiden aunt. You'd do better to think of some way of marking your trail, so that you don't get lost in these caves and give them something real to worry about."

The sand here was damp but well above the water, and the interior caves were lit by gleams of outside light coming through cracks high above her. All she needed to do was to draw an occasional arrow on the sand.

Tessie's hand covered her mouth, and she bit down hard on her lower lip. *There* was an arrow, inscribed in the damp sand at her feet. And she could have sworn it hadn't been there a moment ago, when she entered the passageway. No—the sand was still crumbling at the edges; even as she watched, a few grains of sand fell into the fingertip width of the groove.

"Morgan?" Tessie whispered, as loudly as she dared for fear of drawing the attention of the men she'd left behind. "Morgan!" She tiptoed forward, toward the opening in the wall indicated by the pointing arrow. It was low and narrow, but she got through with only a little damage to her braids and a few hairpins left on the sand.

She found herself in a long, low cavern with perfectly smooth walls, not a crevasse or another opening to be seen anywhere, illuminated by a dim blue radiance that had no discernible source. The smooth sand before her was innocent of footsteps. There was nothing to be seen but a long line of sea-worn rocks, hundreds of them, perched on the sand like so many fat little miniature Buddha statues.

"Morgan?"

"Morgan, Morgan, Morgan," the walls of the cave whispered back in a ripple of echoes.

"Morgan, Morgan, Morgan," splashed the waves at the edge of the sand.

Tessie tried to collect her thoughts. She'd been led to this cave; there was no doubt in her mind about that. But Morgan did not mean to meet her here. Was there another clue in this room? There was absolutely nothing to be seen but smooth walls and roof, smooth sand, and that line of rocks. Perhaps the rocks were a clue. Another arrow? No—they pointed toward the blank wall of the cave. How many were there? They reminded her of something, but she couldn't think what.

She tried to count them, but there were so many and the light was so dim that she kept losing count. There must have been a thousand rocks—no, maybe half that number.

The answer flashed into Tessie's mind. Of course! Five hundred sea-worn stones that looked like statues of Buddha, lined up beside water. It was a clear pointer to Nikko, the famous city of five hundred Buddhas. Every tourist to Japan had heard of Nikko's five hundred Buddha statues, lined up along a stream, and of the legend that no one could ever count them. Years ago Morgan had told Tessie of the day he spent there, trying to count the statues and failing every time. He could be sure that she would remember the story and interpret the clue.

"Tessie? Tessie! Damn that girl! What sort of trouble do you suppose she's gotten into now?" Jason raised his voice and shouted, "Tessie!" so loudly that the echoes reverberated into her quiet blue-lit cavern. "She wouldn't have been fool enough to lose herself in these caves, would she?"

"With Miss Teresa," Masao's voice answered him, "almost any sort of trouble is possible, indeed. But I think that she would not act foolishly."

Tessie hurried to meet the two men, making sure that her feet scuffed up the sand around the mysterious arrow mark so that they would not notice it. She finished her task just as Jason popped out of the narrow passageway like a cork out of a bottle, with Masao following close behind him.

"Look, she's right there," exclaimed Jason. "Dammit, Tessie, why didn't you answer when I called you? You gave me the fright of my life! Don't you know it's dangerous to go wandering off alone like that?"

"I, um, I was lost in contemplation of the beauties of the caves," Tessie suggested, "and didn't hear you."

She raised her eyes to the ceiling with a soulful look in support of this statement. Unfortunately, this particular section of the caverns was low-ceilinged, dimly lit, and showed nothing but rough gray stones.

Jason snorted. "A likely story. More likely you just wanted to see how much you could frighten me by disappearing like that."

He did look genuinely upset, but Tessie thought he was more angry than frightened. A lock of black hair had fallen forward over his face, and his blue eyes were flashing with a light that boded ill for Tessie if he should get her alone while he was in his present temper.

"Frighten you?" Tessie inquired. "Oh, of course. You wouldn't want to lose your only link to the legacy, would you? And you realize now that you are not clever enough to find the clues for yourself."

A low grating sound was her only reply. After a

moment, Tessie realized that it was Jason grinding his teeth. "Listen, you redheaded chit," he began.

"Do you mean that you have found a clue, Miss Teresa?" Masao stepped between them before Jason could complete his insulting speech. "And what is this matter of a legacy? I thought you were searching for Morgan Gallagher."

"Come back to the inn," Tessie invited him. "I think it's time we told you the whole story, Masao." Once he knew exactly where she and Jason stood—she trying to rescue her uncle from whatever danger threatened him, Jason looking only for money—she felt sure that Masao would be willing to help her. And with Jason enjoying such an irrational fit of bad temper, Tessie badly needed an ally.

Besides, telling Masao the story might distract him and Jason from asking her again whether she'd found any clues. Tessie was not at all sure that she wanted to share this latest discovery with anyone until she'd had time to think it over. So far Morgan had proved maddeningly elusive; she might fare better if she could go to Nikko by herself. If only Jason didn't control her pass!

On the way back to the inn, Jason maneuvered matters so that he and Tessie sat together in the back of the boat while Masao occupied the single place in front of them. The water had grown rougher since that morning, and Jason used the rocking motion of the boat as an excuse to keep his arm around Tessie's waist—"to steady both of us," he explained. Tessie would have snorted if she hadn't been too much a lady. As if an experienced sailor like Jason needed a woman's support in a boat!

The excuse was flimsy, and at one time Tessie would have thought his real object was to make love to her. But today, instead of charming her with false compliments, Jason murmured in her ear that he was glad she had found no more clues and that he thought it was time they returned to Yokohama. Obviously his real aim was to tease her into revealing what, if anything, she had seen when she wandered away from him and Masao.

What layers upon layers of deceit! Pretending to Masao that he was only trying to support Tessie against the uneven motion of the boat, trying to make Tessie think that he was courting her, and really working on her to discover what she had learned of Morgan's promised legacy. Tessie told herself that only a woman bent on self-destruction would ever take anything this charming liar said seriously. Then she told herself that she did not enjoy the pressure of her arm around her and the enforced closeness of their bodies in the small boat.

Unfortunately, their proximity called up a flood of sensual memories that she could well have done without. Summer, moonlight filtering through a gazebo, Jason's hands on her bare skin . . . Tessie compressed her lips and tried very hard to think of something else, but it was impossible with him sitting so close beside her that she could feel his breath on her neck when he spoke, could almost feel the movement of his lips so close to her cheek.

Then Jason himself distracted her attention most effectively.

"*What* did you say?"

"I said that it's high time we went back to Yokohama, before whoever is trying to kill you succeeds in his attempts."

"What makes you think someone is trying to kill me?" Against her will, Tessie remembered the hand on her back just before she tumbled into the canal at Matsue, the stunning crack on the head that had left her unconscious and at the mercy of the slow, strong current. "I thought we agreed that my fall into the canal was an accident."

"So Masao said," Jason agreed. "And I can't prove

otherwise. But the incident with the rock that nearly crushed our boat was no accident. I saw a man's head in the opening above us, just before our boat passed under and the rock fell."

And for once his words had the ring of perfect truth about them.

Chapter Eleven

The winding mountain path was too steep and too narrow for *jinrikshas;* they had to hire horses to take them over these ridges. Tessie scandalized Masao by hitching up her full skirts and riding astride rather than crouching in the unstable basket he and a coolie had rigged across the back of the oldest and most docile pack horse.

"Carry luggage in that," Tessie advised. "My satchel doesn't mind being dropped, but I should object most strenuously to entrusting myself to that thing." She glared at Jason before he could speak. "And don't *you* voice any objections!"

"I wouldn't dream of it," he replied smoothly. "If you wish your legs to be rubbed raw before we reach this mysterious destination of yours, so be it. I shall simply ride along behind you enjoying the view." His eyes were on her ankles and the curve of her calf that showed whenever her skirts were tugged in riding, but his arm went out in a sweeping gesture that encompassed the dark green mountain ridges, the patches of rice fields in the valleys far below, and the crags of the precipitous path ahead of them.

Tessie had told Masao all that she knew or guessed

about the advertisement, her hopes of finding Morgan alive, Jason's hopes of getting a share of the promised legacy. For a time Masao had been as sympathetic an ally as she could wish for, but she began to lose his sympathy when she steadfastly refused to tell either him or Jason the nature of the clue she'd discovered at the Fountain of Jizo. All she would reveal was that she did have another clue, and that they would have to turn back toward the more populous portions of Japan to follow it up.

This was the best compromise Tessie had been able to think of. Jason had that damned pass, which they really did check everywhere. Even in the tiny seaside village of Mitsu-ura, there had been a lazy constable in a comfortable old kimono who sprang up, disappeared into his house, and reappeared looking very miserable in a stiff starched shirt and trousers, which he wore just long enough to perform the official task of looking over their traveling papers. As soon as that was done, he reverted to his faded cotton kimono and his preferred occupation of watching the tide come in.

Very well. She had to travel with Jason, and at some point in their journey he was bound to notice that they were headed for Nikko. But she didn't have to tell him anything else. The nature of the clue that had pointed her to Nikko could remain a secret; without it, he would not know where she needed to go in that busy, crowded town of tourists and temples. If she put her mind to it, surely she could slip away from his and Masao's guard long enough to arrange this one meeting with Morgan entirely on her own, the way he wanted it to be.

For now, all she had to do was sit back on her ambling pony and enjoy the ride and the ever-changing view. Each overlook from the mountain path presented her with a sight ever the same, yet ever changing in the details: a deep valley, a sloping hillside with terraced patches of rice fields; a cluster of thatch-roofed huts, and a shrine set away from the huts under the shelter of the trees. Once they passed a dancing, icy mountain stream with a narrow mill wheel turning under the silver spray; and once they overtook a group of peasants trudging on pilgrimage to some local shrine.

By noon of that first day's ride, though, she was sore and aching and sadly aware of the truth of Jason's warning. After they stopped in a village for their light meal of rice and steamed vegetables, she was quite unable to make herself get back up on the horse again, especially not with all the villagers watching so intently.

"I'll walk for a while, if you don't mind my slowing us down," she said.

"Not at all," Jason said instantly. "We can stop here for the night if you like."

Tessie shook her head. "I'd rather go on. Masao, you know this part of Japan better than either of us. Are there villages ahead where we can stay?"

"Yes, many little villages," Masao assured them. "In fact, my—"

"Yes?" Tessie prompted when he seemed to be staring indecisively at nothing.

"Oh. My father used to say that this was the most hospitable part of Japan," Masao said, and Tessie had the distinct feeling that while he was telling the truth, it was not what he had begun to say.

It was bad enough to be forever wondering what was the real meaning behind Jason Lancaster's actions; if she began suspecting Masao of secret motives and hidden meanings as well, this journey would become intolerable. Tessie resolved firmly not to worry about Masao; his secrets were his own, after all, and very likely no business of hers.

She was less successful in putting her troubling suspicions of Jason out of her mind. She brooded on them as she trudged up the trail. And the tension generated by those suspicions, and the chance of her decision to walk rather than ride, saved her life.

Somebody *had* pushed her into the canal in Matsue; the firm hand in the middle of her back had not felt tentative or accidental. And the blow on her head could have come from somebody hiding under the bridge, rather than from a knock against one of the bridge supports. It might have been the same person Jason saw peeping through the opening in the sea cavern just before a rock came down where their boat ought to have been. Jason wasn't lying. After all, he didn't want to scare her out of continuing the journey; he needed her to lead him to this supposed legacy of Morgan's. But then maybe he had thought he could frighten her into returning to Yokohama, entrusting the next clue to him.

Tessie frowned at Jason, glanced back over her shoulder at Masao, then looked up suspiciously at the high rocky ledges that leaned over the path ahead. Doubtless it was just her imagination that made this stretch of mountain path seem so dark and menacing. It was a cloudy day. And she hadn't heard any birds singing for several minutes. Doubtless there was a perfectly natural explanation for that. She really must stop letting her imagination get the better of her like this; a little more, and she'd be as bad as Jason, believing in the mountain goblins and thinking they could send lightning and rocks in her path! Why, an overimaginative person could even think that great pinnacle of dark rock, just above Jason, was moving to and fro, when it was really an optical illusion caused by the trees swaying in the wind—

There was no wind.

Tessie shrieked and grabbed the bridle of Jason's horse. The shaggy little mountain horse was as nervous as the rest of the travelers, and quite unaccustomed to being screamed at by redhaired barbarian women. He threw up his head and danced forward in a curious sidewise fashion, dragging Tessie with him to the very edge of the cliffside path. Jason cursed the horse and yanked on the reins. Tessie felt the path slipping away under her feet. She clutched desperately at the bridle and felt it, too, slipping sidewise. Behind her there was a crashing roar. Dust swirled about her face, choking and blinding her, and a hammer blow struck her ankle. Pain exploded up her leg, and her feet slid out from under her. She screamed into the choking dust, feeling herself slipping down into the churning maelstrom of falling rocks. Something encircled her wrist like a bracelet of iron, hauling her up and away from the cliff by one arm. Her shoulder burned, and something hit her in the stomach— Jason's saddle. Why was she lying across Jason's saddle? Something or someone screamed in pain and terror behind her, from the center of the crashing rocks and the dust.

As suddenly as it had begun, the avalanche was over, leaving only silence and drifting towers of dust behind. Tessie scrambled to a sitting position before Jason and rubbed her shoulder. She was grateful her arm had not been pulled out of the socket.

"Did I hurt you?" Jason inquired.

"I think you saved my life," Tessie replied indistinctly through the dust that coated her face. She looked down the cliff and shuddered. Far, far below, a pile of freshly broken and splintered rocks bore witness to the fury of the rock slide that had almost engulfed them. Some of the rocks bore fresh wet stains. Tessie remembered the terrified scream she had heard.

"Masao!" she exclaimed, twisting in her saddle to look behind them. Rocks covered the trail and spilled over the side of the cliff. A thick cloud of dust still obscured the path on the far side of the rock slide.

"Here I am!" called a cheerful voice from the

middle of the dust cloud. A moment later Tessie could make out Masao, picking his way over the rocks.

"Oh, you're alive! Oh, I'm so glad. I thought—that scream—oh, Masao, thank God you're all right!" Tessie's eyes filled with tears.

"I too," said Masao quietly, "was afraid for you, Miss Teresa. A happy reunion." He bowed and took her free hand for a moment, looking up at her with a wealth of feeling in his dark eyes.

"The screams?" Tessie looked down into the rocky gorge, already guessing the truth.

"Your horse and mine." Masao confirmed her guess. "It is fortunate that you were walking! I threw myself free when I heard the rocks coming, but you might not have been able to scramble out of the carrying basket."

"No," Tessie agreed. There would hardly have been time. She looked down the gorge and shivered in the hot still air, imagining herself buried under that cruel weight of falling rocks.

Now that they were all safe, somehow she could not stop shaking. A chill ran through her blood.

"Miss Teresa! You are injured."

Tessie shook her head and began to explain that Jason had wrenched her arm in hauling her to safety, but it was nothing really. Only before the words reached her lips, Masao touched her ankle. Fire shot up her leg, and she lost consciousness for a few merciful moments.

When she opened her eyes, her ankle throbbed with a dull ache. Someone had tied it to a stick. No wonder she hurt. People weren't the same shape as sticks. And Masao had torn the rich purple sleeve of his kimono. It must have happened during the rock slide. Strange coincidence, that something just the same color of purple was wrapped around her leg, binding it to the long stick. Tessie tried to call Masao's attention to the coincidence, but her voice wouldn't obey her, and anyway Masao wasn't looking at her. He and Jason were arguing, very politely and in low voices.

"There is no discussion," said Masao with a sharp cutting-off gesture that made Tessie think there had already been a great deal of discussion. "Miss Teresa is injured. She cannot possibly travel."

"Agreed." Jason cut off the word in that short, snapping manner he used when he was really terribly angry. Tessie had only heard him speak that way once before—in the summerhouse behind her parents' home, the night he told her that he would not wait for her while she nursed Mama. She hadn't known then that he was angry. She'd thought he was relieved to be rid of the responsibility for her. This would require careful thought, but just now Tessie felt incapable of thinking about anything. She carefully stored her new knowledge of Jason away for later and tried to follow the argument between the two men.

"My family home is close. We will take her there."

Jason's expression mirrored that on the face of his balky, stubborn little mountain horse. "There must be an inn closer."

"As it happens," said Masao, "there is not."

"How do I know you are telling the truth?" Jason demanded. "I think you just want to get Tessie into your house."

"I do," Masao agreed. "But I do not particularly wish to have *you* in my home, and I must allow you to remain with her. That should convince you of the purity of my motives."

Jason snorted. "Oh, very well. I don't know this region, so I'll have to let you be our guide. But I think it's damned funny you didn't mention before that your family lived in these parts. And I'm warning you, Masao. If we pass a single village with any kind of accommodation for strangers before we reach your house, Tessie's staying there."

"You prefer to deprive her of the comforts of a family home?"

"I prefer not to subject her to any more travel than is absolutely necessary." Jason broke off the conversation and bent over Tessie. "Feeling better? Can you ride?"

"Of course I can," Tessie croaked. She was relieved to find that she was getting her voice back. For a few minutes there she had not felt at all like herself. And she was still desperately sore and confused. But it was important to keep Jason in his place; just why, she couldn't remember. "Of course I can ride," she repeated more strongly. "It's my ankle that's hurt, not my—well, anyway, I can ride."

But when Jason lifted her onto the horse, the shards of pain came shooting up her leg again until the world was black. The last thing she knew was that she was gently sliding off the horse, and she was quite, quite powerless to save herself.

The rest of the journey was a blur of jostling and pain and strange, sweet moments when she seemed to be floating on clouds above the mountain path. She came out of one of those vague periods and discovered that the warmth that cradled her was Jason's arms.

She murmured a protest. Jason shouldn't be carrying her; she was too heavy, it was too far, the path was too steep.

"Shut up," Jason told her. "I could carry you forever, a little thing like you."

And later, when she protested again that her ankle was much better and she was sure she could ride if he'd only let her try again, he pointed out that they were riding. He was holding her in his arms on the back of their one remaining horse.

"And I like it," he said sternly. "Do you realize this is the first chance I've ever had to hold you in my arms for a whole afternoon?"

157

"Why should you want to do that?"

"Have some more sake," Jason told her, holding a flask to her lips, "and don't try to think. It's not one of your talents at the best of times."

"And this isn't a very good time." She recognized the fiery taste of the sake. They had given her some to drink before they set her ankle; that was why she felt so fuzzy-headed and confused. Probably just as well. Whenever her head cleared, the pain in her leg threatened to overwhelm her. Only it was dangerous to be weak and confused around Jason. She must stay alert. Reminding herself sternly of this, Tessie dropped off to sleep, resting her head on Jason's shoulder.

Later she was dimly aware that he was walking beside the horse, supporting her with one arm. The mountain was dark, but there were torches ahead, and voices of men hurrying toward them.

"Masao went on ahead to send servants to help us," Jason told her when he saw she was awake. "They'll take you in a litter the rest of the way."

He helped her into the swaying *kago* brought by the servants, moving with infinite gentleness so as not to jar her ankle, and as she lay back in the basket his lips just brushed her forehead. "Rest now, my love," she thought he said.

He walked beside the *kago* for the rest of the short journey; his tall form cast a long, distorted shadow on the path, and Tessie felt an irrational sense of security knowing he was there beside her. Wounded and weak and with her head full of sake fumes, she felt for the first time intimidated by all these strange people in this strange land. It was good to have someone of your own at a time like this, even if it was someone you couldn't trust. Why couldn't she trust him? Tessie searched her memory. The anger she'd felt once, the sense of betrayal, had all left her. All she had now was a question that she had to ask. And she was forgetting the question . . .

There was a high plaster wall before them and a gateway of weathered planks held together with curiously wrought iron bars. More servants screeched and ran to see the foreigners, and in the bustle of preparations for their arrival Tessie lost sight of Jason for a few moments. A sweet-faced woman with sad eyes greeted her.

"My mother," Masao said.

Three almond-eyed girls in their early teens hung back behind the woman, whispering and staring.

"My sisters."

"And who is this woman? Is she your mistress?" Masao's mother asked sharply. "Or does she belong to the tall barbarian? Or to both of you together? I do not understand these foreign ways of yours, my son."

"Mother!" Masao sounded so embarrassed that Tessie wanted to giggle. "She speaks Japanese."

Masao's mother put one hand before her mouth and gave her son a chance to go on. "This is Miss Teresa Gallagher."

Masao's mother was so pale, Tessie thought she might be about to faint. To have spoken in such a way before a guest who understood her was a terrible breach of hospitality; she must be feeling quite miserable at her mistake. Tessie wanted to reassure her, to tell her she was not offended, but she was too tired and perhaps too drunk to find the Japanese words.

"Not—"

"Yes, Mother," Masao interrupted. "She is the daughter of the American family with whom I stayed in San Francisco." He emphasized each word as though it was terribly important. "Now we have an opportunity to repay their hospitality. It is an obligation."

"Yes," Masao's mother said at last through pinched lips. "It is—an obligation."

She looked about as happy as Tessie's own mother would have been at having her home invaded by a group of strange foreigners of uncertain morality. Tessie felt miserable and unwelcome, and she resolved that she and Jason would be on their way the very minute she was able to travel.

"Come." Masao's mother gestured to the servants who had set Tessie's *kago* down in the courtyard. "There is a room made ready."

Tessie felt panic rising inside her. Alone, unwelcome, unable to walk, what would she do when they left her in this room? "Masao, where is Jason?" she asked urgently. "I *need* Jason."

"Say that again," said a familiar deep voice, and Jason appeared beside her. "I like hearing it."

"Come with me?" Tessie begged.

Masao's mother threw her hands skyward, as if absolving herself of all responsibility for the strange ways of foreigners, and shepherded her three young daughters back toward another part of the rambling house while the servants escorted Tessie to the room prepared for her.

"Do you want me to stay with you?"

She did, but she didn't want to offend Masao's family any more than she had already. "No. I just needed to ask you something."

"What?"

The question that had been eluding her came back at last. "In San Francisco. That summer . . . When I told you I couldn't marry you?"

"I remember," said Jason.

"You were angry?"

"Of course I was."

"I always thought . . . you were relieved. Not to have the responsibility."

"I told you thinking wasn't your strong suit. What made you change your mind?"

"Heard you quarreling with Masao. You sounded the same way. Cutting all your words off short." Tessie was desperately tired. She wanted to sleep, to forget the throbbing pain in her ankle. But she wanted even more to understand what had happened between her and Jason ten years ago. She was beginning to think there was just a chance she might have misinterpreted his actions. And if that was true . . .

"Yes. I was angry. What did you expect? Men don't take kindly to being jilted, Tessie."

"But *you* jilted *me!*"

"You're tired," Jason said. "We'll talk about it in the morning."

This time his lips brushed hers, and the brief touch was enough to keep her awake long into the night.

Chapter Twelve

Within a few days, Tessie was able to hobble around on crutches. The doctor who had come to examine her injury on the day after the rock slide said that she had a bad sprain and severe bruising, but nothing was actually broken. It would do her good to move about, so long as she did not put any weight on the injured leg.

"It will be painful, perhaps more so than an outright break," he warned.

"I've noticed," Tessie said with a weak grin.

The doctor bowed and hissed politely and told Masao that his barbarian friend had the heart of a lion. "Instead of crying like a woman when I examined her, she smiled and jested with me. In my village, when I was a boy, they would have said that such a brave woman, and redheaded too, must be a Shojo."

"The scarlet monsters of the sea?" Masao queried with a twinkle in his eye. "No, Doctor. Miss Teresa is assuredly not a Shojo, for I too remember the tales of those monsters. They are said to live in the mountains too, and our farmers used to complain that the Shojo were stealing all their sake—for a Shojo can drink a barrel full of sake at one time, they say, and show no effects at all. We gave Miss Teresa sake last night to dull her pain, and she was most thoroughly incapacitated by the time we reached this house. Besides, she is far too beautiful to be called a monster."

"You think so?" The doctor was an old-fashioned Japanese who did not approve of traveling abroad and mixing with foreigners. He could not see beauty in pale skin, round eyes, and flaming red hair.

"By barbarian standards," Masao said solemnly, "Miss Teresa is very lovely." And by his own, too—which somewhat confused him, now that he saw the reactions of his family and their old friend the doctor. Had he indeed, as his mother sometimes charged, lived in America so long that he had become corrupted by the foreigners? Tessie was beautiful to him, not only for her fiery crown of red hair and her wide, generous mouth, but also for her spirit and daring. He admired her for setting off on this arduous quest to save her uncle, for refusing to let setbacks and dangers stop her, for persisting in the face of Jason Lancaster's obvious disapproval. And he didn't want to admire her. It would upset all his plans. Such behavior would be not at all admirable in a well-brought-up Japanese girl who knew her place.

It was all very confusing. Masao retired to his private rooms in the back of the house to think things over, leaving Tessie and Jason Lancaster very much to their own devices for several days.

The period of peace and rest and near solitude was welcome to them both. Awake and sober, Tessie was too shy to ask Jason again about that disastrous night when they had become lovers and lost each other in San Francisco. But she accepted the crutches he made for her and let him help her as she struggled along the drafty passageways of the rambling old house, and when she tired of exploring the house, they sat in a small private courtyard shaded by maple trees and talked of anything and nothing for hours on end.

Jason did not know why Masao was allowing them this quiet time alone, but he resolved to make the most of it. For once Tessie did not seem hostile to him; she was quiet, meditative, and every so often she looked at him with a puzzled expression in her light eyes. Jason didn't know what she was thinking, but he was afraid to disturb this period of equilibrium. For once he had Tessie to himself, without having to fight his way through hordes of demanding relatives, without having to fight her own preoccupation with this insane quest after a dead man. There was nothing but the peaceful atmosphere of the rambling, decayed old house. They sat in the courtyard and fed rice crumbs to one fat old carp and watched the patterns of sunshine and shadow filtering through the maple leaves, and Jason was very careful to say nothing that might disturb their precarious accord.

Seeking for safely impersonal subjects, he told Tessie about the Japan he had first discovered on sailing voyages with Morgan, the Japan he had learned to love during his years of building up the export business of Benten and Company. It was a country quite different from the frenetic, bustling, foreign-dominated life of Yokohama and the diplomatic circles of Tokyo—a world of secluded mountain shrines and quiet country villages, artist-craftsmen patiently working in traditions passed down since feudal days, secret forest temples and seaside fishing settlements.

He could not tell her about his years of travel, about learning to appreciate the traditional arts and crafts of Japan and getting to know the skilled workers who carried on these traditions, without telling her a great deal about himself. And Tessie listened and learned and added to her store of understanding of Jason Lancaster.

He was, she thought, a great deal more than the

impatient young sailor who'd loved and left her in San Francisco. Had he matured, or had these other facets of his character always been there, invisible to her? He spoke of arduous winter treks through snowy mountains, and Tessie listened between the lines and understood his need for solitude and beauty—and also his need to share the beauty of a snowy dawn on the mountain peak with someone. He talked about visiting the shop of one elderly potter a dozen times, getting no farther than the doorstep on the first ten visits, until slowly he gained the old man's trust and was invited in to learn the secrets of his craft. Tessie listened and understood, again, more than Jason had said. He'd wanted more than to buy the old potter's wares; he'd wanted his trust and his friendship. He had genuinely respected the lifetime of skill that went into the work. How many foreigners would have taken the time to look below the surface of Japanese life as Jason did?

Tessie had loved the young Jason. Now, so gradually that she was scarcely aware of it, she began to like and respect the man he had become.

The only trouble was that she wanted so much more than that. In the first few days after their arrival at Masao's house, when she was still bruised and shaken from the accident, it had been safe enough to sit in the sunshine and listen to Jason's stories. As her injuries healed and she felt stronger, Tessie found it more and more difficult to keep her mind from thoughts of what might have been. When Jason's strong hand steadied her on the way down a flight of broken steps, or when he lifted her up to the high bench in the courtyard, she remembered the occasions when he'd kissed her in jest or anger, and her traitorous body longed for those brief touches to be prolonged. When he told his stories of travel through the remote parts of Japan, she wondered what would have happened if she had forsaken her duty and gone with him ten years ago. Could she have traveled with him as his beloved wife, sharing the joys of exploration and discovery during the day, sharing their love at night?

A little persuasion, a little force, and she would have gone with him then. But he hadn't cared enough to exercise that force, nor even enough to come back on his next voyage and see if she was free yet.

Tessie frowned and chewed on the tip of her little finger. For years she'd nourished her indignation against Jason Lancaster, who could make love to her in the moonlight and then abandon her without a backward glance before that same moon had set. But very recently, she had begun wondering if she'd understood everything about that fateful night when they parted. He had been furiously angry; she knew that now, though she hadn't guessed it then. But why? She'd asked that on the night they came to Masao's house, and he had evaded answering, or she'd fallen asleep before he could answer.

She needed to ask him again. But now, just as she began to heal and was plucking up her courage to do so, Jason became unavailable. "There's an indigo dyer in the village," he explained after his first day-long absence. "He knows all the old traditional resist-dying patterns, including a number of designs I've never seen before. I want to commission him to do a series of cloths for Benten and Company, but he's not sure about committing to that much extra work. It may take some time to persuade him, and anyway I want to spend a few days watching the work so I can learn as much as I can about it. You don't mind, do you?"

It should have been a statement, not a question, because he was off to bed without waiting for her answer, and the next day he vanished again. Tessie nibbled on the tip of her finger and told herself all the usual things about how fickle and untrustworthy

Jason Lancaster was, but this time she was having a little trouble convincing herself. After all, why should he stay at her side day and night, just because she had privately decided that she might want him after all? He didn't know what she had been thinking. He probably didn't want to reopen a love affair that was ten years dead. He owed her nothing. And he needed to take care of his business.

She had nothing to complain about; all the same, she resented the indigo dyer very much.

Jason was away for three days and nights this time, and when he came back he looked desperately tired. It was the middle of the afternoon.

"Come and tell me all about your cloth maker," Tessie invited him, hobbling to their courtyard.

"Dyer," Jason corrected her. "He gets the cloth readymade." He sank down on the ground, folding his long legs under him, leaned back against the sun-warmed bench, and gave a deep sigh of contentment.

"Oh. Well, how should I know? I've never seen the process."

Jason tilted his head up and looked her over slowly. "Would you care to visit his house? Indigo dying is a messy, smelly business. I shouldn't think it would amuse a young lady."

"Yes, I would," said Tessie.

"Really? Well, I suppose some of the household servants could carry you down to the village in a *kago*. It's not far." Jason leaned back again. This time his head rested against her knee, provoking a host of disturbing sensations that she could have done very well without. Her thigh tingled, and her fingers wanted to twine themselves through his dark, thick hair.

Instead, Tessie concentrated on her perfectly good reasons for asking Jason to take her to the indigo dyer's house. It made perfect sense. Really. If Jason was going to spend all his time hanging over indigo vats, she might as well hang over them with him. Soon she would be well enough to travel again, and she felt that they needed to resolve their personal relationship before they set off again on the search for Morgan or his legacy. If she could fully trust Jason when they went to Nikko, it would make a great deal of difference to her feelings and to their chances of success.

That was, she told herself, the only reason she was pursuing him so shamelessly. Certainly she wasn't fool enough to think they might begin again where they'd left off.

"Can we go tomorrow?"

A breathy snore was her only answer. Jason had fallen asleep with his head in her lap.

Tessie sat quite still for nearly an hour, feeling a growing cramp in her leg and getting uncomfortably warm as the afternoon sun moved across her face, afraid to move for fear of waking Jason, and quite unreasonably happy.

The dyer's house was a long, low structure, humble enough in itself, but turned into a Japanese version of a gypsy tent by the long pieces of cotton cloth stretched on bamboo poles to dry in the sun before the house. Tessie's *kago* was carried through undulating curtains of rich blue dotted with white *shibori* patterns of butterflies and flowers. A lighter version of the same blue fluttered like a second sky just above her head, and the dyer's porch was screened by gently undulating layers of silk dyed in the more expensive shades of rose and purple and saffron-yellow. There Masao's servants helped her out of the *kago* and handed her the crutches Jason had made so that she could get about without putting any weight on her injured ankle.

"This is fascinating," she told Jason truthfully as

she hobbled after him on her crutches. "I wish you'd brought me here earlier."

Jason looked down at the stained floor mats. "It might not have been such a good idea."

"No," Tessie had to agree. "I wasn't well enough until a few days ago." Though why should Jason look uncomfortable about that?

He strode rudely ahead of her without even looking to see if she could keep up, greeted a stooped old man at the door, and exchanged a few sentences in low-pitched Japanese, too rapid for Tessie to follow. They seemed to be arguing about something; from his gestures the old man was deferring to Jason, but not without protest. Tessie just caught his last words. "Enough! She does not need to know about it; I shall be grateful if you do not mention the matter again."

Now what could that have been about? Tessie wondered as Jason came back to her. Oh, of course! Jason had told her that Benten and Company was in severe financial straits and that he badly needed the infusion of cash that he hoped Morgan's promised legacy would bring; yet he'd also spoken grandly of commissioning this dyer to make him a series of resist-dyed and *shibori* textiles to sell through his company. No doubt he'd promised the dyer payment later, maybe had even spun him a tale of the forth-coming legacy. And he wouldn't want Tessie to know about that, because even though he'd made no bones about thinking Morgan dead and wanting a share of the money, he thought she would be hurt at this reminder.

Jason was really very considerate of her feelings. Or very wily. Tessie nibbled on a fingertip and brooded and scarcely heard most of the dyer's long-winded explanation of his working processes. He and Jason were bound for the shed behind the house, where the dyer had some fresh samples ready for Jason to inspect. On the way they stopped in the back room, and the dyer showed Tessie how he got such complicated patterns onto the cloth. She stared unseeing at the large stacks of stencils he brought out for her admiration.

"Yes, yes, very lovely," she said automatically to the patterns of cherry blossoms and wisteria, the cranes above swirls of water, and the jagged lozenges meant to represent pine bark.

"My daughters use these to mark the undyed cloth with wheat-flour paste," the dyer explained. "It is light work and suitable for a woman. Furthermore, my older daughter is quite talented at drawing the stencils. Dai! Where is the dragon you made for the wedding of Master Masao?"

"Here, Father," shyly answered a young girl who had been standing politely in the back of the room. She held up a large stencil in the shape of a coiled dragon. "Are you the honored wife of our—"

"No, the lady is not my wife!" Jason interrupted, his voice overriding the last word of the girl's question.

"O-Dai! Have you no manners, to be speaking to our foreign visitors before you are spoken to? Go to the kitchen and help your mother!"

"Wait," Tessie intervened as the girl, head bowed, prepared to leave the room. "I should like to know more about Dai's work. Please, may she stay to talk to me?" What she really wanted to know was what Dai had been about to say when Jason and her father interrupted her. Jason had certainly been unchivalrously quick to deny being married to Tessie. That alone might have explained his interruption. Or it might not.

"Why don't you gentlemen go on?" she asked, seating herself with some difficulty on a sack of flour for the stencil paste. "I am tired, and my ankle is hurting. I'll just sit here and rest for a little while, and

170

perhaps Dai will be kind enough to amuse me by showing me the rest of her lovely stencils."

Jason and the dyer both looked so unhappy at this suggestion that Tessie felt sure she was onto something. But Jason couldn't very well bully her into walking when she claimed she was in pain, and the dyer was constrained by the laws of hospitality.

"Do not bother the lady with foolish chatter, Dai!" he warned his daughter with one hand upraised as if he was already prepared to beat her for talking too much. "Answer her questions, then go and help your mother as I told you!"

"This is nice," said Tessie with what she hoped was a reassuring smile as Jason and the dyer left. "The dragon stencil is very fine work, Dai. Did you just complete it?" Strange, Masao hadn't said anything to her about plans for his upcoming marriage.

"Oh, no," Dai said with a beam of innocent pride. "I did that five years ago, when I was still learning."

"Five years! I didn't know Masao had been married so long." In fact, Tessie thought, he couldn't have married five years ago. Surreptitiously counting on her fingers, she verified her first guess. Five years ago Masao had been in America, living in her parents' house, studying Western engineering science in San Francisco, teaching her Japanese in his spare time to pay for his room and board.

"He isn't married," said Dai, pouting. "He was betrothed to Shizuka, and they were to be married when he came back from America, but for some reason he kept putting it off, and putting it off. At first it was a great scandal, because everybody thought he must have found Shizuka misbehaving with some man, but months and months went by and she never did have a baby, and now almost everybody will talk to her again. Though, of course, she will never marry now."

"Why not?"

Dai looked surprised. "Who would have her after such a scandal? Besides, she is getting old—at least nineteen now."

"I should like to meet Shizuka," Tessie said thoughtfully.

Dai looked surprised. "Haven't you? She visits Masao's mother and sisters all the time. Masao's mother insisted on it, so that everybody could see there was no quarrel and the families are still friendly and so that Shizuka would not be blamed—but, of course, everybody knows there must have been something wrong with her. Maybe she has not come to visit recently because Masao is there. But I am sure they will not marry now. I don't think Masao will *ever* marry," Dai said with a pout.

"Do you—er—like Masao?"

"I hardly know him!" Dai laughed. "Oh, did you think I would dream of marrying a man like that, the son of a samurai? No, but I wish he would have a wedding. The dragon cloth I made is rotting away, and no one else around here is likely to commission such interesting designs—and I have so many ideas! Besides, I have learned a lot since I made this stencil. I could do better now, but our villagers do not want such expensive and complicated designs for their clothing."

"You may find it more interesting to make up designs for Jason to sell abroad," Tessie suggested. "Is that why you called him your benefactor?"

Dai flushed and looked down, and Tessie felt a surge of triumph. So she had guessed correctly! She'd thought she heard what Dai was saying, but with both Jason and the dyer interrupting and trying to drown her out, she might have misunderstood.

"I think my father does not wish me to speak of our debt to Jason Lancaster," Dai murmured.

"Perhaps not to strangers. But you may tell *me*," Tessie urged gently.

"Are you betrothed?"

"I—" Tessie found she could not lie to this gentle, shy girl. "No. But I wish we were."

Dai nodded solemnly, and for a moment she looked older than her years. "Shizuka is not happy, but no one can help her. I think you are not happy. Will it help if I tell you what we owe to Jason Lancaster?"

"It might."

"Well!" Dai's animation returned. Her eyes sparkled, and she settled down for a long chat, first looking over her shoulder to make sure her father was nowhere in earshot. "It was just three days ago . . ."

Tessie listened and nodded and felt herself glowing inside as Dai's story unfolded.

Dyers, the girl explained, were favorite targets for robbers. Their houses were likely to contain expensive silks that had been entrusted to them for dying; furthermore, they often delivered a season's work to a city shop at one time and were paid a large sum all at once.

"Of course, my father does not have such a rich business," Dai explained. "How could we send work to Edo or Kyoto from here? And sophisticated city folk do not like our simple country patterns; they say our work is old-fashioned. Father says in the cities now the rage is all for cloths from Eng-land and Ame-rik." She stumbled a little over the strange foreign names and looked up at Tessie to be sure she had got it right. "Still, we are richer than the peasants around us, and we do have some silks here."

Only three nights earlier their house had been invaded by a band of robbers who hoped to find silks and money. Disappointed with their spoils, they took what they could, slashed open a few sacks of dye stuffs, and threatened the dyer and his family with death if they dared stir out of doors before dawn to pursue them.

The next morning Jason Lancaster had visited the

dyer's house to find the family sitting amid the devastation, bewailing the loss of a year's income. Worse, one of the silk kimonos taken by the robbers was an heirloom of Masao's family that had been sent down to have a worn panel matched and replaced. "It had been in the family since the time of the first Shogun," wailed the dyer. "How can I ever make good such a loss? If I were a samurai, I would commit *seppuku,* but fortunately I am only a common man and perhaps honor will be satisfied if I hang myself."

Jason stayed just long enough to extract the dyer's solemn oath that he would not hang himself until the end of the week; then he disappeared into the mountains. Two days later—the previous afternoon—he had reappeared bearing one sack full of money, another one full of the silks that had been stolen, and the precious antique kimono from Masao's family.

"This is more money than was stolen from me," Dai's father said at once. He separated the money into two piles, a small one for himself and a much larger one for Jason Lancaster.

"You may as well keep the rest," Jason said. "I—er —don't think the people who returned your goods will have any more use for the money."

He refused to say any more about the incident and asked the dyer and his family not to speak of it in the village. "The authorities of your country would not be pleased to hear I had done what should have been left to your own police."

"Akita the policeman is a lazy fat rogue who's good for nothing but stamping papers," the dyer said. "It used to be the obligation of the samurai to defend us commoners, but now there are no more samurai. Masao's father committed *seppuku,* and Masao himself says that the old days are over and we must look to the government for protection. I might have died and my children starved before the government helped us as you have done. I think you are an American samurai, Lancaster-*sama.*"

And he had bowed very low until Jason, looking deeply embarrassed, raised him to his feet and begged him to forget all that had passed as though it had never been. "Tomorrow, when you have had time to set your house in order, I will come again," Jason said, "and you will show me the samples of work you were making to sell in my shop, and we will speak only of business, as is proper between two common working men such as ourselves."

"But he didn't come alone," Dai finished with a dimpled smile. "He brought you with him—and I think you did not wish to speak only of business!"

"You're entirely right," Tessie said absently. Her head was spinning with the impact of all the new information she'd received. Jason hunting down robbers for the sake of a man he barely knew, to save that acquaintance's house from shame? The tragedy of Masao's father? Masao's own broken betrothal? And, strangest of all, Jason refusing money when he needed it so desperately?

It was too much for her to take in all at once.

"You are hungry?" Dai asked. "Shall I ask my mother for some tea and cakes?"

Tessie realized that she had nibbled off two fingernails and was starting on a third. Blushing furiously, she folded her hands in her lap to conceal her ragged nails and agreed that it would be pleasant to have a cup of tea while they waited for the men to conclude their business.

She did not get a chance to speak privately with Jason until they were back at Masao's house. She asked him to give her the support of his arm to her room, pretending she was too tired to use crutches. Instead, Jason scooped her up in both arms and carried her bodily down the hall.

"Wait—I did not ask you to *carry* me!" Tessie protested.

"Easier than hobbling down the hall, isn't it?" Jason grinned at her. "I carried you considerably farther than this the night we came here."

"I already know you are strong." They'd reached the entrance to her room; Jason seemed reluctant to put her down. Tessie felt breathless, though he'd been the one doing all the work. "And—and now I know a little more about you."

"Dai talked."

"Why do you object?"

"I'm a trader, not an imitation samurai in Western trousers. Those people want to make a hero out of me. I feel like an idiot."

He seemed to have forgotten entirely about setting her down. Tessie leaned her cheek against his shoulder. She felt like a cat, rubbing up against his warmth, purring with pleasure. "But you were a hero. You saved the dyer's life."

"His honor," Jason corrected.

"In Japan it seems to mean the same thing . . . Jason, why were you so angry that night?"

The words came out in a rush, unplanned. And she didn't have to explain what night she was thinking about. She could tell from the look on Jason's face that he remembered that night as vividly as she did.

Now he did bend over and set her on the sleeping mats. "Don't go," Tessie begged. "Jason, I *need* to know."

He had withdrawn a few paces already. Now he sat down on the floor, cross-legged, with loose-limbed and fluent grace, as easy in his movements as any Japanese. Servants had lit the lamps in this room while they'd been gone, but his face was in shadow where he sat now.

"Why?"

Tessie stared.

176

"Why," Jason amplified, "do you need to know now? Because you think I'm a hero for beating up a couple of poor half-starved robbers and retrieving their spoils from them?"

"Oh!" Tessie felt relieved of a worry she hadn't even known she felt. "I thought—Dai thought you had killed them."

"I'm not quite such a fool as that," said Jason gently. "Mind you, I've already interfered enough to get my pass revoked if the police find out about it, but I do draw the line at actual murder. Of course I was angry with you, what did you expect? It's not every day I offer my hand and heart to a girl who's given me every reason to think she loves me too, and get told politely that on the whole she thinks she'd rather stay with Mama."

The swift change of subjects left Tessie gasping to keep up. "But—but Jason, it wasn't like that! I *had* to stay and take care of Mama—I could not abandon her when she'd just had a heart attack!"

"I told you, Morgan told you, the way she changed doctors every month should have told you if you had any sense, that she was faking the heart problems to keep control over her family. Over you. Don't you know that by now?"

There'd been five more doctors in the next two years, and after the last one left in a rage, Mama had announced that doctors did one no good anyway and she would depend on Cousin Sophronia's herbal mixtures and the devoted nursing of her dear daughter.

"Ye-es," Tessie said slowly. "I suspected—yes, I know it. I'd never have dared leave her for this trip to Japan if I hadn't really known she was pretending. Not faking. Making herself ill, I think. But I never dared think about it before."

"Why not?"

"I would have hated her for ruining my life."

"So instead you hated me for deserting you."

"Yes." But he had deserted her. The naked fact was still there.

"I had a ship waiting."

"You never came back."

Jason made an impatient gesture. "After that first time, I thought it would be useless. When you refused even to see me—"

"I never did!" Tessie gasped. "Jason, I never *heard* from you from that night until the day I met you in Yokohama."

"Yes, you did," Jason argued. "When I got back from that South American run, I thought you might have had enough time nursing your mother to see through her pretense of illness. I thought you might be ready to come away with me. I didn't dare come to the house for fear of precipitating another scene, so I wrote you a letter begging you to meet me privately. The next day Hartley came to my boardinghouse with the letter. It was torn in two, not even removed from the envelope. He said you had refused even to look at it. He said he was very sorry to be the bearer of such bad tidings, and he'd come in person to break the news so that he could try and explain, so that I wouldn't be too hurt. He said that you were about to become betrothed to a young gentleman, a friend of his, and that you were terrified he'd get some hint of your misbehavior with me—that you begged Hartley to see that I didn't ever come near you again."

"I never saw that letter," Tessie said quietly. "You believed him?"

Jason shrugged. "He was very nice and sympathetic. You *were* young; I couldn't expect a girl of sixteen to know her own mind. And you sure as hell hadn't had much trouble sending me away nine months earlier. I wasn't about to mess up your life by reappearing at an inconvenient time." He picked up a rough-cast tea bowl that had been left on the floor and ran his thumb over the unevenly glazed surface, turning the bowl to let the lamplight play over the pattern of light and shadow created by the glaze.

"Perhaps," he said after a while, staring intently at the shining lights reflected in the bowl, "perhaps I was too hasty. But you were so young."

"I'm not young anymore."

"Twenty-six. Hardly the verge of extreme old age and decrepitude." Was Jason smiling? The shadows fell across his face; it might have been a trick of the flickering light. Tessie felt breathless, as though she were struggling up the side of a very steep mountain, as though she were running a race with everything she had ever wanted in life as the prize. But no one was moving at all. The room was very still, except for the dance of shadows where the candlelight flickered. Soft, almost imperceptible currents of air floated through the room from the open windows, moving the warm summer air across her hands and face like the gentlest of caresses. And Jason was very far away, and very close.

"Old enough," Tessie said at last, "to know my own mind now." How plain did she have to be? Perhaps he didn't want her anymore. Perhaps he was afraid of getting seriously entangled with the woman who'd hurt him before—for he had been hurt, as well as she; she understood that now.

Humiliating, to be gently and ever so politely rejected, to be told flat out that Jason's tastes had changed, that he could do better for himself now than to take a redhaired, sharp-tongued spinster.

Even humiliation was better than wasting another ten years on a misunderstanding.

"Old enough to regret the ten years we've lost," Tessie said, "when we could have been together."

Jason stood slowly, uncoiling his long legs with the

fluid grace that characterized his every movement, and Tessie felt something leap within her—panic or delight? She no longer knew.

"Tessie," he said slowly. "Teresa." And her name on his lips was like a kiss traveling through the air. "But are you sure?"

"I told you," Tessie repeated. "I am old enough to know my own mind."

Two steps covered the distance between them; then he was seated beside her on the soft sleeping mat, his arms about her, and her whole body was aflame with expectation. "Somehow I doubt that," he murmured. "What about Ricardo?"

"Who?"

A soft chuckle was her only answer as Jason drew her down to lie in his arms. One fingertip brushed lightly over the swell of her bodice, lingering and teasing until she felt her nipples growing stiff under the layers of confining cloth.

"Do we really need all these clothes?"

It was astonishing, really, how fast one could dispense with layers of buttoned and hooked and starched and frilled garments when the need was really urgent. Tessie didn't think a Japanese girl could have slipped out of her kimono any faster than Jason had her out of her long, stifling dress and layers of petticoats and corsets and knickers and stockings. And even at that, it wasn't fast enough for their mutual need, so long denied. A trail of kisses burned down her arm from wrist to shoulder to the soft curve between neck and shoulder, stopped there by a frill of unnecessary lace on a totally unnecessary undergarment. His hands fumbled on the strings of her corset, his first clumsiness and his last, until he swore and broke the strings.

"I *wish* you wouldn't wear this stupid cage garment."

"I need it."

"I disagree." Jason's long fingers cupped and caressed the swelling richness of her white breasts as they were freed from confinement. Tessie closed her eyes in a long shiver of pleasure almost too intense to be borne. "You are perfect. Teresa. My lovely Teresa . . ." His mouth closed over the aching tip of one breast, and Tessie felt as if she would explode from the shock of delight. She moaned, and her fingers clutched at his black hair.

"Last time," Jason murmured into the valley between her breasts, speaking as though it had been yesterday, "last time I was in too much of a hurry. This time we're going to take our time and savor every minute," he promised.

"I don't think I can bear that!" Tessie moaned aloud as his fingers moved lower, brushing the flaming garden of red curls between her thighs, searching out the secret places that ached for him.

Neither could Jason. Thirty seconds after promising that they would take their own slow, luxurious time in this encounter, he stopped in the act of rolling down one of her long black stockings and plunged forward with an inarticulate cry of desire. Tessie felt him filling her, most joyously, most perfectly, and the intensity of his need joined with hers and drove her on to meet him without shame. The hot aching within her melted into a sweetness that spread through her entire body, rippling outward from the center in shocks of pleasure until she could think of nothing else.

"Now," Jason murmured sometime later, his lips warm against her bare skin, "where was I? Oh, yes. Taking off your stockings."

"Isn't it a bit late for that?" Tessie inquired lazily. She propped herself up on one elbow and watched him kneeling at her feet, slowly and luxuriously rolling the thin stockings down her legs. Sweat dampened the black hair that fell over his forehead, and there were damp spots on the sleeping mat, and the hot still air enclosed them in the candlelit room like a comforter. Soft golden light played on naked skin, white and brown together; outside, a hundred crickets sang a slow creaking melody together. Tessie felt warm and sticky and completely peaceful, unwilling to worry about anything.

"Too late? Dear heart, we've just begun." Jason looked up and gave her a crooked smile that made her heart race again. "This night is ours. We have ten lost years to make up for."

His lips traveled slowly, teasingly up the length of her bared legs, lingering over soft hollows and smooth white skin. "I don't know . . ." Tessie murmured uncertainly. She had never even imagined somebody kissing her on the lips like that, much less kissing her where Jason's mouth was now traveling.

"You will," Jason promised.

The song of the crickets blended with the rushing of blood in her ears as he brought her again to that state of shivering anticipation. This time he had enough control to linger, prolonging his caresses and her own responses, savoring the pleasure he was able to give until her soft cries of need became a fire in his own veins. She was his now, his Teresa, and she could not deny the mutual desire that brought them together. He possessed her this second time with exultant, incredulous joy, taking as much pleasure in the sight of her half-closed eyes and parted lips as in the sweet sensations of his body entering hers. "My lovely Teresa," he murmured as she arched and cried out beneath him, and then, his own passion commanding his taut body, "Mine!"

"You'd better write to him," he said when he had recovered command of his voice.

"Who?"

"Ricardo, who else? You have to tell him you're breaking the engagement. I don't want any other man imagining, even for a moment, that he has any claim on you."

"Oh." Tessie felt sleepy and lazy and as bonelessly relaxed as a contented cat, much too tired and happy to confess her little deception to Jason. "Ricardo . . . I'll explain later."

"Just so you make absolutely sure he doesn't show up expecting you to marry him."

"I think I can promise that." A sleepy smile curved up the corners of Tessie's lips. Jason looked sharply at her, looked again, and began to smile himself. He didn't need to nag Tessie now; he had no fear of being supplanted by any other man.

All the same, the night was not over yet, and it was as well to make sure of her. Besides, the sight of that creamy skin and drowsy smile was having an effect, predictable and all too familiar, on his loins.

"Again?" murmured Tessie, sleepy and surprised but hardly protesting, when Jason drew her on top of him and ran his hands down the generously curving lines of her back and bottom.

"You have . . . a certain . . . effect on me," Jason told her.

Tessie giggled. "Yes. I can feel it!"

"You're going to feel more than that in a moment, my girl!" Gently he coaxed her into a sitting position astride him, raised her hips and guided her down over his erect manhood. Her eyes widened, and her lips parted slightly in surprised delight at the new sensations afforded by this position. A moment later she was discovering the freedom it offered, moving above him and bringing her own sweet rhythm to their love.

The urgency of desire too long denied was past now, but Tessie discovered she was as far from being sated as Jason was. And now she discovered, too, the delights of slowing and prolonging their mutual pleasure, of seeing his face grow taut with desire and feeling the little uncontrollable movements of his body as she

moved above him. Somewhere there were waves
rocking a boat back and forth, waves thrusting higher
and higher and roaring in her ears; the rocking
became a storm, the storm a tidal wave that she rode
out of control until it exploded into white surf and
white light and strong hands holding her and Jason's
voice crying out with hers.

The candles had burnt out. The crickets still sang,
and a full moon filled the room with luminous pale
light, still and peaceful. Neither Tessie nor Jason felt
any urge to sleep. They lay entwined on the sleeping
mats, talking quietly, recalling with fond laughter
incidents from their courtship ten years earlier and
from their recent journey through Japan.

"I wish we could go on traveling like this forever,"
Tessie said with a yawn.

"Why not?"

"I have a feeling that when we reach Nikko, our
search will be over. And then I really ought to go back
to Yokohama. Hartley and Sophia need me."

"*I* need you," Jason said, mock-severely. "But we
will certainly have to go back to Yokohama. It's the
nearest place where we'll find a Christian minister to
marry us. After which, Tessie, you will be *my wife,* not
the overworked drudge of the rest of the Gallagher
family."

"Perhaps," Tessie murmured half-heartedly, "we
should wait a few months. Until Hartley and Sophia
are settled and don't need me anymore . . ."

"Do you want to wait?"

He wouldn't force the decision on her; he simply
waited himself, hands flat and open, face open, for her
to make up her own mind. Tessie swallowed. Of
course she loved Jason. Of course she wanted to be his
wife. But it was one thing to leave Hartley and Sophia
in the lurch because of her duty to find Uncle Morgan;
it was another thing to abandon them because of her
own selfish desires. If Jason would only put his foot

down and say firmly that she *must* marry him at once, that he wouldn't allow her to go back to Hartley's household! Then she wouldn't have to fly in the face of her lifelong lessons about doing one's duty and serving others first. She wouldn't have to be selfish, merely obedient.

Tessie looked at Jason's expressionless face. No, he would not do that for her; he never would. And for a moment she hated him for it.

"I want to marry you."

"Then," said Jason, "when we return to Yokohama, that's what you'll do."

They should have been at peace, but the moment's strife remained, gritty as sand in the bedclothes. To take her mind off it, Tessie began talking at random about the next stage of their journey. She was beginning to feel guilty about dawdling so long in Masao's home. What if Morgan needed her?

"A fat lot of good you'd be to him, hobbling around on crutches," Jason pointed out. "Besides, it looks like a dangerous journey. Somebody has tried to kill you twice now, Tessie."

"I'm not going to give up now, so close to our goal!" Tessie blazed up at this hint of opposition.

"Of course you aren't," Jason agreed soothingly. "I'm just suggesting that you should be in shape to face whatever lies ahead of us. Give yourself another week or two to heal. If Morgan needed you urgently, he wouldn't be wasting time with this chase all over Japan, would he? It might not even be Nikko we're supposed to go to next."

"Oh, yes," Tessie said. "The clue was a line of five hundred little round stones, lined up in the sand just like the five hundred Buddhas at Nikko. That's where he will be waiting; by the river where the Buddha statues stand. I've read all about it in *Murray's Guide to Japan*. It couldn't possibly be anywhere else."

"No," Jason agreed. "It must be Nikko. And while

we're there, I will show you the shrine of Ieyasu, beyond the waterfall, with the five-storied gold pagoda and the stable of the sacred horse of Ieyasu. And then we will go into the hills . . ."

He went on quietly describing the wonders of Nikko and its shrines until Tessie's eyelids closed and her breathing became deep and even. Then, moving with infinite caution, he disentangled his arms from her sleeping grasp and stood up to draw his clothes on again.

Nikko.

The shrine of five hundred Buddhas.

And somebody waiting to attack them on the way there.

He didn't want Tessie to face any more dangers on this quest, but she blazed up like a bundle of dry kindling struck by lightning at any hint of protection. So he wouldn't tell her where he was going. It would be another two weeks at least before she could move about easily; long before that time he should have returned, bringing her either Morgan or his legacy as his gift to his bride. She could quit fretting about this quest, no one would have any motive to attack her, and they could go back to Yokohama and get married at once.

Jason thought it had been one of his most brilliant ideas, getting the clue from Tessie so that he could go off to Nikko while she recuperated here. But then, he'd always known he was a clever fellow.

He scribbled a hasty note to Tessie so that she wouldn't fret over his disappearance, collected his belongings, and quietly opened the great gate at the front of Masao's house. The moonlight would light a path to the dyer's house; the dyer would be only too happy to lend him a horse. By morning he would be well on the way to Nikko, beyond the reach of any inconvenient questionings from Tessie.

Jason was too pleased with himself to keep watch behind him. One person in the great house was still wakeful; one man, kept awake by the small sounds from Tessie's room, by the stirrings of suspicion and jealousy, watched Jason leave by moonlight and resolved to follow him.

Chapter Thirteen

A buying trip!" Tessie exclaimed in the morning, shaking her head over Jason's hastily scrawled note. Really, the man was impossible! She'd awakened slowly, lazy and happy in the warm summer morning, in the expectation of turning toward the man she loved and who had loved her so thoroughly the previous night. When he wasn't there, she felt momentary disappointment but no real alarm. After all, they were guests in Masao's house; Jason might have elected to slip back to his own room to avoid shocking the servants or offending Masao's family.

But then she'd caught sight of the note pinned to one of the sliding rice-paper screens that partitioned off this room from the rest of the wing. It didn't say much, merely that he would be away for a few days, inspecting and buying local crafts from some neighboring villages, and that Tessie was not to worry about anything. This last word was underlined twice with heavy black lines that notched the paper deeply, as though the pen had been drawn down with great pressure.

"Worry about *you*, Jason Lancaster?" Tessie said aloud. "No fear! Obviously you can take care of yourself very well!" Last night he'd said not a word about this projected buying trip. He didn't even know this part of Japan; how could he know there was anything worth buying in these poor mountain villages? No. He wasn't out there on business. He was avoiding her. Last night's tenderness and intimacy had frightened him. He didn't want to face her by morning light, when he might have to live up to the love words he'd whispered by the pale glimmer of the summer moon.

Tessie deliberately tore the note several times over, until it was reduced to shreds scarcely bigger than grains of rice. "Oh, no, Jason," she said. "I'm certainly not going to worry about you."

Having said that, she immediately began imagining other crises that could have called him from her side. Perhaps he'd gone back after the robbers. Perhaps he was trying to hunt down the mysterious ill-wishers who'd dogged their path from Matsue to this house, trying twice to kill her. Perhaps even now he was lying wounded and helpless, calling for her.

Tessie bit her lip. Even if she could have traveled very far on her injured ankle, she had no idea in which direction Jason had gone and absolutely no way to trace him. She would just have to wait for his return to discover whether he'd gone away on some mission of misguided heroism or whether he was simply afraid to face her again after their night of love.

And if he didn't come back by the time she was well enough to travel again, she would just go on to Nikko without him. No, she couldn't do that; he had no doubt taken their joint passport with him.

There was absolutely nothing she could do but wait. Tessie nibbled at the ragged edge of one fingernail and tried to talk herself out of her impatience and anxiety. She'd been waiting on other people's pleasure most of her life; she ought to be better at it by now!

"Duty," Tessie told herself. "Think of others first."

And come to think of it, there *were* some other problems close to hand. This might be a good opportunity to spend some more time with Masao, to try to discover what was troubling him, for there was certainly something on his mind. He'd spent enough of their journey frowning abstractedly into the distance to make Tessie sure of that. And then there was the way he'd been avoiding her and Jason since they arrived at his family home. Yes, there was certainly something wrong, and finding and fixing it would serve to keep her mind off her own worries. Tessie picked up her crutch, which by now she was using more as a cane, and hobbled down the hall toward the public rooms around the large courtyard. Somewhere she was sure to find a servant who could tell her where Masao was keeping himself these days.

She did not find Masao, but she did stumble on a scene of unexpected gaiety, all the more surprising after the silent days she'd already spent in this somber, sprawling mansion. In the main rooms a small army of servants was at work, shaking out the floor mats, polishing the floors with steaming hot cloths, sponging off the woodwork, and mending every little tear in the rice-paper screens that served for interior walls. Their chatter and singing blended with the *pat-pat-pat* of the dusters and the squeaking of the polishing cloths, much as if an army of singing crickets had invaded the house. And they all seemed incredibly happy to be doing this hard, painstaking work.

"We are preparing for the arrival of O Shorai Sama," one of the maids paused to explain.

"I see." Tessie paused politely. "Er—he must be a very important gentleman?"

The maid raised one hand to her mouth and tittered. "Not a person, my lady. O Shorai Sama means—oh, very holy thing!"

"The term stands for the combined spirits of all our

ancestors," said a quiet voice behind her. Tessie turned and saw Masao's mother, dressed in her usual dark kimono, but with a gentle smile on her face instead of the severe expression she usually wore. "We celebrate their return during the festival of Ura Bon, the Welcome to Souls Returned. It is a time when we are directed to show charity to all, and particularly to the guest within our gates. So you have come to us at a fortunate time, my child. Will you help us prepare?"

Masao's mother urged her into a room where several chattering girls sat before a bronze Buddha seated on a gilded lotus. A niche behind the shrine held several framed family photographs and a tablet with Japanese names on it; before the statue there was a fresh mat of pampas grass, and on either side a vase held an elegant arrangement of dry branches and autumn grasses. Apart from these things, the room was unfurnished, even emptier than most Japanese rooms.

"This is our family shrine," Masao's mother said, "where the spirit guest lives during the days of his visit. We are preparing decorations to welcome O Shorai Sama now. You are welcome to help."

Tessie recognized Masao's three young sisters, the shy girls who had greeted her on the night of her arrival and whom she had since glimpsed scampering about the house or craning for a good look at the fire-haired barbarian. Now, seated before the shrine, they were working busily with trays of vegetables, dried hemp stems, and bundles of softened noodles. They smiled and moved aside to make a place for Tessie.

There was a fourth girl kneeling to one side, older than the little sisters. Tessie did not recognize her. She had an interesting face; bright, lively eyes that took in every detail of Tessie's dress and appearance, a sweet smile, and a gentle expression—all of which were belied by the hands that twisted tightly in her lap.

"I am Shizuka." The girl introduced herself in a soft voice that matched her pleasant expression.

Tessie knew her surprise must show on her face.

"My son's betrothed," amplified Masao's mother, who of course did not know that Tessie had heard the story of the neglected betrothal from Dai in the village. "Who *should* be my son's wife by now, save that he has become infected with foreign ways and neglects his responsibilities."

"Shh! Do not blame Masao, Mother," Shizuka said gently as if this bitter woman was indeed her mother-in-law and to be honored in all things. "He has other responsibilities. And you know that I am not unhappy."

But her hands twisted together again as she spoke, and Tessie observed that two of her fingernails were bitten off short—like her own. Before she ever met Shizuka she had had a strange feeling of sympathy for this girl; now it grew stronger. She felt convinced that they were meant to meet, that somehow their destinies were to be entwined.

"Not unhappy!" snorted Masao's mother. "Ha! Is that why you come to visit us only when my worthless son is absent, you who grew up here like a daughter of the family?"

"I did not know Masao was away," Tessie interposed.

The two younger girls giggled, and Masao's mother answered, "Yes, he left early this morning to visit friends. I can only *hope* that he will choose to return in time for the festival."

"I am sure he will do so," said Shizuka soothingly, "for none of us would want to miss such a time of charity and loving kindness to all."

"Yes, and when he returns to the house you will leave it again!" Masao's mother looked as if she were about to cry. "I thought to have you for a daughter, Shizuka, and instead this betrothal has driven you

192

away from us!" She picked up a crooked squash from the tray before her and with quick, angry motions plaited corn silk to resemble a horse's mane and tail, stuck hemp stems into the body of the squash to resemble stiff little legs, and set the completed decoration on the table before the shrine.

No one spoke for a few moments. Tessie felt surrounded by old, bad feelings that she did not understand. Sensibly, she bowed her head and watched the little girls working on their wreaths of fruit and flowers.

After a few minutes of silence, Masao's mother stood. Going to the niche behind the shrine, she drew out a brownish-toned photograph in a silver frame and thrust it at Tessie. "This was Masao's father. He, too, had foreign friends. And his is one of the spirits that will be in this shrine. You must think about these things."

As abruptly as she had stood, she replaced the photograph and left the room. Tessie could not help but feel relieved. The moment of charity with which Masao's mother had greeted her had obviously been a great effort, put on in an attempt to keep the spirit of the festival. Her true feelings, the bitterness and anger that colored her every action, had come out more and more clearly with every moment she spent in Tessie's company.

And here she was, the guest of this unhappy woman, unable to travel on her own, and with both her friends mysteriously disappeared on their own business! Tessie told herself that she was *not* so low-spirited and weak as to cry before Masao's family, but she had to concentrate very hard to keep the tears from spilling over.

A little hand crept into hers, and Masao's youngest sister, a little girl of twelve or thirteen, looked up into Tessie's sad face. "Please, do not let Mama make you unhappy," she said. "It is not your fault. My father had a barbarian friend who caused his death, and I think Mama blames all barbarians equally."

"Ishi!" the next oldest girl reproved her. "It is not polite to call the lady a barbarian! The correct term is *foreigner.*"

"It is all right," Tessie said carefully. "I am not offended. Indeed, I am grateful for your sister's explanation."

Both girls burst into giggles, clapping their hands over their mouths, and Tessie looked at them in bewilderment. "Now what did I say?"

"Your accent is a little strange," Shizuka answered for them. "And you place the words in a strange order."

So Tessie discovered that her command of Japanese, good enough for following stories or arranging travel plans, was sadly lacking when it came to the rapid give-and-take of a family conversation. The little girls enjoyed teaching her, and as Tessie laughed as heartily as anyone else when her mistakes were pointed out to her, they soon began to have a genuinely happy time over the arrangement of the flowers and vegetables.

When the supplies of vegetables and hemp and flowers before them were exhausted, Masao's sisters volunteered to fetch more. They ran off, laughing together, leaving Shizuka and Tessie alone for the first time.

Almost at once Shizuka began to question Tessie about life in America, and particularly about the place of women in American society. Could women go to college? Yes, Tessie said, though she herself had not done so. Hold paying jobs? Yes—although, again, Tessie had to confess that she had spent her life caring for members of her family rather than working in the outside world. Vote? No, but Tessie felt sure that would change soon.

"It does not sound so different from Japan,"

194

Shizuka said unhappily. "I thought American women would have much more freedom."

"Oh, but they do!" Tessie assured her. "You must not judge by me. The truth is that I am rather . . ." She could not think of a way to say *spineless* in Japanese, but that was the word that came to mind. "I am like a jellyfish," she said at last. "I give in to every pressure. Many women have done much better."

Shizuka studied her for a long uncomfortable moment. "I do not think so," she said at last. "You are traveling now, are you not? The days of staying at home with the parents are over. And you travel with a man you are not even married to!" She sighed. "I wish I had such freedom—or such courage."

"Most people," said Tessie wryly, "would not envy my situation so much. Why do you wish to know about America, Shizuka? Do you think you would rather live there?"

"No," Shizuka said at once. "I am Japanese and I love Japan. But my father sent me to study in a missionary school in Edo for several years when I was younger, and I liked what I saw of the American and English women who taught in the school. Instead of bowing before men and always agreeing with whatever the men say, they argued for their own views—yes, and sometimes they won! They are cherry blossoms, and I was a plum blossom."

"What?" Tessie felt that her faulty knowledge of Japanese must have tripped her up.

Shizuka changed to English, which she spoke much better than Tessie did Japanese. "In our country," she explained, "the plum blossom symbolizes duty through hardship, because it flowers when there is still snow on the tree branches. The plum blossom is our bridal flower, and it symbolizes the virtues to which Japanese women must aspire—modest, gentle, bearing hardship without complaint. Self-sacrifice is the greatest virtue to which we may aspire, even if it is useless sacrifice. But American women are free and natural, always changing and always strong, like the cherry blossom."

"Oh! We are not so wonderful as all that," Tessie protested.

"Perhaps not to yourselves," said Shizuka, "but to me, my American teachers were a vision of what women could become, what I wish to see women become here in Japan also. I vowed then, when I was still at school, that I would never bow under the yoke of the traditional Japanese bride—submissive and subservient above all else, a servant to her mother-in-law and a slave to her husband. That is what Masao's mother does not understand. She blames her son because he was unwilling to carry out the betrothal that was arranged before he went to America; she does not understand—and how can I tell her—that I could never marry a man like Masao!"

"Are you sure Masao would be so overbearing?" Tessie asked in surprise. "He has not seemed so to me."

Shizuka shrugged. "He has lived in America; perhaps he has learned how to behave like Americans in some respects. But he is still the son of a samurai, and tradition still rules him. Why, he could not even say honestly that he did not want me; he had to pretend that some debt of honor prevented him from marrying, that he would not be free to marry me until he had restored the honor that his father lost." Shizuka stared at the bronze statue in the shrine, seemingly lost in her own thoughts.

"His father lost honor?" Tessie prompted gently.

"Because of the *daimyo*'s sword," Shizuka nodded. "That is why he committed *seppuku*. But of course you know all about that."

Tessie was about to protest that she knew nothing at all, but just then Masao's sisters burst in with baskets of tomatoes and corn silk and funny-shaped peppers and squash, and the opportunity for private conversation was over.

In the following days, Masao's mother kept back in her own rooms, as if regretting her moment of charity toward the foreign guests. Shizuka stayed always with the younger girls, so that Tessie did not have a chance to talk alone with her; perhaps she, too, regretted her impulsive confidences.

Shizuka's opposition to the Japanese style of marriage worried Tessie for reasons she found difficult to express. All her life she had dreamed of a strong, masterful, heroic lover who would sweep her off her feet and carry her away without listening to her protests. She had hated Jason for refusing to take on that role. But would she really like such a man? Shizuka lived in a world where no man ever listened to what a woman had to say—and she found it a prison, not a romantic dream. Tessie began to suspect that the romantically masterful hero of her dreams would prove a most unromantic jailer, once the honeymoon was over.

Of course, that wasn't to say that one wanted a man like Jason, either. At least Tessie's dream hero would be by her side, not vanishing into the dawn like a frightened fawn after their second night of love in ten years!

Altogether, she might have brooded herself into a state of total misery if Masao's little sisters would have permitted it. But now that she was well enough to hobble around the house after them, they took it for granted that she would want to be involved in all the festival preparations. They kept her busy with all their little tasks: cooking and decorating sweet cakes, twisting streamers of brightly colored paper, and making little boats to sail candles down the stream on the night of the festival. At the same time they laughed and told stories and sang and giggled politely at Tessie's mistakes in Japanese and encouraged her to walk a little farther, climb a little higher, than she had thought possible.

By the night of the festival, she was able to dispense with her cane entirely. At twilight, Masao's sisters urged her to join them in welcoming O Shorai Sama, the mysterious embodiment of past ancestors who came riding on a snow-white horse from the land of darkness. Even Masao's mother extended her invitation to the ceremonies.

Shizuka, too, came to welcome the ancestor spirit with Masao's family. Her own father was a learned man who did not entirely approve of these old superstitions, and she explained to Tessie that since her mother's death when she was a child, she had spent more than half her time in Masao's household, so that it was as much home to her as her father's scholarly establishment on the other side of the village. But Tessie thought she saw something else in Shizuka's face while the girl made this explanation—a shadow of unexpressed longing. *Why, she loves Masao!* Tessie thought. *She wants to marry him, only her pride and her advanced ideas prevent her from saying so. But she treats his mother like her own, his home like hers. Where would she be happier but here? If only these foolish young people could get together!* For at that moment, alone in this foreign twilight, deserted for the second time by her love, she felt eons older than Masao and Shizuka.

The festival of Ura Bon was no time for sad thoughts. Tessie forced herself to smile as she joined the other members of the household for the quiet march to the great entrance gates of the house. There a pile of hemp stems and fluffy dried grass had been laid, ready to be struck into fire by the man of the house.

Since Masao still had not returned, his mother lit the spark that began the welcoming blaze.

In the blue twilight, almost at the same moment,

hundreds of little fires sparkled out all down the long road and across the valley. Tessie looked up at the encircling hills and saw more sparks twinkling across the ridges. Every doorway had its fire tonight to welcome O Shorai Sama.

"Listen!" Ishi, the youngest sister, tugged at her mother's skirts. "I hear O Shorai Sama's horse coming."

Masao's mother began to laugh indulgently at her daughter's fancies, but her laugh was cut off after a moment by the unmistakable thud of a horse's hooves —not galloping, as O Shorai Sama would have come, but plodding wearily up the long, steep trail.

Tessie pressed her hands to her cheeks as a white horse indeed came into view, gleaming pale against the darkness of the trees. The momentary blaze of the grass fire had died down to embers, and she could see only a strange huddled shape, grotesque and too large to be a man, crouched on the horse's back.

Then the white horse stopped before the gateway; the great huddled shape resolved into two figures, one of which slid off the horse's back with a stifled groan and bowed to the women in the arch. "I told you I would come back for the festival, honored mother," said Masao.

Behind them, servants were lighting lanterns for the procession through the village. In their light Tessie could clearly see the other man who had ridden up with Masao. She was not, by that time, surprised by his identity. Jason Lancaster took his own sweet time getting off the horse. He moved stiffly and cursed under his breath.

"Are you hurt?" Tessie ran to his side and threw her arms around him without thinking.

"Tired. Sore. Rode too far today," Jason mumbled.

"Oh!"

"Disappointed?" His black eyes gleamed wickedly with a dancing red light, the reflection of the lanterns that were being lit and passed around to family members at the gateway. "I could always go back again and come back wounded so you could nurse me into health."

"I hardly realized," Tessie said, "that buying crafts from the local villagers was such a dangerous pursuit, that you were likely to be wounded."

"What? Oh! Yes. Well. I wasn't exactly buying craftworks," Jason admitted.

"What *were* you doing?" She could restrain the question no longer. A servant thrust a lamp into her hand, and Tessie held it up to shine on Jason's face. He looked tired and dirty and sad.

"Trying to keep you out of trouble, what else?"

"How?"

"Hush," Jason murmured. "This is supposed to be a time of charity. Let's have the quarrel later." He took a lantern from a servant's hand, bowed, and murmured the appropriate words of thanks. Slowly the procession of family members, guests, and servants moved back to the shrine, where they bowed to welcome the invisible guest.

"You went *where?*" In the doubtful privacy of Jason's room, screened by rice-paper walls that let sound and light through to the neighboring parts of the house, Tessie repeated her question in a furious whisper. She couldn't quite believe Jason had betrayed her.

"You heard me. To Nikko. To the river. To the five hundred Buddhas." Jason sighed deeply and massaged the back of his neck with one hand. "And I don't see what you're so angry about; it seemed like a good idea at the time. You were tied up here with your sprained ankle, fretting that we might be too late to meet Morgan. All I wanted was to spare you anxiety."

Tessie kept her lips pinched shut and breathed deeply through her nose until she could control her voice and her choice of words. "You might have discussed it with me first."

"I am not in the habit," Jason said evenly, "of asking a woman's permission to go when and where I like."

"Even when you go on *my* business?" Tessie shook her head. "I can think of another reason why you sneaked off in dead of night like that. Poor Jason! What a lot of effort you've expended for nothing." Her voice quavered on the last sentence. With luck he'd take the shaking of her voice for anger, not for the sign of the tears that constricted her throat.

"What do you mean by *that* little crack?" His face was immobile again, but his eyes watched her with the wariness of a cat seeing possible danger approach.

"You went to Nikko without me," Tessie enunciated with cold precision, "because you thought, having the last clue, that you might get all Morgan's legacy for yourself. And in order to get that clue from me, you seduced me and pretended to love me." Her laugh sounded as shrill and false as she felt. "I do hope it was not too difficult for you, pretending such great desire for a woman you were only using."

"Damm it, Tessie! Why do you always leap at any chance to believe the worst of me?"

"Why do you make it so easy for me?" Before he could answer, she hit him with another question, words sharp and hard as the blows she would have liked to rain down upon him. "Didn't you already tell me that you were forcing yourself along on this expedition because you desperately needed money for your business? Why shouldn't you have tried to steal a march on me so as to double your proposed income?" He didn't even look ashamed of himself. Perhaps he thought of what he'd done as normal business practice, no worse than spying on a competitor's load of trade goods. Perhaps he truly didn't realize how despicable it had been to trifle with her feelings like that, how deeply he had hurt her this time. To have been wooed into trusting him again, after all these lonely years, and then to find that she had been deceived again!

"I don't need money," Jason said.

"Too late! You already told me that your business was in trouble."

"I lied."

"Oh, so now you want me to believe *that* was the lie! Why would you have invented a story so much to your discredit?"

"I had to give you some reason for my desire to accompany you," Jason said, "and somehow I didn't feel you'd accept the real one."

"Which was?"

"That I loved you. That I've always loved you. And that I couldn't give up this chance to court you and win you back, away in Japan and far from your interfering family."

He offered the words nakedly, without apology or caresses or any persuasion but the bald statement. For a moment Tessie felt the impossibly strong pull of her own desire to believe him, like the drag of the tide; then cold reason won. Of course, she wanted to believe him. But if she did, what would she do next time he deceived and betrayed her? Each time hurt worse than the last. Right now she felt as if sharp knives were cutting into her each time she looked at him. She could not survive another betrayal.

"Too late for that story, don't you think?" she said coldly. "You should have tried it before you went sneaking off to Nikko behind my back."

"I can't prove anything about my feelings for you," Jason said, "but if you'll come back to Yokohama with me, I can easily demonstrate to you that Benten and Company is in no financial trouble whatsoever."

Tessie shook her head. "No, Jason. I've no doubt that you can make papers and balance sheets look good enough. You're a very clever man. But you're not clever enough to make me trust you again. We'll go on to Nikko after the festival—and the only reason I'm allowing you to travel with me," she warned, "is because I need that pass. But I'm not going to trust you out of my sight for one moment. And when we get to Nikko, *I* will find Morgan, as you obviously failed to do. Now if you'll excuse me, it's been a long day, and I'd like to get some sleep before we set out." Tessie picked up her skirts and turned her back on Jason.

"Wait!"

Jason's shout stopped her with one hand on the sliding screen. Tessie looked back over her shoulder, trying to tell herself that all she felt was annoyance at having her grand exit spoiled. She couldn't possibly be hoping that Jason would come up with some incontrovertible proof of his honesty—not now—could she?

"How do you know I failed?" Jason demanded.

Tessie raised one eyebrow. "Why else would you have come back?"

Chapter Fourteen

The last of the summer's heat had passed while they lingered in the mountains. When at last they reached Nikko, the maples were blazing out like tongues of red flame, and the river ran cold and chill from the mountain caves. The foreigners who flocked to Nikko in the summer for picnics and tea parties had returned to the comforts of their snug houses in Tokyo and Yokohama. Tessie and Jason and Masao came to a quiet, dreaming town of shrines and temples, populated by priests and pines, rainbow-tinted with the spray of waterfalls, and gray with the ubiquitous carved stone of steps and shrines and statues.

The river bisected the town, a full cold torrent rushing down between dark green hills and spanned by a delicate bridge of scarlet latticework. While the travelers crossed lower down, Masao explained to Tessie that the scarlet bridge was not for ordinary use; only the emperor might use that pathway to the shrines.

The emperor had not been to Nikko in many years, and the paths leading to the shrine were all overgrown with pale gold autumn grasses that rustled in the lonely breeze.

"I must go down to the place where the Buddhas stand," Tessie said.

"Let's find a hotel first. I usually stay at the Kanaya. It's cleaner than the Nikko, and they don't overprice everything for foreigners," Jason suggested.

"There will be no necessity to stay at a hotel," countered Masao in tones that suggested quiet horror at the very thought of using such public accommodations. "I have a friend in Nikko."

Masao's friend was a Buddhist priest who lived a little way up the mountain from the village, in one of the walled enclosures that had belonged to princes in former days. Now the prince's palace wall enclosed a vegetable garden and two houses, one for the priest and one for those visitors who came to the shrines, to whom he was pleased to offer hospitality.

The setting of the two houses could not have been lovelier. A rocky cliff rose behind them, with willows and maples and paulownia planted on every tiny ledge, and with a little waterfall tumbling down the rocks in a rainbow shower of icy spray. The water was captured in a pool at the bottom of the cliff, and from there, tamed and warmed by the sun, it filled the baths of the household and watered the vegetable garden.

Tessie was happy to leave her shoes on the threshold and to stretch her sore, tired feet on the soft mats. A smiling little servant girl brought tea and a bowl of sweet cakes and told them that she would bring a box of burning charcoal through from the priest's house to heat their baths.

"This is *much* nicer than a hotel," Tessie exclaimed. "And more private, too. Thank you, Masao, for thinking of this. And I hope you will thank our host for me, if his religion prevents him from talking to a barbarian female."

Masao smiled. "I am sure he would be happy to meet you, Miss Teresa, but these are days of prayer and fasting and seclusion for him, in fulfilment of a special vow. It is the anniversary of a very sad day in our family—my father's death. He must remain in seclusion to pray for his soul."

It had been at this time of year, according to the newspapers, that Morgan disappeared. And it had been the end of summer when she and Jason quarreled for the first time, as it had been the end of summer in the mountains when she discovered his second betrayal, just a few days ago. Tessie felt the shadow of all those griefs falling across her soul like a precursor of winter. She had always loved autumn, with its crisp air and the bright colors of the trees. It had always seemed like a season of new beginnings to her, but now she felt that it was the time when everything sad began, also, and that there was nothing to look forward to but the lonely winter of her old age.

"I am sorry, Masao," she said quietly. "Do you wish to join your friend in his prayers? Jason and I would not wish to keep you from your family duty."

"The souls of the family are a priest's concern," Masao replied. "The honor of the family is mine. And I think that will be best served by staying with you."

"How strange," Tessie murmured to Jason after Masao left. "I knew the Japanese took the duties of hospitality very seriously, but don't you think Masao is overdoing it? I'm not even a guest in his house anymore. He is hardly obliged to keep constant guard over me!"

"Somebody needs to," Jason told her. "You're in danger. Or haven't you noticed?"

The only danger that frightened Tessie was that in her own heart. The only man she feared was sitting on the mats beside her, drinking tea and looking as if their quarrel three nights before had not touched him at all.

"Never mind me, but Morgan may be in danger," she said. "And the sooner I find him, the better. I'll go to the river as soon as we've finished our tea."

"That you will *not*," Jason said. "It's almost dusk. You wouldn't be safe. Besides, as there is nothing there to find, you may as well wait until daylight so you can convince yourself it's hopeless."

"You found nothing," Tessie said, "because the clues were not meant for you. I do wish you would stop imposing yourself into my business."

She felt edgy and irritable, gritty from the long railway journey, and more tired than she was willing to admit. She didn't want to snipe and snarl at Jason. She wanted to blast him to the ground with the blazing force of her anger. No. She wanted him to understand that she felt absolutely nothing for him, that what had happened between them in the mountains was a momentary aberration that had nothing to do with her true feelings.

"As soon as we've finished this search," she said, turning away from Jason and speaking into her tea-cup, "I think I shall go back to America."

"What? Forgetting your plain duty to Hartley and Sophia?" Jason teased.

Tessie nodded unhappily. It was wrong, of course. Hartley needed her. Sophia needed her. The children needed their Aunt Tessie. But she could not bear the thought of continuing her stay in Yokohama, where she would have to see Jason Lancaster every day, and every day she would have to put on her mask of cool indifference. What if he decided to amuse himself by stirring up her feelings for him once again? She felt miserably certain that he could do it, if he bothered. She'd been a fool twice already, why not again? No, she couldn't stay in Yokohama and risk that.

"I find I am missing Ricardo more than I thought," she said.

"Ah! No doubt you'll be married soon after your return to San Francisco."

"No doubt," Tessie lied through the growing lump in her throat. Didn't Jason *mind* the thought of her marrying another man? No, he was probably relieved. Toying with her affections was but a momentary amusement for him.

"Good," Jason said. "You—should be married, Tessie. You were never meant to be a maiden aunt."

Was he making some snide reference to the passion he had so easily awakened in her? Tessie glanced sidewise at Jason but could read nothing in his face. He was staring into his teacup as though he could read her future there. "You have too much love and generosity and joy in life to be wasted on other people's households," he went on. "You deserve a man who'll make you happy and children of your own to raise. I'm glad to know you will be going back to that. I wouldn't like to think of you returning to America to wither into one of those lonely, embittered old maids with nothing better to do than to run around sticking their noses into other people's business."

Tessie suppressed a shiver at the bleak look into her future that Jason had unwittingly provided. How ironic that he should be congratulating her on escaping such a fate, when in truth it was all that awaited her! Even if there had been a Ricardo waiting for her—even if she had ever been able to look twice at any other man—she knew in her heart that she could never do so now. The only man she wanted was sitting beside her on the soft clean mats, caressing the rough surface of his tea bowl with one finger, staring into the clear green depths of the tea, and completely ignorant of the storm of feelings possessing her.

"If you don't mind," Tessie said, rising and suppressing a twinge of pain from her stiff ankle, "I think I'll leave you and Masao to your tea. I'll just walk down to the bridge for some fresh air."

He saw through that, of course. "You're not visiting the five hundred Buddhas without me. The riverbank is far too lonely and secluded, especially at dusk."

Masao overheard the ensuing quarrel, and all Tessie gained from yelling so loudly at Jason was that Masao, too, insisted on accompanying her. The three of them made the walk together, solemnly staring at the worn statues in the gathering gloom. The two men waited until Tessie had to agree that she could read no further message in those weather-beaten, almost featureless faces.

"Though why you should ever have expected to, when Masao and I had already been there to tell you there was no clue, escapes me," Jason grumbled.

"The message was for *me,* not for you. And I wouldn't be surprised if you two were quarreling too hard to have noticed a message ten feet high written on the nearest statue."

Jason bit his lip, and Masao suppressed a chuckle. Tessie concluded that her guess was correct. They hadn't set out to investigate Nikko together; most likely, Jason had gone off after the clue and Masao had followed him. And whatever else had happened on the journey, the two men had not become close friends as a result.

And there was not, as Masao now pointed out solemnly, a message ten feet high written on the nearest statue.

"Oh, well," Jason said, "as long as we're in Nikko, will you allow me to show you around the shrines tomorrow? Or are you in a desperate hurry to go back to your dear Ricardo?"

"Who?" Masao demanded.

Tessie stalked ahead of the men, back to the priest's house on the hillside, while Jason told Masao all that Tessie had once told him about her fiancé in America. At the moment, she detested them both equally, for discussing her and her affairs and, most of all, for being right about the absence of clues in Nikko.

All the same, it wouldn't do any harm to linger a day or two here, painful though Jason's company was to her. Morgan had been looking for her. She had followed his trail too long, through too many secret ways, to accept that it could all end in this mountain town of shrines and temples. Perhaps, if they stayed in Nikko a few days, he would yet find some way to get in touch with her.

On the way to visit the shrines the next morning, Masao tried to explain the complicated history of Japan and the role that Ieyasu and Iemitsu had played in that history. Tessie had not slept well, and between the buzzing of weariness in her head and her determination to watch for any sign of Morgan, she took in very little. It all seemed a long, confusing string of battles and sieges and foreign names. All she really grasped was that this one man, Ieyasu Tokugawa, was supposed to have been at once the author of Japanese law and the conqueror of the old regime and the founder of the dynasty that had ruled Japan until the revolution just a few years previously.

"Magna Carta, Henry the Eighth, and George Washington all in one?" Jason murmured into Tessie's ear, and she choked back a giggle. How perfectly he had mirrored her own confused thoughts! Oh, dear— if only it were safe to laugh with Jason, to travel with Jason, to be friends with Jason . . .

Tessie bit her lip and reminded herself that enjoying Jason's company always ended the same way—with her in Jason's bed, vulnerable and loving and open to his selfish manipulation. When would she learn to stop liking him and look for a man she could trust and depend on, a man who would take control of her life and leave her without any of these miserable doubts and vacillations?

The trouble was that even when she hated him, it was all but impossible to stop liking Jason. He kept doing sneaky things like looking after her little comforts, or making her laugh, or pointing out some subtle beauty in the landscape that nine men out of ten would never have seen.

As they climbed the giant steps leading to the shrine of Ieyasu, Tessie tried to put both Jason and Morgan out of her mind and to concentrate on nothing but the beauty surrounding her. It should have been easy enough. They ascended steps built over and around a torrent of clear mountain water, with rows of dark green trees guarding them on either side, the temple grounds before them gleaming like an enchanted castle of high white walls and red-and-gold roofs.

Within the outer walls was a whole little world of shrines and storehouses, heavy bronze gates framing miniature vistas, and courtyards opening off other courtyards, until Tessie was quite confused with the complexity of the shrine. A delicate little building of black lacquered panels and golden gratings was, Masao told her, the stable of the sacred horse of Ieyasu—and there was indeed a horse within, a quiet little white pony that whickered and snuffled at Tessie's outstretched palm in friendly, quite ungodlike fashion.

They passed the sacred horse and continued on to the temple font, a perfectly balanced massive stone set so that the mountain stream overflowed it evenly on all sides. From a distance it looked like a mass of solid water, mysteriously defying the laws of gravity to flow in a liquid cube.

Over this wonderful font was a canopy whose roof glittered in a radiant glory of bronze and gold, supported by painted waves and sculptured dragons in scarlet.

"Do me a favor, and don't stand too near that thing, Tessie," Jason teased. "Your hair clashes with every color in the canopy."

Tessie made a face at him and wandered off in another direction to where a new courtyard opened out. She passed through gates and terraces, through courts shadowed by tall trees and past great moss-covered stone lanterns, until at last she found herself alone in the final shrine. A small enclosed terrace was filled with gilded screens and pierced stone walls, bordered by painted sculptures of birds and flowers whose shadows seemed to dance upon the polished granite of the walls. The interplay of light and shadow, sparkle and darkness, created a tiny artificial world of mystery where it seemed to Tessie that the stone carvings might at any moment speak to her, the birds carved with such realism might fly to perch on her shoulder, and the flowers dappled by sunlight dancing through gilded screens might bend their heads to a passing breeze.

A tall shape draped in brilliantly colored cloths did indeed move, and Tessie started, then realized that what she had taken for a statue was actually a young Buddhist priest who had been standing so still in contemplation that he blended perfectly with the decorations of the court.

"Do you like our shrine?"

She nodded, too startled by the sudden apparition to think of the incongruity of his address. How had he known that she would understand Japanese?

"I have never seen anything more beautiful," she said honestly.

The young priest's smile was as warm as the sun. With one hand he gestured wordlessly, inviting her to raise her eyes. Tessie looked up and saw that the stone wall bordering the terrace was itself bounded by the face of the mountain. The slope of the mountain was covered with ancient trees, tall and wind-bent in a thousand different forms. The lichens and mosses of the forest grew right down to the edge of the stone wall.

She nodded slowly in acknowledgment of the priest's unspoken message. "Yes. All that men have made here is beautiful, but the mountain surpasses the temple."

"It is an error to worship the mountains and the beings of the mountains," said the priest, "but when I stand here in meditation, sometimes I think I can understand that error. The priests of Shugendo had their own wisdom."

Tessie started again at this mention of the outlawed cult. Her search for Morgan had begun with instructions to seek out a Shugendo priest. Was it to end here, in this calm Buddhist shrine? Breathless, she waited for the young priest to give a further clue.

"If you appreciate the beauties of nature," he said with a faint smile, "I think you really should visit the five hundred Buddhas by the riverbank before you leave Nikko."

Tessie swallowed. "I-I've already been there," she said faintly.

"Sometimes," said the priest with a reproving frown, "nature gives up her rarest beauties, her secrets one might say, only to those who are willing to pursue them in solitude. Go to the riverbank, my daughter, and meditate upon the transitory nature of all things. *Alone.*"

The long line of gray Buddhas stretched onward from the bridge, dappled with moss and sprinkled with spray from the rushing river. Tessie walked solemnly down the line of statues, not even attempting to count them. The noisy rush of the river dazed her; the red and gold stars that hung in the sky above her dazzled her until she had to remind herself that they were only maple leaves. She was surrounded by fire and jewels and rushing water; every quiet eddy in the river was a mosaic of bronze and gold leaves from the trees above her, and the path on which she walked was a crimson carpet of fallen stars.

Here, if anywhere, she would find what she had

been seeking. She felt it so strongly that she could almost have held out her hands; but the image that she saw before her dazzled eyes was not Morgan, but Jason Lancaster.

He was waiting with Masao, just beyond the bridge, out of sight and barely within earshot, for Tessie to call at once if any danger threatened. And she was surprised he'd acceded to that much.

So—having fought so hard to come alone to this quiet god-haunted place beside the river—why did she now long to see him? If she had any sense she'd be delighted to be free of his overpowering company for a few moments, overjoyed to think that her long search for Morgan might be coming to an end and that soon she would no longer have to suffer the torture of being close to a man she loved against all the dictates of sense and reason.

Tessie concluded soberly that she had no sense whatsoever. She preferred the sweet torture of Jason's company to the long desert of his absence, the hopeless years that stretched before her once this quest was completed. She was almost ready to turn now and flee to the comfort of the bridge, to tell Jason and Masao that she had been unable to see or hear anything at this appointed meeting place.

But that, too, would be an end to the quest, in failure rather than success.

Tessie squinted through the mist of spraying water, trying to make some clue out of the silent stones and the flaming glory of the maples. She could almost persuade herself that she saw a stocky figure in the white robes and black skullcap of the *yamabushi*—or was it a trick of the light, a dazzle of sun on water too far away for her to see clearly, a black branch momentarily clothed in the glare of smooth water reflecting the sun? Would a priest of the outlawed Shugendo sect dare to come to Nikko, this heart of Buddhist shrines and true believers?

A crackle of leaves distracted Tessie for a moment. Her head whipped around, and she just glimpsed something red and gold that was not an autumn leaf: the brush of a fox crossing the water. When she looked back, a folded paper lay by her feet, and she heard a rustle like a long robe being drawn hastily over the fallen leaves.

"Wait!" she called hopelessly. But the messenger was already out of sight, as if whisked away by magic. Tessie took up the paper and unfolded it slowly. It had been folded into the shape of a fox. On the inside one word was written in Japanese characters—the name of a town or village, Tessie thought.

"Kasadake," she read aloud. "Less subtle than the earlier clues." Suddenly angry, she raised her voice. "Morgan! You're losing your touch! Why don't you just lay down a paper chase through the countryside!"

Morgan—if he was listening—did not answer, but Jason and Masao burst forth from their place of concealment behind the bridge and were at her side within seconds. And after that, of course, there was not much hope of being contacted again.

Chapter Fifteen

Kasadake was a mountain, not a town, and it lay back behind them, in the untraveled hill country where ghosts and demons owned the silent nights and peasants stared in surprise at the sight of strangers. And it was, Jason insisted, too late for them to set off on another grueling journey that night.

Masao concurred, but Tessie had the feeling he had reasons of his own for wishing to linger in Nikko for another evening. Once the decision to leave in the morning had been agreed upon, when they were all back sipping tea in the comfort of the priest's guest house, his hidden reasons slowly emerged.

"You want to go to the *puppet show?*" Tessie repeated, choking back a gurgle of laughter. The only puppets she had seen were a pair of dolls in a seaside booth, cavorting and shouting silly jokes while they pretended to belabor each other with toy umbrellas. She couldn't imagine the dignified Masao being seduced by such a cheap, noisy children's show.

"In Japan," Masao said rather stiffly, "the puppet theater is an ancient and respected art form."

"Like Kabuki," Jason put in from the corner where he lounged.

Masao shot him a grateful glance. "Yes, precisely, except that it is, of course, more respectable. A samurai would never have attended the Kabuki."

"The difference is obvious," Jason agreed with the merest glint of a smile hidden behind his solemn eyes. "So you want to go off to the theater, Masao? Have a good time."

But Masao wasn't to be dismissed so easily. He wanted Tessie to accompany him. "It will be an educational experience," he told her, "and I think the play that is to be presented tonight will help you to understand the problems you may be dealing with here."

After that prelude, Tessie had expected a mystery, or some modern play about the problems between Japanese and foreigners, or something that would have some faint relevance to Morgan's disappearance and the chase that had led them across Japan and back again. She was rather surprised to learn that they were to watch a scene from an eighteenth-century play called *Imoseyama Onna Teikin.*

"The title means 'An Example of Noble Womanhood,'" Jason told her when they were settling into their places.

"I had already translated that much." Tessie had accepted Masao's invitation as much to avoid being left alone with Jason for the evening as for any other reason. She was not pleased that Jason had chosen to accompany them. At least, she felt it would be wiser not to be pleased. They might have to travel on to one more place together, but this journey would end soon enough; she might as well start getting used to being without Jason. She had meant this evening at the puppet theater to be a test of her ability to enjoy life without Jason. She'd wanted to prove to herself that she could go out with a young man who was merely a family friend, make polite conversation, enjoy a play, and soak up Japanese atmosphere, all without longing for Jason's presence like some silly girl who cared for nothing but love.

Instead of the quiet, civilized evening she'd planned, she now had to deal with Jason sitting beside her, taking her hand in his, making irrational shivers of desire and excitement run up her arm while he leaned too close to murmur his unwanted translations into her ear.

Masao didn't look terribly pleased at the arrangement, either.

The sharp beating of wooden clappers interrupted the murmuring of the settling audience. Silence fell over the crowded theater as two men in black removed the screens that had concealed the stage, revealing a low reading stand behind which sat a man dressed in a plain white kimono.

The austerity and simplicity of the setting startled Tessie, who had been expecting something like the Punch and Judy shows of her childhood, all gaudy tinsel and noisy display.

A man dressed all in black, with a black hood drawn over his face, walked onto the stage and knocked his two wooden clappers together, calling out, "Tohzai! Tohzai!" The meaningless syllables were followed by a short announcement of the scene they were about to watch. Masao had already told Tessie enough about the play for her to follow the singsong prologue. The hooded man was saying that they were about to see a young man who had followed a girl home from a festival, only to discover to his distress that she was the sister of his greatest enemy.

"Tohzai, To, To-o-o-," the hooded man chanted again, walking offstage so that the last sharp syllable, "-zai!" came from behind the screens on the left side.

Complete silence fell on the theater.

The man in the white kimono moved for the first time. He lifted a book to his forehead and bowed, then placed it on the lectern before him and opened it with a snap that echoed through the theater. Somewhere, unseen, a stringed instrument was plucked in a run of plaintive sharp notes.

As the man in white began to chant to the music, the first puppet appeared. Almost lifesize, it was like a large wooden doll representing a young man in old-fashioned Japanese dress. Tessie was startled to see that it was not manipulated by strings; instead, a second man in white stood behind the doll, moving it so that it appeared to walk about the stage. There was no attempt to conceal his movements. What was more, he was followed by two other men, dressed in black with black hoods covering their faces, who helped to move the doll's limbs and head.

It seemed impossibly artificial and clumsy to Tessie. How could one ever forget the presence of the three assistants and believe in the reality of this carved and dressed wooden doll? But she could hardly say so to Masao, who with a deep sigh of satisfaction was settling into his seat and whispering explanations to her. "The man in white is the *omo-zukai*—head puppeteer. He operates the head and the right arm. The *hidari-zukai* takes the left arm, and the *ashi-zukai* manages the legs and moves the hem of the kimono. The *omo-zukai* here is a master puppeteer. He trained in Osaka, the center of the art. I saw him many years ago there, when he was only *ashi-zukai*. I have never seen anything to equal the delicacy with which he moved the female puppet's kimono to simulate her kneeling before her husband. It was a most moving scene."

Tessie smiled and nodded and rather wished Masao would stop talking. Despite her gloomy expectations, she was beginning to get caught up in the scene. The other puppet had entered now, a doll painted with the delicate features of a young girl and dressed in a hand-dyed and embroidered kimono that shimmered like moonlight and roses under the theater lamps. The narrator's voice changed from the man's deep bass to a girl's light, uncertain tones as he shifted back and forth, taking both parts of the dialogue with amazing virtuosity.

The young man was called Nakatomi Tankai. The girl's name was Tachibana-hime. Tessie thought that it was a good thing she'd been in Japan long enough to get used to peculiar names; then the Tankai puppet knelt, and the Tachibana puppet wept, or seemed to, and Tessie forgot everything but the story.

Tankai had seen Tachibana at a festival, not knowing who she was, and had followed her to her home. She had fallen in love with him at sight and was overjoyed to see him again, but he seemed unaccountably distressed. What, he asked, was she doing in the garden of this palace? It was her brother's palace? This could not be. Her brother was his greatest enemy. Tankai was sworn to kill him and every member of his family.

"Then begin by killing me," Tachibana cried, "for I would sooner die by your hand than live without you."

Torn between love and honor, Tankai finally came to a solution. His feud with Tachibana's brother had begun with the theft of a precious sword, a family heirloom. If Tachibana would help him to recover the sword, his debt of gratitude would give him sufficient excuse for sparing her life.

Masao was as caught up in the unfolding of the scene as Tessie, but for different reasons. Every line, every gesture spoke to him too vividly of his own vows, the debt of honor he had rashly sworn before he went to America and actually met his enemies.

As the narrator chanted the lines and the puppets gestured, Masao's mind drifted back to his own secrets and the hideous dilemma he faced now.

It had seemed very simple when he was a boy in his teens, with his head stuffed full of honor and duty and the ancient glories of his samurai family. Before the revolution, his father had been a samurai in the service of the *daimyo* of Shiroyama, one of the Japanese nobles most fiercely opposed to making any concessions to the barbarian invaders. After the Shogun was deposed in the early 1870s and the feudal order of *daimyos* and samurais came to an end, the lord of Shiroyama had hated the Westerners more than ever, blaming them for the disastrous changes that had ended his private world. His anger had been turned even on Masao's father, who had made friends with an American named Morgan Gallagher.

Somehow, Masao never knew how, his father had become convinced that it was his duty to the *daimyo* to show where his heart lay by killing the American. The *daimyo*, pleased with that resolution, had entrusted Masao's father with a samurai sword that had been passed down in the family of Shiroyama since the fourteenth century. "By striking with this sword, you strike with my hand, and the blood of the American will wash out the dishonor that has come upon our country!"

Well, Masao thought uneasily, it had seemed to make sense when he first heard the story. Before he found out what Americans were really like.

What moment of weakness had fatally slowed the attack? Had Masao's father paused at the last moment, unable to deliver the death blow to a man who had trusted him as a friend? Masao never knew; his father had not said. All Masao knew was that the fight had ended with the other samurai dead in the street, Masao's father given up for dead, and Morgan gone, having disarmed Masao's father and taken the priceless heirloom sword with him.

In the long weeks of recovery, there was still no word of Morgan or the *daimyo*'s sword. And so the long time of nursing his father back to health had ended as Masao, even then, had known it must. As soon as he was able to sit up, Masao's father had sent for his son and had related the whole story as far as he knew it, enjoining Masao to take up the burden of revenging them and restoring the *daimyo*'s sword; then, with a hand that hardly trembled at all, he had plunged his own sword into his body.

It was an honorable death. It had left young Masao burdened with the care of a mother and three baby sisters and an impossible vow, but he had never hated his father for that. Instead he had hated the American. In those first angry, grieving moments, Masao had extended his vow, swearing not only to recover the *daimyo*'s sword but also to kill Morgan Gallagher and every member of his family.

The recovery of the sword came first. That was why he had arranged to meet the Gallagher family and to live in their house when he went to America. For that matter, it was why he went to America in the first place; his study of engineering had at first been only an excuse to search out his enemies. But in his three years of study he'd never heard any clue that any of them knew anything about Morgan's death. They were just what they seemed: a loud, quarrelsome, excitable, lively, uninhibited Irish-American family, with nothing more on their minds than roasting the joint for Sunday dinner and starching the lace curtains in the parlor.

Masao couldn't bring himself to kill these innocents, especially not in America, where revenge and blood feuds seemed like something out of the distant past. He'd returned to Japan, his vow unfulfilled, his life effectively halted—for how could he take a wife or carry on a profession, a man who'd failed to take the revenge for which his father's ghost cried out?

When he heard, through an American acquaintance in Yokohama, that a man named Gallagher was coming to Japan, his interest had pricked up. Could it be that, after all these years, the Gallagher family had managed to find out what had happened to Morgan and the heirloom sword?

It was easy enough to keep track of the Gallagher man's movements through his friends in Yokohama; though when Masao realized it was *Hartley* Gallagher who'd come, he began to lose hope. He'd never thought Hartley anything but a pompous fool. Surely the family wouldn't have entrusted him with such a delicate task? As for Tessie, the little sister—he remembered her fondly, but of course a woman wouldn't be burdened with the responsibility of tracking down Morgan Gallagher and the *daimyo*'s sword.

As Tessie darted about Japan from one obscure spot to another, though, it had seemed quite likely that she was indeed the member of the family charged with making contact. Masao had come to Matsue with every intention of arranging a meeting. He had been watching Tessie and Jason when she fell into the canal. A lucky accident for him—if it was an accident. Masao scowled at the puppets on the stage. A fall into a canal, a rock dropped into the sea caves, a second rock slide in the mountains. Somebody was interfering in his plan to follow Tessie until she found Morgan and the sword.

And his other plans, too, were falling by the wayside. He had not the least objection to killing Morgan Gallagher, if the man still lived. He didn't much care whether Hartley lived or died. But he *could not* carry out his sworn revenge on brave, sweet Tessie. Outgoing, cheerful, stubborn, she was the exact antithesis of everything he'd been brought up to revere in women. And she was infinitely more fun than the meek Japanese women with their downcast eyes and murmuring voices—women, Masao thought with scorn, such as his betrothed, Shizuka, had no doubt turned into by now. He had barely seen her in the past years. She'd been a child when he left for America, and since he came back only to confess failure and put off their marriage indefinitely, she had avoided him. But this prolonged journey with Tessie Gallagher was confirming what he'd suspected ever since he returned from America. Even if he were free to marry, Masao would be inexpressibly bored with a quiet, proper Japanese wife who had nothing to say for herself.

Not that he wanted to marry a redheaded barbarian, either. If only there existed in the world a girl with slanting black eyes and smooth black hair and a porcelain face of pure Japanese beauty, a girl with spirit and liveliness and a mind of her own but also with a good grasp on Japanese manners.

Masao sighed and shook his head to rid himself of his fantasy. In any case, marriage was not for him. His destiny led him wherever Tessie was going, to the long-delayed confrontation with Morgan Gallagher, to the return of the *daimyo*'s sword. And then? He could see only two paths, both of them intolerable. He might let the Americans live, in which case his father's ghost would haunt him, vengeful and thirsty for blood. In that case, he would be a man without honor and could not possibly assume a normal life with a wife and children.

The other path, the one of duty, required him to kill the Americans. Masao thought he might even be able to strike at sweet Tessie, if she tried to deny him the *daimyo*'s sword. But he had become too much a man of the new Japan to do such a thing with an easy conscience. If he killed the Americans, Masao knew, his next step would be to turn himself in to the nearest authorities with a full confession. The new Japanese laws took no cognizance of honor and revenge and duty; he would be simply a murderer, destined for death himself. Not that he'd want to live . . .

There was just one way out. If Tessie understood the play—if she would voluntarily invite him to take back the *daimyo*'s sword—then, like Tankai in the play, he could claim that his debt of gratitude to her was stronger than the blood debt of revenge.

Please, Tessie, Masao prayed silently as the scene on the stage came to its moving close. *Please understand what I am trying to tell you. Please offer, of your own accord, to give me back the sword that your uncle stole. Please spare me the duty of killing you once you have led me to the sword's hiding place.*

The lights brightened; the puppets became lifeless statues of wood and brocade; the puppeteers came out from behind their creations and bowed. Masao turned to Tessie. He was encouraged to see tears in her eyes, discouraged to see that her hand was tightly clasped in Jason's.

"Did you enjoy the play?"

"Oh, yes," Tessie said without removing her hand from Jason's.

"I thought it might be hard for you to understand," said Masao. "It is rare for Americans to face the conflict between love and honor that we Japanese know so well." How could they face such a conflict, indeed—a people without honor?

"Not so rare as you might think," said Tessie, remembering a girl of sixteen who had lost her lover when she chose to stay with the family who needed her.

Masao saw how sad she looked and felt joyous in proportion. Perhaps she did understand what was really going on, why he had insisted on traveling with them.

"What if the conflict were between an American and a Japanese?" he hinted. "Would you always choose your own countryman, or would you choose the one who deserved to win?"

Jason's hand squeezed Tessie's like a symbol of possession. For the first time she realized that they had been sitting like lovers, hand in hand since the play began. She flushed angrily and withdrew her fingers. What was Masao hinting at? Did he know about her and Jason? Did he think that now, because she'd quarreled with Jason, she might be available to him? The thought hurt her deeply. She'd thought better of Masao than that.

"I would not choose any man," she said. "I go my own way."

She swept out of the theater well ahead of the two men, head high and cheeks flaming to match her crown of red hair.

Masao watched her departure with a heavy heart. However much Tessie might deny it, he thought, it was plain for all to see that she was deeply in love with Jason Lancaster. What was this talk about "going her own way?" A woman was too weak to choose for herself. A woman would always act to please her lover. And Tessie's lover was Jason Lancaster, and Jason wanted to sell Morgan's legacy—the *daimyo*'s sword, the heirloom of the family, the honor of Masao's family—for *money*.

He might very well have to kill all three Americans.

Chapter Sixteen

On the way to Kasadake, Tessie had to admit that it was just as well that they'd lingered so long at Masao's house. The first part of the journey had been easy enough by *jinriksha*. But as they penetrated deep into the mountains, the road became a path, and the path a rocky track. They had to scramble out of the *jinrikshas* over and over again to clamber over slides of fallen rock or to struggle up a nearly vertical stretch of path where steps were carved into the rocks and the gorge beside the path fell down in dizzying swoops of cliff to a gurgling river. If Tessie hadn't been fully recovered, she would never have been able to manage it.

The last stretch of the pathway was the worst, and the loveliest. The *jinriksha* coolies turned back when they reached a certain pile of standing stones, muttering, "Jigoku! Jigoku!"

"Why do they call this lovely valley Hell?" Tessie asked. "I don't think I have seen a more beautiful place in all Japan." Above them towered densely wooded mountains; below, the blue-green of the trees was broken by the flash of tumbling water. All was peaceful, remote, and inexpressibly serene. Tessie felt she was beginning to understand the *yamabushi,* the priests of the outlawed mountain cult of Shugendo, who retired to lonely mountains such as these to live alone while they cultivated their mystical powers. It was easy, here, to believe that the mountains were alive with their own tutelary spirits; easy, too, to picture oneself settling into this solitude for a life of prayer and meditation. Tessie almost wished she were free to do so herself. Here, alone in the mountains, with no distractions but the spray of waterfalls and the call of the birds, perhaps she could heal her bruised heart and get over the childish longing for love and trust that kept getting her in so much trouble.

"It is very beautiful," she repeated softly.

"You haven't," said Masao with a grim smile, "seen the path before us yet."

Only a few hundred yards past the cairn of stones, Tessie began to understand why this lovely ravine had received the appellation of Jigoku. The path was nothing more than a series of steps and handholds right along the face of the rocks that hung out over the foaming river. A single misstep, a missed handhold, and she would be dashed to pieces on the rocks beneath the water.

"Can't a better path be made?" she gasped after one particularly trying passage over rocks made damp and slippery by a trickle of water from some mountain stream above them.

"The government has many plans for improving the roads," said Masao without a smile. "The *daimyo* of Shiroyama, who once ruled this province, had similar plans. Road work is expensive, and this is a poor province. Don't hold that root; it's about to pull out of the cliff."

He took Tessie's hand and guided her fingers to a better hold, a deep crevice in the rock itself. Still looking at her, he felt his own way forward, casually conversing about road work and the old *daimyo* as if he didn't even need to think about his next step.

"You seem to know this province very well," Jason commented when they had passed the last of the precipitous steps and were once more on a level path above the gorge.

"My father—" Masao bit his lip for a moment, then shrugged imperceptibly and went on as if there'd been no pause. "My father was a sworn man of the *daimyo* of Shiroyama."

"But you are not?"

"The old ways are over," said Masao. "There is no more *daimyo*. There is a governor now. The *daimyo* is a private citizen."

"I wonder who wanted us to come this way?" Jason said to the tranquil air.

"I have been wondering the same thing," said Masao as if he did not catch the suspicion in Jason's tone. "The path we have just traversed would have been an excellent place for an . . . accident. Tessie, are you sure these messages come from Morgan?"

"No one else could have known the phrases he used," Tessie said quietly. Then she wondered if that were true. The first message, the newspaper advertisement, had been like that. The other clues could have come from anybody. But who else would have any interest in her movements? It had to be Morgan.

After that one difficult section, the path widened again, and they had a fairly easy walk to the next village. Here, as everywhere in these remote hills, the entire population of the village turned out into the single street to get a sight of the barbarians. Tessie was used to this kind of unwanted attention by now; she smiled at the old grandmothers, pinched a baby's fat cheek, and was rewarded by squeals of laughter from the baby and from the half-dozen other children who

crowded around her skirts. She finished the perfor-
mance by fishing in her satchel for a handful of sweets
wrapped in shiny paper, a gift that convinced the
children, at least, that fire-haired barbarians were
most desirable visitors to their village.

This village had no inn, but they were told that
there was a teahouse at the far end of the street where
they could rest and eat before going on. They threaded
their way down a muddy lane lined with wooden
houses whose thatched roofs almost brushed the cliffs
behind them. The eaves were hung with bunches of
radishes and beans, and from each house came a
plume of blue smoke from the center hearth fire. The
villagers' faces were wrinkled and dried from years of
sitting around those smoky fires.

The teahouse was just another wooden house, made
grand by the addition of a porch shaded by a rickety
bamboo trellis. The old man dozing at one end of the
porch proved to be the proprietor; waking with a start,
he bowed and invited the foreigners to rest inside
while he made their tea.

"I wouldn't go in," Jason advised Tessie in an
undertone. "Fleas."

Masao had to concur, but he made a few remarks
under his breath about the insects that inhabited the
beds in American hotels.

They sat on straw mats on the porch and listened to
the proprietor bustling about inside, heating water for
their tea and shouting abuse at two heavyset men who
had been monopolizing the little charcoal fire. Scraps
of his aggrieved sentences came out to them in
disjointed phrases, broken by a rumble of discontent
from one of the men he'd disturbed. "Take your sake
kettle and—I don't care *whose* servants you are, the
foreign guests want their tea—all right, you may tell
him I said so; he's not the lord now, you know!"

Eventually the old man came out again with a tray.
They leaned back against the mud-plastered walls of

the teahouse and drank hot, weak tea with an unfamiliar taste to it.

"Tea is not grown in this province," Masao explained, "and anything that must be bought for money is too expensive for these peasants to use it generously. They add mountain herbs to make the tea go farther. It is a very healthful drink," he added, seeing Jason's dubious look at his cup.

"It probably is," Jason agreed. "It smells like new-mown hay, which is a most invigorating odor. The only trouble is that it tastes like new-mown hay, too, and that's not quite so attractive."

When Masao was not looking, Tessie passed Jason one of her remaining sugar candies. "Dissolve this in the tea," she whispered. "It helps disguise the taste."

Jason gulped down the sugared tea and made a face. "Morgan Gallagher will have a certain amount of explaining to do, if we ever catch up with him. *Why* does he want us to climb Kasadake?"

"Do you want to go back?"

"Do you?"

"Absolutely not," said Tessie. "Morgan is my uncle. I have to find him. But you don't have to come with me. I'm sure your business is suffering from this prolonged absence."

Jason gave her an enigmatic smile. "Ah, but think what the infusion of money from Morgan's legacy will do for the business!"

At least, Tessie thought drearily, he wasn't pretending any longer that he had come on this long journey for love of her. It should make her feel better, not having to fend off Jason's pretense at love. Instead, she just felt as though all the brightness and beauty had drained out of the day, leaving her too tired to go on.

"Those men the teahouse keeper was shouting at," Masao said in a low voice. "They've left, did you notice? While you and Jason were talking."

Tessie was too dispirited to care much about the movements of a couple of strange Japanese. "What of it?"

"Probably nothing. I wonder if we should go on."

Tessie roused herself sufficiently to look into the dark, smoky interior of the teahouse. "I don't want to stay here tonight, do you?"

"No. You're right; we'd be safer to keep moving."

Masao was tense as they set out again. Tessie privately thought he was imagining things. The only danger posed by that dirty little teahouse had been that of picking up some unwanted fellow travelers. She resisted the urge to scratch and told herself that she was imagining things. Just because the place was muddy and smoky didn't mean it harbored fleas—or that she did, having rested there for half an hour.

It was Masao's nervousness, though, that saved them. The path on the far side of the village was broad and level, and they walked along at a good pace. Tessie thought about the weight of the satchel over her shoulder, and about the possibility of stopping in a proper inn with a bath so that she could get rid of the imaginary fleas that plagued her. She also thought about the beauty of the wind-blown trees clinging to the mountainside above the path, and about anything and everything except Jason Lancaster, who was not—so she swore to herself—*not* going to occupy her wayward heart for another minute.

Jason strode ahead, scowling at the mountains and occasionally glancing back impatiently to see that his companions were keeping up. His grim, black-browed face gave no clue to his thoughts. Probably, Tessie supposed, he was eager to finish this journey, collect his money, and get back to his business.

And Masao walked behind them, constantly scanning the path on both sides, looking back and peering ahead, listening with the intensity developed during his early samurai training.

"Tired?" Jason asked after they'd trudged up a long, steep way to come out on the crest of a hillside, just a bump in the side of the larger mountain, from which the deeply wooded hills stretched out before them like a sea of blue-green trees.

"Yes. No. It doesn't matter." But when he took her elbow and guided her to an outcropping of rock where she could sit, she didn't protest.

"Well, *I'm* tired, even if you aren't." Jason threw himself down on the ground beside her and rested his head on her knee. He closed his eyes and relaxed into the embrace of the ground with an almost palpable, sensual pleasure.

A well-behaved, proper young woman would have told Jason Lancaster to sit up and take his face out of her knees. A sensible young woman would not have allowed herself to enjoy the treacherous pleasure of feeling Jason's cheek against her leg, of pretending for a moment that they were lovers and friends and that she could trust him as much as she needed to.

The events of the last few weeks had demonstrated time and again that Tessie was neither proper nor sensible; so she decided that it was pointless, at this late date, to aspire to virtues that were clearly so far beyond her grasp. The sun-warmed rock was warm and comforting at her back, and Jason was half-asleep and took no notice when her fingers drifted across the crisp tangle of his black curls. Masao was not looking at them; he was pacing up and down as if he thought he had to keep guard at all times.

The outcropping of stone where Jason had seated her was carved by wind and water into a natural chair, a bowl shape that cradled Tessie and offered a rest for the back of her head. She leaned back and closed her eyes and gave herself up to sensation; the warm sun on her face, the soft rustle of the breeze and the crackling of autumn leaves, the whisper of water in the gorge, and the soft, crisp feel of Jason's hair under her hand.

In this moment of peace, even the aching of her legs was almost pleasant. It was good to stride over hills and valleys, using one's body as it was meant to be used, to become tired in the fresh autumn air, and to look forward to food and a bath at the end of the day's travel. All the little ordinary pleasures of life seemed sharper and brighter because it was Jason who shared them with her now. When the beauty of an ancient *torii* or a weathered wooden house caught her eye, she could beckon Jason to her side and know that he would share her pleasure. A steep hill that would have been merely tiring and boring with another companion became an exercise in friendly competition with Jason, as they scrambled to the top together and both pretended not to be the slightest bit short of breath— until he made her burst into laughter at her own pretense.

Jason never missed anything around him. A hidden flower, an ancient monastery, the flicker of expression that meant Tessie was about to laugh at one of his outrageous tales—he savored each moment of life to the fullest, and he was teaching Tessie to do the same. She had never felt so alive, so aware of the minutest details of physical sensation, as during these happy weeks of travel through Japan with Jason Lancaster.

Happy weeks? Tessie questioned herself, startled at her own thoughts. But yes—despite strain and worry and heartbreaking disappointment, despite lost love and betrayed trust, somehow what she retained of this journey was a feeling of joy. Silver flash of a waterfall, red-and-gold fire of the maples at Nikko, turquoise depths of the sea caves, and, running through all like a golden thread, the laughter and companionship and firm support of Jason's presence.

I'm glad it happened, Tessie thought. *I'm grateful for it all—yes, even for those mad nights when he made me think he loved me. It hurt, in the end, but at least I have that to remember. Maybe I'll never know real love*

*and a family and a home of my own, but I will always
have these moments to treasure in my heart.*

And after all, what harm could there be in remembering the sweetness of love and forgetting the pain
and betrayal? Tessie's hand smoothed over the wayward curls of black hair on Jason's forehead, and she
knew that there could still be great harm in her
selective memories. She had to keep on guard against
him. And Jason was so natural and friendly, so easy to
get along with, that he could still be very dangerous to
her.

The stream far below them rippled and gurgled, the
wind brushed Tessie's cheek, the autumn sun warmed
her face, and the leaves crackled behind her. The real
danger came upon her so fast that she had no warning
at all. A branch snapped under a heavy foot, a hoarse
shout broke the air, and as Tessie instinctively threw
up one hand to cover her face, something shining as
brightly as the sun slashed downward so close that the
breeze of its passing cooled her sun-warmed cheek.

"Hai!" Masao shouted. Tessie saw him only as a
blur of movement through the autumn air. Something
struck her on the shoulder, knocking her off the stone
outcropping and sideways to the very verge of the cliff.
She clutched at roots and small plants to save herself;
something had thorns, it was biting into her hand, but
she dared not let go. Jason was on one knee between
her and the burly man who had come out of nowhere.
The strange man was whirling a sword around his
head and chuckling, savoring the moment before he
brought death down on the head of an unarmed man.
Masao was some distance away, facing another swordbearing man with nothing but his bare hands. He
wasn't even wearing his kimono to protect him. Two
of them, thought Tessie, and both armed. It's hopeless.

But her body wouldn't let her give up hope. She
clung stubbornly to the thorny branches, and as the

235

man before Jason drew his sword back for the death blow, she found the strength to get her feet under her again. Still dazed and breathless, she threw her whole body toward the attacker's legs in a clumsy, twisting motion. She barely grazed his ankles, but the unexpected movement was enough to deflect the blow slightly. The big man, grunting in surprise before the blow even reached his victim, slumped forward on his knees and dropped the blade even as it touched Jason's arm. Blood spattered Tessie, and she screamed in hopeless denial.

"You shouldn't have interfered," said Masao's voice from somewhere above the swaying, hot, sticky hell she inhabited. "I had everything well under control." He knelt before her and took her face in his hands, gently shaking her back and forth until she opened her eyes.

"Tessie, it's all right now."

"Jason," Tessie said hopelessly. *"Jason."*

"My coat will never be the same again," said Jason. Tessie dared to look for the first time. He was white as his shirt, and the sleeve of his coat was soaked through with blood, and there was more blood on the ground.

"Tessie, *Tessie,"* Masao said urgently. "He is bleeding badly. You must stop the bleeding. I have to see to these two worthless brutes." Even as he spoke, the man who had wounded Jason stirred and moaned. Masao kicked backward with his bare heel, casually, not even looking, and hit the man in the jaw with a soft thump that sent him back to the ground.

Gritting her teeth, Tessie knelt beside Jason and tried to take his slashed coat off without hurting him. Every time she moved, a fresh spurt of blood pumped over them both. In desperation, she yanked at the fabric where it was cut through. It came away in her hand, coat sleeve and shirt sleeve together, exposing a long, vicious gash that ran from wrist to elbow.

"Take my shirt to bandage it," Jason told her. His

teeth were clenched, and he was breathing in short gasps.

Tessie shook her head. "Petticoat's easier." She lifted her skirt and began ripping strips off the long flounces of cotton eyelet. "Isn't it a good thing it was already torn?" she said. "Makes it easier now."

"When did that happen? Just now? You're hurt?"

"Don't leap about like that," Tessie said severely. "It makes the bleeding worse." She wrapped a long strip of lace-edged cotton around Jason's arm and secured the knot with her teeth. "And no, I tore it in the rock slide."

"But that was—"

"Weeks ago. I know. I'm not," Tessie confessed, "very good about mending clothes."

Jason regarded her through slitted eyes as she tied another strip about his upper arm, twisting as tightly as she dared. "That feels as if you're trying to cut my arm off. Are you trying to finish the samurai's job for him?"

"Do you want to leave any more of your blood on this mountain?" Tessie retorted. "Act like a man. You can bear a little pain in the interest of saving your life."

"Bad-tempered, a bad mender, and with a cruel streak, too."

"Altogether," said Tessie, "a poor prospect for matrimony. Aren't you lucky that I'm going home to marry Ricardo?"

"Desperately," Jason agreed with a twist of his lips. "Not to mention that you're an expert at bandaging wounds, and that Masao is a master of unarmed combat. I can't tell you when I've felt so lucky."

Now that the bleeding had stopped, Tessie was able to give in to the trembling that had threatened her steadiness ever since Masao forced her into awareness. How close they had all come to death! She could scarcely credit it now; both the vicious attack and their present safety seemed unreal. The peace of the autumn afternoon surrounded them again. But the hot smell of blood covered the scent of drying leaves, and a few paces away Masao was speaking harshly to two unarmed, sick-looking, and sheepish men. The most puzzling thing of all was that they spoke as if they knew one another, or at least as if they all knew what this was about. Could Masao have planned this? Surely not. He had just saved their lives.

Jason seemed to have fallen into a light doze, his head resting against the same rock where Tessie had been sitting just before the men came at them. She leaned back against the rock and tried to make sense of the rapid, angry Japanese flowing back and forth between Masao and the two strangers.

They all seemed to be angry with one another, but not about the fight. The methods of fighting were what they seemed to be arguing about.

"I am ashamed of you, Tasadake Masao," said one of the two strangers. "To think that the son of a samurai would stoop to fighting like a peasant!"

"You cannot feel more shame than I feel for you. Since when does the *daimyo* of Shiroyama employ samurai who can be disarmed by a child's tricks? A man like my father would have killed the three of us before we had time to feel alarm. And *he* would not have attacked by surprise, but honorably, face to face."

"Ah, yes," said the second man, the one who had tried to kill Jason, "we all know about Tasadake Kokushi and his great prowess against foreigners!" And a hideous sneer distorted his already ugly face. "Why, he could not even keep the *daimyo*'s sword— and you, his son, instead of redeeming his honor, have made friends with the foreigners and defend them!"

Masao's face had gone hard as carved stone, but he spoke in a level tone that betrayed nothing of the pain he must be feeling. "It is not the place of a low-ranking failed samurai to taunt me. I know my duty, and I will act as required when the time comes. I have been hoping for this meeting. You will return to the lord of Shiroyama and tell him that these two foreigners are under my protection and that his attacks on them dishonor him and me. In the meanwhile—"

His bare foot flashed out in a blurry motion, and the two swords that lay on the ground went spinning away in tumbling silver arcs, flashing and dancing over the very edge of the cliff. The first samurai gave an inarticulate cry and plunged to the cliffside after them, stopping just short of throwing himself after his sword.

"As you consider it so easy to retrieve a sword," Masao said, looking between the anguished faces of the two samurai, "I suggest that you occupy your time in climbing down into the ravine to get your own weapons. Surely, when you go before the *daimyo* to announce your failure, you do not also wish the dishonor of going unarmed?"

He turned his back on the two men and strode to where Tessie and Jason awaited him. "If you can walk," he told Jason, "I think we should be moving on now. The night comes quickly in these mountains, and it will be cold. We should be able to find shelter in one of the villages ahead."

"What about those two?" Tessie asked.

"They made a mistake," Masao said briefly. "They will cause us no more trouble. Now, if you will excuse me while I dress, we really should go on. I apologize, Miss Teresa, for appearing before you like this, for I know that you Westerners are peculiar about the body; but one really cannot fight in kimono!"

Until that moment, such had been the shock of the attack, Tessie had not really thought about the fact that Masao had shed his kimono and sandals in the first moments to fight the two samurai clad only in his tightly wrapped loincloth. Now she blushed to look at the play of muscles across his dark gold skin, the heavy thighs and broad shoulders that had been concealed beneath his traditional Japanese garments. She stole glances as he crossed the clearing and put on his clothes again. And when she glanced at Jason, she was pleased to see that he was looking distinctly cross.

"He keeps himself in good shape, Masao does," Jason commented. "I thought you said he was an engineering student?"

"He appears to be many things that I did not know," Tessie said quietly. She wondered how much of that puzzling argument Jason had taken in, and what he made of it. She was longing to be alone with him so that they could talk it over. But in the meantime, she was not above annoying him by stealing a few more glances at Masao. "He saved our lives."

"I'm very grateful," Jason grunted, not sounding in the least so. "If I'd been awake—"

Tessie decided not to ask just what Jason thought he would have done, awake but still unarmed, against two trained fighting men with swords.

"*Can* you walk?" she asked, to change the subject. "Perhaps we should rest here a little longer?"

"Don't care for the company," Jason said, glancing at the two samurai who had attacked them. They were now standing at the edge of the ravine, looking gloomily down at their lost swords and conferring in low voices. "Besides, Masao is right—wouldn't do to be caught out in the cold in these mountains." He stood with his usual fluid grace but spoiled the effect by turning white and grasping Tessie's shoulder for support.

"Wait!" The older of the two men, who seemed to be in charge, came forward as they were about to set forth on the path. "You spoke of walking to the next village for shelter, Tasadake Masao? That will not be necessary. You must know that my lord's home is closer than any village. He will be pleased to offer you hospitality."

"I think," said Masao, nose in the air, "all things considered, we would prefer to stay in an *honorable* house."

The samurai's skin flushed from bronze to dark copper, but he persisted. "I beg you, Tasadake Masao. We were wrong to attack you. We did not understand that you had good reasons for acting as you did. But since you have not deigned to tell us what your good reasons are, how can we return to the *daimyo* and explain ourselves to him? We can only report that we have failed. He will probably order us to commit *seppuku*."

"That seems entirely appropriate to me," said Masao.

"But our swords are lost!"

"Yes. A most distressing situation, is it not? As you took pains to remind me, my father faced the same dilemma. He found an honorable solution. I feel sure that you will do the same."

"Masao!" Tessie grabbed his arm and pulled him to her so that she could whisper in his ear. "Masao, did I understand what those men are saying? Will their master order them to commit suicide if they go back without us?"

"Probably. It is no concern of ours."

"But he won't hurt us if we are his guests?"

"No. Not once I explain the situation to him."

"I *wish* you'd do that for me," Tessie said. "But if you think we would be safe with this—this *daimyo*, Masao, then I think we really ought to go back with these men. *I* do not wish to have anyone's death on my conscience. And besides, if you don't explain to the *daimyo*, what's to prevent him from sending other men to attack us, more men, better armed? Please, Masao. I am *tired* of perfect strangers trying to kill me. I just want to find my uncle and go home. If talking to the *daimyo* would settle things, let's go and do it. Besides—" She glanced at Jason. "I really don't think he should walk too far, Masao."

Masao acceded to her request at last, with a great show of reluctance, but Tessie felt that he was not ill pleased with the way things had turned out. One of the samurai who had attacked them volunteered to run on ahead, to tell the *daimyo*'s servants to prepare rooms and send horses for the guests; the other followed them, scowling at the trail while Masao discoursed airily on techniques of armed and unarmed combat in Japan.

"I can see that you were rather puzzled by our argument," he told Tessie. "You must understand that these two men, lowly worms that they are, come originally from the class of samurai—the warriors of Japan—like my own family. Samurai were the only persons permitted to bear arms in old Japan, and so they thought it a mark of honor to fight only with their swords. The peasants, being more interested in surviving than in honor, learned ways in which an unarmed man could face a samurai with no weapons but his bare hands and feet. Some of these fighting techniques are very interesting. I myself began to study them as an aid to meditation, since it is desirable to control both body and mind. But when I was in America, I used to practice daily so that I could keep my body strong, and since I have returned to Japan I've found it amusing to keep up the practice."

The man behind them snorted in disgust. "No true samurai would lower himself to fight like a peasant."

"*When* will you learn that the old days are over?" Masao demanded. "There are no more samurai. There is no *daimyo*. You are a servant of a private gentleman, and if you kill somebody you will be treated by the law just like any peasant who strangles his wife in a fit of rage. The old ways, the old privileges are gone. We must learn new ways of surviving in the new order."

"Ah. I suppose you new young men consider *honor* one of those outmoded old ways. That explains why you are consorting with the enemy."

"You talk nonsense, and it is not for such as you to question me!" Masao snapped. He strode out in front of the party, setting a pace that Tessie and Jason found hard to keep, and he did not speak again until they reached the present home of the lord of Shiroyama.

Chapter Seventeen

Beyond the clearing where they had been attacked, the path widened again, and soon they were met by grooms and horses led by the returning samurai—really, Tessie commented to Jason in an undertone, she did not know what else to call him! Masao might say that those days were over, but here before her stood a man who clearly lived only to fight at the command of his lord.

"Ah," replied Jason, "we may know the old days are over, and Masao may know it, but . . ."

"Are we absolutely sure the *daimyo* of Shiroyama knows it?" finished Tessie with an involuntary gurgle of laughter. He was right. All through this quest into Japan, they had been running into people who didn't seem to know that the old Japan was finished, wiped out to make way for the new industrial nation. But really, it was unfair of Jason to keep reminding her of the little jokes and silly comments they'd shared all through this mysterious journey. How was she ever going to put him out of her heart and go back to America alone if he kept being so *nice*?

They rode up the mountain to the *daimyo*'s residence in a blaze of glory suitable for visiting royalty. Evidently he had sent his most gorgeously equipped horses in a manner of apology for the attack on Masao's friends. Certainly Tessie felt rather drab and plain when she sat on her magnificently attired steed. The lacquered saddle that rose in high crests before and behind her was gilded with the *daimyo*'s family crest, a circle enclosing two flying cranes. The same motif was repeated in gold thread on the embroidered saddle cloths of crimson leather and worked into a tiny mosaic of gold beads on the sides of heavy bronze stirrups. The bridle was a scarf of scarlet silk that matched the scarlet ribbons tying up the horse's mane into a sequence of tufts. Even the horse's tail was encased in a long bag of red brocade, with gold cords dangling from the corners.

The man who had been *daimyo* of Shiroyama still dwelt in a mansion that must, Tessie thought, put to shame the modern residence of the provincial governor. A white-plastered square rose up to crown the mountain, with tier after tier of curved roofs rising in sharp, threatening points. The castle was surrounded by a dark stillness of water, shaded by tall, dark green pines. It was crowned by bronze statues that shone in the last rays of the sun.

As they came closer, she saw the outward signs of decay and poverty. The white plaster was crumbling off the walls to expose the stonework beneath, and a section of the moat had been filled in for a vegetable garden.

The interior of the house was equally gloomy and forbidding. Instead of the rice-paper screens, which let the light shine through and to which Tessie had become accustomed in Masao's home and in the inns where they stayed, there were heavy painted wooden screens on which dark, gloomy old battle scenes were dimly visible. Once, perhaps, the screens had been bright with gold lacquer and the halls had been lit with lanterns; now all was shadowy, dusty, gloomy, with age-darkened paintings and tarnished ancient suits of armor set up, over which Tessie stumbled as she hurried after the servant who was guiding them to their rooms.

She and Jason were housed in adjoining rooms. But in the bustle of arrival, somehow they had been separated from Masao, and they had not even greeted their host yet.

Host—or assassin? Tessie shivered and wondered if she had been wise in so quickly taking Masao's word that they would be in no danger from the ex-*daimyo* once he had "explained the situation." Suddenly she wanted very much to hear that explanation. She had a feeling that Masao had been keeping many things to himself on this journey. It was time to find out what he wasn't telling.

"You're worried," said Jason softly. Servants were running in and out of the room, dusting mats and laying out trays of soup and rice. Probably none of them spoke English; all the same, Tessie waited until they were alone for a moment before replying.

"I want to hear what Masao is telling this *daimyo*. But I don't want to leave you alone."

"There's no need," Jason told her. "We'll go together. Two inept eavesdroppers are better than one, don't you think? And I'm not having you wander the halls of this place alone."

"You need to rest!" Tessie protested.

"Tessie, I'm not an invalid. I've lost some blood; I'll be all right tomorrow. I can rest as well in the *daimyo*'s public rooms as here." There was a lacquered tray before them now with bowls of clear soup and rice. Jason picked up one of the bowls of soup and drank it down in three swallows. A serving maid who had been hovering in the back of the room tittered and covered her mouth politely.

"There! I'm fine. Drink your soup and let's go. We can finish the meal later."

The central room of the *daimyo*'s residence looked out on a wide courtyard lined with decaying walls and splintered doors. Here, once, the gentlemen who attended the *daimyo* would have dwelt when they were called upon. Masao's father would have served his times of duty in one of the rooms behind those collapsing walls. Now the rooms were empty, and no one had bothered to repair the walls where they began to crumble. The single maple tree in the center of the courtyard had already lost most of its leaves to the chill of the mountain air. Instead of the scarlet and bronze carpet of leaves they'd seen at Nikko, there was a dull brown sludge of damp, decaying leaves trampled into the mud where the paving stones had come away. Two lonely scarlet leaves still trembled on the lowest branch of the tree, defiant holdouts against the passing of their time of glory.

Masao stared at the desolate courtyard and tried to find words that would convince the *daimyo* of his mistake.

"Someone has sent this woman messages in the name of her uncle."

"Gallagher Morgan."

"Morgan Gallagher. They place their names backward, giving the family name last."

"What a curious people," the *daimyo* mused. "No wonder they have no proper understanding of honor." He sat cross-legged on a low dais at the end of the room, holding an eggshell-thin teacup between two long fingers—a tall yellow spider of a man, all bushy brows and long, pinched features.

"I am not sure of that. They are different from us, but I believe they may have their own kind of honor."

"What," inquired the *daimyo* rhetorically, "can be the honor of a barbarian, a person by definition without a lineage? As for the honor of a woman, surely you jest, Tasadake Masao?"

"I believe that such a thing may exist," said Masao quietly, "and that I may discover it on this journey. If I am wrong, I shall still be able to recover the sword. It is only to kill the three Americans and bring the sword back to you."

"At one time I should have been able to offer you a place of honor in my court for such a deed, wiping out the dishonor of your father. Now—" The daimyo waved one long hand sadly at the dilapidation of the open courtyard. "I have dwindled, as you see. I have made the mistake of outliving my season, Tasadake Masao." A hollow, painful cough interrupted him for a moment, and he bent over the teacup to ease the spasms. "I shall not cling to this world very much longer. Like those last two leaves on the maple, I feel that my time is past. Still, I do not wish to go to my ancestors and tell them that I allowed the Gassan sword to be stolen and did not even take revenge on the thieves."

"Would it not be better to let me bring back the sword?"

The *daimyo* regarded Masao through glittering dark eyes whose unblinking stare made Masao feel uneasy and very young. "Do you really believe that you can do that, Tasadake Masao?"

"The woman is being guided, either by Morgan Gallagher or by someone who possesses his legacy and wishes to give it to her. What could that legacy be but the Gassan sword? We know that when he disappeared he had no valuable possessions of his own. And he did have the sword."

"Is the woman necessary? Can you not go alone to Kasadake? A barbarian in such a small place would be easy to find."

"Kasadake may not be the final place; we have come

248

a long way already. As your servants must know, if it was they who tried to kill her before."

"I am surrounded by incompetents." The *daimyo* sighed.

"You should be glad of their failures," Masao said firmly. "It has been made clear that the clues she receives will be given to no one else. If she dies, you may be avenged, but the sword will be lost forever. Do you wish to tell your honored ancestors that the Gassan sword remains in barbarian hands because you acted impatiently?"

Masao had never spoken so bluntly to a man of the *daimyo*'s rank. He felt a quivering in the pit of his stomach, a deep uneasiness at going against everything he had been taught. Why was he arguing with this man who had been his father's lord? His place was to bow and accept.

The Americans did not bow and accept a command they thought to be wrong. Perhaps, as his mother continually charged, he had been corrupted by his years in America. Or perhaps, Masao thought, he had learned something of value.

"In my days of power," the *daimyo* mused, holding his teacup aloft to see the light passing through the thin sides, "in the old days, a young man who spoke so to a *daimyo* would have been grateful to be allowed the honorable death of *seppuku,* rather than being torn to pieces by the *daimyo*'s war horses. Even if the young man happened to be right, he would have paid with his life for disputing the *daimyo*'s decision. You," said the *daimyo* sadly, "are right. And you will be of more use to me following the barbarians than dead by your own hand—if you would accept such a command, Tasadake Masao?"

"With all respect, lord," Masao answered, "I think that I would not accept the command to commit *seppuku* at this time." He was not even the *daimyo*'s man, sworn to accept any command. He was merely the unimportant son of a disgraced follower. That made no difference. For hundreds of years, the Tasadake family had served Shiroyama; now he, the last and least important representative of that family, was setting his will up against that of the *daimyo*. The trembling in his midsection increased until he thought he might disgrace himself by becoming violently ill.

"I thought as much. So be it. The barbarians may go in safety from this house, and you will go with them, Tasadake Masao. I agree that it will be better to allow them to live until the sword is recovered. Then you will, of course, kill them."

"That may not be necessary," Masao said. "If they give the sword to me—"

"You would give up the chance of taking revenge for your father's death?"

"None of these three killed my father."

The *daimyo* gave a long, disgusted sigh and set the porcelain teacup down, very gently. He looked at Masao and shook his head sadly. "You have given up Japanese honor for Western ways, Tasadake Masao. Now who are you? Are you an American or a Japanese —or nobody? You cannot ride two horses."

"My lord has many horses in his stable still, does he not?" Having once successfully defied the *daimyo*, Masao found that the taste for argument was growing on him. "Among them, perhaps, there is a black stallion, fiery and spirited, the pride of your house and the sire of many fine colts. In another stall there may be a good, strong, gentle chestnut, trained to pace as you desire. You do not ride both horses at once, but each has his place in your stables. So it may be with Japanese and American ways. I believe that one may be a good Japanese and still take what is good from the Americans."

* * *

It was convenient that Japanese custom dictated the removal of shoes indoors. On their stockinged feet, Tessie and Jason had approached the *daimyo*'s audience room quite silently. They paused for a moment on the far side of screens and listened to the argument.

"They're talking too fast for me," Tessie confessed. "Can you make it out?"

"Nothing important. They're just comparing Japanese and American customs."

The *daimyo*'s voice came clearly through the layers of curtains and screens, high and imperious. "I say to you, Tasadake Masao, that you and those like you who accept the Americans are like a man who eats poison disguised as a sweetmeat. You see only that they are strong and rich, and you want to be like them—and so you have eaten the poison! Wanting to be American will eat away at your Japanese soul!"

"I do *not* want to be American!" Masao replied, sounding angrier than they had ever heard him. "I want only to take what is good from both worlds."

"That task has defeated many a cleverer man than you."

Jason shrugged and whispered to Tessie, "They may go on like this forever. Let's go on in and greet the *daimyo*, then we can retire for the night."

As he stepped through the maze of screens, a gilded panel of chrysanthemums and swallows in flight fell over with a clatter. "Who's there?" the *daimyo* cried out sharply. He was half on his feet when Jason stepped into view. One wrinkled hand fumbled in the folds of his rich brocaded kimono for a weapon. Masao had instinctively thrown himself before the *daimyo* as if to defend him.

Jason raised a placating hand. "I am sorry if I disturbed you," he apologized in English. "We wished only to greet our host and to thank him before retiring to our rooms for the night."

The *daimyo*'s bright, black eyes swept over Jason and Tessie, and Tessie felt as if he was reading her every thought—as if that single penetrating glance had told him all about her. "Is this woman considered beautiful in America?" he demanded of Masao in Japanese. "For myself, I do not see why you are so enamored that—"

"She is not only beautiful but clever, my lord," Masao smoothly interrupted, "for she speaks Japanese fluently."

"Ah!" The *daimyo* lapsed into silence, but he kept his eyes fixed on Tessie with a stare that she found very disconcerting.

"We were just comparing Japanese and American customs," Masao said. He looked very uncomfortable. Well, the *daimyo* had been berating him as they entered; the old man seemed to disapprove of Masao's friendship with them.

"Perhaps you have something to add to the discussion, out of your great understanding of the Japanese people and your wide travels," the *daimyo* said. His sarcastic words might have been addressed to either of them, but his gaze remained fixed on Tessie, and the short bark of laughter with which he ended his sentence said, as plainly as if he had spoken his opinion aloud, that he could not conceive of a woman's having ideas worth contributing. "What does a modern American woman think of old Japan?" he prodded as Tessie remained silent.

He wanted her to appear foolish, or rude, or worse —just to score a point off poor Masao, who had been defending them and himself. And how could she make a good showing, for Masao's sake, speaking a foreign language, stumbling amidst half-understood customs? Tessie felt her hair, uncombed and knotted from the day's travel, coiling into tight fiery ringlets. Blood rushed to her cheeks and burned through the palms of her hands.

She gave way, in one joyous rush, to a loss of temper so complete that it left her no time to feel self-conscious or awkward.

"Masao, you must interpret for me—my Japanese is not nearly good enough to speak on such matters," she said in English. "Tell the *daimyo* that the customs of the two countries are so different that it is impossible for me to compare them. In America it would be thought cowardly to attack an unarmed and unwarned party of travelers merely because one dislikes their nationality, and unmannerly for their host to interrogate them the minute they set foot in the door. In Japan, apparently, such behavior is so common that the lord of Shiroyama does not even feel the need to apologize for his servants' attack. How can I possibly compare two nations with such different standards?"

The *daimyo* watched her, impassive, unmoving, as Masao translated. Behind him, a wall covered with antique swords and lacquered shields reflected the last light of the setting sun. He raised one hand to point at the display. "A country without a past cannot understand the requirements of honor."

There was no need to wait for Masao to translate the cold, disdainful syllables. Tessie felt as if her coiled, tangled hair were turning into a basket of hissing red snakes. The blood burned in her cheeks and in the palms of her hands. She wanted to hit somebody. Instead, she marched past the *daimyo* and picked up the sword nearest his hand. "And a country where disputes are settled with *this* instead of with decent courtesy and discussion cannot understand the rudiments of civilized behavior." She glared at Masao, including him for the moment in her hatred of everything strange and foreign that surrounded her. "Tell your lord that he should train his people not to pick up the sword so quickly. We Americans may be barbarians to him, but at least we have learned better ways to settle our differences." With mocking care, she stooped and laid the sword on the floor before the *daimyo*'s dais. "Treasure this if you wish. Worship the past. But don't expect me to stand in awe of you because of it."

She spun on her heel and marched out of the room without waiting for the *daimyo*'s answer. Halfway down the long hall, she became aware of Jason silently keeping step behind her, and paused so that she could take his offered arm. She had thought he might need her support, but instead it was she who was trembling and leaned on him.

"I don't know what got into me," she confessed. "Are you very angry?"

"Angry?" Jason laughed. "Admiring. You were magnificent. You put that old man in his place as nobody has dared to do in all his life, I'll wager."

"Yes," Tessie said miserably. "It was inexcusably rude of me."

"Well, as you pointed out, his servants did try to kill us, and in America that's considered terribly bad manners."

Tessie could not repress a gurgle of laughter, but she choked it back as quickly as possible. "Yes, but it was not *clever*. We were going to chat casually and try to find out what's really going on, remember? Instead I fired a few salvos and left without learning a thing."

"Oh, I don't know," Jason said. "We learned one very important thing, and I don't think we'd have gotten much more if we'd stayed with the *daimyo* all night."

Tessie stopped before the door to her room and regarded him uncertainly. "We wouldn't?"

"No. The first thing Masao said was that we speak Japanese. After that, the *daimyo* wouldn't have said anything interesting while we were within earshot."

"Maybe not. But what did we learn?"

"Don't you think it was strange that Masao was so quick to warn the *daimyo?*"

"No, I don't," Tessie said crossly. She removed her hand from Jason's arm.

"You don't have any doubt of Masao's own motives for following us?"

"Accompanying us," Tessie corrected. "No, I don't. He just saved our lives—or have you chosen to forget that incident just because you didn't play a heroic role in it?"

A dark flush of anger stained Jason's face. "I'm not such a fool as that. He did save us; I only hope someday we find out why, and how he knew the attack was coming, and why he was so confident of being able to stop the *daimyo.* Unlike *some* members of this expedition, I'm not so blinded by Masao's muscles and smooth manners that I can't tell when a man is concealing something."

"You're jealous!" Tessie accused him.

Jason gave her a particularly nasty half-smile. "Well, somebody has to watch over you—for Ricardo's sake."

For a moment Tessie couldn't think who he was talking about.

Jason prompted her gently. "Your fiancé, in America. You do remember Ricardo, don't you?"

"Of course I do," Tessie claimed, furious at herself for having momentarily slipped.

"Are you sure?" Jason teased. "Just now you looked like somebody who couldn't even remember your precious Ricardo's family name."

Actually, Tessie thought, she was standing there looking like somebody who couldn't remember whether she'd already invented a last name for Ricardo, or what it might have been. This was impossible! Any minute she might give away her invention to Jason.

"I remember Ricardo very clearly," she said at last, "the more so because he is so different from you, Jason. You cannot imagine how much I wish he were at my side now! *He* wouldn't have gone to sleep and left another man to defend me from brigands—nor would he be so mean-spirited as to accuse that other man afterward. Ricardo isn't given to petty jealousies."

"What a good thing," said Jason without expression, "otherwise he might take exception to our prolonged travels together, don't you think? What *are* you going to tell him about me, Tessie?"

"Nothing! You would be of no interest to him whatsoever. Ricardo," Tessie said scornfully, "is a real man, not a petty businessman with his head in the till. You are no sort of threat to him at all, Jason, and he'd never worry about you for a minute. Ricardo—"

Jason cut her off with a shake of his head. "All right. I believe I've heard enough of Ricardo's virtues for one night, Tessie. Let's get some rest."

His face looked very white in the dusky glimmering of the hall. Tessie felt a momentary pang of guilt for railing at him like that; as he moved across the hall to his own room, she wondered if his wound was paining him.

The room allotted to her was most unappealing, with its trays of congealing food and its one window half screened by some kind of tall rushes outside and the oil lamp flickering in a corner. Tessie stood uncertainly in the middle of the floor, biting her lip. Perhaps she had been too hasty in dismissing Jason's suspicions of Masao. No! Masao was her friend; she felt that to be true, and she had to cling to what she knew in this dizzy maze of shadows and mysteries. But Jason was also her friend, and he had been injured that afternoon. He wasn't himself. She ought to go and see that he washed his cut arm properly and bound it up again with clean linen.

There were many little lamps lighting Jason's room, and three girls with glossy black hair knelt around him, giggling softly as they unwound the stained bandage. Tessie retreated soundlessly from the doorway and prayed that no one had noticed her; but as she left, she heard one of the girls say something with an inquiring tone, and the words, "fire-haired barbarian woman" were all too clearly audible.

In the few minutes while she'd been standing, unseen, at the doorway to Jason's room, someone had removed the trays of food and had brought hot water in a great bronze bowl. Tessie told herself how nice it would be to wash and take off her dusty clothes and go to sleep. But before she began, she pulled one of the heavy lacquered screens across her doorway, for privacy, and then set another one behind that.

The precautions were unnecessary. Jason did not come tapping at the screens to find out why she had come to his room. No doubt he was too busy, laughing and flirting with the three girls who'd fluttered to his side on the pretext of waiting on him.

He didn't come until the middle of the night, when Tessie was deeply asleep.

Her dreams had taken her into a strange, misty country of aching loss and grief. Morgan was there, somewhere out of sight just beyond the gold-and-crimson screen of maples; he was calling to her, but she could not hear what he said above the sound of the rushing river. Then, without her seeing or hearing anything different, somehow she knew it was Jason calling her, and she ran joyfully through the crackling carpet of autumn leaves to reach him. As she ran, the leaves rose thick about her feet, muddy and brown now, and the trees before her dulled in color to a tarnished bronze. They were only a painted wooden

257

screen after all, and she could not pass through to find Jason. The *daimyo*'s sword was heavy and cold in her hands, and she tried to raise it to hack through the screen, but she could not manage the blade. It seemed to turn in her hands so that the sharp edge was always menacing her. And she could not hear Jason any longer; he was gone too far away. She would never catch up with him now. Tears spilled out of her eyes and trickled down her cheeks.

A broad hand gently dried her face.

Tessie blinked twice and opened her eyes to a moon-dappled darkness and the warm, comforting reality of Jason's fingers brushing across her cheek. For a moment she hardly dared move, afraid that this was the dream and that the loss she'd just felt was the reality. Then she sat up in one swift motion.

"How did you get in here?"

"Through the door." Jason's voice was low, amused. He sounded perfectly in command of himself and the situation. Tessie was neither. She wanted to throw her arms around Jason and hug him for being there, real and palpable and alive. She wanted to remember that he was dangerous to her peace of mind and that she had not intended to allow him to get past her defenses again. And she wanted to know how he had got past her barrier of screens and stools without awakening her.

"I'm not totally clumsy," Jason said in surprise when she voiced this last question, "and you were sleeping very deeply. Actually, I was surprised myself that you didn't wake up when I moved the screens."

"And what made you think you could come barging in here in the middle of the night, invading my privacy?" Tessie demanded.

"Hush! You'll disturb the household."

Jason's lips came down on hers, muffling further protest. She knew she should fight against the embrace, but it was so sweet, and the poignant memory of her dream loss was still so sharp within her; how could she help but answer his kiss? Delight ran through her veins and stilled the protests of her wary mind. She clung to him and did not fight when he raised his head for a minute, then fell to kissing away the traces of tears on her cheeks.

"I heard you crying in your sleep," he murmured into the soft unbound coils of her hair. "Could I leave you to weep alone?"

"I didn't ask you to come . . ."

"I'm tired," said Jason with sudden ferocity, "of waiting to be asked. You keep taunting me that I'm not a *real man*, whatever that phrase means to you. You've been angry for years because I accepted your decision to stay at home with Mama. I suppose you wanted me to force you into doing what you really wanted. All right. I give in. If that's the kind of man you want, that's what I'll be. Starting *now.*"

He had already started, in fact; his hands were moving over her body with practiced skill as he spoke. Ribbons fluttered loose, and muslin shivered away from her shoulders, and his palms were warm and rough against her bare skin, allowing no more argument, no more denial. The weight of his body held her close, and he took her with a desperate urgency that Tessie could no more have stopped than she could have halted a river in full flood.

She could have cried out. She could have fought. He might even have freed her if she'd resisted him. But the little strength of mind she possessed, barely enough to resist his teasing courtship, was no stronger than a bare branch caught in the current of their mutual desire. There had been too many strained days of suppressing her feelings at the turn of his head or the lilt of his laughing voice, too many lonely nights of lying awake and staring at the cool moonlight. Now he was with her, and she did not have time to think, and she did not want to think. She slid her arms around his neck and pulled him down to her and let him do whatever he would.

She even did a few things herself, shameless in the urgency of her need—fingers tracing the long line of spine and buttocks, tongue and teeth nibbling at his earlobe, breasts springing to life at the feel of his crisp-curled dark hair. She was not Tessie now; she was an extension of the cool moonlight that played over their bodies, free as shadows in the wind to take and seek and give delight where it might be found. Jason gasped once, and the movements of his roving hands halted for a moment, gripping her hard.

"Did I hurt you?" Tessie murmured. She knew so little, really, of men's bodies.

"N-no," Jason replied with the ghost of a laugh shaking his voice. "No, I wouldn't say that exactly. Can you do that again—yes, *there—*"

The mastery was hers as he quivered with desire under her fingertips; and he took it back a moment later, searching out her own secrets with lips and fingers and limbs all bent to do her pleasure until she cried out and drew him close to her again. And then they were equal partners, giving and receiving pleasure in a dance of fire and moonlight, wind and water, until all the needs that had been building unslaked for so long were sweetly quenched, and they lay together, hearts pounding as one. The long shadows cast by the moonlight had hardly moved across the room in the eternity since they began.

As Tessie's pulse slowed and her breathing began to return to normal, so did her powers of reason. And some of her unthinking happiness slipped away. She moved slightly, fractionally withdrawing from Jason, and he sensed the beginnings of reserve before she could sit up. His arm encircled her, holding her close against his chest. "What's the matter now, Tessie?"

"Nothing. That is—"

Nothing, Tessie thought, or everything. She had

wanted Jason's love. She had wanted him to be a man she could trust. What had just happened between them was glorious if it included love and trust, but there had been no word of either in Jason's approach to her. "You took me by surprise. I wish you had given me time to think."

"If I had," Jason said with the air of a man presenting an irrefutable argument, "you would only have sent me away."

"Exactly!"

"Well, then. Isn't it a good thing you didn't think?"

"No." This time Tessie freed herself and sat up. She drew her opened nightgown about her shoulders. "I don't like being—hustled into things. I don't know why you came to me—"

"Don't you? How very slow you must be!"

Tessie refused to be drawn into sharing his amusement.

"I don't know what you mean by that, what we're to be to one another. I don't like being forced into things."

"Don't you? I thought that was your main quarrel with me—that I expected you to make up your own mind, instead of sweeping you off your feet. Haven't you held it against me all these years that I accepted your choice to stay with your family instead of carrying you off to marrying me?"

"That was different," Tessie protested miserably.

"Was it?" The amusement was gone from Jason's voice now, and the rustling noises she heard meant that he was dressing himself again. "In the last few months I've heard altogether too much from you about what a *real* man would do. You never seemed to tire of telling me how far I fell short of your ideal— but when I act as you say you want, you quarrel with that, too! The trouble with you, Tessie, is that you don't know what you want in a man. When I try to act like a gentleman and wait for you to make up your own mind, you despise me. You tell me that a real man like your precious Ricardo would just take what he wanted without waiting for the woman's consent! But when I act like that—and I might say that you certainly seemed to be consenting at the time—then you take offense at that, too. Well, I'm through playing your guessing games. Make up your mind what you want in a man—a real person or a romantic hero— then come tell me. God help me," said Jason, "I'll probably try to play whatever part you wish. But I think I'll just wait until you're through dithering about it."

And he was gone as silently as he had come, slipping between the screens like the ghost of her sad dream.

Chapter Eighteen

Tessie lay awake long after Jason left, telling herself that *she* had nothing to feel guilty about. If Jason had really loved her, he wouldn't have taken offense so easily. He was just looking for an excuse to put some distance between them, in case she thought his love-making implied some real commitment. The same thing he always did!

Or, at least, the same thing she always told herself. This time her old arguments were not entirely convincing. Perhaps she really had been wrong all along, expecting Jason to be something neither she nor he would have liked. Did she really want a romantic storybook hero who would sweep her off her feet and stifle all her words of protest with a masterful embrace?

It had been rather exciting when Jason behaved like that. It had been wonderful—at first. But afterward she hadn't been quite happy about it; she'd felt rushed and surprised, as if he were treating her like a toy rather than a friend and lover.

It was what she'd dreamed of, but was it what she wanted? Tessie tossed and kicked off her sheets. Being married to a man who never troubled to ask what she wanted would be distinctly unpleasant. It would be, in fact, just the sort of marriage that Shizuka was desperately determined to avoid, even at the price of being considered a scandal and a failure in her village.

Marriage to a man who could laugh with you and travel with you and take your hand and walk side by side with you as an equal seemed, suddenly, much more appealing to Tessie than the dark romantic dream she'd cherished for so long. Marriage, in fact, to a man like Jason—friend, companion, confidant.

Tessie was kept awake by the remorseless promptings of her own logical mind. If she didn't really want a man who would sweep her off her feet and ignore her objections, then she could not in honesty complain that Jason had abandoned her ten years ago. She had refused to marry him. He had even come back, a year later, to see if her situation had changed. True, he had been too quick to believe Hartley's lies about her—Tessie still did not feel that she should take *all* the blame for their separation— but he couldn't very well have thrown her over his shoulder and carried her off by force, as the hero of her imagination would have done. Or rather, if he had done that, she would have hated him for it.

When you got right down to it, she was probably too independent and stubborn for most men. Papa wouldn't have stood for a wife who set her own will up in opposition to his. Neither would Hartley. In fact, Jason was the only man she'd ever met who, faced with opposition from a mere female, would have grinned and said, "Let's discuss it."

And she had just driven him away.

Perhaps she should call him back.

Tessie's lips compressed against the urge to call Jason's name. *No.* It would be too humiliating, especially if—as seemed all too likely—he still rejected her after her apology. No, she would say nothing, not yet. They still had to climb the mountain of Kasadake together; they still had to solve the puzzle Morgan had set before them. If Jason really loved her, he would have ample opportunity to make some sign of his love, to give her some reasonable opening to discuss the matter again.

In the morning, Jason gave Tessie no openings whatsoever. As they prepared to set out on the mountainous way to Kasadake, he remained quiet and self-contained. He was pleasant enough, but there was no trace of the teasing fun and ebullient good humor that had enlivened earlier parts of the journey. His expressionless face was like a sheet of smooth glass from which everything glanced off.

Masao was equally silent, wrapped in his own thoughts and disinclined to offer any explanation for the strange attacks they had suffered from the *daimyo*'s servants. He did admit, when pressed, that he now knew all of the attacks upon Tessie to have been made by the two men he'd faced and disarmed the previous day. But he admitted that much only so that he could reassure Tessie that they would face no danger from now on.

"I have spoken with the *daimyo*. He understands that he made a mistake. His men will not trouble us again before we reach Kasadake."

"An interestingly limited promise," said Jason with a flash of his old spirit. "What about afterward?"

"I will be responsible for your safety afterward," said Masao. And it was true enough; he could look Jason in the eye while he said the words and not feel like a liar at all. If they found the Gassan sword on top of Kasadake, and if Tessie understood that she must give it back to Masao, then honor would be satisfied and Masao would protect the barbarians with his life. If she and Jason meant to take the sword and sell it for the money that Jason said his business needed, then Masao would personally kill them before the *daimyo*'s men got anywhere close to the party.

Either way, their safety was entirely his concern.

Jason looked as if he meant to question this promise, but Tessie intervened before he could say any more. "I'm glad to hear that everything would be peaceful from now on," she said hastily. "Let's get started. I understand it's a long climb."

They meant to walk all the rest of the way, partly because it would be simpler than managing horses on the steep paths and partly because, though he didn't say so to Masao, Jason did not altogether trust any horses and grooms that might be provided by the *daimyo*. As they set out in single file, the morning sun turned Tessie's braided crown of red hair into a glowing halo about her face and silhouetted the generous, strong lines of her body against the gold of dawn.

She had not, Jason supposed, intended to dress seductively. Perhaps she hadn't; perhaps it was just that he found the sight of her in any garments intolerably seductive. She probably thought she was being plain and straightforward and sensible in her stout walking shoes and a divided skirt, one of the new fashions for liberated women that Jason had jeered at when they were first seen in Yokohama. "All right for some sexless female who can't think of anything better than imitating a man," he'd said to a friend.

Tessie was definitely not sexless, and she didn't imitate men. She simply did what she set out to do as well as anybody, male or female, could do it. And one look at her made Jason swallow hard and eat all his mocking words on the unsuitability of curvaceous women in clinging skirts.

It was going to be, he reflected morosely, sheer hell to climb all the way up Kasadake behind a woman who twitched her bottom like that with every step she took, a woman he lusted after more each time he managed to get close to her. It was going to be damned near impossible to remember that she was a mixed-up, confused, unreasonable woman who didn't know what she wanted in a man and who couldn't be pleased no matter what he did. By the time they got halfway up the mountain, if he didn't do something, he was going to be ready to turn himself into anything from a court jester to a knight in shining armor, depending on Tessie's wishes of the moment.

And she still wouldn't be pleased.

There was only one thing to do. Jason took the lead. He set a punishingly swift pace that should have had them at the top of Kasadake by midafternoon.

There were, however, a few interruptions.

First a black kite exploded out of a tree directly into Jason's face and sent him and Tessie scrambling down a miniature rock slide. Jason helped Tessie up, she thanked him with frigid courtesy, and they made it back up the steep slope to the path with perfect dignity marred only by a few scrapes and bruises.

A few minutes later, Tessie thought she saw Morgan himself, seated between two pine trees on top of a nearby ridge. She left the path to beat her way to the top of the ridge, followed by Jason and Masao; but when she reached the trees, there was nothing to be seen but a black kite circling lazily just overhead.

"Tengu," Masao suggested, and Tessie had no better explanation.

That detour had cost them some time, and the rain-swollen brook that next blocked their path cost even more time as they had to climb up the side of the mountain until they found a possible crossing place.

"Strange to see a brook flooded like this in autumn," Jason muttered. "Rest of this mountainside doesn't look as if this area had seen rain for weeks. And it wouldn't be melting snows, not at this time of year."

Masao's lips formed the word *tengu* again, but he forbore to voice his suspicions of the mountain goblins. By the time they'd been working their way downward for an hour, Tessie was about to agree with him. Thick underbrush and rough ground kept forcing them away from the brook until they were thoroughly lost. Even Jason had to admit, when they passed the same great moss-covered boulder for the third time, that he had no clear idea where the path was.

"Not to worry," he assured Tessie. "We can use the sun to keep us going in one direction. The main thing is to avoid going in circles anymore. Sooner or later we must come either to the path or to the bare upper slopes of the mountain, where we'll be able to see our way plainly."

Tessie hoped he felt more confident than he sounded.

"I don't think—" Masao began, then fell silent. Tessie strained to see his face.

She could see nothing but a pale blur against the darkness of the trees. Even far above their heads, the green-black darkness was absolute now, untouched by any gilding from the sunlight.

"Jason," she said gently. "Jason, the sun has set."

Before Jason could think of a new and insanely cheerful suggestion, like waiting for moonrise to guide them in the same way, a man stepped out of the clearing on the opposite side from Masao. Tessie gasped. Jason whirled to face the intruder, and Masao dropped into his fighting stance, knees flexed and hands slightly raised.

"My greetings to the honorable strangers," said the placid voice of a very old man, with shrill wheezing sounds and the crackling noises of old age interrupting the words. "May this humble person offer to guide you to the village?"

"There's a village near here?" Jason sounded surprised, and no wonder. In all their long day's wanderings they had seen no sign of human habitation.

"Hirayu," said the old man reprovingly. "Silver mining, and an inn with hot baths fed by the springs.

It is listed in *Murray's Guide to Japan*. Don't you barbarians read anything about this country before you set out?"

His tone was so prosaic, so matter-of-factly reproving, that all their half-expressed imaginings about *tengu* and miraculous waterfalls seemed the games of children frightening themselves into believing their own ghost stories. Without discussion, the three of them followed the old man along the path that seemed to open before him through the dense woods. He walked as surely as one might who had lived his life on this mountain, and they followed him with the absolute trust of children. Tessie was directly behind him. She found that even when she could not see the ground beneath her, the old man's robe was easy to follow. It was decorated with some sort of white pattern that stood out against the dark background, clear enough to see even in this twilight.

Soon they came out onto a rocky slope, barren of all but the smallest twigs of trees, and Tessie found another reason to keep her eyes fixed on the old man's robe. If she looked to her left, she could see lights twinkling—the lights of the village he had named, no doubt—but they were far below, and the cliff fell away into a dizzying expanse of empty blue air.

And she was so tired! Too tired to look behind her for Jason's encouraging smile, too tired to ask the old man how long it would take to reach the village and why they were taking such a roundabout route; too tired to do anything but place one foot in front of another in blind trust.

Presently the old man paused and reached out his hand for hers. "We are coming to a difficult place," he told her, and Tessie could see by the glimmer of starlight that the ledge they'd been walking on was broken just ahead of them. "You had better let me steady you."

She shuddered, reached out to lean on the proffered

arm, and felt two strong hands close on her wrists. A sharp tug jerked her forward; she had no time to feel fear before she was dangling out over empty space.

"What are you *doing?*" she cried. "Help me back up!" If he let go, she would spin down the rock face, plummeting and whirling through a hundred feet of blue emptiness. The lights of the village of Hirayu were far beneath her, the rock was smooth against her feet groping for purchase, the hands of the madman who held her out over the abyss were as steady as iron about her aching wrists. "Jason!"

"Your friends have been deceived," said the crazy peasant calmly. "They followed an illusion which they took to be you and have gone by the correct path to the village."

This was not possible. Jason had been only a step behind her. *"Jason!"* Tessie screamed. Her voice echoed off the rocks before and below her.

"Jason—Jason—Jason," the echoes repeated as if mocking her cries for help.

And far away, far below her, she thought she heard an answering call.

"You see? Your friends are too far away to help you now," the old man said. "Think of your sins!"

He was going to drop her to her death. However he had misled Jason and Masao, they could not get there in time to save her. Tessie's head whirled, and her arms ached, and each painful breath she drew was inexpressibly sweet.

"It is not yet time to resign yourself to death," the old man said above her, as though he could read her thoughts. "You must be purified. Think of your sins!"

Jason and Masao stared upward toward the cliffs from which Tessie's cry had come.

"Is that Tessie?"

"How did she get up there?"

"How did we get down here?"

Jason rubbed his eyes and looked back along the path they'd been following. He could have sworn that Tessie and the old peasant had been just a few paces ahead of them, vague shapes glimmering in the dying light. Now he saw nothing but trees, a bush with white flowers, the pebbled path. He felt like a man awakening from a dream.

"Jason!" The cry echoed, sharp and terrified, and Jason's mind cleared all at once. Later they could discuss how they came to be here; what mattered now was that Tessie was not with them. She was that blur of white petticoats dangling high above them. What had happened? Had she wandered away to pick a flower or something, slipped, and lost her footing? What was she clinging to now?

"Hang on, Tessie!" he called. "I'm coming!"

Masao's hand on his arm stopped him before he'd taken three paces back up the path. Jason spun, fist cocked to smash into the smaller man's face, but Masao caught and deflected the blow without losing his firm stance.

"Wait."

"I can't wait! Damn you, Masao, that's *Tessie,* and I don't know what she's hanging on to or how long it'll hold!" He could taste fear in his mouth, like cold, bitter, rusty metal, and his heart thudded out the insistent drumbeat of panic and despair. Tessie so far above them, clinging to some ledge or branch, Tessie about to fall onto the sharp, cruel rocks.

"I know," said Masao. He was strong; Jason could not throw him off without hurting him. He was not even sure he could do so then. The little Japanese had some tricks of fighting Jason had never seen.

"The old man is holding her over the cliff. Can't you see?"

Jason squinted upward. Yes, he could just make out the pattern of the old man's blue-and-white robe, glimmering fitfully in the shadows.

"If he drops her, I'll kill him."

"That won't help Miss Teresa," Masao pointed out with infuriating logic. "We have to surprise him."

This time, when he drew Jason back into the shadows of the trees along the path, Jason did not fight him.

"Think of your sins," the old man had said, and Tessie tried to compose her mind for the death that surely awaited her. But all she could think of was the sweetness of life. Remembered sights, sounds, smells, tastes, and feelings whirled through her mind, and she was in a dozen places at once. She knew sweet jasmine and starlight and a green-shaded, overgrown summerhouse, and Jason kissing her. She was in a blaze of red and crimson leaves, with mist and the river and the stone statues of Nikko, and wanting Jason. She heard the roar of distant waves echoing in the blue light of a sea cave, and Jason's arm was firm about her waist to save her from the rock that hurtled from above. She was in a puddle of moonlight on the sleeping mats of the *daimyo*'s house, and Jason was her last and only love.

How pitifully few had been their good times together! And now that had to be a lifetime for her, all the life that she would ever have. Why had she held him off? If she hadn't been so proud, so wary, so concerned that he treat her exactly as she imagined a lover should treat his lady, she could have gone to her death with the whole of this sweet journey through Japan to remember as a time of love and laughter.

Her wrists ached, and she thought the old man's grip was loosening. She felt with her feet, hoping against hope to find some crevice of a toehold, but the rock face was sheer as far as she could reach. Beneath her, the lights of the village winked like a promise of the love she would never have now.

* * *

Masao slipped through the trees like a ghostly samurai. Unarmed and stripped to his underclothes, he knew the night's chill against his skin only as the most distant of distractions. A slightly less distant distraction was his nagging curiosity about the man who threatened Tessie. How could the *daimyo* have been so dishonorable as to allow another of his servants to attack them after he had promised to let Masao settle the matter in his own way? How could he be such a fool as to let his servant kill the one person who might lead them to the Gassan sword?

These things would be settled later, and Masao grimly promised himself that if Tessie died, he would plant the *daimyo*'s head above her grave. Her ghost would rest in honorable peace.

But Tessie was not going to die. Not if Jason could get to his place in time. Only this traitorous servant of the *daimyo*, attacker of women who masqueraded as an ancient peasant—*he* would die. Masao was coldly certain of his ability to kill the man, no matter who he was, how armed or trained.

He was so certain that he did not even think consciously about the matter. All his consciousness was agonizingly focused on the problem of lifting up and setting down his feet without noise, of slithering between branches and gliding over rocks so that he could approach Tessie and her attacker without giving the man warning, without giving him any reason to drop Tessie before Jason reached his own place.

The ache was a double line of fire that ran through her elbows and shoulders. Her wrists were growing numb; she might not know when the old man decided to let go. Why was he waiting so long, torturing her like this? Why didn't he just get it over with?

The old, angry, impetuous Tessie wanted to shout at him, to kick out and break his hold, even at the price of falling. The new girl who was just being born in

273

these last moments of her life knew how sweet that life was, treasured each breath even at the cost of pain and fear. Each long breath she took was one more moment in which she could remember Jason and the little happiness they had had together.

Everything else was unimportant now. What did it matter if he was using her or laughing at her or if he would have forgotten her in a month? At least she would have had that month. Now she was going to her death with only those few sweet nights to remember.

"Think of your past life, remember your sins," the old madman chanted monotonously above her. Tessie wished he would stop. She didn't want to think of anything else but Jason and the love they had almost shared. She wanted to hold him close in her mind as she fell to her death.

Jason's fingers were slippery with sweat, and he could not hear the small sounds he made over the racing of his heart. *Keep calm,* he told himself. *It won't help Tessie if you panic and alert the old man.*

Masao had taken the quicker way because he knew nothing of rock climbing. Jason had climbed for fun in America, but always with ropes and tools and a guide, never pitting his nerve and his bare fingertips against the sheer side of a cliff like this.

Never wagering the life of his beloved against his ability to climb an unknown cliff in the dark.

But, slender as it was, Tessie's one chance of survival depended on this climb. Masao had been right. If the man who held Tessie heard them coming, he would surely drop her. They had to surprise him, one on each side.

"Why doesn't he drop her anyway?"

"I think," Masao had said, "he wants to ask her something."

Once Tessie was safe, Jason promised himself, he would personally hold Masao upside down over the same cliff until the Japanese explained just what was going on here. There was more than some *daimyo*'s hatred of foreigners, and Masao knew what it was.

He thought about that in some detail while he made his agonizing way up the cliff, praying for footholds and handholds, fingertips bleeding, knees aching. It was better than thinking about Tessie, whom he had not heard screaming for some time.

"I hope you have contemplated your past life," said the old man almost casually, "and are purified in mind and spirit."

Jason, Tessie thought, and braced herself for the plummeting fall and the rocks that would break her body. Instead, she felt a tug that burned like fire through her outstretched arms, and the lip of the cliff scraped across her waist, and she was lying on the solid ledge again.

"Your friends are almost here." The old man stood looking down at her, a shadow in the gloom. "Tell the Japanese," he said thoughtfully, "that he walks too loudly."

He was gone then, melting into the shadows as though he had never been, and Tessie lay on the ledge and gulped deep breaths of the cold night air and began, thankfully, to catalogue each of her separate aches and bruises and scrapes. Each throb of minor pain was a blessed reminder that she was still alive in this world, that she had been given another chance to take what love and happiness she could find with Jason.

A few minutes later, Masao glided out of the trees and fell to his knees beside her with an exclamation of fear.

"It's all right," Tessie told him. She almost resented the effort of wrenching her mind back to ordinary conversation, back from the wheeling stars overhead and the blessedness of life unexpected and the joy of love. "I'm all right." She lay back on the ledge, in no hurry to get up and reawaken all her little aches, and considered what else would be useful to tell Masao. "He said you walk too loudly; he heard you coming several minutes ago."

Masao used several phrases, unknown to Tessie, that bit like raw sake in the mouth.

"Where's Jason?" You'd think he would have the courtesy to show up at the moment of her rebirth and dedication to love.

"Ouf!" Jason heaved himself up over what she'd been thinking of as a perfectly sheer cliff.

"How did you get up that cliff? It's impossible!"

"You can say that again," said Jason with feeling. He mopped his forehead with one sleeve. "I was highly motivated. I thought I was saving your life. Where's the old man? I want to kill him."

"He left."

Jason took one of Tessie's hands and rubbed it gently between both of his. The contact was like a new spark of life glowing between the two of them, belonging to neither one alone.

"Masao thought he might want to ask you something."

"He wanted me to consider my sins."

"That's all?" Masao sounded incredulous. "I thought he—well, never mind. Can you walk? It might," he said with delicate restraint, "it might be wise to go on to the village now."

Chapter Nineteen

It seemed to Tessie that they had been walking and climbing, losing their way and scrambling over cliffs, for an eternity since that bright calm morning when they departed from the *daimyo*'s house. But it was early evening when they entered the little village of Hirayu. Candles and lamps twinkled in windows up and down the long street, the villagers were eating their simple dinners of rice and vegetables, and the children were still playing outside. At their shrill cries, the parents came out into the street, hitching up their blue robes and carrying food bowls, to see the astonishing sight of three exhausted travelers, two with round eyes like demons, making their way to the inn.

"Hush, dear, they are not devils, only foreigners," Tessie heard one mother telling her small son. "I think . . ." she added in doubtful tones that trailed off uncertainly.

"Look, look!" the boy screeched as Tessie paused under the bright lamp that marked the inn. "The devil woman has hair like fire!"

The whole front of the inn was open to the street, and attendants hurried out at the sound of the commotion outside. In full view of the villagers, Tessie,

Jason, and Masao sat to have their shoes taken off and were ushered back into the private rooms of the inn. A narrow, dark passageway opened out into three large, light rooms whose outside walls were only rice-paper screens.

Tessie was ready to sink down and fall asleep at once, but Jason was saying something to her. With a bone-wrenching effort, she turned her head to pay attention to him.

"What did you say?"

"Did you hear the people outside?"

"Yes. They think we might be devils. Nothing new in that."

"One of the children," Jason said, "asked if we were going to visit the other fire-haired devil, the one who lives on top of the mountain."

"What?" Tessie was wide awake in a second.

"And his mother," Jason went on, "slapped him and told him not to talk like that about the holy *yamabushi.*"

"I can't believe I missed all that!" Tessie's head was whirling. Fire-haired devils and *yamabushi.* Surely they were very near the end of their quest. This time they would find Morgan waiting for them.

"When can we start?"

"Not until tomorrow. It's too dark now to go up the mountain," Jason said, and Masao concurred. For once Tessie did not argue the point. She wanted only three things tonight: a hot bath, a bed, and Jason near her. Morning would be soon enough to confront her uncle and find out why he'd led them on this wild chase across Japan.

"What?" said Jason with a secret smile for Tessie. "Not arguing? You must be more tired than I thought." He passed one hand lightly over her tangled hair and down her back. "I expect, after all you've been through, all you want tonight is a hot bath and a bed."

"Two out of three," Tessie murmured, but she refused to explain herself.

The innkeeper brought their dinner while they waited for the bathwater to heat. Unfortunately, the waiting time also brought the curious villagers, who had found their way by a side passage into the courtyard at the back of the inn. There were holes here and there in the old rice-paper screens, and by the time they were sitting down to rice and soup, every hole was filled with a curious black eye and every move they took was commented on by a chorus of onlookers.

"Look, they drink soup like people!"

"No, they are just pretending to eat. Presently all the food will turn into a hard egg, and they will vomit it forth again. Demons eat nothing but air."

"No," disputed a third voice. "They eat small children, too."

Jason turned and made growling noises and wagged his fingers at the rice-paper screens. "Give me boy to eat!" he growled. "Demon hungry!"

Half a dozen children fled with squeals of delighted fear and laughter, only to have their places taken by grown-ups who continued commenting on the action. The innkeeper, coming personally to supervise the service of the next course of steamed fish and cabbage, bowed seven or eight times and apologized profusely for the bad conduct of his fellow villagers.

"You there!" he shouted at the watchers in the garden. "What are you watching for? There are no marvels here! This is not a theater! There are no jugglers! There are no wrestlers! These are honorable guests, and they wish to eat in peace!"

Soft laughing voices pleaded with him.

"But we want to see!"

"Looking harms no one!"

"The guests will not be used up by only looking!"

"Open the screens, we want to see!"

Jason shook his head sadly. "I think I could ignore the villagers," he whispered to Tessie, "but the villagers and the innkeeper arguing over our heads, that's getting a bit much. Do you think they'll want to share the bath house with us?"

"Go for a walk," Tessie said. "I think I can deal with them."

"How?"

"Never mind. Just go!"

Tessie had been listening to the voices outside. It seemed to her that most of the men of the village, having established that foreigners ate rice in the same manner as Japanese, had sensibly gone back to their own meals. Only the women and children were left. The children would obey their mothers, and the women, Tessie hoped, would be sympathetic once she explained why she wanted privacy for this night of all nights.

Jason had little faith in Tessie's ability to send the villagers away, but he did think going for a walk with Masao would be a damned good idea. It was high time he found out exactly what Masao was concealing, and he would prefer to shake it out of the man without Tessie watching.

Unfortunately for Jason's plans, the open front room of the inn was full of men standing and drinking and discussing the amazing appearance of the foreigners. As soon as Jason and Masao emerged from the passageway, the men of the village surrounded Masao.

"Ho, young master, what are you doing with the *Mahotsukai,* the wizard?" one of them demanded.

"Come and drink sake with us and tell us about foreigners!"

Masao was swallowed up in the crowd, one black-haired Japanese in a blue kimono surrounded by black-haired Japanese in blue working clothes and loose robes.

"Hey! Come back here! I want to talk to you!" Jason shouted. He caught Masao by the shoulder and spun him around—too easily. The shoulder was too light for a man as solidly muscled as Masao, and he was looking into the almond-shaped black eyes of a total stranger, and an unfriendly one at that.

The Japanese villagers pressed closer together and stared at Jason, a wall of black opaque eyes.

Picking Masao out of that crowd, even if he had been able to identify him, would have been like trying to extract a cork out of a bottle with a pair of tweezers. Being a sensible man, Jason gave up. He could talk to Masao later.

For now, it might be interesting to circle around the inn and find out just how Tessie planned to disperse their spectators.

In the darkness outside, Jason followed his nose down a narrow alley, guided by the slight fragrance of the night-blooming flowers that twined up the posts of their rooms in the back of the inn. A few steps took him to the courtyard. He could see Tessie's figure outlined by candlelight against the translucent white screens, and an old and familiar wave of longing swept over him. God knew, he'd had women enough in his life. Why was this sweetly curved redhead the one woman he could never forget, never get enough of? Even now, after all the rebuffs he'd suffered and after all his resolves to let her go her own damned way from now on, the sight of her struck him with an ache of desire so deep it hurt.

"Shh!" one of the Japanese women reproved her crying child. "The barbarian devil woman wants to say something to us!" She turned back to face the white-lighted screen. "We do not hurt you, foreign woman. We only want to see. Why must we go away?"

"Because I want to lie with my husband in privacy!" Tessie said irritably, in excellent Japanese. "And I can personally assure you that we foreigners do it exactly the way you do, so you will learn nothing by spying on us!"

"How do you know that?" another woman called from the far side of the courtyard. "Did you watch us with our husbands? Perhaps we do it differently!"

"Perhaps we . . ."

"Perhaps you . . ."

Jason choked and found himself blushing as the women laughed and called out their bawdy suggestions. He hoped Tessie did not understand all they were saying. She must not understand it, because she didn't sound embarrassed at all as she answered them by laughingly repeating her demand for privacy.

"You really want to lie with husband tonight?" demanded one bent old woman. "Or is it duty?"

"I want to. I love him."

"Is he a good husband, the barbarian? Does he love you?"

Tessie paused, and Jason found that he was biting his lip. "I don't know," she said slowly.

Oh, Tessie, Tessie, how can you not know? Won't you ever trust me?

"It doesn't matter. He is my man."

The women nodded, and their whispers of agreement rustled through the courtyard. Jason had barely time to get out of the way, pressing himself flat against the wall that divided the courtyard from the alley, before they began filing out.

One woman, the old one who had questioned Tessie the most, paused as the others left. "If he is not good to you, the barbarian," she cackled cheerfully, "tell us women, and we will come back and watch him until he shrivels up from shame!"

"Oh, brave demon killer," teased her companion as they left.

Their voices, cackling and recounting bawdy jokes, faded into the night and the chirping of the crickets.

Jason eased his way into the courtyard and silently slid open one of the rice-paper screen doors.

Tessie was not there. Her dusty dress was heaped on the floor, and the towels the innkeeper had brought were gone. She must have gone to the bath while he was blushing at the women's last few bawdy jokes.

Jason settled himself on a mat, supple as any Japanese from his long practice, and folded his hands to wait.

He had not long to wait. Crickets sang outside, the yellow globe of the autumn moon peeped over the courtyard wall, a breath of wind blew the last pale night flowers from the vine outside and scattered them over the sleeping mats. And with that breeze came Tessie, fresh and pink and glowing from a steam-hot Japanese bath in a wooden tub, with something white wrapped about her and her hair tumbling down to make a gilt-edged crown for her sweet face.

"Oh!" She was startled to find him there. "I didn't know you were back already. Is Masao—?"

Jason shrugged. "He's gone off with the locals. You have the privacy you asked the women for."

Too late he remembered that he wasn't supposed to have known Tessie's plans for the night. A flush bloomed on her face, roses mixing with cream and gold. "You were listening!" she accused.

"I was curious to know how you planned to persuade them away."

"And I suppose you found it very funny!"

"No," said Jason. "Very sad."

"Sad?"

"To hear that you still, *still*, don't know how I feel about you. After—"

"It doesn't matter," said Tessie swiftly. She sank to her knees beside him on the thick, soft mat and placed her fingertips over his mouth to stop him. The touch was so sweet that Jason wouldn't have dreamed of resisting. "No, truly, Jason. I don't mind if you can never care for me as I do for you—well, that's not true. I do mind, but *it doesn't matter.* It took that old madman on the mountaintop to make me come to my senses. All that really matters is that all the happiness in my life has come from being with you, and I haven't had nearly enough yet. Giving you up," she said, looking at him over her outspread fingers with sweet, grave eyes that made something hurt deep in his soul, "giving up the happiness we could find together is too great a price to pay for my pride. I've decided not to care whether we spend a day together, or a week, or a year, before you grow tired of me—"

"Grow tired of you, *tired* of you!" It was more than Jason could take. He caught Tessie's wrists and put her hands away from his face, keeping her prisoner while all his feelings exploded into speech. "As if I ever could! Tessie, even you can't be *that* stupid!"

"What do you mean, *even* me!"

"Well—oh, let it pass; we'll have that fight later." In the midst of his passionate outburst, Jason grinned, thinking that a fight with his redheaded spitfire could be as stimulating as making love with any other woman. "Tessie, I loved you ten years ago, and you sent me away."

"You could have come back."

"We'll have *that* fight later, too. Will you for God's sake let me finish? I spent *ten years* trying to forget you, Tessie, and I failed miserably. The moment I heard you were still unmarried, I could think of nothing else but hatching up some crazy scheme to bring you to Japan and into my power, all unknowing. Oh, yes!" He laughed at her astonishment. "Did you think I, or my agents, could be fools enough to think *Hartley* had learned Japanese and educated himself about this country? It was easy enough to find out that he was taking the credit for his little sister's accomplishments. I gambled that he'd be too tempted by the job offer to resist. I gambled that he'd be desperate for your help and that you, with your damned sense of duty, would decide he needed you worse than any of the rest of your clinging family. I've always been something of a gambler at heart. The only throw of the dice I consistently lose is when I'm playing for your love."

"Jason, you've always had that. I just had to learn not to let my pride get in the way."

"Haven't I spent this entire journey jumping through your hoops, trying to become the kind of man you thought you wanted?"

"I wouldn't say that exactly," murmured Tessie, remembering how shamelessly Jason had bullied and tricked and manipulated her into traveling with him. And a good thing, too, or she'd never have found out what really mattered in her life! "But anyway, you can stop now, because I don't think I want a masterful brute anymore."

"Poor Ricardo!"

"Oh!" Tessie blushed even deeper. Jason observed with interest that two shades of pink could mingle with the cream of her skin and the fire-gold of her hair without clashing at all. "Ricardo never existed, Jason. I made him up. Because you were looking so dark and handsome and confident, and laughing at me and feeling superior because I was a poor old maid who never found another man after you—"

"Laugh at you? I never did," said Jason intensely. "I was only trying to find out if some other man had found *you*. And I ought to beat you for the bad moments your Ricardo gave me, except that I did realize quite some time ago that he was only a figment of your imagination."

"You did? And kept teasing me? Oh, you—" Tessie aimed a mock blow at Jason. He caught her hand and kissed each finger separately, then smoothed them out and kissed her palm.

Catherine Lyndell

"You're a very bad liar," he told her. "You kept forgetting his name, for one thing."

"I never forgot yours," Tessie murmured as Jason's kisses traveled up her arm, lingering on the curve inside her elbow, then up again until the white foam of lace at her shoulders stopped him momentarily. "It's written on my heart."

"Just," said Jason with deep satisfaction, opening the lacy white wrapper to place his hand approximately over Tessie's wildly beating heart, "just so it's also written on our marriage certificate, my dearest love. You're not getting away from me again!"

"I don't want to get away." Tessie kissed the dark head that bent over her breast. "I don't want to be anywhere, ever, but where you are."

It was too much to believe and understand all at once, this gift of love in return for the foolish pride she'd finally laid aside. Incredulous joy rushed through Tessie's heart, and the sweetness of love long denied bloomed within her. Jason slipped away from her for a moment to open the top half of the long sliding screen that was the back wall of the room, and silver light flooded the sleeping mats and outlined him, black and clear as any demon shadow, as he came back to kneel beside her. Tessie reached up to draw him to her and caught her breath with delight at the touch of his lips on her breast. Crickets sang outside, and the sweet, earthy, resinous scents of the rain-washed mountain forest drifted and swirled through the room like friendly spirits.

There was no need for greedy haste now that they were together. With delicate, savoring calm, Jason parted the white folds of Tessie's lace-trimmed wrapper, twined his fingers through coils of red hair, caressed the softness she had so long tried to keep hidden from him. She felt each slight movement with an uprush of joy so exquisite that she could hardly desire more. And yet the hunger for him was growing

286

within her, and his hands trembled now and again as he touched her with wondering, half-disbelieving gestures.

"You are the other half of my soul, Tessie," he whispered, "and I could not live without you again. For mercy's sake, don't change your mind and turn against me in the morning!"

"Why would I do that?" But Tessie thought she could understand his fears. She'd been scathingly sarcastic about a man who would follow his old friend's tracks through Japan for nothing more than the money he hoped to gain at the end of the trail. Now she saw what a fool she'd been. Just because Jason needed money, did that have to mean he needed nothing more? Whenever he'd spoken of his love for her, she'd laughed at him and denied the truth of his feelings. Naturally he would not speak to her of his friendship with Morgan, his hopes of finding the man alive at the end of their journey. But people were more complicated than Tessie had been willing to admit. Jason might well be a man who needed money, who loved her, and who wanted to help an old friend sending mysterious messages. The three were not inconsistent.

But it was all too complicated to explain just now, especially while Jason was doing such deliciously perfect things to her body with nothing more than lips and fingers and the warm stir of his breath coming quicker and quicker over her bared skin. And there was another, simpler way to convince him.

"Come to me, Jason," Tessie whispered, "for I cannot bear any more!" She was open to him now, wherever he wanted to roam over her waiting body, every sense alert, wanting nothing but to join herself with him in love. Yet still he delayed, caressing and kissing. She could feel his muscles taut and shaking like an overtightened wire, could sense the tension of this restraint.

"What is it?"

He was all black and silver in the moonlight, without softness or pity. "Tessie. I meant it. I *cannot* love you tonight and have you reject me again in the morning. Flesh and blood and human spirit," said Jason softly, "can only bear so much. Are you sure, Tessie, that you know your own mind this time?"

Tessie raised herself on one elbow to stare at his moonlit face. "God and Saint Joseph, Jason, what would it take to convince you?" she demanded. In her angry tension, she heard herself reverting to the accents of her childhood, the Irish lilt that a succession of American-born governesses had schooled out of all the Gallagher children. So be it! That hard-won gentility was part of family and pride and all the things Tessie had renounced. "Must we have the Buddhist priest out of the temple to marry us now before you'll deign to lay your pure fingers upon my body? It does seem a pity to wake the poor man up to satisfy your foolish fears—and I'm not sure a heathen marriage would count with the Gallagher family, anyway. You'll have to trust me to wed you when we find a decent American priest, or else you'll take yourself and your doubts out of my room and have the kindness not to trouble me again this night!"

"Oh, well," said Jason in a voice choking with laughter and desire, "if that's the hard choice you leave me, Tessie, I'll just have to be taking my chances with you!"

And as if her flare of anger had burnt away the last memory of restraint, he took her, not roughly but urgently, with a need that swept over Tessie and engulfed her in the joy of their coming together. They were truly one now—not two lovers who doubted and feared each other even as their bodies longed to touch, but one soul, one body, moving with perfect harmony under the gentle silver wash of the moonlight that poured through the half-open wall.

And with all those barriers deep within her removed at last, giving herself to Jason with the exultation of one who has seen death and knows life all the sweeter for its shortness, Tessie found something she had never known before in their loving. This time it was not just her body that was lifted to the heights of pleasure, but her soul, too. Her eyes opened wide and unseeing to the silver flood of moonlight; the small sounds of the village settling to rest, the scents of burning charcoal and cooking rice and wet soil and drying autumn leaves and resinous pine needles and cool, rain-washed sky, the song of the crickets, and the soft cold wind over the mountain all entered into her with Jason. She was the mountain and the wind, the moonlight and the song; and Jason was with her.

Rainbow hues of glimmering iridescence washed over her in the place beyond time and space where she found herself. She cried out and held tightly to Jason through a spinning, turbulent fall that ended, not on the rocks that had threatened her that day, but close together on the sleeping mats in a little village inn. Wordless, still unsure what had happened between them, she caressed his cheek with one finger and felt a line of dampness.

"Were you crying, my love?" she whispered. "But why?"

Jason put his own hand to her face and then set his fingers upon her lips, and she tasted the salt of her own tears. "I-I don't know what happened to us, just then," he said shakily.

"Don't you?" Tessie teased. She was rapidly coming down to earth again, and the solid simplicity of floor and mats and Jason beside her was comforting after the strange realm to which they'd been transported. "You're supposed to be the experienced one, remember? If you don't know, I'm sure I can't help you!"

Jason's kiss stopped her laughter. "Tessie. Don't deny it."

And with his lips on her own, she saw again that rainbow glimmering, heard the chirping of the crickets transmuted to a music just too high and sweet for human ears. Words could not express that glamour, but words could tear it down and destroy it.

And so for once, sensible, dutiful Tessie Gallagher put aside her common sense and said nothing at all, but sought the rainbow again in Jason's arms; and they found it.

Chapter Twenty

Tessie woke with that unpleasant and wrenching sensation of having been dragged from the depths that comes with being awakened too soon from a badly needed deep sleep. All the aches and pains that had soaked away in the hot bath flared into life again as she moved, bright lights of pain to match the lanterns that bobbed about outside.

"What—" she mumbled sleepily.

Jason covered her mouth with his hand. "The villagers. A child is missing. Some of them blame us."

"What?" Tessie was jolted into complete wakefulness in an instant. "They can't."

"Demons, you know. Foreigners. The innkeeper is trying to talk sense into them, but I do think," said Jason, "we had better get dressed. It might be as well to leave this room while we can do so quietly."

"You do have a talent for understatement," Tessie whispered as she slipped into the torn and travel-stained dress she had worn the day before. "Masao?"

Jason was not there. A moment later, he was beside her again, having moved in and out of the room as quietly as a big cat. "Not in his room. He may have been awakened already. In any case, he has little to fear from the villagers."

Neither had they, by the time they had dressed and gone over the wall in the back of the inn. The gate had been locked long since. As Jason was silently helping Tessie over the wall, the innkeeper was showing the villagers into their room to demonstrate that there was no child hidden there. The tearful mother explained for the fifteenth time that she had thought her boy was staying with his aunt, as he often did when he was angry about something. She had only discovered his absence a few minutes ago, when her sister dropped in to borrow the big kettle and said innocently that she hadn't seen the boy that evening.

"He must have gone up the mountain," she sobbed. "Just because I raised my voice to him a time or two—"

"You slapped him, too," said the innkeeper reprovingly. "Didn't you? I've seen it before."

Among the Japanese, such treatment of a child was all but unknown. Children were treasures, to be petted and ruled by gentleness until they reached the age of reason and took on adult duties. The villagers disapproved of this woman with her quick temper and quick hands, and there were some mutterings that she deserved it if her little boy had indeed run away.

"We've got to stop this," Jason muttered to Tessie. "They're nervous about something, looking for a scapegoat. Somebody will be hurt before this night is out if their thoughts aren't distracted."

Before Tessie could stop him, he'd swung over the wall again and had entered the conversation as easily as if he were one of the villagers. No doubt, he agreed, the poor woman had deserved to be worried, but what of the child? Would a child really have the courage to hide out all night on a mountain known to be infested with *tengu* and lesser demons? The boy might have fallen and hurt himself so that he was unable to come home. It would be better to search for him than to waste what remained of the night in useless recriminations.

Soon the villagers, animated with new purpose, were spreading out across the lower slopes of the mountain, calling to the missing boy and searching every ravine and cranny in the rocky hillside. Jason took a lantern and joined the search himself. With somewhat less willingness, he took Tessie as well.

"You," he told her sternly, "should sleep. You need your rest."

"Do you think I could, thinking about that little lost boy?" Tessie demanded. She set off ahead of him, up one of the steep paths that wound through pines and boulders, with only the faint, flickering light of Jason's lantern to keep her from a misstep. Jason muttered a few arcane Buddhist curses between his teeth and hurried after her.

Distances and directions were deceptive, once they got among the thick stands of pines that clustered over the lower slopes. Here and there in the distance, they could see the flickering of other lights or could hear the villagers calling out. But the mountain was vast, and they could hardly begin to cover it in the darkness. Tessie and Jason were alone, more alone the farther they went, and the night seemed to press down upon them like a palpable weight, heavy and smothering as a velvet quilt stitched with diamond stars. The lights of the other lanterns were indistinct now, and the calls of the other searchers were muted by distance.

"Look." Tessie pointed when they paused, uncertain, at the branching of two narrow paths. "Is that a lantern? Somebody has already taken the lower way. We should go farther up."

The distant light to which she pointed was green and vaguely flickering like a ghost light, but Jason did not argue. After all, what else could it have been?

At the next turning point, Tessie thought she could hear a weak cry from even farther up the mountain. Could it be the boy they sought?

"We've been climbing for some time," Jason objected. "I don't think he could have got this far. We might do better to turn back and search the lower slopes more thoroughly."

Tessie's face set in the obstinate expression he knew and dreaded. "Let's just make sure that *wasn't* him," she suggested, and Jason knew he'd have to drag her back down by force if he wanted her to turn away without investigating that faint, possibly imagined cry.

An exhausting hour followed during which they went back and forth along hairpin turns, sidling over boulders and scrambling past small scrubby trees. The sky was pale above them now, and they had not heard the boy call out again—if ever they had. Jason thought more and more that it might have been the cry of a sleepy bird.

"Birds don't cry out at night," Tessie pointed out. "They sleep."

"And so should we. This is useless. We're turning back *now*, Tessie, before you slip and break a leg in one of these crevasses. It's almost daylight; the boy may have been found by now, and if he hasn't been, the villagers will search much better than we could." Jason took Tessie's arm and urged her down the steep path.

Black wings exploded out of the rock cliff at their feet, and a harsh cawing noise rent the predawn stillness of the mountain. Tessie shrieked and put up her hands to shield her face from the furious onslaught of a huge kite. Jason beat at the bird, and it fluttered away, but not until they had retraced their steps did it give up the attack.

"We must have disturbed its nest," Tessie said

unsteadily. "Perhaps we'd better find another way down."

But there was no other way, at least not at that point; on one side was the cliff, on the other a pile of smooth boulders too large to scramble over. Muttering to himself, Jason accompanied Tessie up the narrow path until they could find another fork leading downward. Ridiculous, to be put to flight by an angry bird! But he had no wish, himself, to be assailed by that furious beak and those sharp claws. "Too kind to animals, that's my trouble," he muttered. "Too respectful of motherhood. Somebody ought to teach that bird about rook pie. Somebody ought to—"

They rounded a curve in the path and came out into the first glory of the breaking dawn. For a moment, even Jason was speechless, while Tessie stood beside him in awestruck silence.

A rocky slope rose to their right, pockmarked with the dark openings of caves and shaded by gnarled trees. Before them and to the left, the mountain fell away into gorges shimmering with mist. The first rays of the rising sun glowed through that mist, illuminating it like the golden clouds of a dream. Above that red-gold glow, clouds blanketed the horizon and cast a violet shadow on the tips of the distant peaks beyond the mist.

And seated placidly amid this splendor, cross-legged on an outcropping of rock, was an old man in the long white robes of a Shugendo priest. Grizzled hair streaked with red peeped out from under his black skullcap. The conch horn and the rosary of bone beads hung from his belt, just as Tessie had seen such mountain priests equipped in old engravings. But his curiously carved staff had been laid down beside the rock, and his arms cradled a sleeping child with black hair falling into his closed eyes and a thumb stuck between his pursed lips.

"Morgan," Tessie said at last.

"Morgan Gallagher," Jason echoed, moving forward slowly, as if he expected the old man to turn into a kite and fly away with a shriek of disdain.

"I wondered if you would know me," said Morgan Gallagher placidly. "It's been a long time. Good to see you again, Jason."

He stood with unhurried ease and gently lowered the sleeping child to rest on the cloak that lay beside his rock—not such an old man after all, despite the silver that had obscured his flame-red hair. He was still strong and vigorous, broad-shouldered and deep-chested. And Tessie's heart leaped with joy to see him again, but they had a few small matters to settle before she would cast herself into his arms.

"Oh, yes, I know you," she said. "I wonder that I didn't recognize you earlier."

"My dear child!" Morgan's weather-worn face assumed an expression of childish innocence; his blue eyes twinkled with gentle amusement. "Whatever can you mean?"

"You were the old man in the inn at Kiritsumi, the one who played *tengu* jokes and sent us on to the Fountain of Jizo and then vanished," Tessie accused. "And I think you were watching us there also. And the priest at Nikko—"

"No, Tessie! You can't accuse me of impersonating a handsome young man, and him half a foot taller than myself, to boot! I'm innocent of that at least!" Morgan's ringing laughter echoed over the cliffs and came back to them magnified. He seemed younger with every minute. "Ah, but it's good to see you at last, girl! Won't you give your old uncle a kiss?"

He enfolded her in his arms and thumped her on the back. The smell of tobacco and sea salt that she remembered from her childhood was gone, but it was still Morgan, hugging her with tears in his blue eyes.

"And what about yesterday?" Tessie demanded

when he let her go again. "Why did you half kill me over the cliff?"

For the first time Morgan looked uneasy. "Er—I'll explain it all in good time, dear girl. Won't you sit down?"

"Yesterday!" Jason started forward. "It was *you* who pretended to guide us to the village? *You* risked Tessie's life like that? You blackguard! I ought to—"

Morgan caught his raised hand and twisted slightly. Jason stumbled backward and found himself standing several feet away from the old man. "Tessie was never in the least danger," Morgan said calmly. "As you see, I am still reasonably strong, and I've learned a few things since we parted."

"You have indeed," put in a third, familiar voice. Tessie whirled and saw Masao standing at the curve of the path, arms folded. He was dressed all in black, and his face looked as severe as an executioner's. "If I had known you then, we might have been spared this meeting. But it does not matter, since these two have led me to you anyway."

"Led you to him? What do you mean, Masao?" Tessie gasped.

Morgan did not seem confused by Masao's strange statement, but he looked old and tired suddenly. "Ah. Masao, you said? You must be the son of Tasadake Kokushi. I was expecting you someday, though I did not think to see you in the company of my niece." He put both hands on his knees and bowed in the Japanese fashion, and Masao returned the gesture.

"Masao is an old friend of ours," Tessie said faintly. "He boarded with us when he was studying in San Francisco."

"And his father," said Morgan, "was my first friend in Japan. Now, Tessie, Masao, Jason, do sit down. It is a long story. I think you will not deny me the chance to tell it in my own way before you—complete your business, Tasadake Masao?"

Masao bowed again. "You understand that it is a matter of honor."

"Oh, yes," said Morgan with a hint of irony in his gentle smile. "I understand."

Somehow—Tessie did not quite understand how—Morgan got them all settled around his favorite rock. He chatted as comfortably as if he were entertaining them in a Yokohama living room, lit a small fire in one of the crevices of the cliff behind them, extracted kettle and tea and cups from another dark opening, and soon was handing around rough country earthenware cups full of steaming green tea. When the little Japanese boy stirred and murmured sleepily, Morgan produced a piece of sugar candy from one of the long sleeves of his priestly robe and cuddled the boy while he chatted about trivialities and poured the tea.

"I don't think it was very nice of you to steal the boy just to lure us up here," Tessie said abruptly.

Morgan looked pained. "Oh, I did not do it just for that. His mother is too harsh with the child. She needed a fright. She will be gentler with him now. Besides, I did not steal him. I found him wandering alone in the forest. Shugendo priests don't steal children; those are the tricks of *tengu*."

"Some of the people in this country don't seem too clear on the distinction," Jason remarked.

"What a pity, what a pity," Morgan mourned, gently stroking his frizzled graying hair where it peeped out below the black skullcap. "I was once as ignorant myself, of course, or even more ignorant. But I had no intention of killing your father, Tasadake Masao. Kokushi was my friend. I sought only to defend myself."

"You did not kill him," Masao said.

Tessie's eyes opened as she took in the meaning of this interchange. So Masao's father had been the samurai who attacked Morgan in Yokohama—so Morgan had been the American friend whom Masao's family blamed for his death! Why hadn't she put those pieces together earlier?

Morgan looked relieved at Masao's announcement, but his face drew down into gloomy lines as Masao went on. He explained how his father had felt constrained to try to kill Morgan in obedience to his lord's command. "If he had succeeded, I think he might still have killed himself afterward, for the guilt of slaying a friend. But as things turned out, he was doubly dishonored, having failed to carry out his *daimyo*'s commands and having lost the *daimyo*'s prized sword. When you disappeared, he tried to trace you so that he could retrieve the sword; when he failed, he returned to his home and committed *seppuku.*"

Morgan shook his head sadly. "Then his death is still on my conscience. That damned heirloom! I never thought about it at the time; it was just something he meant to kill me with, and I had to take it away from him to save my own life. It wasn't hard; I think he wanted to lose the fight. I disarmed him almost accidentally, struck at him with the sword. It came away covered with blood, and he fell to the ground like a dead man. My first friend in Japan, and I had killed him, and I didn't even know why he had set upon me! It was too much. I ran—I don't know where—away from Yokohama. It was night. I suppose, by the luck that attends children and madmen, I was not seen. Or perhaps those who saw me did not have the courage to stop a mad foreigner waving a bloody sword. I will never know. When I came to my senses again, I was in the country; it was raining, and I had a fever that burned me from inside. I stumbled into a disused shrine in the hills and lay down to sleep. An old man found me there. I don't think he had been ten miles from the shrine in all his life. I don't think he knew what a foreigner was. He nursed me back to health, and when I was well enough to travel, I found that he assumed I was a *tengu,* a mountain demon, because, he said, I had such a big nose and was so atrociously ugly."

Morgan shrugged. "Weeks had passed; my ship had sailed. I felt it was a sign that my life as an American was over. I had only two desires: to do penance for killing my friend and to find out more about a faith that could make a man nurse even a demon, as he thought me, back to health. The old man called himself a *yamabushi* of Shugendo, but he was a very ignorant one. He could not himself teach me very much of his faith; and since the religion had been outlawed by the new government of Japan, the old teaching centers were no more. But that very fact made it easy for me, a foreigner, to enter the religion. Superstitious villagers and isolated mountain peasants and wandering priests in disguise passed me along, one to another, in such secrecy that I don't think either the Japanese or the American authorities ever knew about me."

"They didn't," Tessie confirmed. "You were thought dead." A lump rose in her throat, choking her. "*I* thought you were dead. Morgan, how could you do that to us—to me?"

"I was a self-centered fool," Morgan said frankly. "All I could think about was my own crime; and then, as I began to be initiated into the Six Ways of Shugendo, I think I ceased altogether to be an American. Only in the last few years I have begun to understand that one cannot renounce the world until one has also renounced all responsibilities to those in the world. You were one of my responsibilities, Tessie, because I loved you and I always suspected you'd become a slave to your family if I wasn't there to put a little backbone into you. And you, Masao, were another one of my responsibilities. I should have found some way of helping Kokushi's family, but in my guilt and grief I was afraid to face you."

He sighed. "It was easier, as it turned out, to do something about Tessie. I have—friends—around the country; I even get occasional copies of the Yokohama English-language newspapers. The social column mentioned your name one day. When I learned that you were coming to Japan, Tessie, I felt that I owed you something. You needed the means to break free of your family—"

Tessie stood and interrupted him. "This famous legacy?"

"Why, yes."

"If the legacy you promised me is the *daimyo*'s antique sword, Uncle, I don't want it. I know enough about Japan now to understand that it means much, much more to Masao and the *daimyo*—and it is theirs by right. You must give it back to Masao so that he can return it to the *daimyo*."

"I always intended to," said Morgan mildly. He rose and went into the largest of the dark openings in the mountainside. When he returned, he was bearing a long, awkward bundle wrapped in dark blue cotton and secured with cords. Kneeling before Masao, he offered the sword to him.

"Here is your honor and your revenge, Tasadake Masao. I ask only that you allow me to finish my story to Tessie before you take your vengeance."

Masao's dark eyes gleamed suspiciously as he fumbled with the cords. When cords and cotton wrappings fell free, the blade shone and rippled like living water in the morning sunlight. Forged five centuries earlier by an anonymous hermit on Gassan mountain, it had been a treasure of the *daimyo*'s family since the earliest days of the Tokugawa Shogunate. Now, in the new modern Japan, it would have been esteemed—a most valuable curio. But to Masao it was much, much more; it was the shining symbol of his family's honor, miraculously restored to him without bloodshed or resistance.

301

"You will be able to verify," said Morgan, "that it is the *daimyo*'s sword."

"Yes," said Masao in a voice choked by emotion. He turned the blade slightly, so that it caught the sun like a streak of flame. *"Horimono* says 'Gassan Saku.' Shape of blade is *shinogi-zukuri. Ji-hada* is pattern of waves cresting in open sea."

He laid the sword down carefully, reverently, on the square of indigo-dyed cotton cloth that had wrapped it. Palms on knees, he bowed very low toward Morgan Gallagher. "I do not need to examine it further. My father described the sword to me before he died, and every day of my life I have repeated the specifications to myself. This is the Gassan sword belonging to the *daimyo* of Shiroyama, and you are an honorable man, Morgan Gallagher. It is not necessary for me to hear more of your story."

Morgan paled. "Very well. You have the right to say when it shall be." Morgan knelt before Masao and bent his head forward.

"No!" Understanding at last, Tessie ran forward and threw her arms around her uncle's shoulders. "You can't kill him!"

"His father's ghost demands vengeance," Morgan said. He tried unavailingly to push Tessie away.

"There will be no more killing." Masao raised his eyes to the mist-shrouded mountain peak, as if speaking to the golden wisps of cloud that still clung around the rocks. "The sword has been returned to me freely and honorably, and I shall return it to the *daimyo*. My father did not wish your death, Morgan Gallagher, even though he tried to follow the commands of his lord; and I do not believe that another death now would bring peace to his shade. The return of the sword wipes out the blood debt between our families. I, Tasadake Masao, son of Tasadake Kokushi, have chosen this way."

He knelt before the sword and began carefully

wrapping it again in its cotton cloth. "This will have to serve until we get to the village, where I will get a craftsman to make a case for it. It is rather a pity that you did not take the scabbard as well." He tried to smile, but his voice was trembling slightly with suppressed emotion.

"Now, Tessie," said Morgan, "if you'll stop trying to strangle me, I will tell you about your legacy and explain why you had to come to me by such a roundabout path."

"I think we would all appreciate that," said Jason.

Tessie looked up and saw Jason quietly setting down a large, jagged rock. Without speaking or interfering, he had silently moved behind Masao while all eyes were focused on the Gassan sword. Before Masao could have harmed Morgan, Jason would have knocked him out.

Tessie thanked him with her eyes as he returned to her side, as quietly as he had left, taking up his cooling cup of green tea as though nothing out of the ordinary had occurred.

"All I wanted to give you, Tessie, was your freedom —and Japan. I wanted to make you leave your family for long enough to understand that they could manage without you, and I wanted you to see a little of this country that I have grown to love. If you had come directly here, you would have seen nothing of Japan, and you would have hurried back to be an unpaid nursemaid for Hartley and Sophia. Now, tell me." Morgan sipped his tea carefully, twinkling at Tessie over the earthenware bowl. "Has it been such an unpleasant trip?"

Thatched houses in the mountains, blue sea caves haunted by beneficent goddesses, the misty shores of the Inland Sea, the autumn glory of Nikko. And Jason, and Jason's love.

"Parts of it," Tessie replied slowly, "were rather pleasant." And she gave Jason a secret smile.

"But I'd still like to know why you had to hang me over the cliff!" she burst out at last.

"Ah. Well. The old priests of Shugendo would say that a woman cannot be a *yamabushi,*" Morgan told her, "but I know you, Tessie, and you can do anything you want to. I want to give you the secrets I have learned in my years of study. Yesterday was the first stage of initiation, the purification. Tomorrow we will begin the *koku-dachi,* or fast. When you have mastered the art of abstaining from food without hunger, we will proceed to *mizu-dachi,* the abstention from water. After that—"

"Thank you very much," said Tessie faintly, "but, Uncle Morgan, I really do not think that I want to become a priestess of Shugendo."

"It is difficult, I grant," said Morgan, "but I believe you can do it."

"And illegal," Jason mentioned.

"And *most* improper for a woman!" Masao said indignantly.

"And all I really want," said Tessie, "which should please you no end, Masao, is to get married and have six children."

Masao looked horrified for a moment. "To Jason," Tessie added quickly.

"And to live in Yokohama, but *not* on the Bluff." She turned to Jason. "And to go around the country with you helping you buy Japanese arts and crafts, and—"

Jason rolled his eyes at Morgan with a comical look of dismay. "You see, Morgan, you're well out of it. When Tessie gets started wanting something, there's no telling where she'll stop!"

"And to bring you home where you belong, Uncle Morgan!" Tessie finished as soon as Jason gave her the chance.

"My dear Tessie," Morgan said gently, "I am where I belong. I am a *yamabushi* of Shugendo, and I belong to the mountain of Kasadake. Here is the only man who will come back down the mountain with you." He lifted the drowsy boy to his feet and patted him gently on the bottom, sending him stumbling to the refuge of Tessie's open arms.

He would not be persuaded, and when Tessie argued beyond the limits of his patience, the sun was obscured by gray clouds and a stinging shower of rain spattered over them.

"You'd better be going," said Morgan with a half-smile, "before I get *really* annoyed. It doesn't do to talk back to a master of the Six Ways, Tessie."

"You'll—I'll see you again?" Tessie begged.

"I'll keep in touch," Morgan promised.

All the way down the steep paths, Tessie held the child, savoring the weight of the little head on her shoulder and the sweaty warmth of the small body in her arms.

"Aren't you tired?" Jason would say from time to time. "You'd better let me carry him."

Tessie shook her head. The child's weight in her arms was a promise of continuity, something to comfort her for finding and losing Morgan all in a morning.

"I need the practice," she told Jason finally, but she could see he didn't understand her hint. That was all right. Morgan had his little magic tricks and his secrets of the Six Ways, and Jason had his knowledge of Japan, and Masao had had his family secrets all this time. A woman needed one small secret of her own to keep even with this crew, even if it was more a hope than a certainty, even if it couldn't be kept secret for very long.

Epilogue

The sea breezes of Yokohama softened the heat of the summer. When a blue haze covered the hills and a cool, salty wind blew from the harbor, Tessie could almost imagine herself in San Francisco again. But the overgrown, weed-infested backyard of her family home in San Francisco had little in common with the meticulously groomed and raked Japanese garden where she now sat with Jason. One corner had been turned into a meditation garden, a restrained pattern of raked sand about sea-tumbled boulders that Jason had placed with many mutterings and calculations and consultations with his Japanese friends. The other side of the garden was Tessie's, and she had made of it a shady wisteria-covered arbor, framed in green and roofed in drifts of white and lavender blossoms. Even in midsummer it was a cool and pleasant retreat.

"You look sad," Jason observed, returning from his study of the sand garden to drop down beside Tessie in the broad hammock that swung under the shade of the wisteria. "Missing your uncle?"

"He *did* promise he would keep in touch." Tessie

nodded. "And now it's been nine months, closer to ten. I had hoped to hear from him by now. Especially now. I hope he's all right, all by himself on that mountain."

"Time probably means something completely different to a master of the Six Ways. And remember, he lived perfectly well on Kasadake for ten years before you even found out he was alive. We'll probably get one of his mysterious messages any day now. You know how Morgan operates. He'll write you a letter in the sand, or send a kite flying down from the mountain with a rolled-up note in its beak."

"Anybody would think," said Tessie severely, "that you really believed he could do magic and control the weather."

"I haven't come up with any better explanation of some of the queer things that happened on our trip," Jason pointed out. "Have you?"

Tessie was silent.

"But if you're really concerned," Jason went on, "why don't we go to visit him?"

Tessie's face lit up. "Jason! Do you really mean it?"

"I don't see why not. Remember those *raku* bowls he used to serve tea? I wouldn't mind finding out the name of the potter in that region. Now that you're able to travel again, maybe we should do a buying trip in that general area. Morgan wouldn't be able to resist seeing you and his little namesake."

Tessie's glance drifted toward the open window of the room they had turned into a nursery. She could just hear the little girl who looked after the baby singing a monotonous cradle song to rock him to sleep. "It's a terrible name to saddle an innocent little baby with," she murmured. "Morgan Kokushi Lancaster!"

"Mmm. He'll have a long history of obstreperousness to live up to." Jason lifted Tessie's red curls and kissed the back of her neck. The pages of the letter she had been reading slipped from her lap. "What news from home?"

Tessie blushed. "Mama is to marry again! Her doctor—her new doctor—well, you know how often she changed doctors? Just after I left for Japan, she found this man—famous, I think, in the East. I gather he'd come to California to retire, but so many people asked him for help that he started a new practice in San Francisco. Anyway, he told her there was nothing wrong with her that a brisk daily walk and a sensible diet wouldn't cure, and that he couldn't waste his time attending neurasthenic ladies when there were so many sick people needing his care."

"I remember when she wrote you about that. She was most indignant. But what does it have to do with her marriage?"

"It seems," said Tessie, striving to repress her giggles, "that she set out to prove him wrong. She started walking around the block every day, and she told her cook to follow the diet instructions he left *scrupulously*. She thought after a month or so, when her symptoms had not abated, she would call him back and he would have to confess that he had made a mistake and that she was a very sick woman. Instead, she lost twenty pounds and felt so much better that she walked all the way downtown to his office to tell him what a fool he was."

"And?"

"And he asked her to marry him on the spot," Tessie said in a bemused voice, "saying he didn't dare lose the only patient who'd ever followed his instructions for an entire month—and she accepted."

"Maybe," Jason murmured, "this doctor would like to take on Sophia's case next?"

Tessie laughed. It was strange how trivial Sophia's complaints seemed now that she'd lived her own life for a while. By the time Tessie and Jason had returned to Yokohama, Sophia had discovered that it was actually possible to care for her own house and children with the help of a dozen Japanese servants and the German governess. She had magnanimously announced that she forgave Tessie for her heartless desertion. As for Hartley, he too had pulled himself together when he lost Tessie's support. He confessed to Mr. Nakamura that he knew no Japanese, asked for a tutor, came into the office every day, and applied himself with so much energy that he was soon a very able assistant manager.

"I think all Hartley and Sophia needed," Tessie mused, "was for me to stop helping them long enough for them to discover their own strengths."

"Hartley certainly has done well," Jason agreed. "I shan't at all mind leaving him in charge of the Yokohama office when we go inland on our buying trips."

Tessie picked up another letter, one written in elegant black Japanese characters on a handmade paper of cream with green borders. "And I saved the best news for last. My uncle may have forgotten us, but the baby's other godparents have sent a length of silk painted with cranes and waterfalls for his christening present. I *think* Shizuka is hinting that we may have to return the favor soon, but she's being so oblique that I cannot be sure. Anyway, she and Masao seem to be doing well enough together," Tessie said with smug satisfaction. "I felt sure they would after I talked some sense into them! Really, Jason, it was so stupid—there was Shizuka refusing to have Masao because she didn't want a traditional Japanese marriage, and Masao staying away from Shizuka because he felt sure a little country girl wouldn't have an idea in her head beyond being a traditional, subservient, silent Japanese wife! *Somebody* had to make them see sense!"

"If anybody can make a successful blend of Japanese tradition and Western science," Jason agreed, "those two have the best chance at it. Masao and Shizuka are the best hope for a new Japan, a country that can meet the Western powers on terms of equality instead of bowing to our demands. Someday . . ."

While Jason went on about his vision of the new Japan, Tessie rocked in the hammock and day-dreamed about the future. Someday, she thought, Jason would become bored with buying and selling. A man who could make speeches like that to no audience except his wife and the baby sleeping just inside the window was a man who ought to go into politics. She hoped it wouldn't be soon, though; she was in no hurry to give up their pleasant life in Japan for the hustle and bustle of America.

Tessie's musings and Jason's peroration were interrupted by a shriek from the little nursemaid who sat beside the baby's cradle. Tessie all but fell out of the hammock, and they both raced inside.

"What's the matter?" The baby was sleeping peacefully, but his nurse was yelping with hysterical sobs.

"The goblin looked in the window," she gulped out. "The long-nosed goblin, the *tengu* who comes down from the mountains to snatch babies!"

"Nobody could have looked in on you," Tessie said patiently. "There is only one window, and Jason and I were sitting just outside in the garden. We would have seen the *tengu* if it had come." Some other time she would have to work on educating the child out of her superstitions.

"The goblin came," the girl insisted, "and he touched the baby."

Tessie felt her heart contract with irrational fear. She knelt by the baby's cradle and brushed her own fingertips across the rosebud lips. He blew a milky bubble at her in his sleep and went on peacefully snoring. But there was something hard tucked into the cradle, between the baby's lace-trimmed dress and the white knit blanket that he had kicked off in his sleep.

Tessie reached down and drew out a yellowed ivory carving, marvelously detailed, of a fox with paws tucked together and long, bushy tail wound about his body.

"A *netsuke,* a belt ornament," said Jason thoughtfully. "Antique, quite valuable probably."

"A fox?" Tessie murmured.

"Tengu," they both said together, and then, rushing to the open window, *"Morgan!"*

There was no answer from the empty garden.

About the Author

Catherine Lyndell relates that when she worked for a major computer company, "I noticed that my colleagues used to give me strange looks every once in a while and say, 'You certainly have a vivid imagination.' Eventually I sold two books, quit the job, and gave all my gray suits to Goodwill." Her enchanting historical romance *Tapestry of Pride* was followed by *Border Fires,* which *Rendezvous* called "a delightful book." Then came *Stolen Dreams,* acclaimed by *Romantic Times* as "Catherine Lyndell's most impressive and powerful novel to date." Catherine Lyndell (Margaret Ball) lives in Austin, Texas, with her husband and children. Her newest enthralling romance, *Midsummer Rose,* is coming soon from Pocket Books.

The Duchess

Jude Deveraux

Claire Willoughby, a beautiful young American heiress, had been trained her whole life for one thing— to be an English duchess. But when she travels to Scotland to visit her fiance, Harry Montgomery, the duke of McArran, she finds out his family is more than she'd bargained for. Fascinated by his peculiar family, Claire is most intrigued by Trevelyan Montgomery, Harry's mysterious brilliant cousin who she finds living secretly in an unused part of the estate. As she spends more and more time with the magnetic Trevelyan, Claire finds herself drawn to him against her will, yearning to know everything about him. But if Trevelyan's secret is discovered life at Bramley will never be the same.

COMING IN HARDCOVER FROM POCKET BOOKS IN FALL 1991

POCKET BOOKS